Antonia Senior is a former staff writer for *The Times*. She is now a freelance journalist, and her columns, features and book reviews have appeared in a number of national newspapers. Antonia lives in London with her family. She has travelled extensively through Scotland's Highlands and Islands.

Also by Antonia Senior

Treason's Daughter

The Winter Isles

ANTONIA SENIOR

First published in Great Britain in 2015 by Corvus,
an imprint of Atlantic Books Ltd.

This paperback edition published in Great Britain in 2016 by Corvus.

'We Will Walk', *New Collected Poems* by Iain Crichton Smith, reprinted by
permission of Carcanet.

10 9 8 7 6 5 4 3 2 1

A CIP catalogue record for this book is available from the British Library.

Paperback ISBN: 978 1 78239 660 4
E-book ISBN: 978 1 78239 659 8

Printed and bound by Novoprint S.A, Barcelona

Corvus
An imprint of Atlantic Books Ltd
Ormond House
26–27 Boswell Street
London
WC1N 3JZ

www.corvus-books.co.uk

For Colin.

Coisichidh sinn eadar dà thonn
far nach beir am muir oirnn.

'*Coisichidh Sinn*', Iain Mac a' Ghobhainn

We will walk between two waves
where the sea will not reach us.

'We Will Walk', Iain Crichton Smith

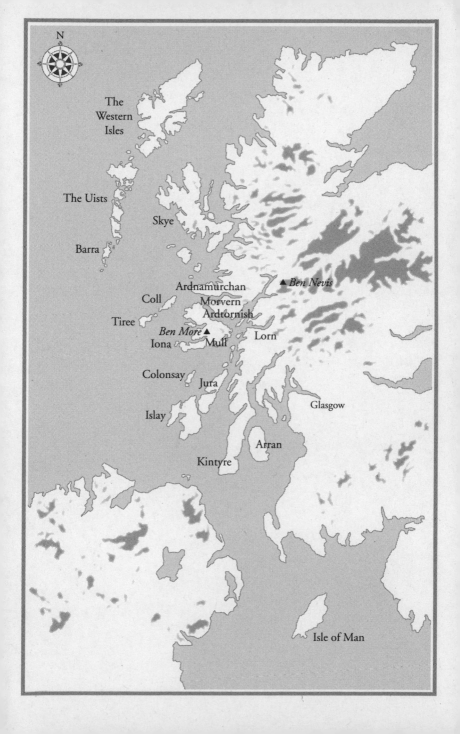

PART 1

1122

SOMERLED

How long had he been there?

Four days. A lifetime. Time stretched impossibly, bleeding slowly into the flat horizon. He sat perched on his rock, scanning. Nothing. A seal popped its head up and seemed to smile at him. How comical, to be stuck on this tiny rock. How absurd not to swim off, with a casual flick of a tail.

'Bastard!' he shouted at the seal. 'Bastard!' It slipped under the ruffled grey sea.

'Sorry,' he said. 'Come back. Come back.' He felt the weight of his solitude descend like a westerly squall.

The tide was out now, weed rippling across black rock where the sea had been. He should look for more food, though he had circumnavigated this fucking rock endlessly, stripping it bare. Limpets gouged out and forced down his gagging throat; mussels crushed under rocks so that the shells splintered into the rubbery flesh.

His stomach growled with hunger and nausea; he could no longer tell them apart. Most of what he had eaten had run right through him, streaming brown back into the sea.

He stood, the sudden movement sending him reeling like a

drunkard. Light-headed with emptiness and misery. He could see right round the island, standing. A rock, really, with green scrub clinging obstinately to serrated black edges, and lichen creeping up the higher stones.

Boats had passed by. But they had been small craft – fishermen's curraghs – hogging the shore like he should have done. Deaf to his wailing; blind to his waving. No deep-water craft. What would he do, anyway, if he saw a Norse knarr, kitted out for a sea voyage, its screaming prow beast turning empty eyes on him? Beg them for water and mercy, or sink into the hollows of the rock and pray they didn't see him?

The boy had witnessed the Northmen's mercy. Last summer, he and the priest were out hunting when they came across their leavings at a village high up the peninsula. A sheltered spot beneath a crag, with a waterfall streaming down its jagged face. They were far enough inland to fancy themselves safe, poor bastards. Stripped and flayed, burned and raped. Some left to twitch, skinless, in the sun's heat while everywhere the midges swarmed and eddied in blood-drunk tides.

Afterwards, he had wept. Father Padeen had laid a hand on his shoulder and talked of souls and judgement. But the boy had wept for his own fascination with the horror, for the compulsion to look, to savour, where he should have been repelled.

Overhead, a gull shrieked. He looked across at the ruin of his boat, where it lay cracked open on the low-tide rocks like an egg. White water hissed around the split planks; the once taut hide of its skin was limp and wet, trailing in the waves.

He remembered the fierce joy of the wind at his back, and the island hovering beyond the steep curve of his bow wave. He remembered thinking, I can weather this, and the sense of mastery – the sea and the wind bending to him. He smiled now, to think of it. The gods were watching, laughing at his arrogance. Mocking him. The first scrape of wood on rock threw him to his knees. He held on to the planks as they broke and split. Spitting salt water and curses, the spray blinding him.

And now, he thought, here I am. Will I die here? Across the Sound he could see the mainland. On the cliff, crooked trees bunched together, reeling perpetually backwards in surrender to the wind. The slopes curled around the bay opposite, cradling the dunes that were so familiar to him. In that cleft on the left, he'd first kissed a girl.

They had played at going Viking, he and his friends, hiding and rolling through those sandy hummocks. He smiled, a little bitterly, to think of their innocence. Even the most inventive of the gang's insect maimers could not have dreamt of the Vikings' leavings in that village under the crag.

Standing, he swayed against the wind. He barely noticed it. A boy bred on this sea expects his hair to whip from his head, expects the sand to blow in his face like midge bites. He stretched and yawned, his dry lips cracking painfully. Perhaps I'll die here, he thought. Thirteen years old, and to die in ignominy.

He imagined his bones bleaching white in the sun and salt spray, like the gannets on the beach or a lamb trapped in a fold of the rock. Would his soul float to heaven? Or to the warm hearths of Helgjafell, the Holy Mountain? Not Valhalla for him, at any rate. Not yet.

Sitting alone on his rock, he let his mind range across the gods competing for his soul: the white Christ of his father and the warrior lords of his mother. He was strung between two certainties, like linen flapping on the line. Hanging between two faiths, the boy thought, threw up the weaknesses in both. Perhaps bones were all that counted after all. They were the essence, the bare picked bones, and the rest so much weaving.

There was, the boy decided, only one sure, proven immortality. When a man died, he lived on in the minds of those who remembered him. Or in the songs of those who did not. But I have no songs, he thought, no name to skip down generations.

He shivered, lost in the misery of dying nameless.

'Fool,' he said aloud, shaking himself like a wet dog, and looked again for a ship. If I could swim, I would chance the rip tides, he thought. Better to die trying than slowly of the thirst and the boredom.

To the west, where the sun was beginning to set, some ugly clouds were bunching. He longed for rain, and feared it. He was cold enough out here at night without being wet. The golden autumn was a dry one – days between rainfall instead of the usual hours. He'd sucked the green stuff for moisture, but his throat was raw and his tongue lolled huge and dry.

At the top of the rock was a pool of water, which was once fresh, before time and the gulls had fouled it. He'd disdained it on the first day, and on the second. By the third he eyed it, and on the fourth he dreamt of it, for all that it was creamy with the birds' dropping. Thirsty was not a word vast enough to cover it.

The seal's head popped up in front of him, watching in that way they had. Wise souls trapped in playful bodies. It rested there, calmly bobbing, only its fathomless brown eyes and sleek grey pate above the waves.

'Hello,' said the boy. 'I'm sorry to have shouted.'

The seal, speechless, watched him.

'Answer me this, seal. Should I drink the droppings? What matters most? Pride or life? What is pride worth, if no one is watching?

'The boys will call me Shit Guzzler. What if that becomes my name? Not The Mighty, or Fierce Beard, or Bloodaxe. And what if they don't know and I do, seal? What matters most – the name you are given, or the one you call yourself in the night?'

He paused and held out a hand, as if trying to coax the seal further inshore. The seal floated casually on the swell.

'But to die on this fucking rock through fear of name-calling seems a poor enough way to end it. That's no path to Valhalla, seal. And we should do something with life, this life, before we seek heaven, should we not?'

The seal, seeming bored, slipped under the water, and the boy sat on his haunches, watching. Sure enough, the seal bobbed up again, a little closer, so that the boy could see the particular brown of his staring eyes.

'So I ask you,' said the boy. 'Here I am on this rock. Am I the same boy as the one on land? Do the same codes apply if you're wholly, entirely alone?'

The seal's head seemed to jerk sideways, and the boy looked up to the horizon. The weather was swooping in on him. He could see the sun and rain playing tag across the sea, streaking it blue here, grey there, so that alone on the rock he felt like a spectator at the edge of the world. Clouds scudded overhead, dropping lower and lower until at last they engulfed him. Barely a rain, though; just a damping. A kissing rain, his mother called it. He raised his face to it and opened his mouth, letting the drizzle spritz his chapped lips. Barely enough for a swallow, but a blessed, glorious relief. He put out his tongue and recoiled from the pure salt of his falling tears.

They were following the gulls, the brothers from the Point. It was a desperate business to come this far out when the clouds were skimming the sea. But on shore there were eight hungry mouths open like gasping nestlings pushing them on to chase the herring.

They neared Scurry's Rock, slow and careful, the younger conning from the bow. They had worked together too long for words. An incline of the head, a jerk of a finger was all it took for the elder to jiggle the steering oar. This patch bristled with underwater rocks, sharp and malevolent. The boat crept forward, close-reefed and cautious.

Inside a new cloud they blinked against the wetness, droplets falling on their searching faces like dew. The world seemed muffled white; the slapping of the sharp waves against wood, the rush and suck of the tide on the rocks, the cackling gulls. Beyond the dampened sound came something new. A thin bark, like a wounded seal pup.

The elder watched the back of his brother's head as it cocked to one side. His hair was frazzled by the damp, springing in crinkled clumps from its long plait.

'What—' began the elder.

'Shh.' The younger shook his head, his impatience clear.

The barking fell into the silence between them. This time, the sound took shape. 'Help. Help me.' A thin, cracked whisper.

'Jesus,' whispered the younger.

'Mary and Joseph.' They both reached for the hollow at the base of their throats where Thor's hammers used to lie, before the priest crushed them between two giant rocks.

When they hauled the boy into the boat, he gaped soundlessly at them, his parched mouth working. The younger brother held a flask of water to his lips, and the boy drank, spluttering fast.

'Thank you,' he said. The skin was drawn tight across his face. At first they only noticed his swollen, black lips, with cracks so deep you could see to the red beneath. But as he spoke, they looked

7

at him, front on. The younger brother reached for his missing hammer as the boy turned his sun-bleached face on them. His green eyes held them, perfectly still. A man's eyes staring from a sun-speckled boy's face.

The brothers glanced at each other. The boy looked, like them, a half-blood. A foreign Gael. The reddish hue of the Gael leavened by the yellow of the north. 'Take me to my father,' said the boy. 'He will reward you.'

'But our catch, boy,' said the elder, thinking of his wife. His brother smiled, thinking of her too, and the tongue on her if they came home bare-handed.

The boy stared at him; a level green stare.

'Our catch,' the elder mumbled again, drawing his arm around in a wide arc as if to point out that this was, in fact, a fishing boat. The boy ignored his arm, staring at him until the older man shrugged and looked at his brother.

The younger asked: 'Who is your father?'

'Gillebrigte. Son of Gilleadoman.' They drew sharp breaths. 'You know where to find him?'

They nodded in unison. The look on their faces, like brothers who had fished for herring and caught a shark, made him smile. His grinning seemed to unnerve them, so the boy lay down on the nets and turned his face to the sky, the tension and fear leaking out of him. His father's name was like a talisman; a wind to carry him home.

He was cold, and wet and tired. The boat, a scrap of sail to keep her manageable, drifted into a patch of blue sea and sky. Lying on his back, he watched the clouds, higher now, stream through the sky. That one looked like a dragon, he thought, the wisping cloud trails its smoky breath. He heard the two men whispering to each other.

One, the grizzled elder, looked at some point behind the boy's right ear. 'We will take you, lord,' he said. 'Aye.'

The boy felt a blanket come over him. It was rough, and reeked of herring. He smiled as he closed his eyes, anticipating the warmth creeping back into his limbs. Safe now. A song floated across the waves from his past, the harmony sung by the creaking of the boat and the rustling of the sail.

His old nurse, with her thick accent of the Antrim glens, singing Patrick's song, the deer's cry:

I arise today
Through the strength of heaven:
Light of sun,
Radiance of moon,
Splendour of fire,
Speed of lightning,
Swiftness of wind,
Depth of sea,
Stability of earth,
Firmness of rock.

He heard speech, breaking through the remembered honey hues of his nurse's song. The voice, harsh as pebble scratching on pebble, said from a great height: 'And if you're sleeping, little lord, how shall we name you to your father?'

'Somerled,' he said. 'My name is Somerled.'

~ ~ ~

'Lie back.'

'Jesus wept.'

'Boy!'

'Sorry, Mother,' he said, not sure if he was apologizing for the blasphemy, or the invocation of the Lord's name.

Somerled watched her in the light from the fire as she bustled around. They were at the warm end of the hall, where the big fire was perpetually burning and pots of liquid hissed and steamed. He lay on a shaggy rug, and he idly picked and stroked at the strands, twisting and plaiting them.

Her hair was escaping, as usual, from its long plait. There was flour on her dress, and charcoal on her forehead. She was smudged and smeared, flustered and competent all at once. Her face, reddened from the fire and the thin threads of broken veins in her cheeks, was so familiar that, before the island, he had forgotten to look at it. But the days on the island seemed to have brought everything to a sharper focus, as if, before, he'd been watching the world through a skin of falling water. He looked at the yellow of her hair, and the freckles on her nose; the fresh lines scratched around her eyes and the crease in her forehead made from frowning – usually in concentration, not anger.

She muttered to herself in that way she had, a tangle of Gaelic commentaries, half-snatched songs in her native Norse, smatterings of proverbs. 'Now, where was it . . . *And the moon sang on the* . . . Oh, here it is . . . Now then . . . *And the great jarl came* . . .'

'Mother!'

'Hmm?' She stopped to stir something, and taste it. Turning to the slave girl, Aedith, she nodded. Aedith's pale, thin face transformed itself with a smile so bright that Somerled felt an answering grin rising and his mother was moved to chuckle.

'How long must I lie here?'

'Until I and Father Padeen judge you are well enough,' she said.

'Can I not judge?'

'No. Eat this.'

She handed over a bowl of stew, thick with meat and barley, and he fell on it. How he had eaten and drunk since the fisher brothers brought him home, carrying him up the stony beach at the head of the loch to the sound of screaming and weeping from the women. Her reaction to his being missing, and the shock of his return, was to feed him. She had slaughtered a hogget, and in the past few days they had steadily eaten it. First its livers, quick-cooked on sticks in the fire while the legs roasted and crisped. The smell filled every crevice of the hall with a promise so glorious that grown warriors near wept with hunger. Somerled slept, fill to sicking point with water from the burn, and the smell of the lamb sank into his dreams, so that he was riding a giant sheep through a bog when his sister woke him.

They had eaten the legs with the rump of his father's war-band – the old and the tired ones – left here to guard the family while his father and the rest were off scouting.

He drained the last of the stew, biting a sliver of meat off the bone and sucking the marrow. He began to entertain the possibility that he might, finally, be full. Sated. Replete. He had thought, over the past two days, that he could never eat or drink enough; that he must be tied to this bed forever, swallowing and licking, quenching and devouring. But now, finally, he was full.

He lay back, warm and sleepy. His limbs felt heavy, as if they had finally lost that hollow brittleness bred by the island. His mother came over and sat next to him, crouching down on her haunches. She pushed his hair back from his forehead, and smiled. Near-death, the boy decided, was reason enough to allow this tenderness. At least when no one was watching. He grabbed her hand and kissed it. He could feel her bones shift under the skin as he pressed her hand.

'I thought we'd lost you,' she said.

11

'Sorry.'

'No matter, though you are lucky your father was not here. Who would be a woman, hey, my darling? We're schooled from the womb to accept that our children may die, and I, who have escaped it so far, found that all the preparing is as naught. The world was made of grief when you were gone.'

She shuddered, and he saw that she was beginning to cry. She never cried, his mother. Not even in the days after they landed here first from Ireland, two years ago. The days when their initial rush at the usurpers had been rebuffed, and they had found themselves living in caves so cold that freezing water dribbled down the walls and icicles stood to attention at the entrance.

He squirmed at the sight of the tears.

'Father Padeen says that children sit at Christ's right hand,' she said. 'I told him he was using my grief to befuddle me with fairy tales. He said—'

'And here he is himself,' said Somerled, looking over her shoulder to the doorway, where the great bulk of the priest paused.

She turned and smiled at him, and he walked forward. Somerled could not fathom these two: priest and pagan. They spent their days wrangling endlessly. She clung to the gods of her grandfathers, resisting the near-universal pressure to convert. She was convinced that they had spoken to her, the gods, in a fever dream, when she was young and sick and expected to die. On her recovery, her faith had become unshakeable, despite the pressure of her mother and her husband, and the motley band of priests and wise men both had sent to fight repeatedly for her soul.

Yet they liked each other, Father Padeen and Sigrdrifa, the jarl's natural daughter from Orkney. Somerled suspected that if ever he won the battle for her soul, Father Padeen would be disappointed at losing his sparring partner.

12

Father Padeen crouched by his side, sighing heavily as he eased into the squat.

'And how is the Culdee himself?'

'Don't be filling his head with that nonsense, you oaf of a priest.'

'What is a Culdee, Father?' asked Somerled.

'A holy man, boy. Who seeks to find God in the wilderness. Some live on islands like yours. For years, not just a few days.'

His mother grunted.

Father Padeen said: 'They model themselves on the desert monks of the Great City.'

Somerled looked a question, and Padeen, his great moon face smiling, said: 'Well, then. They believe, these godly men, that they can be closer to God in the quiet of the wilderness. Did not our Lord stay in the desert forty days and forty nights? The desert is hard to picture in this fruitful land of rain and bog. It is a place all of sand, where no rain falls. And the first and greatest of them all, boy, was St Simeon Stylites. He lived on top of a pole for forty years, praying and singing, and telling the Lord of his love.'

Fascinated in spite of herself, for she loved Padeen's tales of life beyond the seas, Sigrdrifa listened. Aedith crept forward, keeping to the shadows.

'A pole,' said Father Padeen, 'so wide.' He held his hands as wide as a butter churn.

'And how did he eat and drink?' asked Sigrdrifa.

'Forty years!' whispered Aedith.

'The people loved him, and they put food and drink in a basket and he hauled it up to the top of the pole.' Padeen mimed the people watching the basket rising, necks craned. Aedith's head followed, and she stared at the ceiling, where the meat hung in the smoke reaching the rafters, her mouth a great round O, the awe as real as if Simeon himself perched in the beams like a pious bat.

'And then,' said Sigrdrifa, 'he shat on their heads.' She laughed, a great roaring laugh that drew Aedith and Somerled in, and even Padeen's face cracked a little, though he tried to look severe.

'You are hopeless, and faithless, woman,' he said.

'True, true,' she said. 'But what a ninny. What a berk, sitting up there on that pole for forty years. If that God of yours has any sense, Padeen, he was pissing himself laughing. If you can show me proof that your tortured Christ found it funny, that stupid man wasting his life praying on top of a pole, then I will let you put the cross on my forehead.'

He spread his hands in defeat, and she moved back to poke at the fire, still laughing and muttering. 'What a fool, what a fool!'

Padeen shook his head in exaggerated despair and turned to Somerled.

'We were worried, boy.'

'Sorry.'

'No matter. And what have you learned?'

'Learned?'

'Yes. For what use are misadventures if we do not learn from them?'

Somerled thought for a moment. 'That prayer comforts us. That I must not always trust my own judgement. I thought I could weather the island, and I was wrong. Desire to do it clouded my weighing of the risks.'

Padeen nodded. Silently the boy added: That left alone I am not as brave as I thought I was. That if no one watches, I weep like a girl. That I want songs to be sung of me. That fame and bravery go hand in hand; the two cannot exist without each other.

Aloud, he said: 'But most of all, Father, I learned that I must learn how to swim.'

~ ~ ~

Padeen pulled the girl out from behind his back. She was, at first sight, unpromising.

'They call her the Otter,' said the priest.

Somerled eyed her. She was small and red, and fiercely freckled. One of the little ones he paid no heed to. Despite his father's lack of progress in subduing his birthright, his followers remained with him, their families deposited here in the safest of the glens. A gaggle of children ran wild under the benign hand of Father Padeen, the distracted mothers and the few slaves left of those they had brought over the sea. Somerled ignored the littler ones, mainly. He ran with the boys, and, when they would let him, the older girls. This little sprite was one of his younger sister Brigte's friends.

'Your father?'

She twisted a little, and he thought her shy until he realized that she was squirming from the priest's grasp. Level-eyed, she said: 'My name is Eimhear. My father is Fhearghais, son of Fionn.'

He nodded. One of the lordless Antrim warriors who were following his father more in hope than expectation. If, by the grace of God, Gillebrigte won back these lands, despite the odds against him and despite, the boy whispered to his private heart, his weakness, then they would be rewarded. In the meantime, this little freckled otter was wearing a gown too small and a cloak so patched you could not tell what colour it started at. About nine, he thought. Ten perhaps.

'And you can swim?' he asked her.

'Aye,' she shrugged.

'How?'

She raised her shoulders again. 'If a seal can do it, how could I not? The daft creatures.'

Father Padeen laughed. 'Watch this one,' he said.

Together they walked towards the shore. With no preamble, she shrugged off her cloak and her dress and stood in her undergown, wind-whipped and tiny against the vastness of sea and sky, smudging together in shades of grey. She glanced at him and threw a silent challenge, then turned and ran straight at the surf. She skipped over the first few waves, and flung herself forward under the biggest, bobbing to the surface with an inarticulate shout to the sky.

'Jesus.'

'Somerled!'

'Sorry, Father. Are you coming?'

'If the good Lord had wanted us to swim, would he have walked on the stuff?'

Somerled stripped down to his tunic and started to walk in. 'God's bones, but it's cold!'

Father Padeen began to laugh.

'Go quicker!' shouted the Otter. 'It's the only way.'

'Wait until it reaches your balls, boy,' said Father Padeen behind him, through great sobs of laughter.

He's right, thought Somerled, fighting to keep going. Lord, but he'd like to run out again.

With the water at waist height, the pain of the cold began to ease.

'Like this,' she said, showing him. He flung himself at the water, only to sink in a whirl of bubbles and fear.

He felt a small hand grabbing his chin, pulling him up. She wasn't laughing. Her fine-boned face was serious, contained. 'Let's float first,' she said. 'Imagine you're made of driftwood. You're just trying to bob. On your back, like this.' Her freckled nose poked up from the water as she rippled on the waves. Clear brown eyes appraised him.

She held his head, and he lay back in the water.

'Trust me,' she rapped as he began to panic and twist. 'Trust me. Just let every muscle relax. It only works if you give in to it. Listen to the sea. Can you hear it?'

He heard the scrape of the pebbles beneath the waves, and the rushing hiss of where the water met the land.

'Lie still, Lord.'

She let go, and for a moment he felt suspended between sky and sea, his body undulating on the swell like seaweed. Then the strangeness overtook him, and he began to tense, caught between laughter and fear. He lost his sense of balance, his closeness to the sea, the waves. He began to turn and sink, the bubbles rising and the salt water rushing up his nose.

She pulled him up again, and this time she was smiling. 'Do you fight better than you float, Lord Somerled?'

'I find floating doesn't answer when the swords are singing,' he said, liking her. He wanted to keep her smiling, he realized. This strange otter child, with her solemn eyes and shining smile.

'Shall we try again, Lord?' He nodded and lay back, her small hands holding his head above the cold water.

By the end of that autumn, he could float unaided, swim confidently as long as the tide was with him and even, when the spirit took him, turn icy somersaults and come up laughing. The Otter liked to dive beneath the waves and jump up behind him when he was not expecting it. She turned back somersaults too, staying under to walk on her hands across the shingle, only her skinny white legs poking up above the waves. Sometimes she climbed up on to his shoulders and plunged into the water head first and arms extended.

They liked it best when the seals came to play. Soon Somerled was comfortable enough to swim beneath the water, his eyes open and salt-stung, watching the irresistible rippling of their underwater bodies. They would come close, the seals, so close. He watched the Otter once, treading water, as a young pup came so near their noses were almost touching, before it swam away and left her laughing so hard she had to fight to float. The seal would laugh if it could, he knew.

They swam until their lips turned blue and the shivering became uncontrollable. The evenings were the best time, after his lessons and her chores. He soaked away the Latin in the cold water, forgot the roll call of the ancestors and the great reams of poetry, the swordplay and archery. She left her spindle, forgot the hated loom; forgot even the plaque made of whalebone which she used to straighten the linen as it lay in damp mounds from the washing.

Until, at last, the days grew shorter and it was too cold even for the Otter. Then they had to make do with talking instead. They hid in the dunes, bunkering down where the wind did not reach. It was better to hide; the boys did not understand his friendship with the little girl. But they did not know her fierce, searching mind. They did not know that within the small freckled package sat a questing soul so insatiable for life, for knowledge, for experience that Somerled felt humbled when he allowed himself to think of it.

They travelled, those two, hunkered down in the hollows. They went to Vinland, the fabled land so far beyond the horizon a man could die of hunger on the way. They went to Miklagard, the Great City that the Franks call Constantinople, sharing tales of emperors and intrigues, of coups and decadence, of pleasure gardens and sewers. They tried to make sense of it by looking at the stars, that all those people could crowd into one small place, living on top of each other, side by side. They travelled to the lands of the Rus, and to the far north, where white bears ruled. They talked of Rome; of the fountainhead of their faith. And even of Jerusalem, where the Lord pulled down the Temple. But most of all of Miklagard, where the emperor ruled from a golden throne.

'One day,' he said. 'One day, I'll take you.'

And she looked at him, fierce and trusting all at once, so that he swelled with the pride of being the anointed one, the one who could take her roaming.

In the spring, their thoughts turned to the water again. One night, on the beach, waiting for the whistle home to bed, she said: 'My father says that I am becoming too old for the swimming.'

'You're a scrap still, Otter. Tiny.'

'He hates that I'm the Otter. Says a woman must stick to her given name.'

'You are not yet a woman. Besides, men find their own names.'

'Men find their own everything.'

'Would you rather be a boy, Otter?'

'Of course. Foolish question.'

'Why?'

'Who would not want to settle their own fate?'

'I cannot, and I am a boy.'

'Oh, I know. Poor, poor you. To be the chief's son. To be the chosen one, the tanist. To be put in the way of fame and glory and riches.'

'And failure.'

'Pah. That's what worries you? Don't fail, then.'

'What of you?'

'They will marry me off to some fool who goes off raiding, leaving me at home to pray he is knocked on the head, while I spin and weave and pickle and smoke, until at last they bury me with my spindle, so I can spend eternity as well as this life being bored witless.'

The moon was bright, and he looked sideways at her. She scanned the skies with restless eyes. She took him off guard, this imp. He could not always tell when she was speaking seriously, or to amuse herself. She was so unlike the other ten-year-olds. He thought back to himself at ten; how simple and uncomplicated seemed this world, bordered by sea and moor, with all the joys in between.

He tried to explain it to her. How, that now he was growing, the world was becoming troublesome.

'Is it me, or is it the world? Which is becoming complicated?' he asked.

She turned her face to him, smiling and sad all at once.

'It's you, stupid. You're learning to see the shadows.'

eimhear

L ast night, I thought about being young. I remembered Somerled promising to take me to Miklagard. How he turned to me in the darkness and said it with a solemnity that made sense under the stars. 'I will take you,' he said, and I believed him.

A blessing on that little freckled sprite that was me. One thousand kisses for her frowning brow; her trusting face. I can see her in my daughter. I love my child in her every mood, but the one that makes me jolt, that makes me think of falling backwards from a high cliff, is her serious face. That point of concentrated innocence. Absorbed in her letters, or her wool-work, she pushes her hair from her eyes. A single line, off-centre, creases her forehead. She is unaware of me, of the background hum of wave and wind. There is only the quick working of her hands and a quietness of soul. Her mother, standing unnoticed behind her, rages at the trials she will face, the scratches to skin and heart, the violent intent of the world to crush her grave joy.

Breathe, Eimhear, breathe. Perhaps she will be unscathed. Perhaps she will sail through the storms flecked with gold, the wind behind her, dolphins dancing in the bow waves. Perhaps.

What made me think of Somerled's promise? We had a visitor last night. A pilgrim on his way to Iona. It was late and rough-waved when he arrived, and he stayed the night. Fussed over and cosseted by the women, who were desperate for news, for stories, for anything he could give.

He was old, tanned bronze from a stronger sun than ours. He had the unwarranted pomposity of a man who thinks himself clever among the clattering of women. But, after all, he had come from Miklagard. He was an envoy for the king over in Alba, he said. Sent to treat with the emperor. He shifted in his seat as he said this, and I caught Eua's sliding eyes and we tried not to laugh openly at him. He was a servant to the envoy perhaps. Rough hands; a creaking way of talking, like a man unused to being heard.

Still, he had been to Miklagard in the past year. I have been to the beach on the far side of the island; and that only once. We listened to him talk, threading gold in our heads from his halting weave.

He told us of the size of it – he said it would take a day to walk from the first house to the last; and the houses all crowd on top of each other. Families live above families above families. We stared in wonder, and I tried to imagine it, but I couldn't. How could that be? I looked up into the rafters and imagined a whole other floor beyond, and another beyond that. Like ants, they must be. But do they know themselves ants, or do they think themselves gods? If I lived in Miklagard, perched on top of other people's souls, I would think myself a god.

He told us of gold, and silks. Of strange beasts with green spit and humped backs. He told us of men with black faces, of priests and warriors. Then he said: 'There is a princess, there, named Anna. She is an abomination.'

How so? we asked, thinking salacious thoughts of a high-born whore. It was long since we had seen a man worth tupping.

22

He leaned forward, looking around at us, enjoying the pause. Doubtless imagining himself as the tupper.

'She is more learned than any man in Christendom,' he said, in a low and growling voice. 'She fancies herself a philosopher. What is a man? she asks. What is God? She knows more about the stars than the priests. She does magic with numbers, thinks herself a healer. She has seven tongues, they say. She reads old poets; stuff where heathens boast about their false gods.'

He built each sentence on the tutting of the women, waiting for their disapproval before starting the next.

'She is not even ashamed of this. She boasts of it. She parades herself as a scholar and a teacher. She runs a hospital, where she tends to sick people, even men.'

Exhausted at last by his invective, he sat back. I stood then, disorientated, a pitcher of hot water in my hands. I swayed and quivered with the urge to throw it at him, to douse the irritating, pompous bastard. I moved forward, feeling like the champion of this foreign princess, as if her honour rested with me. Lord help me, I would have done it too. But Eua, sensing something in my mood, stood suddenly between us, hands on ample hips.

I ran outside, pulling on my shawl, into the howl of the gale. What was I thinking? Rage against the pilgrim, though he was beneath it. Rage against her, too. That learned princess with slaves for her chores and a free mind that roamed and dug and roamed some more. A furious, violent envy. I looked behind to the hall. Dimly lit, a star-prick against the cavernous horizon. I felt the familiar press of hill and sea and sky, and thought that this time – this time – I would be crushed.

I found a hollow in the hill, curling myself into it, out of the wind. And I let myself think of Somerled, and when we were young.

~ ~ ~

'Father, what are the stars?'

'God made them, Eimhear.'

'Yes, but what are they made of? Why do they shine only at night?'

He was combing out his long beard, and I saw the irritation in his face. I moved closer. 'Let me do it.'

He grunted, and I climbed on to his knee, facing him. His face softened, as I thought it would. I took the comb and pulled it through the long hair, with its streaks of auburn and grey.

'Plaited?'

He nodded.

I divided the hair into sections, and set to plaiting it. I was awkward with the maths of it; three strands, two hands. His eyes were smiling now; I soothed him with my incompetence.

'Where do they go in the day?'

'Jesus, Eimhear. Who knows? Maybe the fairies steal them. Why does it matter? It's enough that they are there. It is enough that they help us know which way to go.'

'Yes, but—'

His face hardened again, and I quietened. 'No matter, Father. There, done.' I hopped off his knee again, looking at his plaited beard. Lord, but it was rubbish. One thick, proud plait and one little one, like a rat's tail.

'I'm just . . . going walking,' I stuttered.

'Don't be bothering the priest again while the boy is at his lessons.'

'They won't mind.'

'Aye, but I do. Why can't you be friends with the other girls?'

He pointed over to the long hall, to where two girls my age sat with their backs against the wall. I liked them well enough, but they would care less than Father what the stars were made of. I had to dip in and out of their talk about boys and gowns and marriage prospects – immersion in it would make my ears bleed.

'I am.' I ran over and kissed him. 'I won't be long.'

~ ~ ~

There was a moment in the walk up the hill behind the hall I always loved. The ground flattened and then sank down for ten paces, as if you were walking across the bottom of a bowl. In the hollow, the wind couldn't find you. In the summer, the sun caught in the depression. You could lie in there and feel it seeping through to your bones; until the midges found you, of course.

They say that Somerled's father once found himself betrayed by a man. He hunted him down and buried him to the waist in a sheltered spot, and let the midges turn his brain to a single scream.

The spring was the best, for lying in the hollow. No insects, just the trapped sun. You couldn't see or be seen there, either. I loved that moment of feeling yourself alone. No eyes watching, no tongues gossiping, no close press of the jumble of families living all together hemmed in by hill and sea.

I walked on, up the steep back of the hollow. I could see the hall again, and some of the cleansing joy of being alone left me. On I went, following the path of the burn upwards.

I could hear them before I could see them. Padeen's big laugh rumbled over the heather. I had a fear they wouldn't want me, but when I came closer, they turned and smiled. Somerled was sitting on a wide rock, and he shifted over, the invitation clear. I ran the last few paces.

'Father Padeen, what are the stars?'

'And good morning to you, little Otter.'

'It's been burning me.'

Somerled grinned at me. 'Go back to your weaving, little girl. Ow, you can't hit me, I'm the lord's son.'

'You're a fool. Father, please.'

'Well, child. No one knows for sure. God's mysteries are profound. They move across the skies. You must imagine a series of celestial spheres. The stars, which shine through God's will, are set in these spheres like jewels in a torque. As the spheres move, the stars move.'

'But who moves the spheres?' asked Somerled.

'Well, I corresponded once with a man who believed that they were moved by the angels in the Book of Revelations. But in truth, we do not know. God makes them move, and that is as far as we can go.'

I tutted, impatient with him.

'It's the answer to everything. God made it so.'

'And that, my child, is because God is the answer to everything.'

Somerled thought about this. 'But Father, even though that is true, you can see why Eimhear finds it frustrating. God made it so is the answer when we are ignorant, just as often as it is the answer when it is the true and only answer.'

'But what else do we have? Life is frustrating, child.'

I knew that, but I said: 'That's the type of thing adults always say. Life is frustrating, life is not fair. Get used to it. Well I don't want to. Why can't we shape our own lives so they are not frustrating, so they are not unfair? And Father, if you tell me it is because God's ways are mysterious, I shall jump in the burn.'

He laughed. 'Well I shall remain silent then,' he said. 'Eimhear, we were talking of mathematics when you arrived. You may join us, if you forget to mention it to your father.'

26

I nodded, and settled into the borrowed lesson. Later, we walked back down the hill, the three of us, still talking. Dusk was falling, and the smoke was rising from the long hall. I found myself glad to be home, impatient to fight for my place by the fire and hear the gossip of the day. We raced the last yards, Padeen's laughter chasing us down the hill.

~ ~ ~

He was rotten at swimming, at first. He didn't always have the patience for learning difficult things. He wanted to be the best too quickly. The quickest, the fastest, the bravest. When he was not any of those things, he dropped out early and made a joke of it. When he was young, people underestimated him, I think. They thought him flippant. They thought him lightweight. They didn't always see him coming.

With the swimming, however, he was determined to learn. He didn't speak, often, of what happened to him when he was missing.

It happened before we were friends, but I felt his absence. Who could not? He already had a presence, even so young. When he was in a room, the air found him first. When he left, the light leached away. It was not just me who felt it. At least, I think not.

When he was missing, his mother walked the shore like one of the lost folk, holding in her giant scream of despair. The rest of us did the endless sums. Two days, three days, four. If he was wrecked on the mainland, how long would it take to walk back? How long could a body go without water before it shrivelled? Five days, six. Still she paced. I was envious of him, even when he was thought lost forever. It seemed to me, then, the most glorious thing in the world to have a mother's mourning.

27

When they carried him up the beach, weak and pickled by wind and sun, he was smiling for her alone.

I asked him about it, later. Out there on the rock was scouring, he said. He had thought he would die, but that was not the worst of it. It was dying without a name that bothered him. Dying small and insignificant, so that, a hand-span of years later, only his mother would remember him. I would remember you, I told him. He smiled at me, and even then I knew that it was not enough for him. Not enough to be mourned by the woman who bore him and the girl who loved him.

The talks were snatched things, at first. We practised swimming until our lips were blue.

'Hold still,' I said, letting him go.

He sank, spluttering. I wrenched him up to the surface.

'How am I ever to make you float?'

'And why must I float, when it's swimming I want to do? Jesus, I'm cold. Do you never feel it?'

I shrugged. 'You have to float. It's the basis of all of it. If you can't float, you can't swim.'

'It's all the staying still.'

I laughed at him. 'It would be good for you to be still, sometimes.'

'Show me again.'

I upended my legs, wondering not for the first time how something so easy, so very like breathing, could be so troubling. I loved to float. Finding the exact pitch of stillness within the muffled ruffling of the waves.

'Now you,' I shouted. My ears were deaf with water. I was absorbed in the undulation of my limbs.

'I did it! I did it! Jesus, Otter. You weren't even looking.'

'Do it again, then.'

'It's too cold. Besides, I might not be able to.'

28

I splashed him. 'Once you have done it once, you can do it again.'

He looked at me with his green eyes smiling and his bleached hair slick against his forehead. There was such trust in his expression it made me breathless.

Quickly he kicked his legs upwards and made himself still in the waves. I pushed myself up and next to him, reaching for his hand to keep us lashed together. Above, the different greys of the sky played tag. Rain threatened. We floated, Somerled and I.

1124

SOMERLED

The boy stared. Somerled stared back. *Kill him. Do it. Oh Lord, help me kill. Mother Mary, give my sword arm strength enough. I am Somerled, the summer warrior. Deep thinker. Man-killer.*

His legs began to quiver, a quick, uncontrollable pulsing that took him by surprise. It emphasized the curious detachment he felt of mind from body. While his mind barked orders and mumbled prayers, his body ignored the summons. It shook and procrastinated, fumbling and trembling. And there was the boy, lying still, staring.

He was a similar age. Fifteen, say. Clear-eyed. He had sleep clinging to his eyelid on one side, and smudges of dirt across his forehead. A snot trail from nose to chin, and reddened nostrils. He has a cold, thought Somerled. Mother would counsel a basin of hot water, swirled with honey. But a poke in the neck with a sharp sword would do the trick. He grinned, then retreated from the joke. Ashamed.

Perhaps it was his first time with the war-band, too. Perhaps this morning he too had sharpened his blade and practised his throwing, polished his helmet and checked his shield. Each detail necessary, and yet also a prevarication, a distraction from the essential business of being terrified. Perhaps he too had walked with exaggerated confidence, looking slant-eyed at the warriors to the side of him to check he was not dreaming a terrible and longed-for dream.

The boy looked whole. Unconcerned, almost. As if, walking on a warm day, he'd found a perfect bed of springy heather and settled down for a sun-baked nap. Yet further down, his hands scrabbled at his leaking stomach, as if he could repack the spilling, stinking mess and wish the skin whole again. Somerled looked down at his reddened blade, astonished at the colour. The longed-for, troublesome, vivid redness of it.

Why did God make blood red? he wondered. To bring out the contrasts? To signal that on the inside we are fire and heat, whatever our outward dull show? If blood were beige, like skin, would it be so shocking to see it spilt? Is it the colour that shocks or the fact of the blood? Why does is dry to be dark and dull?

Jesus. Get back to the task in hand. Somerled looked at the boy. That expression in his eyes, then. Was it fear, or incomprehension? Was he already halfway to eternal bliss, so that the sharp thrust of a sword would just help him along? Like the gust of a land breeze filling a limp sail, or the bite of oars as the caller wound up the pace. That was all. A sharp prick and it would be done. Over. A kindness.

Jesus. Mother Mary. St Colm Cille. He was whispering their names over and again, without registering the nervous fluttering of his lips.

He summoned his will. Commanded his body to obey. He changed the grip on his sword, ready for a downward strike. He nestled the point in the hollow place at the base of the boy's throat. An inconsequential image came to him of Aedith, the slave girl, and how she arched her neck when he entered her, pushing the back of her head into the sand. The hollow flattened out as her neck stretched, and the contours changed, like dunes shifting in a gale.

Somerled shook his head. He hoped the boy would give him a sign: that it was all right – he was ready. That the angels were already singing lullabies and picking him off the bloodied peat. The boy's eyes narrowed as if suddenly registering Somerled's existence, and he jerked his head away. Too soon. Somerled wasn't ready, and the point of the sword scored the boy's neck, drawing beads of crimson blood across his white skin. A necklace.

'Just do it, boy.' Aed. The champion. He rasped it close to Somerled's ear, his sour breath strong enough to overpower the stench of the boy's inside-out stomach. 'Quickly. Like a sheep.'

Like a sheep.

Somerled turned to glance at Aed. He saw the man's great shaggy mass of hair, and the unkempt beard and the battle-mad eyes. He saw, as if at a distance, the champion watching the lord's son, to see if he had the balls to take his first kill like a warrior. He imagined the Otter's contemptuous face, questioning the code, mocking the men. She was right, perhaps, but . . . I am Somerled. The summer warrior. What am I, if not a warrior?

He changed the angle of the sword, and forcing his trembling legs to a kneel, he pulled the blade fast across the boy's throat. He heard the boy gurgle and choke, and watched the blood spill. Like a sheep.

In the long hall, the warriors' spears beat the time as they growled the songs. And at his father's right hand, Somerled sang too, giddy with joy and mead. They sang of St Colm Cille, who'd given them the victory.

'*Leafy oak tree, soul's protection, rock of safety, the sun of monks, mighty ruler, Colm Cille!*' They spat the words out, roaring through the epithets. The steady thump of the spear shafts on the hard-packed floor paced out the words, danced with the flames, pulsed with his heart, until he was lost in the roaring.

But in his head he sang his own song.

I am Somerled, summer warrior, man-killer, seal-tamer.

Over and again he repeated the refrain, until it became fixed and true as the North Star.

I am Somerled, summer warrior, man-killer, seal-tamer.

Suddenly they roared his name. The drinking horns were raised, and as they drank to his first kill, he saw the Otter looking at him from the far side of the hall. Something in her expression sobered him. He looked beside him to his father's mead-washed face. His mouth hung open, laughing at some joke told by Iehmarc, his steward. Somerled saw the man's mirthless smile, as Gillebrigte creased with laughter. He could see a sliver of gristle caught in his father's far molar, and he turned away. The sudden sobering came in a rush of despondency that left him gasping for air in the hot, smug hall.

And what was it, after all? Cattle-rustlers, and not many of them. What was this frenzy of back-slapping, of congratulations? As if they had taken on the Fianna and beaten back the giant-slayers themselves.

How long had he known that his father was going to fail?

He remembered the war-band that had set off from Ireland; the galleys full of warriors, packed in like garrulous herrings. Their boasting filled the air, turned the clouds blue with curses and the sun pink with shame for their talk of the women they were leaving. The gulls shrieked overhead as if responding to the callers, a celestial waulking song, and the oars bit eagerly at the sea.

How passionately he wanted to be like them, the eleven-year-old boy, his blunted child's sword hanging pathetically at his waist and his small fist pounding the planking in time with their roars. He remembered setting his high treble in competition with the deep basses, singing the rowing.

The fifteen-year-old Somerled looked back with fond contempt at his younger self.

His father. Gillebrigte of the Caves. He couldn't shake the name. They had lived in the caves when they arrived on this coast, after their initial rushed assault had failed and they were beaten back into the hills. But they had carved out this sliver of territory, and built a hall. A small victory, sliced from the dreams of conquest and glory.

Gillebrigte looked the part, at a distance. With his sandy hair and firm chin, his broad shoulders and fine air. His unmistakable air of a man who should be heroic. He swaggered, and he talked and he bragged. In the practice, he was deft. His sword edge was blurred as it moved; his parries were firm, his attacks fierce. He could drink, and eat to keep up with huge Aed and his bottomless stomach. Several of his natural children ran around the hall; Gillebrigtes in miniature.

So why then did Somerled find that he pitied him? It was a slow burn, this pity. It had begun around the time of his rescue from the island, when his father and his war-band returned five men lighter with nothing to show for their trouble. And over the years, as the numbers began to shrink, and the victories came even less frequently, as the dream of recovering their ancient birthright receded, and as Somerled grew taller and wider, the feeling could not be mistaken.

He could no longer blame indigestion for his unease when his father called on Alfric the Bard to sing his second-rate songs about their ancestry. He watched his father's face in the firelight, listening to the roll call of heroes stretching back to Colla Uais and the high kings of Ireland. Even the bard, thought Somerled, was rotten. A man of the clan that served their erstwhile host, the lord of Antrim, he had followed them across the sea, professing a love for adventure, suppressing his lack of any discernible musical talent. A man trapped by his birthright.

Somerled could no longer blind himself to the signs of his father's inadequacies: the hesitation before the orders, the scrabbling at small details, the disastrous failure to play his men to their best ability. Gillebrigte misread them at every turn. He mistook sycophancy for cleverness, disagreement for rebellion. He was too prickly and yet too hearty, with forced attempts at overfriendliness that fooled no one but himself.

Soon he would have to admit that his self-appointed mission, which he had laden with boasts and empty prophecies, was a failure. That he, Gillebrigte, son of Gilleadoman, was a failure. That he was no Fionn mac Cumhail, nor even close. Just a small, unsuccessful man living in a leaky hall with reluctant retainers who were themselves out of options.

There were just twenty left of the forty who had set out from Ireland four years before. Gillebrigte of the Caves. It was a good name, for a man backed into a corner. A man riven by the chasm between his ambition and his abilities.

But Somerled owed him loyalty. And, he supposed, love. He watched his father with the little bastards, throwing them skywards until they giggled, tickling them, chasing them. It brought back memories as soft as dreams of his own infant-hood, before all the expectations of the clan fell on him – the only true-born son.

He turned away from his father, to Father Padeen on the other side. Padeen had welcomed him back from his first kill with a smile and a pat, and a reserve that had seemed excessive to the jubilant, elated boy. Now, with the warriors' roaring turning sour for him, he sought the priest.

He leaned across to him, putting his head close to the priest's ear. Without preamble he said: 'What makes a leader?'

'Lord, boy. And what a question. The ability to win fortune and glory for his followers.'

Somerled and Father Padeen talked quietly in Latin, the boy thankful now for all the hours they had spent on the language. Knowing his young pupil, Padeen had taken the lessons outside. They had invented a new technique for salmon fishing, boring the poor bastards to sleep with the endless conjugating and declaiming before hooking them out. God knows what use it would be in his life, but he liked being able to talk to Father Padeen quietly.

'But what is that ability made of?' he asked the priest.

'Skill at arms, cunning, the power to read men.'

'Can you learn these things?'

'The first, yes.' Padeen spread his arms wide. 'The others are God's gift.'

'What else?'

'Something . . .' the priest paused, 'indefinable.'

'Define it.'

'Puppy,' said Padeen, smiling. 'All right. Luck, I suppose. A sense inspired in others, real or imagined, of divine favour.'

'Yes, yes!' Somerled leaned forward. 'So you can do everything right, and not have that luck?'

'Ye-es,' said the priest slowly. 'But some men can forge it for themselves.'

'Who? How?'

'Well, Alexander. Octavian.'

Somerled waved a dismissive arm. 'Them! Ancients. But how?'

Padeen shrugged. 'A mystery.'

Somerled slumped backwards.

Padeen, his voice slow and considered, said: 'Alexander shared his men's hardships – he asked nothing of them that he would not do himself. Yet the emperors in the Great City never see the common people. They are separated by a tribe of eunuchs.'

'Eunuchs?'

'Men with their parts cut out.'

'Jesus!' Somerled shivered.

'Boy! Although perhaps the blasphemy is, in this instance, understandable.'

He laughed loudly. Somerled sensed Gillebrigte leaning in to catch the joke, and he turned closer in to the priest.

Padeen, the hint taken, lowered his voice. 'My point, boy, is that the people of Constantinople expect their king to be distant, impossibly regal. If he jumped down from his palanquin and tried to share their pot, they would assume his wits were gone. The Macedonians wanted one thing, today's Greeks another. To lead a people, you must first understand how they want their leader to be.'

'You must play a part?'

'Yes.' They were silent for a space, both, perhaps, thinking of Gillebrigte. But Somerled would not voice his thoughts even to Father Padeen.

'Perhaps,' said Padeen, at last, 'the part can only be played convincingly if the player feels conviction.'

'So the playing becomes real?'

'Yes.'

A voice barrelled into their midst. 'Now is not the time for God, boy.'

Gillebrigte stood and raised his horn. 'My son!' he shouted. They drank again, noisily. As Gillebrigte sat down, he glanced across at Somerled, who thought he saw something ugly in the old man's gaze; something hidden and vicious.

~ ~ ~

As soon as he could slip out unnoticed, Somerled left the hall. He had long been anticipating the sensation of stepping outside. By Christ, it felt good. The cold air licked his forehead, the quiet was soft on his ringing ears.

He walked down to the beach, easy in the darkness. The familiar stones crunched underfoot. It was a soft, enveloping night. He could see the white of the breakers in the darkness. Above, the stars were just where they should be, unconcerned that he had killed a man. He had killed a man.

Suddenly he felt a bubble of something rising in him – shame? Fear? It was hard to name, but it came spewing out of his mouth in a froth of mead and mutton juice. He knelt on the stony path and retched.

'Better?' A small voice behind him.

He nodded.

She ran down to the sea, becoming more indistinct as she neared the luminous breakers. For a terrible second he thought she meant to swim away, to join the sea fairies and leave him here, on this beach, alone. Just as he stumbled to his feet, he saw her coming back through the gloom. She had a cloth, wet with seawater, and she used it to wipe his face, to smooth the hair back from his forehead. He ran his tongue across his lips, eager for the salt.

'Thank you,' he said.

They sat in silence for a while, on the flat-topped rock beside the dune. Her knees were pulled up under her chin, and she looked up, beyond him, to the stars. She liked watching for the shooters, on clear nights like this one.

A new song thrummed in his head.

I am Somerled. Puke-heaver, boy-killer, death-fearer.

He looked towards her, his skinny, freckled shadow.

Otter-lover.

'Well?' she said. 'What was it like?'

'Christ love me,' he said, 'but it felt good.'

'Why?'

'He was dead, and I was alive. And him being so dead made me more alive.'

She nodded.

'Who was he, do you know?'

'He looked well-born. Cattle raiders, Father said, but . . .' He trailed off.

'But?'

'I thought they could be scouts. It's raiding season.'

'They were Northmen?'

He nodded. 'Not newcomers, from the look of them. From Man, perhaps, or the Outer Isles.'

'But if they were scouts . . .' She paused, and looked at him.

He nodded. 'Father said no. But if it were me, I would be posting proper sentries. Waiting before I unleashed the mead stream.'

'They needed a victory,' she said, and they paused to listen to the chorus of a drinking song, seeping out of the hall.

'Yes,' said Somerled. 'Perhaps he is right then. But if it were me . . .'

'And yet it is not.'

'No.'

He remembered another day, when they were younger, when he had boasted of what he would do when he was a man, and King

39

of Argyll. And she had not mocked him, but had asked him to explain it all to her. So he had drawn a map in the sand, like the one Padeen had taught him from. He had drawn the contours of the Great Sea, and the islands stretching down from the strange, wild Norse ones at the top, past holy Iona and giant Mull, down past Islay and all the way to Man. The islands were misshapes in the sand, Mull too big and Man too small. 'And yet,' he had said, 'the power in the isles comes from Man. Olaf Crovan, whose father was Godred, the Norse warrior of warriors. He came out of Dublin, the stronghold of the Norse – here.' He pointed to the mainland.

'My father went there once,' she said, nodding.

'Well, Godred Crovan, from the tree of Ivar, took Man in our grandfathers' time, and now it takes tribute from the southern islands.'

He traced the finger of Kintyre down to where it pointed at the Irish mainland. 'We are here,' he said. 'Not far from where we first landed.'

She looked up at this.

'Once, it is said, we ruled, in name at least, from here to here.' He pointed from the tip of Kintyre, up along its ridge, towards the great sea lochs, and over them into Morvern and across to Ardnamurchan. 'But my grandfather, Gilleadoman, lost these lands thanks to Macbeth, the traitor, and his brother Donald Ban, and their weasel dealings with the Northmen, the Lochlannaich. Here, in the north, he lost the last of it, when Magnus Barelegs came rampaging through the isles from Norway.'

'That was when you came to Antrim?'

'I was not born. But yes, my people came to Antrim, to our cousins descended from Colla Uais, the High King of Ireland.'

'And here you are.'

'Here we are. We've claimed back this beach, hey. And the warriors dribble away. The whole coast is a pit of rival groups, Lochlannaich and Gael all mixed and snarling at each other. It should have been ripe for the taking. It should have been.'

A giant roar from the hall. They were still going. He leaned against the Otter on the flat-topped rock. Silent and comfortable, back to back. *I am Somerled. Puke-heaver, mead-dodger, soft-bellied, Otter-lover.*

He remembered the fierce twelve-year-old boy who had railed against his elders' weaknesses. But was the twelve-year-old so wrong? They had landed with a host, but caution and attrition had whittled down the band. They were clinging on now. Another small thane with a few cows and a straggle of followers.

It should have been one throw. One bold bid for the queen. One fierce king-move on the tafl board.

Again, was he being fair? Father Padeen always said that it was easier for the young to gamble, because they never truly believed in the possibility of failure. Ageing, he said, was the wearying accretion of small failures.

They heard the dogs barking, the sound drifting down across the machair.

He felt the Otter stiffen. 'That's Cip,' she said. She loved the dogs, the Otter, and they loved her, pushing their wet noses into her hands, fighting to be the one to lick her.

'Well?'

'He does not bark for fun, Somerled. Never.'

The boy scrambled to his feet and grabbed her hand, and they ran back towards the hall. Thinking as he ran, Somerled veered up the steep bank to the right of the hall before they reached the door, which streamed with light. He wanted to preserve their night vision, find out what was happening. They flitted up the path, their childhood games turning serious now. At the bluff, they crouched, wordlessly, and inched forward.

Somerled looked out, scanning the dark horizon. Nothing. He felt the Otter move away, along the top of the low cliff. He scanned, straining his eyes to see. The moon was a sliver, and hidden anyway behind a dark cloud with silvering edges. Nothing. He relaxed, aware suddenly that the heather was wet, and seeping through at the knees. He cursed softly.

Suddenly the Otter was back. Sliding next to him, she put her mouth to his ear, so close her words tickled.

'A boat. Some sort of galley. Beached in the bay across.'

'Mary and Joseph,' whispered Somerled. They had beached, and now they must be circling. The small crew this afternoon had been scouts. Jesus, the boy he'd killed could be the jarl's son. His firstborn.

'Stay here,' he said to Otter. She made to stand, and he gripped her skinny shoulders. 'Stay the fuck here.' He hissed the words, and she nodded.

~ ~ ~

He ran into the hall, shouting for silence.

'To arms!' he screamed, his voice cracking into a high note. 'An ambush.'

A heartbeat of stunned silence, and then a roaring, swearing panic. At the head of the maelstrom stood his father, still and silent. Why wasn't he moving, the daft old bugger? Move.

Aed, huge and mead-crazed, like something out of the legends of the north that his mother spun, jumped across a table and stood near him. 'Where are they, boy?'

'Their boat is beached on the strand beyond the bluff. They are coming.'

'Do we have time?'

'I don't know. No.'

All around them were the muttered curses of men trying to find their gear and their wits. And still Gillebrigte stood motionless. At the far end of the hall, the women were shushing the clutch of children, whose wails were fuelling the panic. Somerled ran over to them. His own mother, bright-eyed but calm, came forward to him.

'Take them out. Hide in the far dunes. The watchword for friends is "Otter". Do not emerge until you hear the word.'

She nodded, and turned. From behind him, a voice. 'Giving orders, are you, boy?'

He looked at his father, at the broken veins in his flushed cheeks and the watery eyes. 'Are *you*?' he asked, lightly.

Aed shouted: 'We are ready, lord.'

They both turned to look at him. The men were ranged up, helmeted and swaying, the firelight glinting off their steel, shining from their mead-rich eyes. Along with them were some of the boys, Somerled's unblooded childhood friends. Domnall, Diarmait and Ruaridh. Where they had found their arms from, he did not know. Ruaridh, yet to grow, was dwarfed by his helmet, which tipped over his eyes, giving him a raffish air. Somerled would have laughed at him, called the banter down on his head, but now was not the time. Father Padeen, his helmet covering his tonsured forehead and his great axe jumping from hand to hand, nodded at him, then hazarded a wink.

Gillebrigte stood next to him, breathing heavily. Suddenly he sank to his knees and began to puke noisily on the heather-strewn floor. Jesus wept, thought Somerled. He waited a pause for someone else to speak; Aed or Iehmarc. He looked at Iehmarc, the weasel man, his father's pet sycophant, who raised an eyebrow.

Jesus. Breathe. *Straw leader. Fake warrior.*

'Storm out,' he shouted. 'Defensive shields, in a half-circle. They'll see us better than we'll see them as we come out. We need to get the women away. Mother, come out behind us.'

'Aren't they safer here?' asked Iehmarc.

'We don't know how many there are. If they fuck us up first, what's the next thing they'll do?'

'We'll take our chances with the night faeries, Iehmarc,' shouted his mother. 'Not wait here to be spitted.'

Breathe. Breathe. Breathe.

'Now!'

Outside was shockingly quiet. For the second time that night, Somerled felt the cold air slap him alert. In the rounded half-circle, they paused, taking stock. Behind them, the women and children flitted. The baby – Aed's child by his pocket-sized wife Oona – shrieked, breaking the silence. The warriors flinched, waiting for the spears. They stood in close, shields up, fidgeting and grumbling softly, checking their hastily donned gear, looking out over the tops of their shields into the darkness. The mountains loomed black against the ink-blue sky, the summits circling in on them like crook-backed ancients. From behind them came the the susurrant hiss of a calm sea.

Slowly, the tension began to unwind.

Somerled peered out at the nearest shadows, where rocks lurked in tricksy silhouettes and hillocks promised cover to phantoms.

Beside him, Aed shifted weight from one foot to the other, the pebbles scrunching with the movement. The grumbling became a little louder – fewer muttered incantations and more whispered whines.

So, thought Somerled. Would I rather be wrong and look foolish, or be right and be facing a horde? It was, he thought, an interesting question; one to unpick later.

Thorfinn the Catcher, a big man with more Norse than Gael, was the first to speak. 'Well, little lord,' he said. 'And did I not have a full horn of mead? Are we done with your joke?'

Aed grunted his disapproval.

'Hold fast,' said Somerled.

'There!' shouted Iehmarc.

Somerled whirled round.

''Tis a fairy coming to murder us,' Iehmarc hooted. 'Show it your arse, Aed, that'll send the bugger running.'

The laughter ran through the line. Somerled felt Aed grappling for a comeback.

'Sheep-raper,' said the giant.

'Is that your best?' said Thorfinn.

'Hush!' hissed Somerled. He closed his eyes tight, and counted to five. Opening them again, he found the scene clearer; the shadows resolving themselves into recognisable shapes. He heard, somewhere, the crunch of a foot on stones. The women?

Iehmarc began to sing a quiet song about drinking. Somerled had noticed that when his father was not around, the steward seemed to widen and coarsen, as if the man burdened with flattering Gillebrigte had a counterbalance, a shape-shifted identity who lashed his tongue at underlings and kept his smiles on a tight leash.

This drunk, rash Iehmarc was a new thing. His song grew louder and louder, until at last he was shouting through Somerled and Aed's shushing. As the chorus came, Iehmarc's brother, young Niall, stepped forward out of the line, holding his shield above his head like a serving tray. He danced a jig designed to make his few mates laugh, and they obliged.

'Well then, puppy,' said Iehmarc, grinning at Somerled. 'Are we done? Can we bring back the women?'

He was still grinning when the spear took his brother in the throat, with a savage tearing that sent the boy reeling to the floor. They came like summer rain then, spitting on to the raised shields, seeking out bare flesh.

Behind the spears came the men. It was, in the darkness, like being attacked by something mythical. A sea serpent with coiling metal scales that flashed and screamed and bit. It snaked round them, screaming, screaming, a great looping ululation that drove the wind from Somerled's stomach and wiped his mind blank. Sparks showered in the black night air as steel clanged on steel. Around him, men were falling.

Not Aed; oh God set a flower upon his head. Not Aed. The warrior screamed back, and whirled and danced with death, his great shaggy coat soon matted with blood. His own? Theirs? Somerled screamed too, and the screaming helped him push forward; to parry and hack and thrust with the roar pounding in his head like a fist. A man's face, close. Not his man. He jerked his shield up, taking his opponent's nose with it, watching it spread across his face, watching the blood spraying like mucus and the man's crazed eyes above. His sword came from under, and took the stranger in the ribs. Punching and slicing, and pulling back, his grip on the pommel slippery and slimy.

The serpent whirled him round and spun him about, so he could not tell which way was sea and which mountain. Another man, coming at him. A stupid, careless man, with a raised arm and a pit begging to be skewered. Somerled, trained, looked for the trick, the feint. No, he was that stupid, and he died quickly.

A new something now, tugging at his mind. What? He couldn't concentrate, not for a second. Little Ruaridh, pinned back, howling. Somerled bunched small and pounced large, knocking Ruaridh's man down, stepping on his face as the rush carried him forward, grinding his heel as best he could and feeling something snap. 'Finish him,' he screamed at his friend, who, wiping the blood and tears from his face, could only nod and stumble forward with his too-large sword.

'To me! To me! Men of Lorne! To me!' screamed Somerled, and the serpent seemed to coil back, its scales in the darkness glinting less, and quiet now. Suddenly he could concentrate on the new something, and as they flocked to him, he recognized it. Burning.

Turning, he saw the brushwood piled against the sides of the hall. He saw the flames dancing towards the roof and heard the cackle and spit of damp sticks. And there, staggering through the open doorway, like a crazed and fiery offering to the old gods, was his burning father.

~ ~ ~

Dawn came slowly to the beach. The sun rose, he supposed, but it was hidden behind a thick tapestry of grey and black clouds. As the sky brightened, he watched the grasses on the sand that grew perpetually sideways, buffeted by the wind. He saw how they did not even try to stand tall, but hugged the earth as if wary of growing upright.

As it grew lighter still, he could see the faces of his people; their poor, soot-grimed, defeated, tear-tracked faces. Some slept, curled in the sand. Others watched the sea, as if the rhythm of the retreating waves held a clue, a portent. His sister, Brigte, twelve years old and resilient as a scallop shell, skipped along the top of a far dune, as if this were an adventure fresh for the taking.

His father slept now. His cries had echoed over the strand, his sobs and curses rising to the stars. It was as if he was waking himself,

Sigrdrifa had whispered to her son. One side of Gillebrigte's body seemed to have melted, the skin scoured and crusted with melted wool. Father Padeen had cleaned him by the light of the fire that burned him, and kept him topped up with whisky to muffle the pain. Until, at last, as light glimmered fitfully on the horizon, he had slept. Or slipped into unconsciousness. Either way, it was a guilty relief when he stopped screaming.

Somerled and the Otter sat side by side, holding hands. Her father, Fhearghais, watched them with narrowed eyes. But the night was too raw, too exceptional, to hold them to normal rules. When death came so close, thought Somerled, life seemed like an affectation. A succession of small rules that didn't really matter.

He faced away from the hall, towards the sea. He could smell it smouldering, and the ash floated down upon their heads like a charcoal rain. The heat of it reached across the sand, and his back was hot.

'At least we didn't need a fire,' he whispered to the Otter.

She gripped his hand a little tighter, and leaned into him, avoiding her father's eyes.

At last, when it was light enough, Somerled let go of her hand and stood up, shaking the sand from his clothes and hair.

'We had better go and look,' he said. Bleak faces tilted to look at him. His mother and the Otter were already standing. A handful of warriors lumbered to their feet, and in that he knew the best of them. Aed, of course. And little Ruaridh, who barely reached past the giant's waist. Domnall, just thirteen, with his father Oengus; the two of them standing, dark-haired and grimy, side by side. Thorfinn the Catcher, who grumbled as he rose, but rose nonetheless. Sigurd Horse-face, who looked nothing like a horse; and Alfric the Bard. He might be rotten on the harp, thought Somerled, but he had heart.

The rest, eyes darting to Gillebrigte's sleeping body, set their shoulders away from Somerled. Iehmarc spat into the sand. His face and clothes were blood-soaked from the cradling of his brother's corpse. He looked away. Who would be led by a fifteen-year-old boy? They had lost enough without that final absurdity.

So be it. 'Fhearghais,' said Somerled. The Otter's red-haired father looked up, casually. 'Will you and Sigurd here relieve the lookouts?'

'What are we watching for? They are long gone,' said Fhearghais. 'They did what they came for.'

'And if they are not? What if they want slaves, hey? How much do you think Eimhear would fetch in Dublin?'

'A sight more than you could pay, boy,' said Fhearghais, looking towards the Otter and beyond her to the rising smoke. But he climbed to his feet and picked up his spear, and walked off slowly towards the high bluff.

Somerled left the others to sulk, and walked towards the hall. Over the brow of the dune behind the beach they saw the flat land where the cattle should have been. The pasture was empty. Had they taken them, or just driven them away? The sheep pen was pulled open. Empty.

The hall was charred and twisted, beyond redemption. The heart of it still burned in red embers; the rest smoked and hissed.

Sigrdrifa, beside him, was muttering: 'The dogs, the fucking dogs. All the work. All the work. Oh great Thor, bring thunder on their heads. Carve them up. Strike them down. All the work. And how shall we feed the children?'

She moved through the blackened ruin where she could, picking up fragments, lamenting each one. She had been working all through the spring and summer to get ready for winter: pickling and smoking and curing; piling up food and wool against the lean times. And now it was all gone.

Aed came up from behind him. 'The fishing curraghs are sound, Somerled. Four of them. The big galley . . .' He shrugged. His father's war galley. Gone.

'He should have posted lookouts, Aed. You know it. Why didn't you tell him?'

'Because, little lord, I was worried he would make me do it, if I spoke. And I wanted a fire, and a bucket full of mead, and to see my woman.'

Disarmed by the big man's bitter honesty, Somerled just nodded. He imagined Father Padeen's voice. *What have you learned?* To be wary of the easy road. *What will you do?* Weep on the inside. *What will they see you do?* Stand tall.

There was the priest himself, kneeling, praying. Somerled walked over to him. In his hands, Father Padeen cradled his dearest possession, a wrought-iron cross with the Lord's body twisted on it. The iron had melted in the heat, fusing body and cross, scorching the Lord's face. Padeen wept.

Behind him, the Otter shouted. She held up some pots, blackened but intact. 'Food,' she said.

Sigrdrifa crossed to her and rootled about, pushing her hair back with charcoaled fingers. Somerled joined them, picking his way past the ruin of what had been his parents' sleeping area. She smiled at him. 'We have some left,' she said. 'How I hate to face a winter unprepared.'

'Is it worth such a smile?' he asked.

'Tsk, boy. Look at Padeen there, weeping away over his little statue. That's the problem with your God. You expect him to be kind and loving, then you're disappointed when he's not. Fools. The old gods, they showed us to expect nothing. *Nothing*. Then,' she said, waving a slice of smoked herring at him, 'you can be surprised when they throw you a nugget of mercy. Here. Breakfast.'

She glanced sideways at the Otter, then looked back at Somerled with a curious tilt to her head. He stared back, saying nothing. 'Well,' she said. 'Why not?

'Eimhear!' she shouted, though the girl was close by. 'Breakfast.' She handed her a piece of the fish. The Otter took it reverently, glancing up at Somerled.

Before he had time to understand what was happening, he heard shouting. Aed's head shot up, and he looked over at Somerled. They ran down to the beach, their feet sticky in the ash-covered sand. There, by the high-tide mark, stood Sigurd, his back to the beached curraghs, his sword in hand. Circling him were five of the band, led by Fhearghais, or so it seemed. Iehmarc sat apart, watching. Smiling.

'Stop!' Somerled shouted. They turned to look at him, and he realized that he did not quite know what to do next. So he walked forward. Swords bristled at him. Fhearghais' face above his shield was set and ugly. Somerled was caught off guard by his inverse resemblance to his daughter: the same red hair, the same cool, white skin. He stopped, uncertain suddenly.

'We are going home, boy,' said Fhearghais. 'Enough of this gull crap. We all of us know that your father is done, finished. We'll take our chances back across the sea.'

'You swore an oath.'

'Your father broke it, by being unworthy of it.' Fhearghais spat the words, and they were terrible. An unspoken truth made vocal, laid bare like the bones of a beached whale. Somerled felt the awe of it ripple around the men, and when it reached Aed, the big man shook with rage and bile.

'No,' said Somerled as the champion moved forward. 'No!' he

shouted, and Aed backed down, shaking his head as if to make the world seem still again.

Sigurd, his face red and taut, said: 'Gillebrigte's son is here, Fhearghais.'

Fhearghais looked at Somerled, and his face softened. 'Aye, and he's a good boy,' he said. 'We can all see that. But he is a boy. And I am a man alone with a daughter in tow, and I need a lord who can give me silver.'

Somerled looked at him with a level green stare. The man paled and fidgeted, his weight shifting from boot to boot. 'A good boy,' he repeated in a quiet voice that tailed off a little.

'Let them go,' Somerled said.

'Lord!' protested Sigurd.

'I said let them go.'

Sigurd dropped his sword.

'Listen,' said Somerled. 'We know we cannot stay here. With no hall, no wood, no silver, no livestock. We will have to head back to the caves at Morvern and start again.'

Aed and Fhearghais nodded; one sadly, the other with the smug air of a man proved right.

'So,' said Somerled, 'we will need only those who are committed. We cannot watch our arses as well as our noses. Go, Fhearghais. But know this. When I am king of all the lands my family lost, I will find you, and I will drown you in molten silver. You will choke on silver. I will give you so much silver that you will beg for your mother while it sets solid in your throat.'

Fhearghais forced a laugh, but the boy's face was hard and implacable, and the four men with him wilted.

'Enough,' said a voice behind him, and the Otter stepped forward.

'You're staying here,' said Somerled.

'And am I a slave that you can order me?'

'No, but you must stay.'

'He is my father, Somerled. I must go.'

'No.' He sounded like a petulant boy, he knew. He felt the smirks of the men at his back.

She stepped forward, and drew him away to the side. The older men's eyes were on them. Some were indulgent, some scornful. He knew that Iehmarc was watching. He tried to shrug off their scrutiny and concentrate on her. She put her lips to his ear and whispered low, so that her voice was like listening to the sea trapped inside a shell. 'Let me go, and I will come back, my summer heart. I will come back.'

eimbeaR

We sailed away. We left him standing there on the shore looking after us. We left him with nothing: some provisions, a handful of men. A furious mother who capered on the beach and shook her fist at us as we set off through the breakers. A melted wreck of a father.

The boat sailed under a cloud of guilt and oath-breaking. They wrangled it endlessly. 'Our oath was not to the boy. Our oath was to the father.'

Nods and grunts.

'He broke his oath first.'

'He did. He allowed this to happen. What kind of lord sets no watch at a feast when there's raiders around?'

'Aye, and where was he in the fighting? Inside asleep, with the skin melting off him.'

'Jesus, but he was a terrible sight.'

They all fell silent at this, remembering him staggering and screaming out of the hall, his clothes still flaming. The smell of him punching through the wet, smoky air. The popping hiss of his burning skin. The stench of him, like crackling.

The youngest, Magnus the Red, looked as if he might cry. Such

54

an awful thing to break an oath. He stroked his auburn beard, as if to remember he was a man with man's choices. I wanted to make him cry; I wanted the pain of his betrayal to bite.

I said nothing; huddled into my father.

He was quiet, too, and unusually tender. He stroked my hair back from my face. He let me be quiet and still. He said nothing as I cried, just held on to my hand and let me weep.

I do not know what I wept for. My friend, my home? I was too young, I think, to understand that it was for Somerled and me. I was too young to know that what hurt most, as I sailed away, was the end of dreams I had not known how to dream.

~ ~ ~

We settled, at first, with some distant cousins in a glen too far from the sea in the land of the Ulaid. They were old, childless and bitter about it. Conchobar was the younger son of a dispossessed younger son, and was in a state of permanent half-rage at his small life. He was bent-backed from work, his face lined under a bald head that proclaimed to the world his inability to grow hair or make sons. His wife, Aine, was a silent woman. Taller than her husband, but quiet; weighed down by the viciousness of his tongue and the guilt of her barrenness.

She would not talk to me. When I tried, she slid her eyes away from me and found a new chore. Perhaps she is shy, I thought. I tried, again and again, until at last, when she ran from me, I gave up.

When I first understood that my father was to leave me with them, to go and fight for the local lord, I cried for a day.

'I cannot take you with me, my darling. You'll be safe here.'

'Please don't go.'

'And how will we eat? I will be back soon, my treasure, you will see. Carrying silver, and jewels for your hair.' He left, and as he went, the silence dropped like a shroud.

My best friend was the pig.

'I was loyal to him, Pig. And still he leaves me here. I could have stayed with Somerled.'

Snort, snuffle, scrape.

'I could, Pig. I know my duty is to my father, but is it his duty to leave me here, in this place? Do you know, Pig, that when we eat, there is complete silence. Scrape, scrape. You hear the bread scratch the bottom of the bowl as loud as thunder. It's hard as a rock, this bread, anyway.'

Her head raised at the word *bread*, and she lumbered forward, her massive head lolling from side to side with its great weight as she shifted from foot to foot.

'Sorry, my darling. I haven't any. I was just saying the word. I have some nuts for you. There. They'll make you lovely and fat.'

I rubbed the bristling, rough skin on her back as she ignored me, ploughing into the nuts.

Of all the things I hated about that place, the distance from the sea galled the most. How could they bear it? At night, they were not lulled to sleep by the hissing rush of the waves. Instead, there was a sinister silence that kept me awake and listening for ghosts. In the first summer there, when it was so hot that the pig would not leave the shade even for the choicest stale bread, Lord, how I pined for the sea. I would lie in the stream beyond the house, but it was too shallow. It was just a cooling-down, a functional thing. There was no joy in it. I wanted to float in the bob of the sea. That was all I thought about, all I prayed about that summer. Lord, let me swim soon. Lord, let me turn a somersault in deep water. Lord, let me go home.

But there was no home. Just a burned-out shell and a burned-out shell of a lord, and Somerled scrabbling for a life on a desolate shore.

'Pig, you're lucky. You have a home.'

Snuffle, grunt.

'They'll mate you soon. Did you know that, Pig? You'll have babies, and then you won't be lonely.'

The pig was the only being I told when I began to bleed, the second winter there. I knew what to do; Sigrdrifa had talked to me of it. I should have been surrounded by women, combing my hair, twirling me round, welcoming me to their ranks. Instead, the mute Aine gestured silently to the pot where I should boil the rag clean. She looked at me now with a new intensity.

In the torrid silence of that house, I began to feel watched. Eyes were on me. I'd glance up and see Conchobar looking away. Spin round and see Aine becoming suddenly busy with a neglected task. Was there ever a woman more unfortunately named? It means splendour, brilliance, radiance. She sucked the light in and turned it dark, this Aine.

As I get older, I can find compassion for her. She was named for the fairy wife of Fionn mac Cumhail, the best-hearted, kindest of his wives. And the fruitful one.

Back then, I hated her.

~ ~ ~

'Are you finished with your chores, girl?'

Conchobar stood behind me. There was something about him that made me uneasy. Something about the way his feet were planted so wide; the drawing-up of his hunched-over back.

'No. I have to gather some more nuts. We're low.'

The pig heard the word and grunted, scuffling up the muddy ground with her trotters.

Conchobar came forward. The low autumn sun was behind him, and I couldn't see his face clearly. I could not work out quite why he was making me nervous. I moved closer to the pig and put my hand out to feel the familiar rough scratch of her back.

'We've not heard from your father for months. Since the pedlar at Easter. Seems to me he's probably dead. We heard word of a battle.'

'There's always battles.'

'Seems to me that if he's dead, you need to start paying your way.'

'I do my chores, do I not? I keep your livestock and tend your vegetables. I cook your food and wash your clothes.'

He laughed, a strange, thin sound. 'And do I not have a wife for all that? Why keep a dog and get another to do its barking?'

As if whistled, his dog came round the corner. A sly, vicious thing. He usually avoided the pig. They hated each other, and we laughed about him when he was not there.

Jesus. Sometimes I forgot, in my loneliness, that she was only a blessed pig.

The dog curled himself around his master's shin, and yapped at me and the pig. The pig squealed back at him, and I began to laugh.

'You're always laughing, girl. What is there to smile about? What the fuck is there to smile about, that's what I want to know. Are you cracked? Are you mad? Have you seen how we live? That pig lives better than we do; you fuss that animal.'

He moved a little closer. 'You know we're to eat her? You know that we're to fry her, roast her, sizzle her, salt her?'

'Why else do I fatten her up?'

I turned away from him, looking at the pig's small eyes. Then I felt him close, and his hand snaking round my waist.

'What are you doing?'

'You know well enough.' His voice was thick, throaty. I tried to pull away. He gripped my arm with a surprising strength, and I realized to my horror that this close up he was bigger than he seemed. He smelled of whiskey and dog hair. The dog yapped at my ankles, as if excited by this new game. Pig, the treacherous pig, carried on worrying at a rotten cabbage.

'Get off me,' I screamed. His other hand clamped over my mouth, yanking my head back so I felt his breath judder at my ear.

'Quiet. Do you want her to hear us?'

He had no free hands then. One to grip and one to silence. But I felt him begin to grind his body against the back of mine, and the vomit churned in my stomach.

'I'll take this hand away if you're a good girl. If you're a good girl, I'll give you a pretty necklace. Would you like that?'

I nodded.

Slowly he moved his hand away from my mouth. Whispering at me as if I were a frightened horse.

'Good girl. Quiet now. There's a good girl.'

His hand hovered by my face. Quickly I jerked my neck forward and bit down. My teeth crunched on bone and skin. The dog howled and yapped, the pig grunted and the man let out a scream of rage and pain. He dropped hold of me and I turned quickly, kicking him as hard as I could in his bollocks. He dropped to the ground, bleeding and spluttering.

I ran to the house, bursting in. Aine was huddling in the corner. She looked up at me. I put my hand to my mouth, and it came away bloody. Jesus wept, I must have looked like a wild and vengeful fairy, bursting in there, blood dripping from my teeth. She stood up and walked towards me.

'He tried to. He—'

I don't know what I expected. Not the hard and masculine punch to the face that snapped me backwards and sent the lights of the world spinning round inside my head. She pushed past me to get outside. Blurring with pain and rage, I gathered my pathetic bundle and what food I could grab and ran out. Up the path by the stream. The direction my father had ridden off in, nearly two years before. I paused by the rocky ford and looked back down at them. They stood watching me go; him still on his knees.

I screamed down the hill at them, so fierce it made my aching head threaten to burst.

'I hope the pig eats you, you turds. Roasts you, sizzles you, salts you. You and your fecking dog.'

1125

somerled

O utside, a torment of snow and ice. A wind so sharp it could lay a man's skin open. Inside the cave, a muffled, crouching sort of a life. Mostly they found the blessed torpor that kept minds sane in winter, when the walls closed in.

The rocks of the cave were cold and damp to the touch. There was a crack in the roof, somewhere above their heads. There must have been, for the smoke from the fire found its way out, mostly. The smoke that lingered grimed the walls and sooted their throats.

Low rations. Watching Sigrdrifa's careful splitting of the strips of dried meat and fish. Counting as she doled it out carefully. Trying not to think of the charred stubble of their fields. The splinters of their ruined hall. The lost cows and the dead hens.

The rocks of Loch Linnhe they could reach at low tide were stripped bare. Even the limpets, rubbery and grim though they were to eat. At the ebb of the tide, when the weather relented to let them leave the cave, they could see across to the mainland and its mountains, heavy with snow. There was a forbidding beauty there. A sparkling white world. But, as Sigrdrifa said, hungry bellies made for dull eyes, and most of the time they were cast downward, looking for a string of plump mussels, a tangle of edible seaweed.

61

White was the colour of menace, of cold. White was the colour of death.

Yet, blessed be the Lord, no one died that winter.

The children fretted and whined, but they did not die.

The adults led a crouching existence; a grim cycle of seeking food, shelter, warmth. Hanging on.

Gillebrigte sank further into a disconnected half-life. He was topped up continually on whisky, even when the pain no longer justified it. His burns hardened into pitted scabs, with their own complicated geography of mounds and valleys and dark ridges where the blood had set.

They all colluded, without acknowledging it, in his slow pickling. He was sometimes violent, often lachrymose. Only Sigrdrifa could soothe him, hectoring him in her strange, jumbled language until he calmed. On the rare occasions he was lucid, he was vicious. Iehmarc goaded him, whispering to him.

Pent up in the cave during the winter storms, Somerled thought he might snap. He thought he might launch himself at Iehmarc, limbs flailing like a berserker. He grew envious of the small children, who were allowed to give in to their rage, allowed to throw themselves on the floor and punch the unforgiving stone, to arch their backs and scream, roar themselves hoarse.

He took refuge in elaborate mind plays, in which Otter came back and Iehmarc's whispering malice drew divine retribution. He tried to plan for the spring, but there seemed to be no future in the caves; only a relentless present.

~ ~ ~

They told stories. Bright fables of St Colm Cille crossing the sea. He stood in his curragh as it beached on holy Iona, cross in hand, the Lord's name on his cracked lips. Stories of the old gods, Norse and Gael both. Just stories, said Padeen to the children. Not like our Lord.

Once, Somerled watched his mother turn on Padeen with venom in her eyes. Brigte was lying on her lap, watching the fire, her mother's hand brushing her hair from her forehead again and again.

'Pah,' hissed Sigrdrifa. 'Don't give me that, priest. Your God is so great, and so good. Yet how can he explain us here in this cave?'

'He does not need to explain. He moves in ways beyond our ken.'

'Please.' She closed her eyes as if in pain. 'Always you Christians have an answer. He is your God, and he loves you, you say. If life works, it is the goodness of God. If your life is shit, God moves in mysterious ways. If your life is unbearably, impossibly shit, don't worry, children, there's always heaven. He'll be nice to you in heaven.'

Padeen shrugged. 'And what do your squabbling, childish gods do but behave like toddlers. Worse?'

'But at least it explains things. What else can explain the way life batters us but the trickster God? Your theology has no Loki, and that's where it falls, Padeen. There must be someone spiteful up there. Someone who thinks it is funny when we crawl on our knees. A malicious trickster, laughing, and the rest? Indifferent. What other view of heaven makes sense?'

Padeen looked down to Brigte, whose eyes were closed now. There was a hint of a smile on her face and her skin glowed gold from the fire. Sigrdrifa's hands kept up their gentle, rhythmic stroking. Over and again she ran her hands over her daughter's hair, handling it like silk.

'There is something your view of heaven misses, Sigrdrifa,' said the priest.

'What?'

'Love.'

Somerled watched his mother's hands, hatcheted with lines, calloused with work, pause in their stroking. She made a non-committal noise, and resumed the movement. Padeen, the Lord bless him, had the good sense to turn away from her then, watching the shadows leap and crow on the cave walls.

~ ~ ~

Somerled spent much time that winter with Aed and Oona. She was smaller than Somerled, fine-boned and flinty. She looked at the big warrior with adoring eyes, which turned sour when other women approached. Her life revolved around one central truth: that Aed was the most handsome, desirable man to have ever lived. She found it inconceivable that other women did not agree. They were plotting to entice him, their seeming indifference a mere ploy.

Aed could hold his two hands around her tiny waist. He could pick her up and put her on a high rock, where she squealed with delicious fright. There was something touching and appealing about their evident joy in each other and the baby. He was much longed for, the child. She had miscarried time and again. Her labour with baby Aed had been long and difficult. Baby Aed was a god; a prince. He was cosseted and kissed, and the big warrior grumbled she would spoil him, before rubbing the baby's tummy with his beard and laughing at his squeals.

'I never asked you something,' said Somerled one day, as they cast lines into the icy sea beyond the cave. A rare clear day. Cold, but bright. The wind had dropped, this once, and they could talk and hold their faces up to the weak sun. 'I never asked how you came to be here.'

'No?' said Aed, peering into the shallows.

'Well?'

'Well. Magnus Barelegs. May he be flayed by demons. While my mother was carrying me.'

Somerled nodded. The violent rampage of the Norwegian king still echoed through the islands and coastal settlements of this sea. Laying claim to southern isles to sit alongside his northern holdings, he had torn through the islands like a malevolent gale, wasting and burning, raping and destroying. Forcing his terrified victims to admit his sovereignty.

'Those of us who survived ended up like beggars on the fringes of the Antrim court,' said Aed. 'My family were little kings in their own place. Until Magnus Barelegs. My mother, God bless her, did not let me forget. But we had nothing.' Something in Aed's face warned Somerled against asking questions. There was, he thought, some clear Norse in the great man's shaggy countenance. His father, God forbid?

Aed paused, cursing softly as his foot slipped on the green-slimed rock. 'Your father stood on a table in the court. He offered an adventure to all the landless, to the younger sons and the dispossessed, to the children birthed in the fire of Barelegs' making. The Earl of Antrim told your father that he could take as many of the younger, unwanted band as he could fit in the chapel. I was eighteen, and hungry. I elbowed my way in.'

He turned to Somerled, looking at him through a tangle of hair. 'Remember, boy, that your father was young once. He was confident. Certain of his destiny. Like you now.'

Somerled nodded, but he couldn't imagine his father young. His attempts to picture it dissolved quickly, leaving an image of the drooping, pickled man of the cave.

'Aed, why did you not leave with Fhearghais and the others?'

The big man turned back to his salmon. 'I don't know,' he said. 'Better to have nothing here than nothing there, perhaps. I'm not ready to go back a failure yet. I've cousins who would be too glad to see that.'

They caught three small fish, and rewarded themselves with the smallest. They built a fire in the lee of a small rock and roasted it on a stick, crunching through the blackened skin and into the white flesh.

'My father,' said Somerled slowly, as the fire cosseted warmth back into his limbs, 'should have staked it all on a first strike. One push against the Norse, when we first sailed here. He settled for a long campaign without the means to sustain it.'

'Perhaps,' said Aed.

'And now we are in the same position, just writ smaller. Too few men to strike without risk, yet slow attrition if we do not.'

Aed licked the last of the fish from his fingers, and picked his way through the bones.

'Well,' said Somerled. 'Then we must risk all. Push forward our queen.'

Aed looked up sharply. Somerled felt as if he was being weighed and measured. He kept as still as he could, rigidly returning the big man's stare.

Aed, at last, grinned and nodded.

~ ~ ~

'Spring is coming.' Somerled looked around the watching faces. Noon outside, but in the cave it was dark. The fire was low; their peat stores were running out. He thought about being caught in here with no heat, no light. He imagined the press of the dank walls, the smell of damp wool that never dried.

'We must plan our move. Be ready.'

He saw Aed nodding, his smile visible behind a tangle of hair. Ruaridh piped his approval in his unbroken voice. Sigrdrifa, her hands busy with a pile of wool in her lap, muttered something that might be assent. Behind her, Gillebrigte lay sleeping, a noisy, irritating medley of whistles and grunts.

'We should send a party out in the curragh, to Man perhaps, or Iona.' This from Padeen. He nodded as he spoke, as if to convince himself.

'And what good would that do?' Iehmarc sat picking at his nails with a knife.

'Do you not feel our ignorance? Since the raid, we have seen no one. We cling like limpets to this rock, with as much ignorance as they. When last we heard it, Toirdelbach Ua Conchubair held sway in Ireland. Godred in Man. In the south, the Conqueror's son Henry. Is he still there? The last we heard, his only son had drowned.'

A few men crossed themselves. Fear of drowning shadowed them all.

'Did it send him mad? Is he still king? Is a son of Mael Coluim Canmore still king over in Alba? Alexander reigned when we dropped from sight, but he is childless. His wife is dead, we know that. Perhaps he has married again and whelped. They say he has made bastards.'

'It is strange,' said Sigrdrifa. 'All these kings with no sons.'

Iehmarc made a sound of contempt. 'And why does it matter, priest? Why? We are ants to them. Spawn. We are nothing. We fester in a cave.'

'Of course it matters, man. Kings die, kingdoms fall. Would you set sail without checking which way the wind blows? Perhaps the sons of Magnus Barelegs have been killing and thieving in the isles again. Perhaps the Scottish kings have given up sitting on their arses in Dunfermline speaking French to each other and are marching across the mountains to stake a claim to the west. We don't know.'

Somerled saw something like panic rising in Padeen. He saw the big priest's hands twist on the molten cross he carried like a talisman. He could understand it. It was unnerving, this cave-dwelling. The wind howling at the entrance, the men crouched inside like beasts until the whole world beyond seemed a dream. A Loki-sent, confusing tale told to make children behave.

Sigrdrifa stoked the fire and a sudden leaping of flames threw a dark shadow on the priest's face as he said, in a low voice, 'Jesus keep us, but judgement day itself could be tumbling from heaven and we would not know it.'

The younger boys looked solemn at this, gazing at the priest's shade-dappled face.

Sigrdrifa laughed into the silence. She stood up with a creak and a grunt, muttering to herself in her mother's tongue.

'Enough,' said Iehmarc. 'Even supposing the priest is right, and the world is being unmade out there . . .' He waved vaguely towards the cave's entrance. They turned to look, as if learning for the first time of its existence. Not Somerled. He kept his eyes carefully on Iehmarc's face. 'It makes no difference,' the steward said. 'We have only one choice. There are too few of us. Fhearghais was right. The only thing to do is abandon our claims here, and throw ourselves into the service of another lord.'

'No.' Somerled's voice was sharp, almost petulant. He must learn how to speak like a lord, he thought, catching the off-key tone. 'No,' he said again.

Iehmarc looked across at him, waiting. A curl in his lip, a challenge in his raised eyebrows.

'My father is still the lord here.'

As if hearing Somerled in his nightmares, Gillebrigte grunted and turned in his sleep. Somerled could see the burned part of him now, the sickening, puckered mess of skin.

'Truly?' Iehmarc said. Somerled felt the hatred twisting him round its hilt. He clenched and bunched his muscles to fight it off, struggling to keep upright and calm. He looked around. Nine of them if you counted the boys and discounted his father. If he killed Iehmarc, there would be eight, even if he succeeded in the fight, which was doubtful. Iehmarc was about thirty, battle-seasoned and tough. Let him go and he might take one or two with him. What could Somerled do then, with a sprinkling of men and some boys? Nothing.

I am Somerled. The patient one. The Loki-fired one. The clever one.

'Perhaps you are right, Iehmarc,' he said, quietly. Over his enemy's head he saw his mother suddenly stand upright, away from her chore, looking at him.

'I am sixteen. Untested. My father is indisposed.'

Thorfinn snorted at this, but the others ignored it. Somerled felt the pressure of their eyes boring into him.

'Perhaps I should rely more on your wise counsel, like my father did. Who advised him, Iehmarc, not to set sentries the night of the ambush? Who whispered in his ear that the feast was the thing? Who stroked him and puffed him up?'

Iehmarc began to look uneasy. He looked around the men for allies, but there was something hypnotic about Somerled's tone, something mesmerizing in his eyes. Somerled paused, letting the moment spin itself into a web. He threw it. 'A wager.'

'What sort of a wager, boy?'

'Let me plan a raid, follow me. Give me three weeks. If we are not sitting in our own feasting hall, balls-deep in women and pickled in beer by the end of the third week, then you win.'

'What do I win?'

'Them.' Somerled inclined his head. 'The right to determine the future of the kindred. The right to call me boy.'

'And if you win?'

'You will call me lord. And you will kneel before me, and you will kiss my arse.'

'Three weeks?' Iehmarc shifted his weight, considering. The wager was trapping him. Decline it and he had lost already. That much was clear from the faces of the band. He grunted his assent.

~ ~ ~

They had passed the place on their way back up to the caves. He had barely registered it, lost in the misery and the cold of that voyage. A small hall, clinging desolately to the rocky, wooded shore. A poor man's hall, exposed and barren. But roofed and tended. No beaches up here, just rocky crags that fell away into a violent sea.

He set the younger boys to watch it. From the far side of Lismore island, they would pull across Loch Linnhe before dawn, dropping one of their number off to creep about the heather. Watching. They were too few to leave much to chance, and Somerled wanted to know his enemy. Little Ruaridh was the best of the stalkers; wasted, Sigrdrifa said, on this nonsense, when he could be after some venison.

There were some thirty men, with all their sundry women and hangers-on. Norse settlers, Ruaridh reckoned, though it was difficult to tell at a distance. Christians, he said. Still too many, thought Somerled – even with the advantage of surprise. There were nine in his pitiful band, if you counted the boys and discounted Gillebrigte.

Somerled felt the days drag by. He felt each passing hour as a crease in his forehead, until the frown was so deep it would never lift. Iehmarc watched him from the shadows of the cave, stoking his anticipated triumph.

One clear spring morning, two days before the wager's deadline, Somerled saw the curragh racing for the landing point near the cave, running before the wind with the rigging straining, and the boys aboard standing and waving. Breathless, Ruaridh shouted the news. 'They are gone hunting, Somerled. And with all the kissing and greeting and gear they carried, I'd think they are set for a long haul.'

'How many left?'

'Half, I think. I counted the ones out as fifteen.'

Somerled nodded. This was it. Christ, oh Lord, be with us.

~ ~ ~

The wet, boggy ground seeped through his clothes, leaving him damp and shivery. Somerled ignored it as best he could, concentrating. He wriggled up the hill quietly, keeping close to the ground. He thanked the Lord for the darkness, the absence of the moon.

Ruaridh, the Lord bless and save him, had watched the sentry postings from his mountain perch. He kept calling himself Ruaridh Eagle Eyes, hoping it would stick. Somerled smiled to think of it, and Sigurd's refusal to call him anything but Squirt.

He heard the lookout before he saw him: a great hawking spit. One man only, on top of the small hill behind the hall, where he could watch the sea and the approaches to the glen. He was almost impossible to approach unnoticed. Below him, the entrance of the hall spilt over with light, and the sounds of women singing carried across the night air. A musical, noisy bunch, Ruaridh had said.

Somerled lay on the moist earth, watching the little hall go about its evening joys. The leaking light cast jaunty shadows on the ground. Crouching there, so small amidst the black mountains, it seemed to possess a bravery, an indomitable spirit. It sat, filled with music and light, as the eyes watched from the night. Somerled felt absurdly guilty. We are the thing in the darkness. We are the nightmare.

He waited, trying to ignore his rising unease. It might have been these folk who did for his father's hall, for all he knew. They had a hall, and livestock, and raised beds full of vegetables, and strips of dried peat and a smoking shed, and he did not. They had a galley big enough to take a war-band, and he did not.

They are Northmen, he thought. We live by the rules they brought here. We die by them, too. And so shall they.

He waited. To divert his thoughts from the small lives he was about to take, he thought instead of the Otter, wondering what she was doing. She would be fourteen soon. Perhaps married. Lord, let her not be married.

A new noise hanging in the cold air. Below the top of the small hill, in the darkened hollows, came the unmistakable sound of a woman being tupped. Her low, long moans drifted out across the dark heather. Faster now, with a muffled urgency. Somerled took a risk and poked his head above the heather. Sure enough, the lookout had walked to the edge of the summit, where the boggy ground disappeared into a steep crag. The indistinct figure leaned over, peering into the blackness below, a shower of scree dislodging from under his foot.

Quickly now, Somerled climbed. He grinned as the woman's panted moans grew sharper, timing his footfall to coincide with her ecstasy. He reached the top of the hill, and saw the shape of the lookout black against the dark-blue sky. Almost casually, he pushed, and the man fell with a sharp cry.

A clatter and a pause. Then a low hoot, like an owl, told him the job was done.

They regrouped at the bottom of the hill. Oona, her white-toothed smile breaking the darkness, climbed up to take the sentry's place, her acting done. Or was it acting? Aed looked sleek, the silent banter of the other men's winks and nudges rolling off him.

Somerled hissed into the jollity.

'Concentrate. Form in swine array, at a run. Aed the snout. Me and Iehmarc the ears. Through the door. Kill everything that squeals.'

Iehmarc looked at him, surprised. Somerled stared back.

'Well?'

'Nothing,' Iehmarc muttered. He bounced on his toes, passing his axe from hand to hand.

They formed into a wedge. Aed's sword was sheathed in favour of his great double-headed axe. There was, Somerled realized, a hidden bonus of being in charge. The responsibility of leadership kept him tethered to the wedge. Pride and duty kept him standing, kept him from sinking into the ground to whimper with fear.

As they began to run, his thoughts seemed to soar above his stretching body. Had he anticipated everything? Were they running into a trap? He felt the great weight of other men's souls in his care. Why these men, and not the ones he was running to kill? Were they not in his care too, in a different sense?

Enough. They were on the hall, bursting through into the light. The formation was aptly named. The swine array. They felt like one beast, one great bristling, starving beast, whose snout smelled food and would not be tamed. All the momentum came from Aed, the snout, who laid about with his axe, seeking out enemy skin with all the fury of the world. The sudden transition into the light was blinding, and Somerled, beast-like, roared, hitting out with sword and shield edge. The noise was incredible; a jumbled scream of fear and rage, a tangling of attackers and attacked. Somerled felt his sword punch home. He wrenched it free and swung it around at a new foe, flinging the blood across the room like rain.

A huge man with bare legs came screaming towards him from behind a curtain, axe raised. Satan's arse, he was large, this man, and crazed. Behind him, a woman added her voice to the screaming. She was naked, and a knife flashed.

Somerled threw up his shield arm to take the axe, the shock of it jolting up to his shoulder. He poked desperately with his sword, all training forgotten, and the big man dropped to his knees as the blade bit into his calf. Somerled wrenched his shield sideways and the man's axe followed, his hand still gripping on. Behind the man's head, Somerled saw the glint of the knife coming towards him, and the woman's wild screaming.

Oh Jesus, he thought. I am gone.

A great gash appeared in the man's throat, like a second mouth stretched in a crimson yawn. Somerled didn't understand. Then he saw the woman straddling the man's back, stabbing and stabbing until the skin hung off him in ribbons and the blood puddled on the floor at his feet.

Somerled stood, mesmerized, before registering that the sound around him in the hall had dropped. The shrieks had subsided, leaving whimpers and crying, and in the middle of it, his men were still standing, their ragged breath coming heavy. The only movement was the naked woman, who stood up from the body with blood-speckled skin and a matted weave of black hair to spit, with disarming ferocity, at the corpse's pulpy face.

~ ~ ~

A honeyed buzz of triumph and mead. A warmth and dryness that seeped to their blood.

They killed a calf that night. They were hungry, and victorious. As Sigurd pointed out, if the next part of the plan came off, they would have a dozen cows. And if it didn't, added Thorfinn, at least they'd journey on with full stomachs.

Mebd, the knife-woman, told them that the hunters would be gone two more days.

'Can we trust her?' asked Aed, as they watched the life blood draining from the calf's neck.

Somerled gestured at the sores on her wrists from the ropes that had bound her before they came, and the red, raised weals on her back. And, he pointed out, she had murdered the big bastard as soon as she had the chance.

He remembered the sight of her, straight-backed and red-painted, too fierce, too frightening to be beautiful.

'Who is the leader?' she had asked while they stacked the bodies, her Gaelic thick with disuse, looking at Aed.

Aed had gestured at Somerled, and her eyes had widened in surprise.

'The boy?'

He nodded.

She told them how long the hunters would be gone, then moved away, the welts on her back rippling.

They pushed the bodies into the smoking shed, rather than burn them. Too much smoke might draw the rest before they were ready. Fifteen dead men, including the lookout Aed had dragged in from the place he had been scragged. There were five women too, and, God help them, a couple of bairns. Somerled could not look at their twisted little limbs. You did this, he thought. You should look. Coward.

He could hear the crying of the few remaining women and children, who knew they would be shipped off to the slave pens in their own galley. He felt the cold misery that came after the rush of victory. The pity of it.

They ate the calf's tender bits that night, the stuff that did not need hanging. Fresh, bloody, unsmoked meat, washed down with stolen mead. They were gods, it was true. They were Odin-kissed, Mary-blessed.

His men – *his men!* – were laughing, proud of themselves and of their leader. Fifteen men dead, and they just had scratches.

'Come,' shouted Sigurd. 'Aed, you randy dog. Were you really balling Oona?'

'It was too convincing,' said Thorfinn.

The bard strummed a few chords of a well-known bawdy song and they all laughed, while Aed looked down at his cup and Oona stomped by the fire.

'Convincing, eh, Thorfinn?' she called. 'And how would you know? From what I hear, you've never heard a woman moan with pleasure.'

'He's better with sheep,' said Domnall, ducking as an oatcake came flying at his head.

'I thought we were done for.' Aed shook his great head. 'But the boy had it right. What man could resist a peek, out there on the lonely crag?'

'Jesus knows, I wanted a peek myself, the noises your Oona made.' This from Thorfinn, with a mock-dolorous tone.

'Shame,' she said. 'Never a peek you'll get, Thorfinn the Catcher.'

Aed raised his cup. 'Somerled,' he cried. 'Deep thinker.'

Somerled took the toast, and revelled in it.

Iehmarc, sitting near the bottom of the table, stared into his cup as if seeking something. An omen, perhaps.

'You are not toasting, Iehmarc.' Aed's voice was mellow, conciliatory.

'Apologies. I was thinking about the arse-kissing to come.'

Somerled stood. 'You fought bravely. I saw it. My arse shall remain unkissed. I release you.'

There was cheering at this, and a fresh wave of brotherly back-slapping. Somerled alone stayed watching Iehmarc, and how the smile slid from his face, his eyes hooded and dark.

'What next, Somerled?' Ruaridh asked thickly, the mead tripling his tongue.

'We pick them off as they come back from the hunt, weary for home, and tired, and carrying some fat deer on their backs. Our deer. They'll save us the bother.'

He smiled at his men's faces, the victory shining off them like sunlight on a still loch. He looked behind Aed's head to Mebd, cleaned up and almost pretty. She caught his eye and smiled, coming over with the jug.

This, then, was why men led; why they took the burden. This sweetness. *I am Somerled. Gift-giver, deep thinker, girl-taster.*

Close to, she was lovely, and he ran his eyes over her, dry-mouthed. 'You can have me, lord, if you ask nicely,' she said.

'And will you stab me too?' he asked.

'You are the leader, and I will be your woman alone.'

'What if I don't want you?'

'Have you seen me, lord?' She shook her long black hair back from her pale face, and he laughed.

'Well then,' he said. 'Come here.'

~ ~ ~

Two days later, Mebd pottered by the well; drawing water, bustling, beating a wool rug strung between two posts. An ostentatious display of normality.

'Can we trust her?' whispered Aed. They peered through holes gouged in the stone wall at the girl, and beyond her, at the returning hunters – the laughing, back-slapping, bantering men. They could smell the stew drifting over the heather. They could see the slave girl about her tasks and anticipate all the delights of home and safety and leisure.

And inside their hall lurked Somerled and his band, like malevolent cuckoos.

At the lookout point, Sigurd, dressed in rifled clothes, waved cheerily. As they drew closer, he turned his back on them and squatted behind a rock, his face hidden.

Somerled heard the hoots of laughter directed Sigurd's way. He heard the slap of the dead deer hitting the ground. He saw, with his face pressed against the scratching wood, the big man at the front reach for Mebd's bucket, plunging his head in and pulling it out, shaking his wet hair in streaming ribbons. The dogs chased their tails with happiness to be home, for they knew what the meaty smells meant.

A young boy shouted: 'Mother! Mother! I did it!' He was twelve, perhaps. His face was eager, clean-cut like a spear point. He looked around him, mumbled something to the big man and came on towards the door.

Oh Jesus, thought Somerled. That lad will be the first one through.

It was dark inside the hall. A gloomy dusk outside, thank the Lord.

At the end, near the fire, bubbled the pot. Oona stood in the shadows beside it, her back to the door. Visible but smudged. A woman, any woman. The boy burst in, his mother's name on his lips, his hunting triumph humming about him like a halo. Somerled hesitated, but Aed did not. Quickly, deftly, the big man snaked around the boy – one hand to muffle, the other to slice. The boy crumpled, gurgling, the blood bubbling from his cut throat, falling backwards into Aed's embrace.

They came through the door in twos and threes after that. Somerled could not believe that the muffled thump and slice of their slaughtering could not be heard outside. Being so close to home was robbing the men of their wariness, making them careless and complacent. At last, one got away. Sigurd botched it, and the roar of the man with his cut cheek and astonished rage wakened his friends outside. They rushed in, as they were, half in armour, half out; half-fearful, half-furious. In the gloom of the hall they tried valiantly to resist. But it was too late. When at last the few men Somerled had left hiding in the smoking house burst in behind the Northmen, it was far too late. They met only their brothers, red to the elbow and savage with joy.

How will it be when I am old? thought Somerled then. He stood with blood pooling at his feet, crusting his hands on the sword's pommel. Would this joy see him through to the grave? Could he slide along rivers of blood to a great and glorious future? They will know my name. They will know of Somerled. He was shouting it, shivering with the ecstasy of victory.

eimhear

I skipped across the land on bleeding feet. I danced and whirled. I sang snatches of old Norse songs Sigrdrifa taught us when we were little ones, bloody things dripping with the profanities that made her laugh. I cackled and shook my fist at passing folk. I brayed like a donkey, and once I went a mile crawling on all fours down a busy stretch of road near a market.

I let my hair thicken and tangle, until it hung over my face like a putrid veil. I rolled in fox shit, like a hound, and smeared the mud of passing sties on to my skin. The hunger helped. I was walking for weeks, and I made do with what I could forage. I was high and light, as if the nuts in my stomach were not enough to tether me. I would catch myself in the act of being a madwoman, mumbling of hunger and betrayal, and think with a small, still, rational voice: Am I still pretending?

I did all that. I trusted in the appearance of madness and the stench of the midden. I was foul, polluted. And still some bastard tried to rape me.

A short, squat man wearing a cloak too big for him. I met him at dusk on the final stretch of road before the dun of Áed mac Duinn Sléibe, the lord of the Ulaid. He watched me writhe and caper with a look of horror. I hissed at him through my hair, some gibberish he might take for a curse. I moved past him, the dun in sight and filling me with too much hope. I thought I would see my father soon. I scampered past the man. And he was on me, his hand scrabbling at my thighs, his teeth worrying at my shoulder.

I struggled and bit, but this one was strong. I tasted again the metallic bitterness of a man's blood in my mouth. Fighting made him more angry; he was shouting, and I screamed over him to block out his words. I would not hear them. I swore and cursed and tried to bite some more.

'You.' A deep voice, used to command.

My attacker's hand pushed down over my mouth.

'My wife, your honour.'

A grunt. I could hear the squelching of hooves in mud, the clanking of armour.

'A bit noisy, hey?' came the voice, and the sound of laughter. I couldn't see them, only my attacker's boots with his big toe pushed out through a hole, the long nail yellowed and curling into the mud. But I could hear with a strange sharpness. And I heard feet thumping flanks, and the low hum of conversations resumed, and the unmistakable sound of the horsemen making off.

The anger took me then, and it seemed to give me some sudden swell of strength. I wrenched away from him, pushing him sideways into the mud as I did so. He fell with a soft cry. I straightened up, and pulled back my hair, and screamed at the backs of the riders.

'Cowards. Fools.'

The leader stopped and turned back. My attacker shuffled backwards in the mud. I was too much trouble.

'Do I look like his wife? Did I look like I enjoyed it? Is that how your women scream when you tup them?'

I shook and heaved with the violence of my rage.

81

'And you the lord,' I shouted at the leader, a man in his thirties decked with silver. He frowned above his beard, and I thought I was going too far even as I was beyond caring. 'Is your duty not to people like me? To the vulnerable? To the women being raped by strangers on the roadside as you skip back to your stronghold to congratulate yourself on your magnificence? Jesus.'

A quiet voice from among the riders said with uncertainty: 'Eimhear?'

The sound of my name checked the bile. I stood there, a little foolish, looking among them for the speaker. I saw an auburn beard and a young face, and remembered Magnus the Red, who nearly cried as we sailed across the sea.

'Magnus? Is my father near?'

They were all looking at me. A press of faces. I felt the dirt on me, and the fox shit, and the raggles of my hair.

'Jesus, Eimhear. I'm sorry. It's been a year, more maybe, since . . .' He paused, at a loss. The other men fidgeted and watched him, waiting for the punchline. He looked down into his beard and said softly: 'He's dead.'

~ ~ ~

I joined the household. I was a fourteen-year-old anomaly, with a knife strapped to my calf and a habit of starting at shadows. I was too well born to slave in the kitchen or the byres – my father was some sort of second cousin of the lord. But I had no immediate family, no one to protect me.

At first, the loss of my father was like a fog. It wreathed me, made me invisible. I couldn't quite grasp it; the magnitude of being all alone. I watched the happy tumble of siblings with envy. I turned my eyes away when I saw mothers kiss their daughters.

Dawn was the worst. We all slept together, and in the night-time I could pretend myself into being part of something. The chorus of snores and heavy breath, of childish nightmares and shushing, all was so familiar.

But when morning came, everyone separated out into their own patterns of belonging. Small children like puppies pushing into their mothers' sides. Young couples disappearing under blankets, which bunched and smoothed, bunched and smoothed in the half-light. Grizzled warriors stretching and tousling the nearest child's head. Babies feeding with happy whimpers. And me, creeping into the shadows, tracing patterns in the rushes. Feeling the goose bumps prickle my skin and the starkness of being untouched, unstroked, unaccounted.

At least I could swim.

I found the sea on my first free day. I left behind my chores; the mountains of fleeces, the skeins of wool so vast, so oppressive that I dreamed of them. The wool to be cleaned, carded, dyed, spun and weaved in a relentless, oppressive chain.

It was quite cold that day, I remember, and the autumnal sun was hidden by clouds. The sea was a ruffled grey, calling to me. I ran to it, checking my first impulse to run in as I was. I was not a child any more – I needed to stay hidden. I picked my way along the coast, along the rocky headland, looking for a place I could get out again. Getting in was the easy bit.

At last I found a flattish rock, with an easy scramble-to alongside. I threw off my clothes, chill enough already from the air. I dived, too quick to think about it. The sea's ice hit me, tearing the breath from me. I spluttered upwards, cursing and laughing, the shock of it part of the joy. And there, as if a message from Somerled across the sea to say he was thinking of me, was a young seal. He watched me with big, curious eyes, and I laughed at him until I ached.

We played a while, until at last I could not bear the chattering of my teeth. Pulling myself out, I wrapped my cloak around me and watched the horizon, thinking that if I could fly, or swim like the seal, I could make my way home.

'But where is home, seal?'

He bobbed there as if he wanted me to come back in. Why was he alone? Where were his family?

'Are you lost too? I would go where Somerled is, but I don't know where to find him. I know. He has probably forgotten me. But who else have I got? How can I get across the sea, seal? Can you carry me?'

As if in answer, he slipped under the waves, and was gone.

1125

somerled

He was mazy with sex and blood that spring. He spent his free time with Mebd, intoxicated by her contradictions – she was slender and plump, smooth and textured. She was sweetness and darkness.

He never knew which girl was going to greet him – the tender one, or the spitting one. Both had their advantages. He did not, in truth, care much what she said. He was there to dive into her, to float on her, to lose himself so completely he did not know where to find the sky or the earth. And always, at the back of his mind, was the image of her as he first saw her, blood-smeared and naked, straddling the corpse of the man before him. He told himself the attraction was fierce despite the lingering image.

He tried to tell Aed a little of it. But the big man laughed. 'Christ's bones, boy, you're sixteen. Any woman would get you pumping. She's got her own teeth, and she's smaller than your smallest cow. What more do you need?'

His mother did not like her. But Sigrdrifa was preoccupied with ordering the new hall. She had rifled through it avariciously, like a fat, voluble merchant, holding up treasures and shouting to Oona.

'The cauldron, did you see its like? Did you? Did you? And these . . .' She waved some spoons at the smaller woman. 'Antler, and carved by a master. A master. Thor kissed him on the brow when he whittled these. Kissed him. Kissed him on the arse when he made *these*.' She held some scales, the pans of thin tin-lined bronze and the links made of fine-wrought figures of eight.

Father Padeen scolded her for her greed. 'A thought for the dead, Sigrdrifa,' he said, ponderously.

'Piss on the dead,' she replied. 'They should have set a better watch.'

He mumbled a prayer and raised his eyes.

'I feel sorry for your God,' she said.

'Why?'

'On the first day he made the light, and then the earth, and then all that moves and breathes. And now all the poor bastard has to do all day is listen to you moan at him.'

She skipped from place to place, and Somerled left her to order the domestic horde. The rest he shared out in a solemn ceremony. Thanks to St Colm Cille and the Lord first, and the prayer read from a beautiful bible that made Padeen weep when he saw it, bless him. Then a careful reckoning, weighing and doling out. The rifled armrings. The small pile of hack silver. The tafl boards. The swords and shields and spears. The stocked sea chests that sat in the longship. The longship that made his breath catch in his throat every time he saw her. They had found her pulled up on the stony shore beyond the hall, where Ruaridh said he had seen her. Dragon-prowed, broad-beamed. She had seen better days. She was not big – the timbers that formed her keel were stunted compared to some Somerled had seen. But she was his.

A strange thing, to pull on the life of a stranger. It was the big man, the one that Mebd killed, who had been lord here. An incomer, she said; a younger son of one of the lesser northern jarls, who had set off as a youngster to ravage the southern isles with Magnus Barelegs and stayed when the demon died. The women were mostly captured, like Mebd. She had been seized from the Irish mainland in a summer raid.

She told him of her home; of the river running to the sea and the soft rain that fell like a blessing. And he, when she asked him earnestly to let her go back, would say, 'Soon, my darling, soon,' but not mean it. He would watch her lips move, and wait for her to stop talking so he could kiss her again.

So, here he was. With the Northman's woman, and all his goods. His boots, which moved like supple skins on Somerled's feet. Yet he struggled with his fortune. It seemed too easy, this slipping on of an older man's life. He would catch sight of himself in the river, wearing his stolen finery, and not recognize himself. He would long to tear the boots from his feet, to feel the crunch of heather beneath his toes.

He felt as if success had pulled him into fragments that did not quite match. The warrior, the son, the lover, the leader, the poet. The boy. Broken shards, which, if pieced together carefully, would make something formless.

There were moments of joy, too. Moments when his new life, his stolen life, filled him with a fizzy, spiteful glee.

Mebd told him stories, sometimes, when he could not sleep. He liked to hear of Cú Chullain, the great hero and nemesis of her namesake Queen Mebd. She told him about the druid who foretold an early death for the young warrior.

'Which would you choose?' she asked one sunlit day, as they sat on the boulder by the loch, looking across the water. 'Glory, or a long life.'

'Both.' *I am Somerled. Girl-tamer, Norse hammer, sword-bringer.*

He scrambled to his feet, and throwing his head back as the life surged like a tide, he shouted it: 'I will have both.' And at that moment, he believed it.

Others believed in him. They started arriving not long after the raid, drawn by the story of the boy warrior who had taken on the big man from the north and stolen his life. Sixteen years old and bathed in glory, and his men with not so much as a scratch on them. The tale grew bigger with the telling, and Somerled's men swelled with pride. His band grew.

They came in ones and twos, landless and lordless, wanting to be part of something. Some pure Norse, and others pure Gael, but mostly of twisted parentage. The foreign Gaels, the Gall-Ghàidheil. Fierce and proud. Quick to take offence and slow to forgive. Brave. Odin-touched and reared on tales of Fionn mac Cumhail. A double-headed axe of a legacy to live up to.

And all the while, Gillebrigte sat and stewed himself into a whisky-fuelled agony, watched by a nervous Sigrdrifa.

~ ~ ~

'What shall I do about Iehmarc?'

Padeen clicked his irritation and completed the cast, the line arcing through the sky and the hook sinking into the water with a token ripple.

'Sorry.'

The priest turned to him, grinning.

'No matter. Don't apologize to anyone, Somerled. You are the lord.'

'Yes, of course, I'm . . .'

He trailed off, and they laughed. Somerled felt light, absurdly happy. Like a girl escaping chores. They could see the hall below, the stream from this small loch trundling down the hill to run alongside it. Small figures bustled purposefully. Smoke pushed cheerfully to the white sky. Somerled could almost forget his theft of it. He could almost imagine that he had not been the thing in the darkness, watching.

'Iehmarc,' said the priest softly. 'You should not have offered him clemency, Somerled.'

'A strange thing for a priest to say.'

'I am not talking as your priest, but as your adviser.'

'My mother would accuse you of hypocrisy.'

Padeen smiled. 'If I fart, your mother accuses me of hypocrisy.'

The water ruffled in a gust of wind, sending shivers up Padeen's line. He pulled, gently, moving the hook through the water.

'He would have hated me if I had made him kiss my arse. I am trying to shore it up, not make it worse.'

'Listen, Somerled. Nothing makes a bitter man more bitter than being offered a kindness by a man he hates.'

Somerled thought about this. He turned his face into the rising wind and let it blow his hair back from his face. Why do other men have to be complicated? he wondered. Why can't it be like the Bible? I say jump, they say how high. If I say jump, my crew will ask why.

'I made a mistake then. But how do I fix it?'

'Now I can't help you, Somerled. I cannot, as your priest, give you the advice necessary.'

'I understand.'

'Do you? Well then,' he said as his line began to twitch and jump. 'Just bear in mind that our kind do not take to tyranny. Be clever, Somerled. Always be clever. Brawn is easy, but it is never enough.'

~ ~ ~

They moved through the fog like a whisper. The calm sea was dimpled ahead, furrowed behind, as the oars churned the water. They were moving well, he thought, for all their soft palms and long beaching. Aed looked pleased, he saw, and he mimicked the easy, knee-rolling gait of the big man as they moved forward. Aed held the steering oar with a light touch. Somerled held on to the backstay, which stretched tautly down from the top of the mast, and concentrated on looking the part.

Inside the fog it was warmer than it should be. The last gasps of summer outweighed the cloud. The breeze conjured by the galley's momentum was welcome on his clammy forehead. He raised his face to it, as if drinking in the wisps of cloud that floated above their heads. They were quiet, the men. No songs now, not this close. Just the bite and pull of the oars, the rushing drops as the blades emerged and shook off the sea, and the creaking of the oars in their ports. They were a few men light; this ship could take twenty oars a side. But it was a still day, and the eighteen men he had kept her moving sweetly across the water.

This fog was heaven-sent, he thought. They called him the lucky one. Luck. That gift from God that shone on him like a halo. And now, in this first raid with his new, bigger crew, this glorious fog had come to hide their approach. Sigurd was at the prow, counting the strokes and estimating their speed. They would turn in, soon, to hug the coast and look for the landmarks. They would have to creep slowly then. But this rushing speed was a joy. He looked anxiously towards Sigurd. If the man's renowned sea skill deserted him, they would be in trouble. Luck and skill combined. That was the secret.

Bite, heave, up. Bite, heave, up. Bite, heave, up. He called the rhythm in his head. It dispelled thought, calmed his jittery nerves. Bite, heave, up. Bite, heave, up. Bite, heave, up. *Somerled. Luck-bringer, foe-killer, death-dealer.* Bite, heave, up. Bite, heave, up.

At last they turned landwards. Slowly creeping. Somerled imagined the settlement they were approaching, going about its business in the fog. Perhaps they felt safe – no one would be mad enough to brave the sea roads in this thick fog. Or perhaps they felt unaccountable slivers of fear. The fog was eerie. It enveloped the familiar and turned it into the other. A fairy realm unleashed.

They jumped out into waist-high water, stifling the usual cold-water jokes. Somerled slapped Sigurd Horse-face on the back for his astonishing feat of navigation, and the man grinned as he pulled on the lightened boat, scraping it up the shingle. Ruaridh, their silent scout, set off to show them the path. They had caught him, once, spying on them. But he had pretended to be addle-witted and had run when they had taken their eye off him. Big bastards, he said. Gall-Ghàidheil, from their speech.

A rustling raid, Somerled had told his band. Fast in, fast out. Hit them. When they fall back, grab anything that bleats or squeals and head back – Aed and his crew to cover the fighting retreat. No women, unless they came easily. A short blooding raid – not full war. Not yet.

So here they were, creeping through the God-brewed fog, along the heathery, rocky mounds that littered this coast.

At the top of one of them, they crouched. Silent still. Below them they saw and heard shapes moving in the whiteness. Like ghosts, they were. And if they seem ghostlike to us, what will we seem to them? thought Somerled. He passed the word along. When we run at them, scream like banshees. Scream like the fairy folk come alive. On the signal. On the signal.

Hush now. Hush.

'Now!' he said, and they burst across the brow of the mound, calling and screaming and ululating. The noise would have spooked the dead, and Somerled joined in, raising his voice in a high-pitched scream that juddered as he ran down the rocky hill.

'Fuck!' shouted a voice behind him, as someone fell, and Sigurd suddenly appeared from behind him, somersaulting down the hill with a cry that was genuine. He lay at the bottom, but they didn't have time to stop. They screamed onwards, falling on the warriors who leaped at them out of the mist. One lunged at Somerled, a jabbering, frightened man with wide eyes and the stench of piss about him. Somerled sidestepped his rush and kicked him on the arse as he ran past, and Thorfinn finished him off, the shower of blood startlingly red against the fog.

Suddenly it was quiet. Somerled realized the flaw in his plan, as the fog turned from friend to enemy. 'Quick!' he screamed, imagining an unknown enemy regrouping in the cloud cover. 'Grab and retreat!'

He picked up a chicken, which promptly shat all over his arm.

Around him the warriors grappled with livestock. Somewhere, a woman screamed. 'Retreat!' he shouted. 'Retreat,' and the bastard chicken pecked and shat again, until his arm was covered in scratches and crap and the giggles were catching in his throat.

They met by the galley, laughing madly most of them. Even Sigurd, his face scratched and bloody from his somersaults through the gorse. They threw the animals in, a shrieking jumble of feathers and wool. Aed appeared over the hill, a bull calf under his arm. He slung it over the side and the white-eyed animal scrabbled for purchase on the smooth deck with its hooves, skidding and shitting with fear.

They pushed off, jumping in from the shallows and finding

their way in some order, despite the strange hilarity that had overtaken them.

'All here,' said Aed, smiling. Somerled felt his cheeks flush. He had not thought to check. What kind of leader was he?

They came over the hill then, screaming defiance. Some of the crew not rowing slapped their arse cheeks at them, and the laughter carried across the water like a final insult. Between the chests, huddled around the mast, the animals that the men had caught floundered and squealed.

'Hey, Sigurd,' shouted Oengus. 'Did you train as a tumbler? Couldn't tell your arse from your head as you rolled down that hill.'

Sigurd grinned, a little sheepish.

'Did you see their faces when we roared out of the mist at them?'

'I took yours, Somerled, did you see?'

'Hey now,' shouted Aed. 'Shut your caterwauling, women. Are we not going to give Domnall his due?'

Domnall looked down at his oar, confusion on his face.

'Up oars!' shouted Aed.

They stopped, almost as one, the blades hanging out of the grey sea.

'Your first man, Domnall,' said Somerled. The boy grinned at him. Somerled pulled an arm ring from his arm and tossed it to him across the oars.

Amid the cheering and laughter, he looked at Aed, who nodded, happy.

Later, as dusk fell, the fog lifted and they coasted home. They could see the hall ahead across the sea – welcoming and lonely in the glen.

The wind had risen enough to justify the sail, and the men were sitting and talking quietly.

Somerled imagined Mebd and Oona and Sigrdrifa in that quiet lit hall, and how it would be if he and the others were raiders. He whispered a prayer.

'Aed,' he said. 'Don't you think it odd that we all hug this coast, legs open, waiting to be taken?'

The big man was silent for a space. 'Yes,' he said slowly. 'But who would be far from the sea roads? Trade and news and chat and novelty – they come down the roads too, and more often than bastards like us. Can you imagine sitting in the hills, with only yourself to talk to?'

'Jesus,' said Thorfinn from behind them. 'If I only had you to talk to, big man, I'd rush on to the nearest pirate axe.'

'Pox on your soul,' said Aed mildly.

Somerled nodded, watching the smudged outlines of his home become clearer as they neared. They would have to unship the oars soon, to turn into the bay.

'And how would the young men test themselves,' said Aed, 'if we all sat in the inland glens, raising turnips?'

'There is a reason, I suppose,' said Somerled, 'why the Culdees avoid the sea roads.'

'Aye,' said Thorfinn. 'And there is also a reason why those holy bastards all go mad in the end.'

~ ~ ~

The storm blew in without warning. The wind backed, pushing them away from the hall. They could see it, the blessed place, calling them in, bright against the steel-grey sky.

The sea was malevolent, with a breathtaking suddenness. An angry dark swell. The rain came fast and heavy, pouring into the open boat like a waterfall. Somerled looked up at the blackening sky, blinded by the rush of rain and wind. He knew the lurch of fear that felt like seasickness.

Sigurd, at the steering oar, looked grim. 'Reef!' he shouted against the roaring wind. Hard to know who heard him, but they all knew well enough the urgency. Aed led the party at the sail, handing down its vicious, billowing mass. No time to step the mast. No time to do much but pray that the man who built her knew his business.

Somerled swallowed, his throat dry with the suddenness of it. To make for the hall was impossible; she would take the wind abeam and capsize. He looked over to the foaming black sea. Their only course was to run before the wind under a scrap of sail, parallel to the shore, and beat back up after the passing of the storm.

He looked across to Sigurd, fighting with the steering oar. He rushed over to help, feeling the slip of his feet on the planking. The oar was wet and violent under his hand. They grappled with it together, jamming the blade deep into the water. The ship seemed to yearn for home. They fought her, as her prow sought the land.

Why this yawing into danger? Why did she fight them so, when victory would mean death? Did ships have a soul? Were they yearning, always, to break up, to sink into the sea's violent caress? Not now, man – concentrate. Somerled's palms slid on the wet wood.

Ahead of him, the bailing buckets were being passed with a frantic haste; even from back here, Somerled could see the water sloshing up to the rowers' thwarts with the roll of the ship.

Sigurd screamed something into his ear. Something that called for wide eyes and an edge of fear. Deaf from the rushing of the wind and the waves, Somerled looked up from his task. The hall was far behind already. The Point loomed ahead; oh Christ, the

Point. On this tack they would strike on the rocks. They would have to push her over to clear the edge, but even if they got past, the cross-seas running up from behind the cliff would deal them a heavy blow. Somerled looked at the shore and the great white breakers curling on the shingle. Beaching meant death; striking meant death; weathering the Point meant probable death.

He looked at Sigurd and nodded, pushing the oar across as far as he dared. Sigurd pulled, and the ship turned a little, the wind on her quarter now and the waves pounding with greater violence. He looked along the length of her to the figures of his men, crouching and shivering under the salted lash of the wind.

Now their course was set, now the decision was made, he felt a curious detachment. An acute sense of the division between soul and skin. He thought of his struggling, miserable body with contempt. He soared above it. Let it die, if it must. He was the still, sublime being at the centre of the storm. The passionate heart. The ranging mind. Fuck the rest; let it bleed.

He threw himself into the clarity of the thought, watching the lines between sea and sky dissolve into one roaring, vicious whole. He was smiling, he found, willing the gods to do their worst. He thought of Padeen, and his mother. Padeen's God did not live out here, in the screaming storms. This was where the old gods staked their claims on men. This was the thundering of Thor above and the sucking claws of Ran below; and the men caught flopping in the middle like breathless, hooked fish.

The rocks were nearly on them now, and he watched them come. Lord, how close. You could reach out and touch their jagged edges. He waited for the scrape of keel on stone, waited for the jolting splintering of planks. But they were through, and here was a wave. God help them – such a wave.

It crashed down over the boat, curling into them. He felt his feet whip up from underneath him and he wrapped his arms around the steering oar, clinging, clinging. The wave sucked at him and pulled at him. Easier to go with it. Easier to succumb; then perhaps he could breathe again. Water rushed into his nose, his eyes. Which way was up? Which down?

At last, a lifetime later, the water fell back. His feet found the deck, scrabbling for a firm hold. He drew a breath, rasping. Sigurd grabbed his arm. There was a man over the edge, one arm waving, his mouth wide in a scream. But the other arm clung to a rope, and the man was acting as a drag on the ship. He would pull her round, beam on to the wind, waves catching her two ways.

Somerled lurched to the side, grabbing on to the planking. He tried to pull, but even as he did it, he knew there was no time. No time. Oh Lord, forgive me. Forgive me.

He reached for his knife and with two quick strokes severed the rope. It was only as the water snatched the man away from the ship that he realized who it was.

Iehmarc. A surge of something, which he would later call remorse. As the ship swung back to take the wind behind her, as the pressure from the waves lessened, he knew it for what it was. A vivid delight. His body for mine. His soul for mine. *I am Somerled.*

1126

somerleo

The day was sultry, too still. Grey clouds, heavy with moisture, threatened but did not break. Clouds of midges, lured out of their hollows by the still air, drifted in packs. It was a day to make you scratchy, to make a fight out of the way a man cleared his throat, or hummed a tuneless hum. A day to take offence and give it.

Somerled was talking to two new men, who had arrived that day in a pitiful oared curragh. They were lean and hungry, but there was a toughness there, and an eagerness. Tormod and Iomhar. Brothers from the islands, who had fought as mercenaries for Donnchad mac Murchada, the King of Leinster, but lost their way on his death.

They were by the cliff, where the seabirds called and raced above the water. The band were at leisure. Cleaning their gear, playing at tafl or dice, combing each other's long, matted hair. In the distance he could see the women at work in the field, with the children and the couple of old fellows they had somehow acquired. Beyond them, the high mountains that seemed to box them in, their peaks lost to the clouds.

Somerled hated this clammy heaviness. He longed for a fierce breeze, the type that would have made the Otter's eyes shine and her cheeks flush. He fought to concentrate on the men, who were, he could tell, themselves fighting to keep their wariness at bay. A boy, they were thinking. A strapling.

He would have to take them raiding soon. His reputation was puffed too far, like the thin skin on boiled milk. It rested on one fight and a skirmish. But there were new men now, who had not been there. His old companions were growing restless too. There were too few women here, and too many growling warriors. A raid, then. But where? Ireland? Man? South into the Saxon lands? He thought of Aedith and her much-coveted blondness. She was Sigurd's woman now. But a few more like her might keep some restless souls calm.

They needed to build, too. The hall was bursting, and the land around littered with makeshift lean-tos that would be miserable come the winter. But where to find the expertise? He would talk to the men, see if any knew the knack. Lord, it was hot. He shifted beneath his tunic, feeling the sweat prickling down his back.

'So, Lord,' said one. Tormod, was it? He clawed his way back to concentration.

'Yes,' he said, not entirely sure what had gone before. 'You can fight and row. We will try you out. Go to Aed, the big one, and he will see to your gear. Oona, his wife, will get you fed, show you where to stow your kit. Later, when you are proven, we will look to the oaths.'

'Oaths?' A voice behind him.

Gillebrigte.

This is it, he thought. The crisis. He felt taller, fuller – the way he did before a fight. Gillebrigte stood swaying, hunched a little against an absent wind. His beard was tangled, and his eyes above were red and watering. He looked like a Culdee emerging from his rock hermitage, where solitude and the quest for God had sent him mad. The burned half of him was ugly, livid. A black and red crust instead of a skin.

Somerled sensed Tormod and Iomhar watching. He imagined their gaze flitting between the two of them. The shining boy and his bitter, burned shadow.

'You're taking oaths now, boy? As if I were dead already?'

'Forgive me, Father. I thought you were too soaked in whisky to care.'

Now it was upon them, his clarity vanished. Such a tangled rush of feeling. He floundered, lost in the impenetrable thicket. Love, certainly. Hate. Pity? Impossible to tell. Instead, memories prickled at him, snagging him when he should be concentrating. The rasp of Gillebrigte's cheek. His deep, low chuckle when Somerled the boy begged to be tickled. The shared pride of Somerled's first stag. 'Well done, boy,' rumbled a voice through years and days and into Somerled's hot mind.

A kiss on Sigrdrifa's red cheek. A warrior lifting his shield, so close to a god that the boy Somerled cried for the pride and the envy of it. The time they raced the curraghs across a cut-up sea, and how his father leaned out and shouted, his words whipped away by the wind, so that all Somerled remembered was a wide open mouth that might be laughing or might be calling.

The crack of a belt across his arse, and the biting of his lip to contain the tears. The bristling. The way he talked of Somerled's first man – the pride that seemed a surface thing; an expected thing. The smell of him, hot with sweat and salt and something else that Somerled couldn't name or describe but could recognize on a moonless night with his eyes shut.

The tangle he was in robbed him of speech. There was an irony at play that he could just grasp in his quivering confusion. This rage of love and hate that mired him also made him want to run across and clasp at the man opposite him, made him want to sink his head on that hated shoulder, and feel the rasping of the cheek and the salt-sweat smell of him, and have his father explain it all and make it simple, soothe away the rage that was pulsing, pounding and leaving him breathless.

But he did no such thing. For what else was it to be a warrior than to make things look, to outward eyes, simple. To appear an unruffled man. To convince others of your certainty. Your clarity. Like the smooth lines and sharp edge of a well-made sword. Leave the serrated edges to the women.

What was the old man thinking while he and Somerled stood looking at each other? Was he thinking of the boy he loved, of the sweet baby smell of him, and the tiny fists that clutched at his father's sword belt?

No, thought Somerled suddenly, violently. That is not what he is thinking.

'I am still the jarl here, boy.' Gillebrigte's voice was low and bitter.

Behind his father, Somerled saw his mother approaching. He would not think of her.

'No,' he said. 'You are nothing.'

He turned back to face Tormod and Iomhar, slowly and deliberately. His hand was on his sword hilt, though, automatically feeling for the indent in it, where its maker seemed to have slipped and cut too far. He stroked it with his thumb, listening for the rush and roar he expected behind him.

Tormod's eyes shifted and he looked past Somerled's shoulder. The big warrior was embarrassed about something, unnerved, and he dropped his eyes to his feet, shuffling in the dirt. Somerled turned back and saw his father sitting on a rock, his face lifted towards the sea, openly, violently weeping.

The strangers came up the hill towards the burn. Two of them, both red-haired and burly. Aed strode alongside, but didn't look freakishly large. Somerled turned back towards the water, to where the salmon jostled beneath the foam. He had promised Sigrdrifa a big one. He teased the line back into the water.

Behind him, he heard Aed shout. He turned, reluctantly.

The newcomers were sleek, well fed. Their cloaks, pulled tight against the chill spring air, were new-woven, and the brooches pinning the folds were just ornate enough to signal prosperity without pomp. They were not looking to join the band, then. One was older than the other, streaks of grey in his auburn hair. Father and son. There was something searching, questioning about the older man's gaze. Somerled braced himself against the questing look.

He greeted them, guarded.

'I am Fergus MacOengus,' said the elder, as if beginning a tale. 'And this is my son Callum. You are young. We were not expecting . . .' He trailed off.

Somerled grinned. 'And you, Fergus MacOengus, are old. Shall I hold it against you? Shall we fall out because of it? You are welcome here.'

The old man nodded. 'We are cousins, of a sort. We came to pay our respects. Your grandfather, Gilleadoman, was my father's cousin.'

And where were you, cousin, when we hid in the caves? thought Somerled.

But he smiled, and asked of his cousin's health.

'What news?' he said. 'What news? It has been an age since we last had visitors.'

'Alexander, the king in Alba, is still without an heir, we heard.'

'Him or her?' asked Aed.

'Her, it seems,' said Callum. 'He has at least one near-grown bastard, out to foster in Moray. That's what you get for marrying an Englishwoman. Daughter of royalty or no.'

Somerled looked to the hills that towered over them. He imagined, for a dizzy moment, soaring above them, eating up the heather, bog, scree, loch and rock that stood between him and Alba. Even an eagle would struggle. To sail round would be a feat. Down the Clyde from the lowlands and up the coast, that was the only real way.

'He claims title to these lands – yours and ours. Tribute,' said Fergus.

Somerled jerked his head towards the mountains. 'Let him,' he said.

They walked back down towards the hall, where he could tell by the smell that the arrivals had sent Sigrdrifa into a frenzy of cooking. She cooked competitively; her honour was in the crispness of the skin, the plumpness of the meat, the strength of the ale and the creaminess of the butter.

Fergus sketched the state of the real powers that mattered out here, by the Western Sea. Olaf Crovan was tightening his grip on Man and the isles. The dwarf, they called him. In part because of his size, but in part because any son of that wicked old giant Godred Crovan, who took power in the sea by force of sword and personality, was bound to feel small. 'And now he's had a daughter. Ragnhild, they've called her.' Somerled nodded, not interested in this Norse girl baby.

'Muirchertach Ua Briain still calls himself the high king over the water, but outside of Munster they slap their arses at him,' said Fergus. Somerled smiled at the thought: all the small kings and chieftains, the Norse in the trading ports and the Gaels in Ulster and beyond; even the strange folk with their own garbled tongues, all turning their backsides on Muirchertach and his claims.

As they approached the hall, Fergus looked around keenly. The younger man, Callum, was more self-contained, more guarded. He walked spear-straight, as if determined not to show anything so vulgar as curiosity. As they walked through his band, who sat in clumps of four or five, cleaning their weapons and talking, Somerled was absurdly, boyishly proud of them. They had spent the winter drinking too much and eating too much. But now, with spring here, they were shaking off their winter sloth like hunting dogs padding from a loch.

There was an expectation in the air. They looked at him with amused respect. They were waiting for the next exploit, for the winter hibernation to end with something big, something bloody, something profitable. He hoped the visitors saw it too, hoped they could sense this atmosphere; a controlled tension that Somerled held in his hand, ready to release. He felt it in himself – a hemmed-in violence looking for an outlet. He felt bouncy on his feet as he walked down to the hall; strong.

That evening, they feasted the newcomers. Alfric the Bard gave them a song of Cú Chullain, and although his weak tenor struggled to fill the hall, the message was not lost on the visitors. The harp sang, and Somerled watched Fergus watching. The old man took in Somerled's bare arms, and the coiled silver armlets that reached to his elbows. He saw the heavy rings on his fingers, and the gold torque round Sigrdrifa's mottled neck. He watched the flow of food and drink, even, God love them, wine. It was the one jug, rifled from a ship off Galloway, but Fergus was not to know it – the stores could be piled with amphorae from Miklagard for all he knew. And the old man watched Mebd pour his wine; a sleeker, plumper

Mebd, who bent low, as if to show off the silver cross that nestled there and proclaimed Somerled's ownership.

The tale of Cú Chullain wended on, as Fergus took all this in, the seventeen-year-old hero's feats growing larger and more extraordinary as the poem piled verse upon verse. As if to hammer it home with a double axe, Aed shouted across the table: 'And what age is Somerled? Seventeen. That's how old. Seventeen.'

Further down, he saw Sigurd telling Callum of the raids on Man at the waning of last summer, of the men killed and the spoils shared. Suddenly all the brimming confidence spilled over and left him empty. If they knew, he thought, why we ravaged Man last summer. How I sought to wipe myself clean of the shame. How I sought oblivion in the sound of sword on shield, and good men died because of it. Tormod, and Domnall's father Oengus. And all the while his own father sat in his new-built hut near the beach like a mad yet faithless hermit.

Guilt piled on shame. Padeen had told him that this was a foolish reaction. That Tormod and Oengus had chosen their life, and in doing so had chosen their death. Somerled knew he was right, and hated himself for his qualms. Did Cú Chullain mope about because men died in his war with Queen Mebd? Didn't Achilles save his grief and guilt for Patroclus? Foot soldiers die. Pawns are taken.

He heard his name called, and put on a smiling face.

Fergus was speaking. '. . . and you only lost two, I hear, in your raiding on Man.'

Somerled nodded. Just two. It sounded good, did it not? Two. Grim Tormod, and Domnall's father. Domnall had cried at Oengus's broken body. 'I do not believe, Cousin Fergus, that men should be wasted.'

The old man nodded, appraising.

'Tell me,' said Somerled, 'something of your home.'

'Why?'

'To help me raid it.'

Fergus smiled. 'Fair. You'll have passed it. Up the Sound and round. When you can see Coll on a clear day, then veer right. A good place. A settled place. Some twenty families paying tribute to the hall. Men to fill three galleys when called.'

'Only we don't have three galleys any more,' said Callum.

'No,' said Fergus. Silence settled as Somerled waited for more, and Fergus turned his weary gaze down the hall to where Thorfinn and Ruaridh were taunting some of his men. Somerled watched the warriors' muted response, and caught Aed's eye across the table.

~ ~ ~

Somerled sought out Aed after the meal. He stood beside the big man at the pit beyond the hall, their piss streaming thick with ale. There was something afoot, they agreed. Something coming. A challenge or a proposition. Somerled, feeling the lightness of his seventeen years, didn't say, what should I do? He didn't say, tell me how to handle this sly old man.

But Aed, with the cleverness of a man who pretends to be all brawn, understood his unspoken appeal.

As they walked back to the hall, they paused. They could see the smoke rising, and hear the laughter and the drunken singing. The moon above the sea was thin and painfully crisp. Beside him Somerled saw the big man's head go back, and the happy sigh as he gazed at the stars spread out above them like a complex weave. The gods' own blanket

'You know,' said Aed. 'When I was a little lad, I wanted to be a poet. Don't tell the boys, Somerled. But here was my trouble. I was too big. All the little fellows would set themselves up to fight me,

106

for if they brought down the big man, they won all the fame. So I had to fight, and be the best at it. The bigger you get, the wider a target you make.'

Somerled nodded. He could see his breath pooling in the night air, and he remembered how only a handful of years had passed since he would have thought himself a dragon with such a torrent of smoke appearing.

He watched his breath come and go, while Aed grinned at the stars. 'Come on then,' said Aed, slipping an arm across his shoulders. 'Back in to the slippery bastards, and let's see if we can tickle it out of them.'

~ ~ ~

It came the next day. Fergus had borrowed a line from Somerled, and the two of them sat by the burn, ignoring the misting rain and watching the salmon twisting under the water.

'Spears are easier when they're so plentiful,' said Fergus.

'But where's the fun, if it's too easy?' Somerled replied.

Fergus glanced up at him. That quick, searching look again, as if trying to weigh the boy in front of him – measure him out in hack silver.

Somerled's irritation spilled over. 'Christ's blood, man,' he snapped. 'Don't look at me as if I'm speaking in riddles. We're just talking about salmon.'

Fergus grinned suddenly, and Somerled realized it was the first time he had seen a real smile from the man. His green eyes near disappeared back into their wrinkles.

'You are right,' said the older man, and the grin, if possible, seemed to widen until he was all teeth and crinkles. Christ, thought Somerled, I preferred the bastard when he was dour.

'So here it is,' said Fergus. 'When the old chief died, we were left . . .' he paused, searching, or so it seemed, for a benign word, 'rudderless. The Norsemen, the ones settled between your land and ours, they sensed it – like blood to a hound. The branch that should take the chief's place, well, there's daughters and an idiot. So that leaves a space, and we're all in it, growling at each other.'

'You? Or your son?'

The old man grinned. 'Aye, maybe. But we've a more immediate problem, Somerled. We've had skirmish after skirmish, and we're losing. We're too busy growling at each other to let one man lead. A band with a council instead of a chief.' He let out a mangled yelp of disgust.

'Ah. I see.'

'Now look, you're a young one. I can't very well parade you in front of men twice your age and say, here's a chief for you. But you've been fighting small wars. If you join us, you've enough men to be biggest dog in the pack. This is a chance to prove yourself. These are hard, ugly bastards we're talking of. Based in a glorious sea loch, off the Sound of Mull. Loch Aline.'

Somerled felt the telltale twitch on his line. He looked down into the thrashing water and saw a silvery flash of salmon.

'Why me?'

Fergus grinned again. 'There's no one else. You're a cousin of sorts, so you're eligible. You're not tainted with the tangle of the past years. You have just enough men to claim leadership, but not so many that you can take it by force. And those Norse bastards killed my youngest boy.'

Somerled looked away from the burn, to the old man's ridged face.

'And if I acquit myself, you'll back me for the chieftainship?'

'Well, lad, the rules of tannistry would say you've an even chance against, say, my boy Callum. I'll not promise, exactly.'

Somerled felt the line tug. He concentrated on the fish, not risking another look to the old man next to him. It swerved and slid under the water, seeking a way out but already lost. He registered, as usual, that second when he knew it was caught, but the fish kept the illusion that escape was possible. If fish had illusions. *Concentrate.*

'I tell you something, Fergus. If I land this big sod, I will come with you, and I will fight with you.'

'Well catch the bastard then,' said Fergus.

Somerled thought for one long second that he had misjudged the salmon, that he would lose it. Who had misplaced illusions now? But he held on, gentle and persistent. As it tired, he risked a flip, and out it came, the water sucking at its silver scales and falling back in a shower of drops. It landed with a thump on the boggy grass. Above its thrashing and gasping, Somerled raised steady eyes to Fergus.

'When do we start?'

~ ~ ~

They stood together a while in the morning mist. The men and the women and the children, heads bowed under the sky. Father Padeen led them in prayers, the great man's voice rich and rare as it echoed across the hushed glen.

They intoned Christ's breastplate that morning. There was comfort in the familiar words, in the looping rhythm of the incantation. Sigrdrifa, he knew, found this song moving, despite her resistance to the Christian God. Her face was fierce with not crying, so that the grooves in her forehead deepened into crags.

Those who did not know her would think she was angry. Gillebrigte stood with her, drooping and quiet. He would shake soon, if he didn't get a drink. Quiver and judder, turning his blood-red eyes to the cup. He was insisting on coming along. Let him, said Aed. What harm could he do?

> *Christ's cross across this face,*
> *Across the ear like this,*
> *Christ's cross across this eye,*
> *Christ's cross across this nose.*
> *Christ's cross across this mouth.*
> *Christ's cross across this throat.*
> *Christ's cross across this back.*
> *Christ's cross across this side.*

The words wound on, and Somerled spoke them without thinking, letting them settle his nerves, letting them ease the clenching tension in his body. After would come the work, the packing of the boats with salt fish and cured meat, the oatcakes and the cheese, and the jugs of ale. All the necessary goods to keep their bodies hard and fierce and full. Yet here on the beach was where the real preparation was done; here with the skuas diving and the herring gulls calling and the low, smooth voice of the priest slathering them in Christ's mercy.

> *Christ's cross my sitting,*
> *Christ's cross my lying.*
> *Christ's cross my whole power*
> *Till we reach heaven's king.*

Christ's cross across my church,
Across my community.
Christ's cross in the next world,
Christ's cross in the present day.

From the tip of my head
To the nail of my foot,
Christ, against each peril,
The shelter of your cross.

Till the day of my death,
Before going in this clay,
Joyfully I will make
Christ's cross across my face.

As they made the cross he felt sheltered. He felt whole and unblemished, and as if the words were a powerful spell that would protect him. Fuller, taller, he watched his men prepare the galley. His first test. His first big outing against a seasoned, wary, angry foe. Lord Jesus, he prayed silently, make me worthy.

eimbeaR

I thought often about blood.

Pinned in there, in that fort, all the women spun into the same cycle. In the few days before, the place boiled and hissed. Simmering feuds spilled over, small slights tumbling into unforgivable wrongs. Then, one by one, we started to bleed and the atmosphere lightened and calmed. There was a relief in the bloodletting; it seemed cleansing, somehow, or soothing.

Is it the same for men? Is this why they have to manufacture their perpetual small wars? I understand that there is no option in one sense. Wealth and fame come only in battle; unless you are born to it, what other way is there for a man to advance? But that is not how they approach it – for them it is not a calculated thing, but a driven thing. In the days before a raid, cooped up, they boil and hiss like the women.

Did God plan our monthly blood so that we could understand this male thing that looks so much like stupidity? What other reason can there be for this messy absurdity? Father Padeen told me once that God's plan was infinite. Look at the bee nosing in a flower then spinning an intricate honeycomb. God's work. If it is all a plan, why this need for bloodletting? Where does that sit in his purpose? Why create Adam in all that glorious detail but set within him the urge to destroy? Is destruction the necessary end to creation? Is that why children always break their mothers' hearts, one way or the other?

I tried to talk to the lord's bishop about this, but he shooed me away as if I were the inquisitive bee. I tried to talk to the lord's wife, Gràinne, about it. She looked at me as if I were touched.

'We need our men to fight, to protect us,' she said, slowly, as to a child.

'Aye, but who from? Other women's men. If everyone stayed at home instead of looking for reasons to knock each other's heads off, we would not need protecting, and neither would the other women.'

The women cast looks between each other. Skeins of wool dripped from their fingers as if skin and thread were the same.

Little Sadhbh piped up, her mischievous eyes shining. 'And what if all the men sat at home growing cabbages, Eimhear? Who would we fight over and sigh over? Give me a warrior over a cabbage farmer.'

There were giggles and nods.

'But if all the men farmed cabbages,' I said, 'then there would be other things to find attractive. We only think we must sigh over the warriors because they are the ones with status, with power. What if status and power were granted to whoever grew the most cabbages?'

They were laughing now, at the image.

'Imagine the lord sitting at home growing cabbages,' said one.

Sadhbh put on a low, growly voice. 'I demand manure! Only the best among you are worthy of the best pig shit.'

I smiled along, and fought with the inevitable tangles in my wool, watching the smooth threads looping as if by themselves from the other women's hands. Gràinne thought I was deliberately poor at the work; she could not understand how anyone with sufficient wit could be so stupid with their hands. The laughter died away, and the gossip resumed. Who looked at whom; which husband was playing foul. I tried to join in, so that I would not be different.

~ ~ ~

I remembered the conversation at the next homecoming. The men had been gone for the whole spring, and now most of the summer. The harvest was threatening to come early, and the women were beginning to fret. Where were they? Who would wield the scythes?

The chapel was filled with candles. Prayers rose skywards from dawn to dusk, as if the Lord in all his wisdom would change his plan in reply to our pathetic squeaking. Still, it gave comfort, I suppose.

I felt my lack of concern then. One of the younger warriors had been circling around me. He had fair hair and smiling eyes. I was beginning to think, perhaps, perhaps. But something held me back. Some unarticulated promise made when I was too young to pledge it. I joined the other women looking out towards the southern hills, and I made the right noises. But I called him home with my head, not my blood.

At last, when Gràinne had marshalled the old men and young boys left behind, and handed out scythes to the youngest among us, the cry went up that they were coming home. We scrambled to the highest point, laughing and calling. But the words died on our lips as we saw them. They were ragged and bloody. They were too few. Even from here, we could see they were too few. They had no dogs, no horses. There was just this slow limping forward, like a wounded pup making its way home.

We rushed out, feet wet in the morning dew. Each searched for husband, brother, father. The cries of lament began to rise until Gràinne shouted, 'Enough!' in her bishop's voice, and we quietened down. The men looked at us with dark-pooled eyes and tangled beards.

We propped them up, and walked them in. Inside, Gràinne rapped orders, and the fort came alive with bubbling water and stewing meat and the squeals of dying goats and chickens. We unwrapped foot coverings that dripped with pus, we cleaned out sores as wide as my hands. We swallowed our retches and our nervous giggles out of respect for these poor ruined men.

Everywhere there was blood. Crusted, dried. Fresh, as filthy rags unpeeled the skin.

They fell on the food; more than one of them was violently sick within minutes of gorging himself. We held their heads and wiped their cheeks and set another plate in front of them.

The lord survived. My fair-haired admirer did not. Sadhbh's father and her intended were lost, and I knew her thoughts as she looked about the room at the outnumbered men surrounded by women and saw her future stretch forward into endless solitary barrenness.

They began to tell us what had happened. Who had wronged whom. Who needed revenge. Why it was their battle and not someone else's. How it was not their fault that they had lost, and how these few had escaped. I walked away, looking for ways to be useful. They talked as if it mattered. As if the whys were more important than their tattered bodies and lost friends. As if they had choices. There will always be another wrong. There will always be another battle. And some poor, stupid bastard will always have to lose.

1128

somerled

Somerled followed Callum, flitting between the dark trees.
They moved as if tracking deer, placing their feet with
tender care, wary of snapping branches and the echoing rustle
of bracken.

They came at last to the edge, where the oaks stopped and the
tangled scrub fell away over the edge of the crag.

'There. Loch Aline,' whispered Callum.

Somerled crept forward on his belly and stuck his head over the
side of the crag. There below him stretched a long, shining loch.
His heart leaped like a salmon.

The early sun had found the still water, sheening it with silver.
Low tide, and the edges of the sea loch were left bare where the
water had retreated. The line between land and sea was absurdly
clear: black rock striped with light grey, like a tidemark of grime
on a boy's neck. The absurd comparison made him smile. He set
his face straight again, conscious of Callum's presence.

Be practical. The steep, rocky sides of the loch made for a
sheltered anchorage. It would be some gale that ruffled this water.
And at the back, cupped by the towering crags, was a grassy, fertile
plain begging to be planted. It was about three boats long and ten

times as wide. Behind this, a wood, full of ancient trees that would make a man as many ships as he could take. Such ships!

On the water, ridiculously sheltered, were six galleys, doubtless hewn from those same trees. They barely moved, just swung lazily at anchor.

At the mouth of the loch, a gap to the Sound of Mull. He'd sailed past it enough times, that opening. It was narrow enough that with men on each side the whole entrance would be covered by spear and arrow. You'd need a high tide and a sure hand to thread a path through.

At the side of the loch, in an indent near the neck, there was a hall, and some outbuildings. There were signs of life. A few women clucked about the yard. A big man came out of the hall, walked to the water's edge. He scratched his belly, looking up the loch towards the hills of Mull beyond.

Sheltered, fertile, practical.

Hang that, cried Somerled's heart. All the beauty of the world. The early sun left the land undefined, its edges blurred. Mull, over the water, was a smudge of black rock and white snow, set in a light blue sky. Above, last night's moon clung on in a thin curve, unwilling to let go of this place. All the white-capped, God-raised, Christ-blessed beauty of creation was there in that steep-sided loch. To their left, a nub of high land nosing out into the Sound. Exposed, true. But from there, a man could survey the whole run of ships coming down the Sound. Control them all.

'Ardtornish.' Callum's voice was a gruff intrusion. He pointed at the bluff of land Somerled was contemplating. 'Thor's headland.'

Any god would take this as his own.

'Listen, Callum. Listen. When we win, I will support you. I will help you, by fair means or vicious, to take your place at the head of your hall. But here's my price. I must have this. This must be mine.'

Callum looked sidelong at him, silent.

'This is the better place,' he said.

'Aye, but it's not yours. Not your people. Tell me you don't want to plant your feet as lord in the place where you grew up.'

'Perhaps. But who would pay tribute to whom?'

'Worry about that later. We must take it first. And we are out-manned, out-galleyed.'

'So how?'

A Loki-sent certainty bubbled in him.

'By cunning,' he said, and his smile was as wide as the sky.

They weathered the headland and glided into the bay. Ugly clouds were spritzing a cold rain. Dusk threatened.

'Beach, or push on?' Sigurd shouted from his place at the steering oar.

'How long until we reach Fergus's place?'

Sigurd sniffed at the salty air like a hunting dog.

'Two hours. Perhaps three?' With courtesy, he looked at Callum, who nodded.

Somerled weighed the decision. The tipping thought, for him, was the notion of one last night in the easy brotherhood of his band. Before the politics, before the pulling-on of helmets. He knew it was not a good reason, but there were others in his favour. Better to arrive in a fresh dawn than hungry and tired. Besides, it could be dark before they arrived, and he would not risk a blithe sail into a potentially hostile bay. Who knew what had happened to Fergus's plans in the three weeks since he had left? Callum's presence was not guarantee enough.

They pulled her up on to the muddy flat of sand and shingle.

Ruaridh scampered along the rocks at the bay's edge to watch the sweep of the sea.

Somerled sat with his back to the rock, a pitcher by him. A rough covering of hide propped above his head. The rain pattering down on the skin. Aed by his side. He watched Sigurd outside, scraping at the exposed planking of the galley.

'Come in!' he shouted. 'Out of the rain.'

Sigurd came under the hide, water streaming off him. He grinned at Somerled fondly. Somerled thought the pilot might ruffle his hair, as he had always done until not so long ago. Would he mind it? He should, he supposed. He grinned back at the older man.

'So, tomorrow,' said Aed, and paused.

'Tomorrow,' began Somerled, and even as he gathered his thoughts, there came a cry.

Sharp, the three men's heads cracked towards the sound. There was Ruaridh, waving a warning from the land's edge.

'Fire,' barked Somerled, and Thorfinn quickly dumped a bucket of water over the fire, which hissed and spat in protest. The smoke died as they kicked sand and stone and stamped it down.

Ruaridh was on them. 'Six galleys', he said, gulping at the air. 'Under sail. Thor's hammer on the hide. I watched them bear away, as if to fetch here on a new tack. Perhaps sail off.'

Somerled turned to Callum. 'Any other sheltered bays between here and your place?'

The big man shook his head.

'Thor's mark,' said Somerled. 'The ships are from Ardtornish. They are bringing the war to you.'

Callum nodded. 'It looks like it.'

Think. He watched his men raise their faces, calculating odds, judging the wind, reckoning the tide. Think. He saw them turn to him, trusting and stupid. Even Aed. He wanted to strike them, to shake them up. To grab the straggling ends of their beards and pull, pull. Jolt them out of it. Not now. Think.

'How long until they're round?'

Ruaridh shrugged. 'Twenty minutes?'

They would come sailing into the bay, the wind and the tide behind them. No time to beat out with the oars and win the wind. They would come down on them with sails sheeted home, the warriors free to bristle with spears, free to use their numbers against one pathetic oar-pulled galley. Think.

'Callum. Can you be home across the land and back with your family's fleet by dawn? Surprise them?'

'Aye. But you'll be dead by dawn,' he said, flatly.

'No. Go, go quick.'

Callum, his face unreadable, clasped arms with Somerled and set off, winding his way across the machair to the higher ground. Dead. What did he know, the big stupid bastard?

Somerled turned to Sigurd.

'Sigurd,' he said, his voice almost tender.

'No.' Sigurd half turned away.

'I'm telling you. We can't get away; they've the wind and the tide. There's six of them. We'll die.'

'We'll all die anyway.'

'Aye, but not yet. Scuttle her.'

Indrawn breaths from the slower of the crew, the words ricocheting between them like a skimmed stone.

Sigurd let the wrench of it show on his face. But he nodded. With cold hands they grabbed at her sides, pushing and scraping her down into the water.

'Careful,' shouted Sigurd, then shook his head fiercely, muttering to himself.

Waist-deep in the cold sea, Aed climbed on and raised his double-headed axe to the sky. It paused at the top of the upstroke, seemed to tremble, then crashed down on to the wood they had so carefully seasoned and tended. The wood they had scrubbed and sanded so a man could slide across it in his bare feet and never catch a splinter. Aed laid about like a berserker, as if the fury could ease the sadness of it.

He jumped back into the cold sea, and they helped her sink, pushing her downwards under the murky water, holding her there as the bubbles rose and broke on the grey skin of the sea.

'Quick, quick,' shouted Somerled, and they waded back to the shore, pointedly ignoring Sigurd's tears, the proper weeping of a sailor who had knowingly drowned his own ship. They scrambled up the beach, grabbing their packs, scuffing the marks behind them, covering the scorched earth with sand and rock. They scrambled up and over the hill behind, sinking into the heather and fighting for breath.

Somerled gestured for them to stay put, and crawled back up to the bluff of the hill. They had better be putting in here, the bastards. He would weep like Sigurd if he found it had all been pointless.

There they were, thank the Lord, sweeping round into the bay, in a quiet rush of wind and sail.

~ ~ ~

The sound of their voices drifted over the heather to where Somerled and his men lay huddled below the summit of the hill. Norse, not Gael. He picked out words from their thick accents. His band leaned in together, cloaks pulled tight. It was a dark night, cloudy and moonless. A strange, suspended night, with tension and cold keeping them wakeful and time drifting endlessly.

Aed, next to him, whispered: 'I shall not be able to look at my axe in quite the same way. All the men it has sent to hell, but never its own galley.'

'You love that axe.'

'Is that what you think, Somerled? No.'

Aed paused. Somerled knew that he was smiling. 'A big bastard like me,' he said at last. 'People want me to have a bloody great axe. Scares them shitless, which is half the battle won. Love it? No. I'd like a fine sword, jewelled handle, sharp, slender blade.'

Somerled felt the hilt of his own sword and the mistaken notch in it that seemed shaped for his thumb. His hands were numb and he drew them back under the cloak. Aed shall have his sword. He slept, a little, perhaps. Or else they were thoughts, not dreams, about the Otter, twisting into Mebd and back again. Hard to know.

At last it was brighter. A lifting of the absolute black that held each man cocooned. He could see his fingers distinctly now, as he brought them out to blow them awake. With Aed, he shuffled on his belly to the top of the hill, the sharp branches of the heather snagging at them. Below them, the dark mounds of the beached galleys. Two were anchored in the bay, with no room on the small stretch of flat. The swing and clank of their rigging the only sound bar the rippling of the water. On the beach, small lumps of sleeping men dotted like cowpats. There, where Ruaridh had stood yesterday, a moving shape. No need to post a sentry to landward, in this bleak landscape.

They waited, not moving, for the light to spread. With each passing second the brightness grew, and with it the knot in his stomach. There, at the edge of the horizon, caught in the dawn haze that blurred the edges of the world, were ships. Callum and Fergus.

'Two hours away?' he whispered to Aed.

'At least.'

Somerled rolled on to his back. He'd wanted them closer, sailing into the bay at dawn to spring a trap on the sleeping men. Catch the bastards at the morning confusion. What now?

Above him, a gull circled and turned, floating on the sea breeze. The sky still had the pallor of night-time, but the edges of things, the details on them, were becoming clearer. He could see the gull's open beak as it shrieked.

From where he stood, the sentry would spot the sails within minutes. Should have done already, the dozy sod.

The sentry.

Somerled jerked his head. 'Scrag him, Aed. Quiet. Bring him back.'

Aed nodded, moved off. He was quiet for all his bulk, slipping around the back of the hill like a dark wraith.

Soon across the bay came a muffled cry, and a gurgle. On the sand, the shapes began to shift and move. Somerled slithered back down to his waiting band. He whispered instructions and they got to it, breaking out the black cow hides they had brought as gifts for Fergus. They cut up the brown hides they used to keep off the rain, turning them into makeshift cloaks, which should convince at a distance. Ten makeshift cloaks of black, ten brown and each of his men with his own cloak.

He took half of them, ten in all, up the hill. They stood tall at the summit and watched the men below running for their arms in a scampering confusion. Iomhar, the Irishman, was laughing, and Somerled stared him into silence.

He barked an order, and the ten men on the ridge marched back down it. The next ten came up, and paused, letting the men below register them. Somerled could see the first ten men ditching their own cloaks and donning the brown hides, ready to march back to the summit. The men at the top came down, and switched to the black cloaks, as their brothers in brown climbed up to taunt the Norsemen on the beach.

From the beach, they would look like a fresh set of men. If he could persuade the enemy, in the murky dawn light, that there were twice, three times the number holding the high ground, they would think before attacking up the hill.

He stood at the top, letting his men rotate and march around him. Far below him, a group formed a huddle. The chief and his advisers? He counted all the figures on the beach. At least seventy men. It must be the Ardtornish lord's full war-band. The huddle broke into individual figures, and he watched them. They moved to their ships, evidently deciding that these strange men were not their problem. This was not their war.

He wanted them to stay bottled in this bay, not out on the open sea where they could make their greater numbers count against Fergus. He nodded at Aed, then, who stood next to him, straddling the body of the sentry he had dragged back up the hill. Casually the big man hacked the sentry's head off with his axe, as if chopping wood. Picking it up by the hair, blood spattering his arm, Somerled heaved it down onto the beach, where it smacked into the muddy sand face down and rolled to the edge of the sea. A rising tide.

They could not hear the thud of the head, but they could hear the howling rage, hear the rasping of sword and spear.

Thorfinn's eyes were questioning across the slender shaft of his own spear.

'No,' growled Somerled. Once they began this, the Ardtornish men would know how few of them there were. For now, let them bristle and plot on the beach. Let them fire themselves up for an uphill raid, let them shake and hackle with thwarted battle rage.

Behind them, four galleys with striped sails were on a tack that would bring them sailing into the bay, wind and tide with them.

The men on the beach had spotted the coming galleys now. He watched them pointing, heard the shouting, but missed the sense of the words. The Norsemen paused, and a silence flooded the bay as they understood that they were caught in a trap. Somerled saw one of them pull his foot back and boot the head of the useless sentry into the rush of the rising tide.

He watched from above like a god, as they pondered and whirred like small creatures. He could almost hear them thinking: better to fight at sea than on land. Six galleys to four, fair wind or no.

'We need to delay them. Another few minutes,' he said to Aed, his mind racing as fast as his heart could beat.

'Let me,' said a voice at a growl. Gillebrigte. He was shaking and pallid from the booze tremors. It gave him a wild edge. An air of madness. He gripped his axe and stared at Somerled with red-rimmed eyes that pleaded and watered.

Somerled nodded. Gillebrigte moved towards him, as if to embrace him. But instead he shook his head and threw it back, howling at the dawn like a wolf. The noise swooped across the bay, freezing the men below. On he howled, and the red-black puckered edges of his burned skin were terrible suddenly, even to those used to the sight of him, used to pitying him.

Pumped and growling, he set off down the hill at a half-run. They saw him coming, felt the madness on him, knew that he was offering himself to the gods and would take men with him. As he ran at them, they gave before him, feet scrabbling in the ridged sand. Their champion stepped forward, and Gillebrigte took him down with startling ease. Who could resist the battle frenzy of a god? Already men were heaving at the galleys with desperation, trying to get them floating and away.

Jesus, thought Somerled. We could take them. They are scared. Panicking. His men beside him knew it too, watched Gillebrigte whirling and screaming on the beach, and the fear rolling off those near him. They bounced and snarled; a wolf pack. At a word from Somerled, they set off at a scream, running downhill, slamming into men trying to go backwards. Pushing them over, taking them down, bowling them into the sea.

Somerled took his first man quickly, the spear grinding into his neck with a jarring quiver. He left it there, spinning with his sword, punching it between a man's eyes, stretched wide with a doe-like fear. All around him was a roaring. Men fell into the sea, blood catching the retreating waves, pooling in the indents in the sand left by the cockles.

Some of them were trying to swim, and men leaned out from the approaching galleys to pick them off with spears for the sport of it.

He saw the Ardtornish lord then, the life leaking from his gashed fat belly, the tide washing over his spluttering mouth. Near him lay Gillebrigte, his yellow teeth bared and blood spooling down his chin. His father's eyes were staring at the sky. Was it a grimace, or a smile? No matter. No matter. Oh my father.

The galleys were slowing; hauling their sails and throwing out storm anchors.

Think. Think. Fergus stood at the bow, cheated of his place in the battle, justified in his faith in the boy lord from Morvern. He needed a gesture.

'They are dead, Fergus,' he shouted across the waves. 'And they killed my father. Danes, they are. No Christians. I will give you a gift of his heart.'

He straddled the body of the fat chief, who spluttered no longer. He thrust his knife into the man's chest. It scraped on bone. He could not push through. His hair fell down his forehead into his eyes, which stung from salt and sweat. Jesus. He couldn't get at the bloody heart. What a fool he was. What a child.

Aed beside him, grinning. 'A great victory, little lord,' he said, joy bubbling.

'I can't get at the fucking heart, Aed,' Somerled whispered, and laughter gripped at his belly. Aed caught it too, and bent double with a giggle that looked like a seizure. The blood and fat and bone slipped from the dead man's ripped belly.

'Jesus, Somerled,' said Aed, trying to control himself. He bent over the man's body, and pulled at the ribcage with a great roaring and spitting. Somerled heard the crack and splinter of bone; saw with a pickle of tenderness and revulsion the inner workings of a dead man. How like a pig he was, split down the middle. How pathetic, stripped of his skin and his soul.

Think. Fergus called something from the shallows, wading towards him with outstretched arms, his cloak bloodied at the hem from the red-washed water. Somerled cut and pulled, and there it was in his hand, gelatinous and warm, the blood running down his arm, a spatter of it in his mouth. A man's heart, beating its last in his palm.

I am Somerled. Immortal Somerled. Immovable Somerled. Eternal Somerled. He screamed, then, and the answering cheer carried him up like a gliding eagle as it ran along the beach and above the galleys and over the crimson sea.

1130

SOMERLED

'In Ancient Rome,' said Father Padeen's voice behind him, 'victorious generals parading through the streets employed a slave to stand behind them whispering, "Remember you are mortal."'

Somerled smiled, and looked out over his land. He could see into Loch Aline from up here, and out into the Sound. In the loch, three fat, heavy merchant galleys swung at anchor. Three galleys of his own were beached in the bay, by the Sound, and three more beyond the merchant ships in the loch. There, at the head of the loch, under a roof to keep the timber dry, was the bare frame of his new ship. Not captured, this one. Built from its very skeleton outwards.

He could see Harald, the shipbuilder from Orkney, walking with Sigurd – heads bent and arms waving. They were tiny from here. There were new houses dotted about the glen, and storehouses, byres and stables. Children were playing on the turf roof of one longhouse, led in their game of dare by Aed's son – a big and fearless five-year-old. There was even a smithy now, built by a cheerful fellow called Cinaed, who'd arrived over the mountains with a bag of tools and bleeding feet.

They were coming all the time. Warriors looking for a chief, traders looking for silver, displaced folk looking for a square of turf and someone to protect it for them, monks looking for souls. Success, Aed said, fostered success. And success, Thorfinn added, attracted the less successful buggers to suckle at your hind tit.

Here he was, lording over it all like some fat potentate.

'Father,' he said to Padeen, smiling at him. 'There is a voice in my head telling me I am mortal. All the time. Tell me, did you ever feel like a fraud? Did you ever feel like you were playing a part, and the watchers need only lift your skirts to know you were a lie?'

Padeen sat down beside him, grunting a little as he settled. An old man's involuntary grunt, Somerled realized with a shock. When did Father Padeen become old?

'When I was young, yes, perhaps. When I first left my teachers, to spread the gospel. I did feel like a fraud. Like I was unworthy to say God's words. But that made me unhappy, humble. You, Somerled? I think you find it amusing.'

Somerled smiled at the priest, and slapped his back.

'It won't be very funny when I do get found out.'

'Why should you be? You may think you're acting a part, but they' – he swept his hand out to gesture at the scene, from the fishing boats in the Sound, past the children collecting limpets from the stippled rocks at the water's edge, to the cattle grazing on the grass by the river that ran into the loch at its head – 'they believe you. And that is more important.'

Somerled looked at the priest. 'The voice telling me I am mortal. It's like a song in my head, Father. It sounds like the litany of the Trinity. The same rolling sound.'

'Have mercy on us, God, Father almighty,' began the priest, and they intoned it together.

God of hours.

Noble God.

World's ruler.

Ineffable God.

Creator of the elements.

Invisible God.

Incorporeal God.

Unjudgeable God.

Immeasurable God.

Impassible God.

Incorruptible God.

Immortal God.

Immovable God.

Eternal God.

Perfect God.

Merciful God.

Marvellous God.

Fearsome God.

God of the earth.

God of the fire.

God of the varied waters.

God of the rushing storm-tossed air.

God of the waves from the ocean's deep house.

God of the constellations and all the bright stars.

God who formed the mass, who began day and night.

God who ruled over hell and its rough crowd.

God who governs with archangels.

Golden God.

Heavenly Father who are in heaven.

Have mercy on us.

The priest sighed, happy. 'Ah, but I love those words, Somerled. They are what brought me to God, I think. That is what gave St Colm Cille his power, his voice down the ages. Those words that can settle and rouse a man's soul, and bring him closer to God.'

'Can words take you closer to God?'

'Of course.' Padeen turned and looked at him, surprised. 'What sets us apart from those cows, Somerled? What makes us the Lord's beloved? Words and music. Stories. The Lord handed down his wisdom wrapped in stories, because that is how we can make sense of this earth, that heaven. Any fool of a bull can fight, but can he sing?'

As if on cue, the cow on the slopes nearest to them let out a thunderous call.

'Hey, that milker thinks she can,' said Somerled, laughing. 'Look!' he added. 'There she is. Ruaridh's boys sent a signal, and I wanted to see.'

Down the Sound came a galley, a sleek, fresh-painted joy of a boat. Her sails stood stark against the green slope of Mull behind. No shields hanging down the sides, so Gael, not Norse. And the prow held no beast, so she came in a friendly spirit. Aed was down on the landing stage with an armoured crew to make sure of her intentions. She would need to be a crazy berserker to come alone as an aggressor into this place. It would take more than one galley, no matter how lovely, to touch Somerled now.

He saw his mother come out of the makeshift hall and raise a hand over her eyes to squint at the horizon. He watched her pull back her shoulders and lift her chin; he recognized the gesture and was strangely moved by the sight of her readying herself for action. She turned back and began shouting and waving; women and children and chickens scurried about, looking small and almost comical from his eyrie up here.

'I have to come up here to see anything,' he said. 'It's too easy to be watched. I want to be the watcher. Father, have you been out to the headland? Ardtornish, they call it. The headland of Thor. From there you can see the whole length of the Sound. I am thinking I will build there. Leave this settlement for the quiet folk, and take the warriors to Ardtornish.'

'It's terribly exposed,' said Padeen. 'But what do I know. Will I get a church?'

'Of course,' said Somerled, slapping him on the back.

Padeen stood next to him, peering out towards the ship. 'Who is it?'

'I don't know, Father. Shall we find out? Whoever it is will bring news.'

~ ~ ~

The chief of the strangers came forward. A fair man, a few years older than Somerled. He looked tired, and battle-grimed. There was dried blood crusted on his fine cloak, and the warriors at his back swayed on their feet with tiredness. They approached each other, a little wary.

'I am Somerled, Lord of Morvern.' It felt good to say it.

'You were not, last time I passed this way.'

'Well,' said Somerled, pulling back his shoulders and lifting his chin, 'I am now.'

The stranger nodded. 'So I see. Well, greetings, Lord Somerled. I am Mael Coluim, son of Alexander, King of Alba.'

A ripple ran through the gathered crowd. Somerled was thrown off balance, but he found his poise again quickly. This must be the natural son he had heard of, a fire-spark based in Moray.

'You are welcome.'

132

He lapsed gratefully into the demands of hospitality, taking refuge in the set pieces required by manners. They were tough, bruised men, these Moray warriors, with a strange, thick lilt to their Gaelic.

In the hall at the head of Loch Aline, Somerled drank a secret toast to the dead man who had built it. He remembered with a lurch of his stomach the soft yield of the man's heart in his palm.

After the toasts and the first rounds of honeyed cheese and ale, he turned to the man who sat at his right side. They had danced around each other, swapping pleasantries like an inverse shadow of a flyting. But he still had no notion of why the man was here. Or where he was going.

'What news of Alba?'

Mael Coluim looked at him with guarded eyes, appraising him. At last he shrugged and said: 'You have not heard?'

'We face Ireland, not Alba, out here.'

'Well then. You know that Alexander, my father, died some six years past. And that the English spawn, his brother David, marched to Scone with a power of English lords at his back. He scorned the Gaelic lords. Could barely say the words that made him king. Looked bored as the poets sang of his family. Didn't understand the great alliterative sweep of their words. English prick.'

Somerled sensed the quiet of the men around them, their leaning in to catch the tale. He watched Mael Coluim's big hand twisting the stem of his cup, the light catching on his heavy silver rings. Alexander and David had both been raised at the court of King Henry down in England, forced out by their uncle Domnall Ban. Mael Coluim's father was by all accounts as English as his brother. Perhaps, thought Somerled, he would not mention it.

One of the Moray men growled his assent to Mael Coluim's words. 'Sits on the border looking south,' he said. 'Never turning eyes to the north. Waiting for Henry to shout from England that his arse needs a kiss.'

'They say,' said another, 'that at his acclamation at Scone, the pretender could not be brought to utter the words. The bishops had to coax him to it.'

'First thing he does – the very first thing – was give a big parcel of Scots land to a French knight. Robert de Bruce.'

Nods from the Moray men, indrawn breath from Somerled's crew.

'Good land too,' said the man who seemed to be Mael Coluim's second. 'Prime grazing. Cattle by the hundred.'

Mael Coluim looked around as if to check that the audience was with him. Satisfied, he said: 'So I had no choice. My blood is as good as his.'

He told them of the march down to take on David, a band of Moray warriors at his back. His Moray foster brothers at his side. He told them of the battle that broke him, where his men hurled themselves on to implacable Norman lances. He told them of the Norman armour, great coats of metal links that stopped a man moving or running or rowing, but turned an arrow. He told them of the great horses, armoured too and trained for battle, that reared and kicked at head height.

Looking round, Somerled saw his chief men absorbing Mael Coluim's words. Aed looked serious, imagining a line of screaming Gaels breaking against the Norman horse. Ruaridh and a couple of others looked excited, pumped up; as if they were desperate to test their mettle against such a foe.

Mael Coluim's story tailed off. It had no heroic punchline, and Somerled was too polite to articulate the obvious. The battles were lost, and Mael Coluim was slinking back up the coast in a borrowed galley, keeping out of David's way and aiming to reach his foster family in Moray the long way round.

They talked, then, of other things. Of poetry and prayer. But all the time Somerled noticed Mael Coluim's slight inattention; the constant sliding-away of his eyes and the fight to bring them forward again. Almost like a tic.

As the meal thundered to its close, Mael Coluim's bard stood up, bowing, and offered a song to the house. In honour of Somerled, whose ancestor was Colla Uais, he would give them the tale of the founding of Airgailla. The bard sang of the three brothers, the Collas, fighting seven battles in one week against the the Ulstermen.

So now I have this hall, and these men, and a great herd of cattle, thought Somerled; now this ancestry of mine is set in stone, written in the runes, carved in Ogham on a cross, scratched in Latin onto parchment, swapped from mouth to mouth of the bards.

But when the fellow sang, he stopped thinking, for this man could make his harp rush and sing like a waterfall, thunder and menace like an army, lull and soothe like a songbird. The familiar story looped around the hall, made unfamiliar by the glorious harmonies. All around him, Somerled watched his warriors gape; these hard-living men undercut by a small fellow with sharp teeth who wielded his harp like an angel. Aed looked close to tears, and even as Somerled watched, the big man gave in and silently sobbed as the words of the dying queen's lament echoed around the hall.

But there in the shadows, Somerled saw another face. Alfric the Bard, who had never made Aed weep, who had never strung a hall of warriors tight on his harp string, who would never sound like an angel's twin, dropped from a cloud to make men and women wilt with his song.

The poor bastard. It was writ on his face – the small tragedy of being mediocre.

As the last notes of the song fell away, dropping into a silence more profound than a roar, Somerled stood. He pulled off an arm ring – a heavy, worked silver piece with the head of a serpent devouring its own tail – and threw it to the bard. It was caught with a practised bow, and the man pushed it on to his thin arm carelessly, as if it were his due.

The roar came then; Somerled's men and their guests happy with his generosity, happy with the song, happy with themselves and their mead-rich, stomach-full, fire-warmed bodies. Only Somerled noticed the empty corner, the unbroken shadow where his bard had been sitting, and his case on the floor, unopened.

~ ~ ~

The next morning, as Somerled emerged from behind the curtain and stepped across the snoring, flatulent bodies of the sleeping men – his and Mael Coluim's all mixed up – everything was made clear: the reason for Mael Coluim's inattention the night before, his distracted air. Somerled's sister Brigte was awake and seeing to the hearth, hauling water into the cauldron to set it to boil. Mael Coluim crouched next to her, talking softly. Something he said made her laugh, and she looked up from her task, grinning, her cheeks flushed and her hair escaping to fall over her face in fine blonde strands.

She saw Somerled then, and looked at him with his mother's clear blue eyes. She blushed, turning near purple with embarrassment. Mael Coluim looked over and he too, this confident, cocksure young prince, turned a shade of red to match the girl. Lord save us, thought Somerled.

~ ~ ~

He found her, later, in with the cattle. His mother was milking, her hands working deftly and her forehead resting on the cow's rough skin.

Brigte stood next to her, stroking the cow's neck with quick tenderness. If they were talking, they stopped when he walked in, and Brigte looked towards him, unflinching. She was bristling, ready for a fight. She paused in her stroking, and the cow, aggrieved, turned to look at Somerled, harrumphing its displeasure.

He paused on the threshold, abashed by the hostility of his sister, amused by the hostility of the cow. He didn't really know Brigte, he realized. She had grown into a woman behind his back, while he was looking at other things. He was angry with her, and he did not quite understand why. Perhaps for clouding the political with the personal; for forcing him to worry about the difference between policy and sentiment.

'Well, Brigte—' he began.

'Shut up!' she shouted. 'Shut up! Don't say it. Don't.'

He took a step back, astonished at the invective. He felt his new leather boot slither in some cow dung, and cursed under his breath.

'Children,' snapped Sigrdrifa, her voice sharp behind the cow's belly, the irritation at being interrupted clear.

They both mumbled something. Somerled inwardly sneered at himself. Playing the great lord with princes, then quailing before his mother. What a fraud he was. What a joke. Mind you, he thought as Sigrdrifa cursed the shifting cow, she is pretty ferocious. Brigte caught him smirking, and she grimaced back.

'Thor's bloody hammer, these children of mine. For what are you fighting?' Sigrdrifa tugged one more time: a dribble. She stood

137

up, pushing herself upright and arching her back. A small grunt of pain; irritation flitting across her face.

Somerled and Brigte looked at each other, conspirators suddenly.

'Well,' said Brigte. 'It's Mael Coluim. He . . .' She trailed off.

'Yes. Am I not your mother? Do I not know when your bowels move? Tsk. As if I could miss you two making the moony eyes with each, and that old love-slut Freyja dancing in the hearth.'

Brigte reddened, and Somerled found himself reaching an arm across her shoulder.

'And you, boy. Barging in, looking to tell your sister off as if she was one of those slave girls you scratch your itch on.'

Jesus. Could she make him feel any smaller?

'What then is your problem, if your sister chooses this imp?'

He gathered his scattered thoughts. 'It is such a dangerous road. He has no land. He has no legitimacy. He has no silver. He has half a name, a fierce ambition, a grievance against his powerful uncle. He has a family who fight like a sack of rats. If she marries him, we are bound to him against the King of Alba, for all love.'

'And what is the King David to us here?' Brigte said. 'Are you frightened of him?'

'No. But you should be. He is the last of six brothers, and yet he is on the throne. A bosom friend of that fiend Henry in England. A fighter. A survivor. A ruthless enemy.'

'And what would you have me do? Hide behind these mountains? Marry a cow-herder?' She stamped her foot in a gesture so absurdly childish, it threw him off balance.

'Not a cow-herder. No. But . . .' He trailed off.

'Are you worried for her, or for you?' Sigrdrifa's question was an uncomfortable one.

'Both. David is too big an enemy. And with Olaf growling at us from Man, can we provoke wrath from all sides?'

'David has made enemies of the Gaelic lords,' said Brigte. 'He is weak everywhere north of the Firth.'

Somerled arched a deliberately provoking eyebrow. 'Now who told you that, I wonder?'

Sigrdrifa growled as Brigte opened her mouth to retort. 'Enough. Yes, it will be difficult. She has courage enough for it. You think only warriors have courage.'

She bent down to pick up the pail, holding it carefully as milk sloshed up its sides.

'You know nothing, Somerled. Nothing. When you men go off raiding, we sit here, with your children, trapped between the sea and the mountains. Eyes watch us from the darkness.

'We know in our hearts that we are helpless and defenceless against fate – not like you foolish warriors who think you can make your own destiny. Pah. To know that you are helpless, to know that you are defenceless, that your children are defenceless; and yet to rise, to face the sun, to smile, to smooth away someone else's tears. This is courage, Somerled. And she has it.'

Brigte looked at him, collected and proud, nodding at their mother's words.

'As for the rest,' Sigrdrifa said, shrugging her shoulders violently, so the milk wobbled at the lip of the pail. 'Her sons will be grandsons of the King of Alba. *Grandsons of the King of Alba.* What more needs to be said?'

Brigte stepped forward, and Somerled had the odd sensation that he had been ambushed.

'Listen, brother. Please, let me choose my life. I don't want to be small, to be obscure, any more than you do. I choose a bold life. I choose a big life. You must let me go.'

~ ~ ~

She left barely a week after Mael Coluim had first sailed into the bay with his borrowed galley and his prickly birthright. They pulled away, the leaving song drifting back across the water to where Sigrdrifa stood watching her go.

His mother seemed to wither with each pull, shrink into herself. It was an extraordinary thing; like watching a flower shrivel and close. By the time the galley had rounded the bluff, and the last notes were lost in a tangle of gull cries and wave crash, she had aged. How she had aged. Somerled felt small and weak, standing on the beach. Wordless. Watching his mother, his brave, strong mother, battle her grief and lose.

As she aged, he regressed, until at last he felt a shameful petulance – a child's fury against a sibling who had caused his mother pain. 'We'll see her again soon,' he said, tripping over the lie even as he said it.

She looked at him, wanting to believe. He waited for the lash of her tongue, for the sarcasm. But she said nothing, and turned her back on the frothy grey sea.

~ ~ ~

A few weeks later, a small band of them were sitting on the rocks beyond the beach, idle. They watched the women at their chores. Mebd was outside the hall in the sunshine, churning butter in the keg with big, violent gestures.

'I thank God daily,' said Sigurd Horse-face, 'that I am not a woman.'

'*I* thank God daily,' said Ruaridh, 'that you are not a woman.'

'Hey, puppy,' countered Aed. 'If he were a woman, you'd still tup the ugly bastard. Stoat that you are.'

'Probably,' said Ruaridh, mildly.

'You're lucky, Aed.' Somerled watched Oona as she emerged from behind the hall, trailing children like goslings.

'Are you bored of Mebd?' asked Thorfinn. 'It's been, what, five years.'

'She keeps nagging me to let her go home.'

Aed gave an exaggerated shudder. 'You're lucky she's just nagging.' There were low murmurs at this, as they remembered the girl as they'd first seen her, naked and straddling the body of her dead lord.

Somerled raised his face to the sun, which was hot enough for springtime. He closed his eyes and let the warmth dance on his face. No man who had slept on an open galley in a storm ever took warmth for granted. He smiled, contented. It was a relief to him to be with the few who had started this with him. He could relax with this handful, his brothers in the shield wall. They had been mangled and pulped by the fights they had been in – little Ruaridh had lost part of his nose at the battle for Ardtornish, which gave strangers a rare shudder when they saw him. Thorfinn could no longer raise his shield arm above his shoulder; Sigurd wore a scar across his cheek like a scratch from a dragon. Domnall limped, but his irrepressible boyishness left Somerled breathless and a little envious. Domnall was only a little younger, but with no responsibilities beyond his thirst for blood, booze and sex – in that order.

They were a raggle-taggle band, then, despite the new finery that sat incongruously on their lean bodies. Only Aed, who was beloved of God, remained untouched and seemed born to clank with silver as he moved.

Yet all of this had left them close. Thor's brothers. Christ's warriors. Somerled would go to Fergus for counsel, to Padeen for wisdom. He could muster eighty oars, and pack a shield wall two deep.

But to laugh, to relive old battles, these were his band.

Sometimes, too, they could venture beyond laughter, before retreating hastily. Lying back on the rock, with the sun on his face and an afternoon of leisure stretching ahead of him, Somerled thanked the Lord for them.

Aed broke his reverie. 'Mebd has had no children,' he said.

'That could be my fault.'

'Nonsense,' said Sigurd. 'They have ways, women. Your mother, for one. She's steeped in the old lore. Seidr magic. If the lass wants to go home, she won't want babies to stop her.'

At the edge of Somerled's mind, as always, someone else hovered. Someone small and freckled and fierce.

They were silent for a while, as old friends could be. Ruaridh and Domnall threw stones at a marker, seeing who could land the closest.

Aed said: 'You are set, then, on building a great hall on Ardtornish.'

'I am. Who could surprise us there? Who could pass without us knowing?'

They nodded. They had all stood lookout there, watching the great sweep of water that made the best sea road from the southern to the northern isles.

Somerled looked out towards his chief galley. The younger boys were out in it, practising their seamanship. He smiled as someone caught a crab with his oar, and the blade jumped violently from the water. He imagined the swearing. He sat up suddenly. Straighter, alert.

'Sigurd. Why do we steer with an oar on the side?'

142

'Hey?'

'Why? Think on it? Does a dolphin steer with a fin sticking out on the side? Symmetry, that's the key.'

Sigurd still looked puzzled, but Somerled saw Aed concentrating.

'But Somerled,' said Aed. 'That is how the big boats are always steered.'

Somerled clicked his tongue, impatient. 'That's no argument, Aed. The old ways are not always the best.'

He sensed a stirring at this heresy, but ignored it.

Sigurd, his eyes fixed on the galley, said: 'What do you propose?'

'A rudder at the stern. Dead centre. Why not?'

They argued about it for a while, trying to imagine it, trying to establish if it would work.

Somerled, irritated, broke in to their debate.

'Sigurd, talk to Harald the Shipbuilder. The new galley is almost ready. We can try, at least.'

'He will have a crimson fit,' said Sigurd.

'Aye, well, let him. Let's see if it works. It could help us turn in tighter circles.'

He remembered, suddenly, Iehmarc's open-mouthed horror and the wild, flying end of the rope as he cut it. He fought to control a shiver.

Across the beach they heard the sound of the women singing, and knew that the weaving had started. The slow beat of the call and response drifted over the sand.

'See,' said Sigurd, listening to the words, 'they think it's a difficult life to be a woman, and they should know.'

'True,' said Somerled.

'We were thinking,' said Ruaridh, strangely diffident. He looked towards Aed, who gave him a nod of encouragement. 'I can find anything,' he continued. 'You know that.'

'Except your own arse,' mumbled Thorfinn, but they ignored him.

'Shall I go to Ireland for you, to find her?'

'Find who?' asked Somerled, although he already knew.

'Eimhear. The one they called the Otter.'

eimhear

'Jesus, Ruaridh. I could swim faster than this.'

'And can I control the winds?'

'Can you make the men row?'

'When there's wind enough in the sail? Not even for beauty such as yours.'

'Ruaridh, I knew you when you cried for your mammy over a grazed knee. Do not play bold with me.'

He smiled at me, and looked up at the trim of the sail. He pulled on a rope, and the curve of it tightened and we leaped a heartbeat forward.

'You always were impatient, little Otter.'

'And you were always cheeky. I am impatient to be home, that is all.'

'Home?' He looked at me askance. 'But you have never been there.'

'Is home a collection of stones and byres, then? Or is it all the creatures that breathe there?'

He nodded as if I were a great sage.

'Wait until you see it, Eimhear. It is the glory of the world.'

'He has done well, then, our little lord.'

He turned to me with an unfamiliar, violent earnestness. 'He is a wonder. Cunning, winning. His men would follow him anywhere.'

'You do not have to convince me, Ruaridh.'

'But some doubt him, for his youth. He is changed from when you knew him. More serious. More driven.'

He excused himself and shouted some string of orders. Somerled was not the only one who had changed, it seemed. Little Ruaridh led these men with confidence. It made me feel nervous. All the certainty about this meeting wavered suddenly. Had I dreamed a boy and called him Somerled? Who was this grim warrior waiting for me?

We swung round to settle on a new tack. I let my legs adjust to the roll, and licked the spray from my lips.

'Almost there,' said Ruaridh. Above, the grey sky pressed down. The coast seemed a solid black fortress against us; the gloom hid its folds and creases. I scanned ahead with salt-stung eyes.

'There! The new fort at Ardtornish,' he said, with pride in his voice. 'Beyond it, the entrance to Loch Aline.'

I saw the smudge of a fortress jutting out into the sea. I had the strangest sensation that even if I had not been told, I would have known it was his. I smiled at my stupidity, and Ruaridh, catching my mood, laughed with me. We pushed on, and I tried to concentrate on the approach; the rolling of the sea, the glorious spray of it on my face. I tried not to think of what I was leaving behind; the familiarity of my rather dull life among the women of the Ulaid. Sadhbh and Gràinne, who cried when I left, knowing it was likely to be the last time. The graveless resting place of my father.

But most of all I tried not to think about what lay ahead. About the crush of disappointment that could be waiting for me. About the absurdity of my hopes. About the boy waiting for me who did not exist except in my head. About the strange man who really was waiting for me, across this forbidding sea.

1130

SOMERLED

I t was harvest time when the arrival of a small galley sent the men crashing down from the fields to find their weapons. Somerled pulled his helmet on with arms exhausted from the haymaking, and a back that creaked and bent like he was sixty, not twenty.

Aed appeared, a wide grin on his face. 'Looks like Ruaridh. Domnall's sharp eyes spotted the little fellow capering in the bows.'

Somerled pulled his helmet back off. 'Alone?' he said, and Aed's answering grin unnerved him.

Jesus. What a performance this would be. What an embarrassing idiocy, to be down on the beach with fifty pairs of eyes watching for something out of a bard's tale, as he and the Otter saw each other and greeted each other like performing bears. What a mistake this was. And why was his stomach churning, worse than before a scrap? Why was there this absurd tightness in his throat? Why was he incapable of walking easily down to the beach like a Christian, instead of this absurd lumber he seemed to have affected from nowhere?

It was a glowering, heavy sort of an afternoon, and the surf was high on the shingle. He could see, as soon as he emerged from the hall, the new galley in the bay, close in and oars backed to keep her steady. There was Ruaridh, waving like a jester from the stern, and there, standing straight-backed and unknowable, was the Otter.

When had he last seen her? Six years ago – when she was thirteen.

And now this nineteen-year-old girl, who jumped into the surf like a boy, trailing her long skirts in the water, was walking towards him across the shingle, and all around them fifty pairs of eyes looked on and waited, like fools breathing in at a song's penultimate disaster, waiting to breathe out when the lovers were united, when the monster was defeated, when the gods were placated.

I am Somerled. Light thinker. Fate-breaker. Otter . . . Otter . . . Otter what?

Now she was in front of him, and Christ, she was as lovely as he had dreamt her. She had grown and filled outwards, so the little freckled girl was eye to eye with him, and full with curves that he dared not look at in front of the watching eyes.

He was dry-mouthed. Helpless. If he was a proper, far-sighted lord, he would have ordered all the watchers, all the gawpers, to fuck off back to the fields, to bury their heads in the shingle, to hide under the sheep until he had worked out what in St Colm Cille's own name he was planning to say to this girl. This pale, freckled girl with the brown eyes that stared back at him from under a mop of red-flecked chestnut hair that put the autumn sun to shame.

And now they were standing there silent and the moment had stretched too long and too far, and he was sinking like a bog-walker into his own embarrassment, and feeling the flush creeping up his neck and to his cheeks.

Why didn't she say anything? Someone cleared their throat behind him. Above, the seagulls called and shrieked, as if mocking his inarticulateness, his utter inability to do anything but stare and swallow.

Then he saw it. Her mouth was twitching, and her eyes crinkling. She was trying not to laugh. The thought gripped at his stomach as he saw it through her eyes – the crowds, the stuttering boy-lord, Sigrdrifa coming up behind with arms outstretched, the expectations and the inevitable disappointments. But most of all, the absurd portentous atmosphere that sought to weigh down their first words to each other with some layer of profundity that neither was capable of living up to. It was, he realized, ridiculous.

As he felt the laughter take him, he grabbed her hand and pulled her away from the eyes and up beyond the beach to the wood by the burn, where they sat, hidden, and laughed until the tears came.

~ ~ ~

'Where have you been?'

'Back over the water. I heard of you.'

'There? They've heard of me across the water?'

'Is your head too big for your helmet? I was listening for you. Listening for your name. Asking questions.'

'Why?'

'Why did you send Ruaridh?'

'Why did you come with him?'

'So are we to dance around, Somerled?'

She turned a wide circle on the beach, her arms outstretched and her hair hanging down beyond her waist.

'Come here, then, Otter, if you want to make it all clear.'

'Not yet.'

Yet.

'When?'

'When I say. When Father Padeen has said the necessary words.'

'You care for such things?'

'I am alone in the world, Somerled. If I do not care, who will?'

149

'How is your father?'

'Dead. Yours?'

'Dead.'

She shivered and looked up towards the hall, towering above them and lit like a beacon. Down here in the bay, it was cold but quiet. They had sneaked out after the toasts, ignoring the winking and leering of those who saw them leave.

'You look well, Somerled. Success suits you.'

'Age suits you. You look . . .' He failed to find the word.

She laughed. 'I shall not look to you for endearments, then. The girl. The one who looks so sullen. What is she?'

'Mebd? She is . . . she was . . .' He failed again. Damn the girl.

'No matter. I am here now.'

~ ~ ~

The next morning, he found Mebd down by the burn, washing great slabs of linen, grinding them white. They always gave her the tasks that called for fury.

'So,' she said, looking at him as he walked up. 'I am to be cast off. Shrugged off like an adder skin.'

'Sorry,' he mumbled.

She shrugged and turned back to her washing, slapping it down on the rock and pulling it back towards her.

'I'll set you up with a bride price. Send you home under escort in a galley,' he said.

'You will.'

'I . . .'

She looked up at him as he trailed off. 'Let's not pretend it was something other than it was. She is pure. She is capable of what your daft, sentimental soul is looking for. Perhaps if I had not been initiated into love by a fat, stinking pig as his mates watched on with total indifference, perhaps I could have moped about on mountains talking about fucking stars.'

The ring he had thought to give her bit into his palm where his fist was clenching. He felt like a fool, an overgrown boy. What had he expected?

She looked at him, and something softened. 'Well, you were kind, at least. Kindness. Jesus. Why is there so little of it? What did He die for, anyway?'

It was his turn to shrug now, and she melted a little further. 'Look at you, Somerled. You were so young when you found me, so very young. I thanked God that this boy was the chief. I thought I could contain you, thought I could teach you to be kind. I didn't have to. That was something. It was already there. So if I'm bitter, I'm sorry. It's not your fault. But you could have let me go home sooner.'

'Was there nothing you enjoyed about us?'

She started to laugh, but seeing his face, she stopped herself.

'Of course,' she said. 'Of course.'

He left her then, beating and slapping the wet linen. She was lying, but he would choose to believe the lie. Her tale was not his tale. Her bitterness not his. Not his.

He took Eimhear hunting later that day. He wanted to get away, to put a fair distance between the two of them and Mebd's mocking, cool stare. He wanted a barrier of heather and moss and bracken, of scree and rock, between them and her bitterness. Eimhear looked askance at him, knowing that there was something beneath this sudden whim. He took Sigurd to one side before they left, charged him with taking Mebd home, making sure she was safe. Although her people were most likely long dead.

They set out on the horses, heading for a shieling on the slopes of the mountain, where they would find the deer. She rode, as he knew she would, confidently. A childhood spent ranging bareback across the peat and bog. Aed was with them, and Ruaridh. But they kept their distance, bless them.

She sat straight, relishing the ride through the heather, mumbling endearments to her horse – a grey mare with spirit enough to carry her.

Up by the shieling, they dismounted, tethering the horses to a tree, and walked up beside the burn to a place where the water tumbled down rocks in a great fall. They sat by a pool at the bottom, on rocks clear of the spray.

'I would swim here, in the summer,' she said.

'I have,' he said. 'It's cold. Shall we go in now?'

'Not now.'

He picked up a pebble and threw it into the pool, watching the ripples reach across the face of the water to the rock where she sat.

'It's a great joy for me that you are here,' he said.

She turned to look at him, smiling without reserve.

'It's a joy to me, Somerled.'

They heard scrambling behind them, and Ruaridh's face appeared above the rocks.

'Deer, Somerled. A big herd. Some tasty-looking buggers, ha ha!'

They followed him through the heather until they came to a strange pocket of land dotted with rocky outcrops that fell away into steep crags that led nowhere. Somerled watched Ruaridh, the little man's impish face transformed as he was taken with the hunt. He was serious, concentrating. He lifted his head to the wind, checked its course, listened for the deer.

He signalled them to crouch, and they followed him, snaking their way through the wet, snagging brush to the top of one of the rocky outcrops. Nothing. Somerled looked round. To the left, the high mountains. Across the way, the unshrouded summit of Ben Mòr. Through the glen he could make out the sea, glimmering blue under the autumn sun.

He felt Eimhear grab his arm, winding her fingers into the cloth. Down below he saw the first deer walking into view. They stepped high and careless through the heather, pausing now and then to raise their heads to the wind, trusting it to carry the scent of their foes. The stag, muscled and graceful all at once, seemed to be shepherding his herd – watching and nudging and shaking his head impatiently at latecomers. Somerled felt a moment of absurd sympathy for him, as two of the younger deer ignored the rest and strayed away, towards the crag where four arrows were being fitted to four strings.

He glanced sideways at Eimhear, and felt an unexpected surge of tenderness. She was concentrating and focused, her face itself like the point of an arrow. Her eyes were narrowed slightly, and the tip of her tongue poked out of her mouth. He watched her fit her arrow, never taking her eyes from the deer, feeling with her fingers for the notch. With a slow, fluid grace she lifted the bow and pulled back the arrow, squinting along its line towards the deer. Only then did she look at him; a sideways glance and a grin, and a jerk of her head that meant: go on, you fool, stop watching me and watch the deer.

Somerled looked away and towards the deer. He pulled back and let fly, hearing the answering hiss of the others' arrows taking flight and the thud and squeal of some of them hitting home. The herd were wide-eyed and frightened, running and dodging. He watched the stag check his own flight and wait for the others to catch up, and he willed him well.

Down on the heather, two deer lay still. One was dead, but the other was still alive, looking up at them with wide white eyes, blood-flecked foam at its mouth. An arrow was buried deep in its throat. Eimhear's arrow, he judged from the cut of the feathers. He offered her his knife and she took it, stepping towards the deer.

But then, in a sudden gesture, she threw the knife aside. 'You do it for me,' she said to Aed, and strode away, back towards the shieling.

~ ~ ~

She was moody that evening – cross with herself for being too squeamish to kill the deer. He thought about saying something placatory, but the set of her head warned him to keep quiet. Aed and Ruaridh moved further down the slopes, mumbling something unintelligible and setting up their own fire and heather beds under an overhanging crag.

She butchered the deer with a compensatory efficiency. She left most of the carcass intact to make it easier to carry, but sliced out some prime cuts, which she wrapped and buried under the fire. Some slivers she kept, and they crisped them on sticks in the flames, the smell and the smoke mingling to drift down to the sea.

He was shy with her now. The sun was setting into the sea, bathing the hillside in pinks and purples. It looked almost as if her hair was on fire in that glorious light, and her face glowed gold.

They sat in silence for a while, an uncomfortable one that scratched and bothered him but seemed impenetrable. At last she said: 'And is this how you court a girl in the sunset, Somerled? It's no wonder you're unmarried.'

'But you're not a girl.'

She laughed. 'You're terrible at this. It's all right,' she said, holding up a hand as he began to retract. 'I know what you mean.'

He retreated back into himself, a little cross.

'So you've managed to win yourself a portion of fame, and a host of men, but up here you're silent and gauche, like a goat boy.'

'I don't know what to say to you. Other girls . . .'

'Other girls?'

Oh Jesus. A lee shore and a foul tide and a reef approaching.

'Eimhear, I have been the chief of a band since I was fifteen. Other girls don't need wooing at sunset. Other girls just . . . just . . .'

'. . . just flock to your bed because you're the leader and they want to catch some of your wealth and fame.'

He nodded, miserable about how crass it sounded.

'And do I need wooing?'

'Don't you?'

'No.'

They were silent again for a pace, watching the sun sink into a fiery sea with a hiss that was almost audible. She pushed the embers to one side with a stick and unearthed the meat. He held it on his lap, still in its leaves, and the warmth of it spread through his body. It was growing colder up there, now the sun had gone. The sea was a blue-black blur beneath the darkening sky. The North Star was out already. Watching them. The meat fell apart, tender and delicious. They warmed their mead in the fire, and drank it companionably.

She told him about the years in Ireland. The death of her father, and her small life in the lord's fort. She told him about the years since the great defeat, with purses tight and tempers frayed. She told him of boredom and loneliness, in a voice vibrating with self-mockery.

'Why didn't you come to me at once?'

'Now, sitting here with you, I don't know. It made sense then. There were reasons, there must have been. Stupid ones.'

'And were there not men who wanted you?'

'Of course there were. But not one who wanted me honestly.'

'I do, Eimhear. I want you before God.'

'Somerled. I am a nobody. You are getting on to be a great lord.
You should marry well.'

'But I want you.'

'Well then. I am here.'

~ ~ ~

My kiss across your face,
Across the ear, like this.
My kiss across this eye,
My kiss across this neck.

My kiss across this mouth,
My kiss across this throat.
My kiss across, oh, this breast,
My kiss across, across, across.

Your kiss across my lips,
Across my neck, oh, like that.
Your whisper in my ear,
Oh my Lord, oh my Christ.

My push, your arching,
My pull, your breathing,
My kiss across this breast,
Oh, this breast, this breast.

Your hands across my back,
Your hands across my hair.
Our voices reaching heaven,
Oh my Lord, oh my Christ.

Oh my love.

~ ~ ~

The next morning, the dawn came wet and cold. They lay under their cloaks, twisted into each other, joined by skin and the memories of the night just past, listening to the rain spattering against the cold stone of the shieling.

He kissed her neck. 'I thought you would wait for Father Padeen,' he said.

'So did I.'

She laughed and arched her body into him, seal-supple and warm. 'I was definitely going to wait. I promised myself.'

'But I am too alluring,' he said.

'Yes, that's it.'

'Ow, you Otter. Don't hit me!'

'But you're ridiculous.'

'I'm the chief, you can't speak to me like that.'

'If I cannot, who can?'

'No one. I shall have you all prostrate yourselves, like they do before the emperor in Miklagard.'

She laughed, and gestured at the mossy roof, the stone wall with the rain and wind leaking through the cracks, the heather, which last night was springy and comfortable but now lay sad and hard-packed on the floor beneath them. Skin untouched by skin was hard and goose-bumped.

'Forgive me, great emperor. I did not recognize your glory in these humble surroundings.'

'Did you not? And I thought it shone through like a beacon.'

'Stop talking nonsense, my summer heart, and kiss me. If we're sinners now, we may as well compound the sin.'

'Sinful? This? No, my darling. Shall I show you sinful?'

She laughed as she felt his lips kissing her ribs and moving slowly down her belly.

'Yes,' she said. 'Oh yes please.'

After the handfasting, he built a bower by the river, up behind a fold in the hill. They were hidden there. He felt as if God was smiling on them, sending a last gasp of autumn sunshine in such copious abundance that they could lie on warm, flat rocks by the river. They could slip into the cold water and come out shaking, warming each other with lips and hands and sunlight.

God sent a breeze, too, that funnelled through this cleft in the hill, driving away all but the most persistent of midges.

God sent a rain, which forced them inside to listen to its pattering, wrapped in each other.

God sent a fragment moon, so the stars were unveiled and sharp, and they could lie outside in blankets of fur, watching for shooters as their breath pooled in the air above them.

They talked. They talked so much that sometimes Somerled was reluctant to kiss her, in case a break in the talking would mean it could never start again so easily, so freely. He followed her back to Ireland, across the sea, to the stars. They talked of poems and stories, and the children they would have.

When he started to kiss her, he was reluctant to stop. He liked to make her gasp, liked to hear her breath quicken in his ear, to make her feel as if, in the middle of love, she was floating on a warm and violent sea.

The days staggered into each other, until at last they began to talk about going back down the hill.

'Why must we?' he asked.

'You have work to do. Battles to fight. And then you will be king.'

'Why?'

'Why? Because it is your fate.'

'Fate be damned. I am serious. Why can't we stay here, as we are? Fishing, and loving, and raising little ones?'

'Because you would grow old and bored, and start to hate me.'

'Why?'

'Because a life with no purpose has no colour. No meaning.'

'Doesn't Christ show us meaning?'

'Christ? No. Salvation. Damnation. Not meaning. We make our own meaning.'

'What is yours?'

'You are mine.'

'Well then. You are mine.'

'I am not enough.'

'Why?'

'Why? Because that, my summer heart, is not how the world works. The essence of the thing is meaningless. We are here because we are here, because we are here.'

'Well then.'

'No. Listen. Why must you fight and lead men and leave me behind? Because the alternative is to have some other bastard telling you what to do. That, you could not stand. And I could not stand watching you take another man's orders.'

'Not if you were the reason?'

'Especially if I was the reason. Besides, if you are another man's vassal, what am I? A vassal's vassal. Be damned to that.'

'So there is no escape for us? No endless bower? No perpetual spring?'

'None, my darling. You must fight and I must weave.'

'Perhaps I should weave and you should fight, my fierce one.'

'Would that I could. Trust me, my summer heart, if you stayed and spun, listening to the wittering of bitter, bored women, you would understand emptiness.'

'Does it bore you?'

'Is boredom a word big enough?'

'But the essence is that both our tasks are meaningless.'

'It is all meaningless. This life, this death. We're killing time, my love, until judgement. So we must kill it with style.'

'But the judging, at the gates, that gives us the purpose.'

'You think that, my summer heart, if it consoles you.'

'It is bleak, your philosophy.'

'The truth is bleak. Mostly. But not all. *This* is true.'

'Us? Oh, my love, yes. And not bleak. We must seek out our joy, then?'

'Yes. And I am here.'

~ ~ ~

Back down the hill, at last, to normal life. But a normal life that glowed, that sang its own low song of love beneath the mundane.

Eimhear slotted in at Sigrdrifa's right hand, throwing herself into the hard work that heralded the onset of winter. Somerled was back with his band, drilling and fighting, cleaning and sharpening; getting ready for their own hibernation and the spring raiding that would follow.

Sigurd returned. He had found Mebd's mother and her sister, living where they had always lived. She had embraced them and showered them with Somerled's silver, promised her mother an easier life. She had smiled, Sigurd said, and that smile was fresh and innocent as a twelve-year-old's, there in the place where she belonged. Somerled put aside his guilt. He added it to the list of guilts and regrets that he would worry about, most likely, when he was old. For now, he was too happy for dark-edged thoughts.

The short days meant long nights. Gathering by the fire, there were the usual tales and songs, the usual rhythmic killing of the dark evenings. But now there was Eimhear. Her hand in his. Her shoulder against his. Her amused eyes meeting his over the mangled poetry as his warriors sought to outdo each other in verse-making.

There was Eimhear's hair burning in the firelight. Her long legs in the darkness wrapping around his back, and her whispers in his ear as he fought to keep his passion silent behind the curtain. He would dream, as he drifted to sleep, of love in the empty mountains, where he could shout and groan and scream with the joy of her.

There was Eimhear's face in the still-dark mornings, and the secret smiles that spoke of pleasure enjoyed, and joy to come.

And running through it all was a warning that throbbed in his heart. *This is too rare. This is too precious. This cannot last. This is too much blessing.*

The year turned, too fast. The cold and dark that kept him here, tethered to her side, began to ease. He cursed the lightness, cursed the warmth.

'Fool,' she whispered, in the darkness.

'Witch.'

'Is it a spell, then, my summer heart? If it is, you have cast it on me.'

'I have not. You are me. I am you.'

'If I am you, can I come raiding with you?'

'You cannot.'

'You are full of shit, Somerled. If you were me, you would die of boredom when the men have gone raiding.'

'Is it so bad?'

'It is for me.'

'Because of your deep soul.'

She laughed. 'No. No. Not my deep soul. Here's the thing, Somerled. I am tone deaf. Completely.'

He propped himself up on an elbow.

'What do you mean?'

'Music. Song. It is painful to me. I see other people's pleasure, and I am unmoved. Bored.'

'Seriously?'

'Yes. Completely. I didn't understand, for a long time. Why I was different. I call the time wrong in the waulking songs. Every time. Every single time. It's not funny.'

'Sorry.'

'Well, maybe a little funny. It's all right when the bards are singing. I can concentrate on the words. Even the hymns. But the working songs . . . Oh my life. They are all rhythm. No words. No words that count. In fact the words are supposed to be an endless repetitive loop, to work with the rhythm, to match the loom, or the churning, or the kneading. At first I find it irritating. Then it goes on and on and on until it's in my head, in my belly, and I want to scream. The other women find that the singing is the only thing that makes the grinding repetition of their work bearable. Without the pleasure of the song, I have only the grinding repetition.'

'You are my woman. You could order them silent.'

'Really? Order your men not to mock each other.'

'True.'

'There's no solution. You can't make this better for me. It is what it is.'

'I am sorry.'

'I'm a fisherman who hates fish.'

162

'A warrior who faints at blood.'

'A bard who can't sing.'

'We've already got one of those. Shh, don't laugh so loud. You'll wake the whole hall.'

'Make me silent, then. I am here.'

~ ~ ~

The day came at last when Aed's face told him what he already knew. It was time to go raiding. To set off down the coast and find his men glory and silver. The task of reclaiming his birthright was so close, so near. Some recalcitrant bands, a few Norse strongholds.

He'd sent messengers. To Fergus in Galloway. David in Alba. Olaf in Man. *I am the King of Argyll,* he wrote. *Recognize me.* To the lesser chieftains in Mull and Morvern. Up into Ardnamurchan, down into Kintyre. Inland, to the lesser places, away from the lifeblood of the sea. *Pay me tribute.* They laughed at his audacity, and now he would laugh at their death rattles.

This was his moment. And all he wanted was to stay here, with Eimhear, naked, warm and smiling.

He pulled on his helmet, hard and cold. He hefted his unyielding sword. He set his face in a war growl. He watched his galleys loading, and straining at their moorings. Where he should have felt eagerness, pride, there was only sorrow, regret. What if something happened while he was away. To her? To him? To this bond between them, that was at once so fragile and so unbreakable?

All the women gathered to see them off. He scanned the faces of the men he would be leaving behind. A few looked pleased; most looked pleasingly disgruntled.

163

She stood next to his mother, her face pinched and white. She would not cry now, he knew. But he would bet two silver rings that she would cry later, when no one could see.

He moved over to embrace her, awkward in his war gear.

'Goodbye,' he whispered in her ear, cursing himself for the lack of words.

'Goodbye. Keep yourself safe. Somerled . . .' She paused, struggling for the words.

'Yes?'

'I am pregnant.'

Jesus, Mary, Joseph. A child. A dangerous, woman-killing, love-slaying thing. He had heard the screams of childbirth. Watched women and babies carried away lifeless from the charnel house of a birth room, blood pooling on the floor, splattered on the ceiling. Oh Jesus.

'I must go,' he muttered, and walked away to the galley, where Aed, Ruaridh, Thorfinn and the others were waiting, impatient to be off.

1131

SOMERLED

This is easy, he thought, as the skin sliced beneath his sword. Too easy. Like butchering a deer. He spun on his toes and took another, chest height, the flesh opening and the skin puckering. We are too good, and they are carrion fodder. Gull scraps. Shredded meat.

Aed, beside him, moved with his usual speed. He smashed and parried, soundless, a smile on his face as the frenzy took him. Somerled wanted to pause, to watch. To drop out of the fight and observe the man's grace and the blur as his sword danced. But here was another one who wanted to feel the edge of a blade, whose brain was begging to touch the air as his scalp slid sideways into the mulch at his feet.

Too easy. He threw his head back.

'Argyll! Argyll!' he shouted.

'Argyll! Argyll!' Back came the cry. A sweaty, ragged cry but a victorious one.

They pulled back then. Spent. Their swords clattered to the floor. A few turned and ran. One stood alone, his sword still up, his breath ragged. Their eyes met.

'It is done,' said Somerled.

'Fuck you,' said the man, and he rushed forward, his sword rising and his ribs exposed. He looked surprised when Aed's blade took him one side and Sigurd's the other, so that he sank to his knees spitted two ways.

Too easy.

Then a voice, a call, that shattered Somerled's complacency. His name, called by Padeen, in a voice already rich with sorrow.

Thorfinn. Skewered and sinking fast. A painful ending, this, with his stomach spilling out on to the floor and the stench of his guts souring the blood-smeared air.

The poor, miserable bugger, to sink like this. In a scrap they had won with ease.

Somerled knelt by him, Ruaridh on the other side, grasping the older man's hand. 'I told you so,' said Thorfinn, in a weak voice, with a smile that seemed to crow that his pessimism had, at the last, been vindicated. A triumph at death. Or was it just a grimace of pain? Was it unreasonable to invest a dying man's facial expression with meaning, like attributing pain and loss to a whining dog, or fear to a lamb brought to the knife?

He was trying to speak, and they leaned in, trying not to gag on the stench of his exploding guts. 'I told you,' he wheezed. 'I told you it was all shit.' They laughed, as he wanted them to, offering him that at the last. He went then, with a gasp of pure pain and the smile sliding from his face.

They were angry, now, the band. Thorfinn, one of the finest – not one of the best, but one of the first – was dead. All the relief and rage turned vicious.

In the corner, the survivors huddled. Women and children, and a few hapless men. Somerled, sensing the mood, pulled himself back from the frenzy. Detaching, he felt it still in his thrumming, screaming body. Understood it as it clouded his men's faces, turned them ugly. Thorfinn was dead and someone would pay.

'Somerled,' said Padeen, and the priest's voice was gentle. A warning.

He shrugged.

The priest rushed forward, standing in front of the huddled group, holding up a cross with white-knuckled urgency.

'They arc under my protection.'

'Fuck that, priest,' shouted someone.

The men growled, prowling and sniffing at the women and children, who shook and cried, beyond fear. Like cornered rats, thought Somerled. Trapped otters.

Jesus.

'Stop!' he shouted. 'Stop. Padeen, the children.'

The priest looked mutely towards him. Aed bundled forward, picking up infants, plucking them away from their crying mothers. Sigurd went with him, and they carried the bairns to the galley. Their mothers would come after. After the men were done.

~ ~ ~

He sat with Padeen away from it all. The priest shook as the screams seared across the heather towards them. He mumbled a prayer, stumbling to a halt. The last of the sun had gone now, leaving a chill and gloomy dusk. They hunkered down in the lee of a rocky outcrop, waiting for the cries to stop.

A single howl rose above the rest, a great keening scream of grief and rage. Shrill, it hung in the dusk like a reproach. Somerled closed his eyes and thought of Eimhear. Of Mebd when he first saw her, blood-flecked and vengeful.

Padeen would not look at him. He sat hunched towards the horizon, as if telling himself he had somewhere else to go. As the scream faded, and the quiet filled its place, he spoke. Perhaps to fill the silence. 'And you, Somerled, the lord,' he spat, as if picking up a conversation. 'Could you not stop them?'

'How long would I be lord if I did not let them loose sometimes, when the killing is done.'

'Fucking animals.'

'And would the ones we killed not have done the same to our women. To Oona? To Eimhear?'

'And that makes it right?'

'Father. I did not make this world. Not man's nature.'

'It's God's fault? Is that what you're saying? Mine? For not making them understand his teaching?'

Somerled spread his arms, palms upwards to the sky, the way you would for a shy horse, or a frightened dog. At last darkness came, hiding the blood, hiding the corpses, hiding the dead-eyed misery of the women.

~ ~ ~

He sank next to her into the furs, watching her sleep. He was glad she slept. It gave him time to adjust. The contrasts were almost too much to bear: the soft unblemished skin, the calm rise and fall of her sleeping breast. The warmth rolling off her, the sweetened smell of her body. He closed his eyes and tried to adjust, but it was too recent, too fresh.

She stirred sleepily, and opened an eye. 'You!' She slid a warm leg over him. 'You're cold. Poor darling.'

He wanted to cry. Lord, how he wanted to cry. Instead he reached for her, burying himself in her; looking for oblivion.

'It's clever,' he said afterwards, holding her.

'What?'

'Adam, Eve. The act of love. It cleanses, somehow. Brings a man home from the fight. Centres his mind, through being mindless for a space.'

'Is love, not life, the opposite of death, then?'

'Perhaps.'

'Can a man be a lover and a fighter?'

'You tell me, fierce one.'

'Perhaps. Perhaps a good fighter makes a poor lover?'

'And which am I? Hey, hey?'

'No, don't tickle me! Sorry, I'm sorry.'

'I should beat you, minx.'

'I would leave you.'

'I know. So I will not.'

'It is the only thing that would drive me away. Except . . .'

'So serious now? Except?'

'If I ever find out you have forced a woman.'

'What?'

'You know. You will have other women, I know. You are the king. As long as you do not shame me, or your child.'

Her hands fluttered across her belly. 'But if you force a woman, I—'

'Shh, fierce one. I will not.'

'It is a corruption of love. It is not even about lust, but about hate.'

'True. You are a seer, woman of mine.'

'Pah.'

They lay still for a while. He ran his hand up and down her bare back in the darkness, imagining the line of freckles that ran from her shoulders down to her bottom. He kissed her shoulder.

'Perhaps,' he said, 'love and death are not such opposites.'

'How so?'

'When I fight, when my sword is singing and the battle is turning for me, Jesus help me, but that is a good feeling. A sense of being utterly alive. The only thing that matches it is when I am coming into you.'

'Not this talking? This kiss?'

'Witch. There's a calmer joy in that, and you know it. I mean the touch of God. The divine frenzy. The promise of eternity.'

'Ah. And to think I spent the day milling oats.'

'And the night reaching for the divine?'

'Lord, what import you give it. Do you think the rutting seals dream of their seal god when the seed is spilled?'

'Perhaps.'

'While you find God through killing, I sit here praying to him for you to come safely home.'

'And does he answer?'

'Are you a dream, here naked in my bed?'

'No. I am here.'

~ ~ ~

They heard from Brigte not long after. She was brought to bed of a son, and healthy, she said. Mael Coluim, after his father. He was a little lord, a new hero, a paragon of the age. Everyone said how fine he was, how beautiful, how strong. Somerled looked across at Eimhear's growing belly and smiled. He was still uncertain about it, how it would change things. But he was resigned.

They heard too from one of the last of the local families. They would pay him tribute. They would accept his lordship. He sent gifts: deer and cattle and silver. He let it be known that those who came to him willingly, he would treat well. Those who crossed him would be stamped into the peat.

He sent letters: south to Fergus in Galloway; north to Mael Coluim and Brigte in Moray, and to Sigurd the Crusader, King of the Norse; west across the sea to Olaf, King of Man and the Isles, to Áed mac Duinn Sléibe in Ulster and Diarmait mac Murchada, the new King of Leinster; east across the mountains to David in Alba. The text was of nothing: pleasantries, greetings, the usual verbiage. The signing was what mattered: *Somerled, King of Argyll.*

He counted.

Sixty head of cattle.

Thirty pairs of oars.

Five galleys.

Two swords; one from the forges of Denmark, with a hilt so fine it could clank at the archangel's side.

Three silver torques.

One chess set, with pieces of true ivory.

Six amphorae of wine from Italy.

Forty-five sundry silver rings and armlets.

One Eimhear.

The pains came one night, in the darkest, coldest part of the winter. He heard her indrawn rush of breath beside him. He heard her pray softly, under her breath, and the next, stronger gasp.

He lay there silently, wishing he had not heard, hoping that this was not it. He was not ready. He could not bear to lose her, to hear her screaming. Perhaps she would not scream. Perhaps he would slide out, the baby, in a rush of gold and crimson light, smiling and jolly and clean.

They lay side by side in the darkness for a while. He reached out a hand to her, under the furs, and she took it. Every now and then, when the pain came, she would clench his hand tighter.

'At least,' she said in a lull, 'I will not be pregnant any more. Once this is over I will be able to see my toes. Sleep in comfort. Ride you without crushing you.'

'You are beautiful,' he said, 'either way.' There was something glorious and rounded about her pregnant body, her full breasts and big belly. But he missed the long, light-limbed girl of their first couplings.

They watched together as the room grew lighter. He could see her features now, the way her face crumpled with each surging pain, and then set again as it ebbed away.

'You will have to go out soon,' she said. 'Leave me with the women.'

'I don't want to leave you.'

'I know. Ah, Jesus, here comes another one.'

She clenched and shivered as it took her, unable to prevent an audible shriek this time as it clawed at her.

'Jesus. Jesus. Jesus.'

'Hush now, little Otter.'

'Hush yourself. Fetch your mother, and get out of here, before I start cursing you properly.'

The hall turned into a bustle of women then. The men were ushered out, grumbling.

They packed into Aed's glorious new house, the displaced men. Aed and his eldest daughter, five-year-old Mairi, kept the cups filled as the men struggled to talk above the strangled cries that drifted across the glen. Oona, herself full to bursting with a new baby, was in with Eimhear. It was unbearable, this waiting. Unbearable. Somerled paced and fidgeted. Played tafl, badly and sulkily. Frowned at levity, cursed at silence. Jesus, if he was anyone else, Aed would have slapped him. He imagined Eimhear smiling

172

at him. The women do all the work, the men get all the leeway. And where is the change in that?

A stronger cry now. 'Jesus, Jesus Jesus Jesus.'

'Do you think he heard her?' said Ruaridh, and around him men laughed, until they saw Somerled's scowl.

At last, a quiet, and a summons, and Sigrdrifa's tired face, saying, 'A boy, a boy,' and Eimhear, sweat-slick and triumphant, a new, wrinkled-red creature perched on her breast and a smile on her well-loved face. *I am Somerled. Otter-lover. Son-begetter. Miracle-maker.*

He leaned in to kiss her.

'Careful,' she said, and one outstretched arm kept him at a distance over the baby's head.

He stepped back, perplexed and awkward.

The baby began to cry.

eimhear

I lay next to you, watching you sleep.

I remember it as a perpetual storm outside, although that can't be how it was. I remember the screaming rage of the sea wind beyond the walls. The violent snatching of the waves at the rocks below.

Inside, the soft rush of your breath.

The tangle of blue veins under the stretched cream of your forehead. The red lines traced on your closed eyelids, that only I knew to look for. If the light was right, I could see the beat of your heart reflected in your temple. A miracle pulse of life. The absurd innocence of your slack mouth. The sheen of your milk-white skin in the firelight.

You twitched in your sleep. Flailed. Sometimes your arms were flung so wide, it jolted you awake.

We wondered what you were dreaming about, to make you throw your arms in the air. What do babies dream about? His future as a glorious warrior, said Somerled. Swimming, I said.

You broke out of me already covered in blood. After, when you were clean and sleepy, I lay next to you, praying that blood was not in your future. Great looping prayers with little hope of anyone hearing. A sleepless, befuddled bartering with God. Charm his life, damn mine. Take my eyes, leave him whole. Kiss his brow, oh son of God, and I will prostrate myself before you.

In, out. Shallow and regular as a bank of oars. In, out. I drifted on your breath, half sleeping. Listening for watchers in the darkness. Imagining the breaking of the storm and a bank of strange warriors screaming out of the gloom. Understanding, for the first time, the point of all the violence.

Sharpen your sword on strangers, my husband. Learn your trade. Wade in their blood. Make them pay for not belonging to us.

In the darkness I kissed Somerled's muscled arms and shoulders. Not lust; gratitude. For his strength, for his viciousness in battle. For the violence that kept his son cocooned. I imagined you tiny and naked. Alone. Around you a ring of warriors facing outward. Swords raised and waiting. Your father at their head. Your father, who was awkward with you. Clumsy and diffident.

He always struggled, Somerled, with contrasts. He found it difficult coming to my soft, clean skin after the jagged tearing of his enemies' flesh. He took his time switching from ferocity to tenderness, and I learned to wait for him; not to rush it. And then there was you, so unbearably small, so vulnerable. Impatiently reaching for him. Expecting him to switch his souls on demand. You unsettled him.

My overpowering love for you – from the instant I saw your puckered, birth-slimed face – that unsettled him.

In, out. Your chest's rapid rise and fall.

Sometimes, you seemed to pause on the in breath. I would jolt alert, panic searing my chest. Waiting for the next breath. Helpless. A chasm opening beneath my feet. A whirlpool sucking me in. A mountainous wave rushing down upon me. The pause too desperate for prayers.

A snuffle, a new breath. A relief fiercer than joy.
I lay next to you, watching you sleep.

1133

somerled

As Somerled watched the little frog-like creature grow into a recognisable human child, he was plagued with this one recurring thought: where does the myth that men are simple and women complicated come from? He watched with awe the fierce, untwisted love his wife held for this tumble of skin and screaming. He found the whole business bemusing. He didn't like to think of it: his odd jealousy for this tiny thing – her absorption in it, her unconditional adoration of its every mew, every twitch.

It was beneath him, this absurd, complicated bemusement with which he viewed his son, Gillecolm. He didn't understand it.

Perhaps, he thought, the myth was there because men perpetuated it. They sought to appear uncomplicated, unprofound. Tortured souls were for women and priests. Perhaps, he thought, as he looked at the shining faces of his men as they bantered across the oars, mocked each other by the fire, ogled women together, perhaps there were deep currents beneath. Unglimpsed complications and doubts. Perhaps that was why they liked fucking and fighting so much – it was the only time that life was as mindlessly simple as they sought to make it appear.

Who knew. Other men's souls were a mystery to all but God, said Father Padeen, and likely to remain that way.

So it went on; the boy prised a distance between them. And the worst of it was that she did not seem to mind. She was too busy, too lost in contemplating the miracle, too tired.

Somerled remembered his first days of being chief, how he had walked like a chief and quailed inside – how he realized that sometimes the outward show is all that matters. So he looked the part, and did the right thing, and called himself Dada and chucked the boy in the air to make him squeal.

And all the time, at the core, he felt this twisting bemusement.

It would break them, he thought. Because if all the world was fooled, she was not. Eimhear watched them both with fierce eyes. She who had thought love was a thing of unalloyed joy, of beauty, of sweetness, was learning to carry it as a burden, an improbably enormous weight. Love was etching its fears into the corners of her eyes, marking her.

They didn't speak of it, this hollow in his heart. They spoke of the day's tasks, of the people around them, of the increasing burden that came with the growth of his power.

Sigrdrifa, too, seemed mesmerized by the little prince. He was given leeway that Somerled could not imagine he or Brigte had ever enjoyed. The boy knew to seek out his grandmother for treats, for bread dipped in honey, the crisped skin of the chicken. It was absurd to feel supplanted. Absurd.

Then, one day, a year and a season since his birth, as the little fellow – Gillecolm – was learning to walk, he tottered to the sea when everyone's back was turned. Somehow, while they talked or dreamt or worked, he clambered up on to the black, slippery rocks that edged out into the water, where the tide and the waves spewed and sprayed. He shouted, then, delighted with himself and his big adventure, and they saw him tottering on the edge of the rock, hovering at the lip of it, laughing at the sea.

In that still moment, when Somerled was too far to reach, when the sea rushed hungrily towards his uncomprehending son, suddenly everything was simple enough. He felt a surge of protective fear that stemmed from an unrealized mountain of love. The fear fed the love, which fed the fear. He sprang forward, his feet scrabbling for purchase on the slimy rocks.

He was reminded, in the second he caught his son and pressed his face into the boy's velvet neck, of a serpent eating itself. 'Oh boy,' he said. 'Oh my daft, tiny boy.'

~ ~ ~

A cattle raid. A stupid, small cattle raid. Strangers, and all dead from Aed's vengeful fury before they could be questioned. From Man, he thought, or one of its isles. But he didn't think much more of it, not with the pain.

Jesus wept, the pain.

He had been careless, complacent. *I am Somerled. Sword-heaver, carrion-feeder, fool-reaper.* He had turned, *stupid,* to wink at Ruaridh. *Stupid.* A spear, thrust from nowhere by a small, skinny boy, caught him, ripping through his thigh, opening it up to the bone.

He drifted in and out of consciousness as they jolted him home across the heather. He wanted to be home, wanted to see Eimhear, Sigrdrifa. They would fight over looking after him, and he smiled to himself.

'Are you all right, lord?' Aed's voice from a great distance. His big face all concern. Somerled found it funny, in the middle of the pain, that unfamiliar look on Aed's face. But when he laughed, it hurt, so he stopped laughing and concentrated on trying not to weep.

Oh the pain. Poor Lord, poor Christ. What he must have felt on the cross. The searing, violent pain. The injustice. Why me, God? Why me? Why me? Why inflict this on me?

Oh Lord.

He mumbled the prayer, trying to take his mind off it, using the words to think of parts of his body that did not hurt, the parts that were whole, unblemished.

Christ's cross across this face,
Across the ear like this,
Christ's cross across this eye,
Christ's cross across this nose.
Christ's cross across this mouth
Christ's cross across this throat.
Christ's cross across this back.
Christ's cross across this side.

By the time they got back, he was babbling, he knew it. Christ's cross, mingling with her face, Gillecolm, his father. Jesus Christ, where did he come from? Standing accusing. 'What's he told you? What's he told you, Lord, about me? It isn't true, I swear it. It's not true. It's not.'

'Shh, my darling. I believe you. It's not true.'

'Eimhear. Tell them. Tell them it's not true.'

'I'll tell. I'll tell. Now be brave, my summer heart. Father Padeen is going to clean the wound. It will sting, my summer heart, but it will pass.'

'You're my Otter. My Otter. I know you. I didn't love him, Eimhear. I didn't. But I do now. I do now. Oh, I swear it. I love . . . Oh Jesus. Oh Jesus. Jesus. Jesus.'

'He's cleaning and binding now, my darling. It will hurt less soon. Don't worry. You're safe, dear heart.'

'Oh Jesus.'

'Eimhear!'

'I am here, shh.'

'Where?'

'Here. It's dark. Here's my hand. Here's my kiss.'

'Don't leave.'

'I will never leave.'

'Truly?'

'Truly. Sleep now, my summer heart. You need sleep.'

'Eimhear!'

'I am here.'

'I am hungry.'

'Good. Good.'

Later, full, and propped up with furs, he looked at her, a little embarrassed. 'Did I ramble? Was I dreaming?'

'A little,' she said, smiling.

'I thought I might die.'

'Father Padeen thinks you have a few years before meeting your maker. Which is good. For I am having another child.'

'Good!' he said. 'Good!' He was pleased to find that he meant it.

'I was worried,' he said. 'A man's thoughts sometimes come in a shameful rush when he is hurt. And – don't laugh – I sing my own song in my head. Sometimes, when you are not with me, I cannot tell what is my song and what is a memory. What is a song and what is a plan.'

'Do you tell your bard?'

'Sometimes. No.'

'Do you think that the warriors of song were true? Flesh and blood and fear and bile. Did Fionn mac Cumhail quake before the giant?'

'Perhaps. The songs make us brave. The songs to come, as well as the ones we listen to in the darkness.'

'Does the Scottish king believe in songs, do you think?'

'Not the old ones.'

'Is he right, my summer heart? Why do the songs matter?'

'If they do not matter, then what does?'

'We have been here before. Why does anything need to matter?'

'Women are different. You find immortality in your children.'

'What tripe you talk, my lord. We are too busy wading in swaddling clothes and puke and tears and our men's giant bubbles of pride and ox shit to worry about immortality. We leave it to Christ.'

'You smell very fine for all this wading in puke.'

'You smell of blood.'

'Still? I don't smell it any more.'

'So why do you care for immortality? You won't be here to see it.'

'I won't be here. Does that not make you wince, fierce one? That all the vivid sense of being you could one day vanish.'

'As long as it vanishes before you, and before my children, I am content. I could not bear the pain.'

'I am not going anywhere.'

'You say that now.'

'Tears, my fierce one? Come, that's not so fierce. I am here.'

~ ~ ~

He had to walk with a stick that winter, a stick that skittered on the ice and snow. He used it to play at mock fights with Gillecolm. He put it out to trip Oona as she walked by, earning himself a clout around the head. He gripped it with calloused hands the night Einhear's second child was born, a daughter who slid from her mother's warm womb into a bitter night. She was a grizzling, hungry baby. Sigrdrifa said it was because of being ripped from the warm to bear the cold.

This time, Somerled fell in love quickly, passionately. This time, when he cooed over tiny fingers, when he leaned in to smell her sweet skin, when he ran his fingers over the downy hair on her too-thin skull, this time he was not playing.

He used his stick as the snow melted to slush. He lopped the heads off new spring flowers, as he had a lifetime ago. He watched his warriors sloughing off the winter, and cursed his limping, painful leg. He used the stick to point out their weaknesses in the training, slamming the point into the ground to urge them on.

And one fine, cold morning in the spring, he used the stick to point out to Gillecolm the galley pulling into the bay, a drab little thing that limped under too few oars, its sail badly trimmed and slack.

He threw the stick aside when he saw the galley's passengers: Brigte and two tousle-haired boys. Hobbling forward, he pulled her close, listening to his mother's frantic bustling and questions. He buried his face in her neck, avoiding her reddened eyes with their dark circles, ignoring her patched-up, shabby gown and the bleakness of her expression. He buried his head to swallow the words 'I told you so, I told you so.'

Drawing back, he saw he might as well have shouted them from the mast-top. She looked at him with a face that said 'You told me so. This is your fault.'

'What has happened?' he asked.

Sigrdrifa was kneeling, clucking at the boys, who hid their grubby faces in their mother's long skirts.

'He fought for his birthright,' she said.

'And lost?'

The pain flitted across her face.

'Not yet. He's won some skirmishes. But David, they say, has a huge army in the field.'

'Where is he?'

'I don't know. Coming here, I think. That was what we agreed. If it were lost, he would come here.'

Oh Jesus wept. With an army chasing him. He might be dead, Somerled realized, brightening.

She followed his thoughts on his face, and wordlessly walked past him to the hall. Inside, they were placed next to the fire. Sigrdrifa plied the children with oatcakes smeared with honey; hot spiced mead for Brigte. Gillecolm eyed the two boys warily. The younger, Domhnall who was looking brighter now he was inside and cosseted. The elder, Mael Coluim a boy of about four, looked pinched and miserable.

Brigte was pregnant again, that much was clear. She looked old and tired. How long since they had seen her – five years, six? She sipped silently at the warm liquid as her mother whirled around, discomposed. 'Here you are then, precious thing. Loki's own daughter to turn up unannounced, with the cold snapping at these poor boys. And you were not wrong, my girl, such fine boys. Do you see your grandmother, hey, Domhnall? Domhnall. A name for

184

a Nordic tongue to struggle with, little man. Grandson of a king, that you are, and grandson of mine.'

Somerled met Brigte's eyes, and something softened. The worst was over for her, he realized. The meeting. Now she could relax into her family.

'Was it rough on the boat? Ours have been inshore only for weeks.'

'Terrible rough,' she said.

'I didn't cry, Uncle,' said Mael Coluim. 'But he did.'

'Didn't,' little Domhnall shouted, consumed with the injustice of it.

'Did.'

'Stop,' roared Brigte, and they hung their heads.

'Gillecolm,' said Sigrdrifa. 'Take your cousins and show them about the place.'

Gillecolm nodded. 'There's a new calf,' he said. 'Should you like to see it?'

They went happily, leaving a silence behind them; a fresh awe at youth's resilience, their childlike ability to leave the dark matters to their elders. The dark matters. Somerled sighed, and looked over at his sister.

'Later,' Brigte said, to his questioning face. 'Let me sleep in a warm bed, just for an hour or two. Please.'

She was bundled away by Eimhear and Sigrdrifa, trussed up in furs. Somerled sat and watched the flames dance. What trouble would this bring? Lord save his children. Lord save Eimhear.

1134

SOMERLED

'Thor's arse, Somerled,' whispered Aed beside him, his face barely moving. 'Did you ever see so many men?'

Never. He shook his head, strangely fearful of big movements that might betray his unease.

They stretched out across the plain, thousands of shadows in the dusk clustering around countless fires. The smell of burning oats mingled with the peat smoke; the place was hazy with it, dreamlike.

Somerled's band, fifty strong, fidgeted at his back. He could sense them champing at the ground behind him, weight-shifting, throat-clearing; obvious in their attempts to appear unmoved. Casual.

'How do you fight a battle with so many men?' asked Sigurd.

'Run at them screaming and spike the bastards, just as always,' said Aed.

'But what if the bastards are these English on their horses, with their lances, so they've taken you in the eye, and you swinging your sword like a child being held off by Aed's palm? What then?'

'Frightened, Sigurd?' asked Ruaridh.

'Bloody right I am. So should you be, little man. They'll take you out first, with you the smallest.'

'Shush,' said Somerled.

He was impressed, and that made him feel small. He had only ever met Mael Coluim in his own lands, where he was the lord and his brother-in-law the supplicant. Here he was a wild western chief with an average-sized war-band. The lad had done well, to regroup and reband. Oengus of Moray, the first general of the rebellion, may have died, but Mael Coluim would not give it up.

Four years it had been since Mael Coluim had first rebelled, limping into Somerled's hall and carrying away Brigte. Four years of riding from place to place, hitting David's outposts, feasting the discontented northern lords; of deals proffered and small skirmishes won. And all the while, the English King of Alba skulked about by the border lands worrying about monks.

Father Padeen had tried to explain it to Somerled – how the king was entranced by the monastic orders of the south and the Continent. The great rich orders, with their strict covenants and powerful potentates. David was bringing them north, the Cistercians and the Tironians and the Benedictines. Not a drop of the Gaelic between them. When I've secured Mull, thought Somerled, Iona will be under my sway, and I'll return that holy place to glory. These seas, according to Padeen, needed Gaelic hymns to soothe them – the Latin was not enough.

'There he is,' Aed said, pointing out the most richly decked of the tents. They saw his symbol flying, and walked towards it. Picking their way through the men, who gabbled and fought and bantered in rich, unrecognisable accents, Somerled and his band were silent. He felt like a boy looking at the heavens. How big the sky; how small am I.

He drew confidence from Aed's easy grace. They were noticed as they walked through – the big man drawing stares and compensatory puffing-out of chests. *I am Somerled. Ring-giver, war-*

leader, carrion-maker. He stepped in time to the beat in his head, and he thought of Eimhear, and the way she clapped just past the beat and then laughed at herself.

He was smiling, then, when Mael Coluim walked out of the tent, arms wide in welcome.

'Well met, brother,' he said.

Somerled, waiting for the reproach for avoiding Mael Coluim's rebellion, grinned. He had, true, been using his growing fleet to watch the Clyde estuary, in case David made a flanking run under sail up the west coast. And if foul winds had left him free to roam south and west, raiding here and there, well that was his price. But the real fighting had been elsewhere, and they all knew it. Somerled's raids were beginning to provoke Olaf Crovan in Man, so he had heard. Ah well, he thought, let's fight one battle at a time, hey.

Mael Coluim's eyes slid behind him to the men at his back. He had a general's hunger for men; like a starved dog with a bone. He eyed Aed as if he could lick him, but contented himself with a slap on the big man's back.

'Well met, well met,' he said jovially. 'And here we are. A final push.'

There was a wild, contained excitement in him. He looked like a man caught in a fever. It made Somerled a little nervous, the way he bounced on the balls of his feet, and his too wide smile, like a merchant selling a leaking bowl.

'Where is the enemy?'

'Two days' march south, the scouts say.'

'And their number?'

'Oh, lots, I daresay. But we've been beating them every time, the past few years. We'll smash them for good now.'

You've beaten them in the small wars we're good at, thought Somerled. David's your master in these big set-piece affairs.

188

'I'll leave you – get them settled,' he said, jerking his head back at his men.

'Good, good. You've brought your own food, of course?' Mael Coluim's face was anxious suddenly, tense.

'Of course.'

They found a patch of unclaimed ground. Unloading the peat from the pack horse, they stoked a few fires in time for night to fall. Somerled's fire naturally drew his oldest mates, and they sat in companionable silence for a while, watching the crackle and sparking of the flames. Somerled held his smoked venison almost reverentially in his hands. It was his link to home. He imagined Eimhear killing the deer, out hunting with him on some unnamed cold, clear day. He imagined his mother clapping her hands as they dropped the carcass at her feet. He imagined Oona setting to on the butchery, and the long strips of meat hanging from the roof over the fire in the hall, where the smoke could cure it and keep it. He imagined the children fighting over the antlers, and the careful sharing-out according to age, and the creatures that Aed's boy would whittle from the bone for the little ones.

He bit a piece off, and the peatiness, the familiar, caramelized smokiness of it, caught in his throat. He could have been at home, so sharp was the sensation. It filled his head, his nose, his mouth. He could picture Eimhear by the fire, leaning in to poke it alight, the shadows pooling in the hollow of her throat, her dark hair falling over her face. Jesus wept. Oh Lord, keep them safe.

A long, rumbling belch. Ruaridh. A fat sigh of contentment. Sigurd.

They were family too, this ragbag of warriors. He would bring them through.

Aed, God bless and keep him, said: 'I don't like this over-much, Somerled.'

'No.'

'He's a brave man, Mael Coluim. A good one, I've no doubt. But you'd have known how many they were. You would not have been complacent. You would have had the scouts out till their feet bled before going in blind to a battle.'

There were rumbles of assent around the fire.

'I don't suppose it matters,' said Somerled. 'Knowing the strength of them won't mean there are any fewer of them.'

But he was uneasy as he wrapped himself in his cloak. Nervous. Above, the stars were hidden by clouds, and as he closed his eyes, the rain began to fall.

~ ~ ~

It was a low-lying land, this. Soggy underfoot, and the hills barely a hum on the horizon. No sight of the sea, either. A rotten place to die, thought Somerled, as he saw the army drawn up against them. At its centre, and on its flanks, were great horses – the breath blowing in clouds from their noses and the sun shining from groomed flanks. The men atop them, too, seemed all metal. They had no faces, just metal masks with broad noses and shaded eyes.

The horses stamped and pawed at the ground, as if anxious to be on the move, to deal out death and mayhem. Above them, their masters were still, ominously patient. The drawing of breath before the slaughter.

'How can they move in that?' asked Sigurd, his voice small.

'They don't have to move. We can't get at them.'

'Cowards,' spat Ruaridh. 'Sitting up there all coffined in metal, picking us off with great long sticks. If they got down and fought like men, we'd show them.'

'Aye, but they won't.'

'Hack at the horses' legs,' said Aed. 'If we get the bastards on the ground, we can murder them. They can't move.'

'We'll stick 'em.'

'Roast 'em.'

'Spit 'em.'

The words were right, the snarling venom. But it seemed staged. As if it were expected. And looking sideways, Somerled saw Aed's facc. He was white behind his great beard, and his jaw was clenched. Oh Jesus, oh Lord. Aed was scared.

He must think. There must be a way. Oh God, here was the word rippling along the line. It was time to charge, to run. He screamed: 'Argyll! Argyll!'

They screamed it back, and the deep, full-throated cry stiffened his legs, put some metal in them, and suddenly he was running with Aed at his side across the boggy ground. The mud sucked at him, the heather snagged him. Still he ran, his sword high. He looked up and saw the sky dark with arrows flying like angels' darts towards the enemy. The scream as some hit home lifted him, gave him succour as he ran. The angels were with them, and St Colm Cille, flying at their shoulders as they ran towards the demons, the great snorting metal demons. Damn them. Damn them. *I am Somerled. Horse-killer. Demon-slayer. Ring-giver. King of Argyll.*

'Argyll! Argyll!'

'Argyll! Argyll!'

The demons were coming now, their hooves a thunder in the ground, which shook and trembled. But we won't shake, he screamed. We won't tremble. We will take you. We will send you back to hell.

Aed ran beside him, God set a rose upon his sword.

Around him he heard the screaming as his men gave themselves the fury. He heard the breath coming ragged and fast, and then he

191

heard the scrape of metal on metal and the tenor of the screams changed, coming faster and louder, with edges that bled and cried.

The horses were upon them, and he whirled and bounced, looking for flesh, looking for his way in, looking for pink skin amid the blinding sheen. It was like a wave rolling over them, picking them up and flinging them down, churning them on the stones, keeping them under. He didn't know how long it lasted. A minute? An age? Yet suddenly they were gone, and Somerled looked around at the tatters of his band. Oh God. Oh my God. The ones standing were reeling, white. Too many were lying. Too much blood pooled in the hoof-stamped ground. Ruaridh, not Ruaridh, his head split like a flower, the grey brains spattering his cheeks. All wrong.

'To me!' he shouted, as if in a dream. 'To me! Argyll! Argyll!'

They came to him: the scared and the wounded and the merely confused. And behind them he saw a body of horse wheeling round to face them again, slowly, slowly, as if they were horses from the shadowlands, and their riders the ghouls.

As his body twitched with fear, his mind kept snagging on a Latin phrase he must have read with Padeen. *Testudo Romani.* He shook his head, and the phrase kept thrumming behind his temples. He told it to fuck off, to stop clouding his thinking, and then at last he understood.

The Romans. Those wily old Roman sods.

'Injured to the middle!' he screamed. 'Swine array and shields up and over. Swine array. Shields up and over.' Aed got it, he understood, and threw men into the middle, cursing and swearing at the fear-spawned stupidity in their faces. Here they were, huddled together, close-packed, feet braced and arms tight, their shields like a canopy. Beneath them the ground trembled and shook. Trembled and shook. And they answered with their own tremble, and a rising stink of piss and shit. The smell of fear and blood.

The horses were on them. Hooves and jousts broke on their shields, scraped across with a sickening screech. They broke at one end, and men went down with screams and flailing arms, before their mates, understanding now, moved to fill the gap with shields and aching arms.

At last the noise and the trembling lessened. Somerled looked out beyond the shields and saw the horses moving off. There was one left, though. The last horse reared, brandishing its hooves and a milky belly. Its rider was laughing, a looping, hysterical shout of triumph. Somerled looked sideways at Aed, and saw the big man's answering nod.

Together they surged out of the tortoise as the horse began to rear up again, and they ripped gashes in its exposed belly so that it fell sideways in a shower of blood and guts that caught Somerled in the eyes. As he wiped them, he saw Aed, sword poised over the fallen knight.

'Wait,' he said. But Aed had the look of one lost to the frenzy, so Somerled sprang forward and caught at his sword arm before it could begin its downward plunge.

'Alive,' he croaked, his voice lost with the screaming. 'Hostage.'

Aed nodded, and kicked the knight once on his helmet, to bring a muffled screech of pain.

~ ~ ~

How strange, to pull off the head of a demon and find a boy. A small, dark-haired boy with down on his lip and pimples scraped raw by the pulling of his helmet.

'Who are you, boy?' Somerled demanded. They crouched behind a stone wall, seemingly alone in the expanse of heather. Only the distant sound of metal hammering metal betrayed their situation.

There was something gloriously solid about the wall, something comforting in the thought of normal life happening here in this place of slaughter. Sheep corralled, cattle penned. Somerled fought to dispel the image of him and his men as senseless, bleating sheep.

He asked the boy again.

The boy looked up with frightened eyes, and babbled something.

'What the fuck is he saying?' said Aed.

'Speak sense, boy,' said Sigurd, very slowly.

'It's French,' said a voice. Somerled turned to face it. Fergus's nephew Brian. Somerled's foster son.

The young man shrugged. 'My mother was French. Taken in a raid down south.'

'The first we've heard of it,' said Sigurd.

'Well, would you boast of it?' This from Domnall, and Brian bristled. There was spikiness between Somerled's original band and the later-comers. They growled at each other, and Somerled crackled with irritation.

'Not now. Brian. Come here, boy.'

Brian listened, and talked to the boy in his own thick tongue, ignoring the whistles and nudges – half derision, half awe at his unexpected talent.

'He says his father will kill us all.'

'Oh aye, and who is his father?' Aed scowled as he spoke, and the boy shrank a little deeper into his armour. Like a tortoise.

'He says his father is Walter Espic.'

'Never heard of him.'

'He's a great lord in England, the boy says. A bosom friend of King Henry. Come to help David, our rightful king, against our evil rebellion.'

'Oh he has, hey?' Aed was getting more furious. Ruaridh's body lay broken and unburied on a shit-strewn field.

Somerled put a hand on Aed's arm.

'Your father's banner, boy?'

'The fox and sparrow.'

Somerled stood up, cautiously peering over the top of the wall. There was a silence now, a silence deeper than the fury that had come before. It was unthinkable that Mael Coluim had turned the battle. It must be lost.

'We need a volunteer,' said Somerled, turning back to face them.

It could only be Brian. God grant he was as deep a thinker as he was a talker of tongues. Brave, at least. He stepped forward with a calm face, and two feet planted wide.

'Ask the boy how they signal a truce in their country. Bring this Walter Espic. Tell him that if you do not come back whole, hearty and fuck-ugly as you are now, we will slit his son's throat – slowly.'

Brian conferred with the boy, whose eyes grew wide as he worked out which way the tide was going.

'Christ with you, Brian,' said Somerled, as the young man set off, his hand clutching at the cross they had cobbled together.

Christ with us.

~ ~ ~

The light was failing as they saw Brian coming back, a clanking troop of knights at his back. He ran ahead and vaulted over the wall.

'The fat one's his dad,' he said.

'Well done, boy,' said Somerled. 'I'll see you right when we get back.'

'If,' growled someone, but Brian's face was lit, and he looked at Somerled with something approaching adoration.

Somerled cleared his throat.

'Sigurd. If they play dirty, take the boy as far as the river as a shield, then slit his throat and run for it. Aed. Brian.'

The big man nodded, and they stood, waiting for the whistle of arrows. The air was still.

Close up, Walter Espic was indeed a fat man. Wobbling chins slapped over the neck hole of his armour. Small dark eyes watched their approach.

'Looks like a badly stuffed sausage,' whispered Aed, and Somerled swallowed a laugh.

'Greetings,' he said. 'I am Somerled, King of Argyll.'

He listened to Brian translating, and they exchanged pleasantries that seemed absurd out here on this cold, corpse-filled field.

'He asks, how does he know it's his boy?'

Somerled called to Sigurd. 'Show him the boy.' The boy stood, his head hanging with the unbearable weight of the shame, his hair straggling down about his face.

'He says your leader Mael Coluim is bound and captive. Your army is dead or scattered.'

'Say, and yet I have captured your queen.'

The big man's eyes flickered sideways at this, to a man Somerled had noticed standing a little apart. A slight, white-faced man, with an air of authority. Someone of quality, by the gold dripping off him.

'He says, what do you want?'

Somerled pulled his thoughts back to this Walter Espic.

'I want Mael Coluim to stay alive, and free passage for me and my men.'

'Alive?'

'Yes.'

'Alive, perhaps. Free, no.'

The little man's eyes flickered sideways again, to be rewarded by a nod. God help me, thought Somerled, but a captive Mael Coluim suits me. I'll have done my duty by Brigte, but I can turn my eyes west, where they belong.

'And free passage. How will you guarantee it?'

The man's head rose, and he fixed his small black eyes on Somerled.

Brian stumbled. 'He's, um, swearing at you, Lord Somerled. Says he is a knight of the realm of King Henry, and you, you . . .' He tailed off.

'No matter, boy, I get it.'

They stood for a moment, deadlocked.

Then a voice behind in faltering Gaelic, and the slight man walked forward.

'You have my leave, and my word, Somerled. And perhaps, before you go, we can talk.'

'And who are you?'

'I am David,' he said.

~ ~ ~

'What is he like?' Eimhear's voice was a whisper. They lay close, noses nearly touching.

'Formidable,' said Somerled. Beyond the curtain he could hear low snoring, deep breathing. Little Sigrdrifa, one year old now, had a cold, and she grunted and coughed in her sleep. He heard the hiss of the fire's embers, and the shuffling of cows' feet. He heard his mother's sleep whistle, a sound that ran through his life like a thread. Christ, but it was good to be in a bed and not sleeping out; to know that he would not get wet, or cold. Most of all to know that she was here. If he put his hand out, like that, it touched her

197

real, living skin and not the phantom he conjured on dark nights on the hillside.

It had been a long, hard march home. They had lost all their gear. Of the twenty that were left, five needed carrying. They had known that every step took them closer to breaking the news, to bringing the dark tale into that beloved glen where the women waited, not knowing that most of their men were not coming home.

A new sound now – someone weeping. Brigte, perhaps. Her face had tightened to a skull when he told her about Mael Coluim's capture. Oh Lord, help her. He would not think of it now. Concentrate on Eimhear's soft skin, her hand pushing his hair back from his face, soothing him like a child.

'How so?'

He told her of the king's poise, his air of a man who expected to be obeyed instantly. A man slow to smile, quick to take offence. He told her of David's vision, expanded over a shared meal in his tent.

'He says that all the land, ours included, belongs to him. We are just his vassals. The king owns everything, and we must pay him for the privilege. It's how they do it in the south, apparently.'

'I hope you told him to shove his vassalage somewhere dark.'

'I did not. We lost, remember? I had only his word that we would get home.'

He remembered the king's eyes above his wine cup – glittering and hard. How the passion vibrated in his voice as he talked of wrenching Scotland free of its past, of turning Gaelic eyes towards Jerusalem. He had talked of the rules of knighthood, of the new codes of chivalry that would guide Scotland's nobles in this new time. And Somerled, to his shame, remembered nodding while his heart screamed, this is not my vision. Yours is not my God.

'The terms of peace demand that we pay him a tribute, a cain. And he will leave us alone.'

'But think himself our master.'

'He can think what he likes.'

She moved away slightly, and he felt the air between them shiver.

'Listen, Eimhear. My band was destroyed. His horses are unbeatable. I have scarcely enough men left to attack a chicken shed. And Fergus tells me that Olaf Crovan is letting it be known that I am his enemy. My raids are a thorn in him. If he comes for us, if he even learns of our weakness, everything I have done will be destroyed. Gillecolm's future will be destroyed. We need space. We need time. To regroup, to refinance, to find new men.'

One of the parts of her he loved the best was her ability to sway to a reasoned argument. Most people valued face over reason, he thought, but not her. Sure enough, she slipped closer to him in the darkness, pushing her head into his chest.

'Any new songs, my summer heart?'

'Perhaps I should write one about you. Beautiful, wild, disobedient.'

'Careful. I'll bite next time.'

'Witch.'

'There are no songs about women. Unless we're to be rescued, or married off, or killed.'

'True, the heroes are men.'

'Why?'

'Because we do the fighting.'

'And fights are the only proper tales for the bards?'

'Yes.'

'Well, I shall never be in a song then.'

'No, fierce one.'

'Unless . . .'

'Unless?'

199

'If something happened to you or the children. Something treacherous and dark. I would fight then. I would make the heavens flinch from my fury.'

'Shh, fierce one.'

'Yes. Well, I shall drift on as I am, no doubt.'

'And are you happy?'

'Happy? Yes. I suppose so. When you're not here, though, Lord, sometimes I am so bored. It's the endlessness of it. You cannot imagine.'

'No.'

'And you have such purpose in your life. Such meaning.'

'Hey, fierce one. Not so long ago, you claimed my life was meaningless.'

'I did so. Well, these are deep mysteries. Only a fool sets their mind to one answer and stops questioning.'

'Do fools even ask the questions?'

'You confuse foolishness with stupidity, my summer heart.'

'And luckily, we are neither?'

'Mostly. Would you prefer a stupid, docile, flexible wife?'

'No. Well, mostly not.'

'Fool. Lucky we never got around to a proper wedding.'

'A handfasting is good enough. And who else would put up with you, woman?'

'Fool. Still, I forgive you. And I am here.'

1135

eímhear

I could hear birdsong, and little Sigrdrifa's constant chatter. I pressed my shoulders back on to the rock, closing my eyes to the sun. A calm, unruffled loch. No midges, miracle of miracles. The languid joy of a warm day after a long and bitter winter.

'I see bird. Bird, Mamma, bird. I see bird. Dadda, look, bird. My like bird.'

I listened in to her monologue sometimes, to check no response was required. I let the stream of it wash over me, and I smiled so fiercely it hurt.

'Gil, look, bird. My want swim. My want swim.'

'It's too cold.' Gillecolm's voice was exaggeratedly gentle with her. I drifted, all silence and love.

'He's right, littlest Otter. It's still cold for little ones,' said Somerled.

'My like cold. Mamma, my like cold.' I knew without looking that her face would be crumpling into a tearless wail. I sympathized, as a rule, with children's bewilderment at the world's refusal to adapt itself around their implacable wants. Perhaps, I thought idly, that is the principal part of parenting – teaching them to bear the disappointment of how unyielding and unappeasable the world is.

There is a space within your head, I tried to tell Gillecolm once, where everything makes sense and fairness reigns unchallenged. And then, unfortunately, there is a universe outside your head.

He understood. My shining boy.

They were throwing stones, the three people I loved best. Little Sigrdrifa threw one with such misplaced force she collapsed on her bottom, shrieking with infectious laughter. 'My fall over. My fall over,' she crowed, just in case we had missed it.

These were the things we did not talk about on that golden afternoon. Somerled's shrunken band. Poor dear Ruaridh. The word reaching us from Man that Olaf Crobhan was stirring himself to move against us. The vassalage to David. Old Sigrdrifa's failing strength. Little Sigrdrifa's failure to recognize her father when he came back from his great defeat. Gillecolm lagging behind the other boys in swordplay. The Great Defeat.

These were the things we did talk about. The habits of otters and seals. Who could spin a stone across the still waters. The size of Sigrdrifa's hands. The impossibility of Somerled and I existing before Sigrdrifa was alive. Gillecolm's deep and passionate love for the sea.

They wandered at the shore's edge, those miraculous beings of ours, laughing and picking up stones. Somerled and I sat watching. He held my hand as if we were young. I could feel the calluses, and I raised his fist to my lips, kissing his raw knuckles.

'It seems impossible to be here,' he said. 'A bit like a dream. I will wake on an open mountainside, crying for you all.'

'No use wasting it in thinking it a dream,' I said.

He nodded. 'It's so hard, though, to grasp what is real and what is not. When both halves are so absurdly different.'

I squeezed his hand. 'Let them be separate. No point trying to reconcile the irreconcilable.'

There was compassion in my kiss, and a lurching swell of love for him. Pity and respect mixed together form a powerful brew.

'Thank God for you, Eimhear.'

'And for you, Somerled.'

The children called us across to a flat rock that hung over the water. Sigrdrifa issued fat-fingered commands, and we obeyed, lying down on our stomachs so that our heads dangled over the edge of the rock. And there we were, gazing back at us. The four of us. We four. Laughing into the still depths of the loch.

The commonplace joy of that moment overwhelmed me. I let down my defences to that panic that lurked always on the horizon, from the instant I saw my first child. It raced through my limbs to my heart, which beat wildly.

Keep them safe. Keep them safe. I rolled on to my back, turning away from their smiling faces. Keep them safe. I opened my eyes to the blue sky as my heart thumped and roared its own titanic plea to an indifferent universe.

1138

SOMERLED

The ships were late. Too late. Two galleys, carrying messages to his base at Kintyre. And on one of them was a seven-year-old boy who had begged and cajoled to go along for the joy of the sail. Gillecolm. How he loves the sea, that boy, thought Somerled as he trudged up the hill to where Eimhear sat waiting. He was too young to fear it properly, as it should be feared.

At the lookout point, young Brian stood rigid, mindful and nervous of her presence beside him. She sat on the rock and Somerled watched her for a heartbeat before she saw him. It's easy to forget to look at those we love, he thought, and he scanned her. How old was she now? Twenty-seven.

There were single threads of grey running through her hair, but her face was clear as a girl's. Only a deep furrow in her forehead betrayed her advancing age. She frowned when she concentrated, and it had left its mark. The little Otter, the friend of his childhood, was traceable in her face, but she smiled less now, God help her. There were dark circles beneath her staring eyes; she had not slept much last night, he knew. He thought back to the first days of their love, when he had believed implicitly in her perfection. He knew now that she was riddled with imperfections. She was impatient, and easily bored. She snapped and bridled easily. She was quick to fury, but quick to mellow too. She let folk see her hidden thoughts. Sometimes she drank too much mead, and she cried at shadows. Why did these weaknesses add up to something greater than perfection, to something wholly precious?

He walked forward and she turned to him, her face bleak.

'Where is he? Why did you let him go?'

'I'm sorry. But he is seven. How could I not?'

She turned back to face the sea, compulsively, as if by looking she could will the galley home. 'They are seven days past their time.'

'You know the sea. They could be sheltering in some bay with the tides and wind against them.'

'Seven days,' she said. 'Seven.'

The seven stretched to eight and into nine. She lost weight, lost substance to the point where it seemed as if only the power of her staring eyes was keeping her upright. She clung to the lookout rock like a limpet. No one could talk her down. Sigrdrifa kept her little namesake away; her mother's too-fierce hugs and wild eyes were terrifying the little girl.

Sometimes she clung to him. Other times she screamed at him. Your fault. This is your fault.

~ ~ ~

He woke into darkness, knowing she was not next to him. He knew she was at the rock, waiting for dawn. He shifted under the warm furs, reluctant to rush up, to share her pain. I'm sorry, he whispered to the space where she should be.

A small, warm body climbed in next to him, pushing her face into his neck. Little Sigrdrifa, who believed herself too old now to cuddle up to her father when there were eyes watching, wrapped herself into him.

'Is he dead, do you think?' she whispered.

'Hush, now, my littlest Otter.'

'You never tell us things we might not want to hear. You make Mother do it. You're a coward.'

He could feel her sobbing, the way children do when they know they have gone too far. He pushed her hair back from her face, feeling the astonishing silk of her skin against his oar-hard hands. She was right. A keen-eyed little one, who missed nothing.

'You should sleep,' he whispered.

'I can't. I'm scared.'

'Stay with me, then, littlest Otter. Do you know something? At night, when it's dark and the water's tossing and turning, otters sleep afloat on their backs. Like this, darling one. I've seen it. I know. And they say, though I haven't seen this, that they sleep holding hands, so the tossing of the water won't part them. So hold my hand, little one. There. Shh, now.'

Do you remember? Eimhear said one time, as the dusk brought the promise of another sleepless night. Do you remember when he was born? Do you remember all those nights I sat up rocking him, rocking him? Do you remember how he never stopped smiling as a toddler, how he would pick himself up from a fall and laugh?

Do you remember when we were children and we found that sailor's body on the beach, and his skin had sort of melted from the sea, and the crabs had eaten his nose, his eyes? Do you remember?

Another time, they watched the sea as a squall swept across its surface, trailing a squat, low cloud. The edges of the sky were silver, and the sea clear here, pitted there. They could see Mull, its fierce peaks reaching heavenwards. The whole majestic sum of it seemed to mock their preoccupation with one small boy; one tiny, freckled lost boy. How could he not be lost, in all of this?

'Your mother is right,' she said. 'Our God makes no sense of this. Her gods are fierce and petty, malicious and fractious. They make sense when he is lost.'

'Come. Our God loves us. He watches us in the darkness.'

'You watch in the darkness before you kill.'

'He loves you. He sent his son.'

She looked at him with contempt. 'He can keep his son; I want mine back. Love, Somerled? If God loves me, why is he torturing me? You love me. Would you? Either he hates us, or he views us all with a sort of monstrous indifference. Nothing else makes sense.'

'It's not true.'

'Is it not? There's more sense in the gods being bastards, human-shaped.'

'Could a small, petty God have made this?' He drew his arm across the horizon, taking in the sea and the mountains, and ending with his hand lightly on her cheek.

She pressed his hand, gripping on to it as if he could save her.

'And what is all this?' she said, so softly the wind muffled her words. 'What is all this weighed against my son? Oh my son. My son.'

What will we do if he doesn't come home? thought Somerled. How will it be? She will break. His panic and fear frothed up into an inarticulate cry at the sea: 'What shall we do?'

Ten days stretched into eleven. On the twelfth, she stopped talking. She was sinew and nerves and wild eyes. Her lovely face was a skull and her hair – well, the vivid glory of it was streaked with grey.

207

And then, at last, a mast and a shout of joy from the lookout that brought him running up the hill like a boy. He couldn't look at her as the ship drew closer and they registered her unfamiliar lines, her stranger's prow and, at last, the banner of Olaf Crovan streaming to the south in the fresh wind. He couldn't look, couldn't bear to see how it would break her.

'They may have news,' he said at last. 'Why else would he send a galley? Look! They're unshipping the prow beast. They come to talk, perhaps; perhaps there is news.'

They walked down the hill together, her hand a shivering claw on his arm. They stood on the beach and waited as the strangers moored, as the chief of them jumped into the shallows and waded ashore.

He was about an age with Somerled; a tall, powerful man with an easy smile.

'You are Somerled?'

Somerled nodded, weariness in every limb.

'I am Thorfinn Ottarson, sent as an emissary by Olaf, King of Man and Lord of the Isles. He sent me to tell you that we picked up some castaways on a beach down in Islay, under the cliffs at Oa.'

Somerled felt Eimhear's hand tighten on this, heard her indrawn breath like a death rattle.

'One of them,' said this Thorfinn, with a glance at Eimhear, 'is your son, Gillecolm.'

'Oh Jesus, oh Jesus,' she moaned, all the tension leaking out of her in the sound, and her knees gave and she sank to the ground, doubled up and weeping.

Somerled crouched down next to her and smoothed back her hair, shushing her as you would a child. He looked up at Thorfinn. 'And he is well?'

'Quite well, Lord Somerled.'

'Where is he?' Somerled's eyes slid past Thorfinn to the galley behind him, where Gillecolm clearly was not lurking.

Thorfinn looked embarrassed suddenly. Shifty. Oh Lord, what now? thought Somerled. Am I to play Job? Or, God help me, Abraham? Where will I find the strength?

~ ~ ~

In the hall, Eimhear found her poise. She straightened her spine, cracked her head into place, pulled on a polite mask. Sigrdrifa, rare tears streaming, bustled round to make the visitors welcome.

They exchanged the usual pleasantries: the wind, the tides, the likelihood of a blow. Somerled paced through them impatiently. Fergus was with him, at his left side, and he leaned on the old man's wiliness, let him do most of the talking while he tried to piece together the implications of Gillecolm being Olaf Crovan's hostage.

He heard, with half an ear, Fergus talking Thorfinn round to the main point, pushing him to the bounds of politeness. Eimhear's fingers rolled out an impatient tattoo on the edge of her chair. She stared at Thorfinn with the intensity she had turned on the horizon, boring through him as if she could force him to produce her child with some magical sleight of hand.

Sigrdrifa brought warmed ale for Thorfinn, and something in her face told Somerled she had spat in the horn.

Jesus, he thought. Let's get to it.

'. . . my king is desolate at the ill feeling between our two houses. Desolate. He feels that we would be better placed to be friends. He has some trouble with the northern isles, and suggests, Lord Somerled, that as friends, the two of you might be well placed to teach the wild Northmen how to be good Christian subjects to their Lord.'

Somerled nodded. God, he could do with an alliance with Man now. He could do with some raiding, too. Some hack silver to replenish his coffers, some slaves to trade for arms and men. But, but? There was something else. Why would Olaf trust him? How?

'The king is treating his hostage, Gillecolm, with all the courtesy due to the son of a respected enemy. But how different it would be if he were the son of a friend.'

Somerled laid a hand on Eimhear's arm. They would get nowhere if she sprang at this Thorfinn and ripped out his throat with her sharp otter teeth.

'And how much better, how infinitely better for all concerned if the boy were a relative. As a relative, of course, he would be free to come and go between our two lands, honoured in both. Free as the wind.'

A relative?

'The king,' continued Thorfinn, looking at Fergus with a studied, casual air, as if they were having a fireside chat in a port far from home, 'has a daughter.'

A daughter?

Somerled's mind was foggy with lack of sleep. He didn't understand, but he saw others did. He saw it in their indrawn breath, in their eyes, which swivelled to Eimhear. She looked calm, as if an old, suspected truth had been revealed to her.

'A daughter,' said Somerled, slowly. 'For Gillecolm?'

'No, Lord Somerled. For the boy is a product of a handfasted marriage, we understand, and my king is a very strict Christian, who doesn't see such unions as quite the thing.'

Somerled nearly laughed at this blatant lie, but held it in. He watched Thorfinn's face tighten.

'No, Lord Somerled. Ragnhild, a lovely girl, would be for you.'

Oh Christ.

~ ~ ~

'We must,' she said.

'No.'

They lay pressed against each other in the darkness. How often had they lain like this? He thought of all the times, now that their love was worn and comfortable, that they had just slept. All the missed hours of talk and sex and togetherness.

'No,' he said again, his voice muffled in her hair.

'Somerled, if you do not let me do this to save Gillecolm, I will hate you. And then we will be broken anyway.'

'We will rescue him. Fight Olaf Crovan.'

'You wouldn't get in the harbour. He's too strong. Leaving my fate to one side, this alliance would suit you.'

'No.'

'Yes. I am not a fool, Somerled. We have never recovered from the mauling by David. You need this. Otherwise you will be like your father, and wither to a nonentity.'

'Better a nonentity with you.'

'Perhaps. But not with a me that you have robbed of a son.'

'What if you stay here? I will build you a shieling above the loch, my darling, and come to you there.'

'Oh, my summer heart. And have you dishonour Olaf Crovan's daughter? He would eat you. Spit you out. I must go to the Island of Women.'

'Oh Lord, no. Not there. You don't belong there. Marry someone else. I will try not to kill him.'

'No. I will not marry someone else.'

She cried, then, for the first time. Shuddering sobs that he felt through his skin, into his bone.

211

'So we are caught in a trap, my Otter.'

'Utterly. Completely caught.'

They slept a little, perhaps. He was wrapped in her, and when he spoke he did not know if he was awake or asleep. 'What will I do without you? How will I bear it?'

'Shh, my summer heart. You will bear it because you will bear it. And so will I. At least you will not be on the Island of Women. You will be tupping some little Norse princess.'

'Don't.'

'Sorry. Kiss me. I am here.'

But you will not be here. You will not be here.

~ ~ ~

The severity of the place oppressed Somerled. The long, narrow hall had plain walls, with a small fire at one end and deep slits for windows. A bleakness of white, and grey and weathered stone. And if it oppressed him, what of her? She who loved beauty and colour, who he'd seen cartwheeling down a beach, laughing at a pink sunrise.

Beside him he saw her face clenched tight, her eyes narrowed.

'Jesus,' she muttered. 'Would a bit of scarlet kill them, the creatures?'

'The setting, though, love. There's a beauty . . .' He waved his arm towards the door, closed on the beauty of the island-scape; the riotous autumn colour of the hills sweeping down to the sea. A small island, hemmed between Iona and Mull. The Island of Women. Like an afterthought, a stray comma between the huge mountainous island of warriors and its small holy sidekick.

Across the strait, with its startling turquoise waters, the men of Iona prayed and worshipped. The women here did all the backbreaking, soul-sapping, spirit-crushing work women do everywhere. The clothmaking and the peat-cutting and the cheesemaking and the child-rearing and the backside wiping and the cleaning. His mother liked to point out that the monks wouldn't have the women on the holy island, but they would take their labour.

There were cliffs to the side of the main hall, low echoes of the sheer faces of Mull. He waved his arm inarticulately at the birds circling above. 'Beauty . . .' he tried again. He trailed off as he saw her face turn to him, and the cold contempt on it.

'Don't. There's nothing you can say.'

They were ushered towards a stone cross, before which knelt a cluster of holy women. Here, there were tapestries and furs and attempts to soften the stone. It was as if this was the only part of the place that mattered, and all the rest was a dull waiting room before the prayers. They could only see the backs of their bent heads, and the flicked-up eyes of the grey-haired woman at the front, which registered them and flicked back down again.

This was a mistake, he thought. A terrible, God-cursed mistake. She would suffocate here. She would slowly die of it. He thought of a landed salmon and its desperate clutching at air.

But the letters had gone to Man. And the reply expected to be held in Gillecolm's hand, their beloved boy home again. Too late. Too late. To back out now would mean the end of everything: his honour, the strength of his word freely given, the fledgling kingdom, peace, his standing with his war-bands, who knew that this treaty meant fame, the chance to breathe and plan fresh plunder, the bride price to build castles and reward his men. All that balanced against her being locked up in this place. Jesus.

He looked at the cross, imagined the figure of his Lord twisting on its severe stone angles. You're the only one whose sovereignty I admit, he thought. So tell me what to do. Speak. So many prayers. Tell me what to do, Lord. How onerous was the burden of being the one to make all the decisions. Sometimes he felt crushed by their weight, the volume of them, so that the simplest became impossible. Venison or hare? Mead or wine?

But now, with this huge, looming choice, he felt clear-headed. Certain. He grabbed her wrist and pulled her back outside

Under the grey sky, they turned to face each other. She was flushed, her eyes bright.

'No,' he said. 'We cannot do this.'

'Why?'

'Lord, your endless whys, woman. Because we cannot and we cannot and we cannot. I cannot leave you here. Sail away. Leave you in this cave.'

'We met in a cave, do you remember?'

'Of course,' he said, impatiently.

'Well then, do you think I am frightened of caves?'

'No. But how can I leave you here?'

'We were decided. All those reasons remain true. First of which is our son. This is what we must do.'

'But this place . . .'

'Yes.' She laughed. 'I daresay I'll make something of it.'

'But—'

'But. But.' Her voice rose to an angry hiss. 'Do you think I am any less capable than you of doing what is necessary? Of being brave enough to face it, and laugh in its fucking face.'

'No, no.' He put out his hand and stroked her hair, as if he was calming a hawk.

'Well then,' she said, her head in his shoulder and her voice cracking. 'Do not make it harder for me by pretending we have a choice.'

They were silent for a space, then. Listening to each other's breathing.

'Goodbye, my summer heart.'

She turned, and walked back towards the cross, where the women were singing a hymn to St Colm Cille, its tune plush with the rhythm of the oars and the beating of the waves. A stale echo of those heart-pulsing sounds.

She did not look back.

PART 2

1138

Ragnhild

I am beautiful.

We draw nearer to the landing place, and I tell myself again: I am beautiful. I can see at this distance a group of men on the beach. Which is he? They are too far to be distinct. Most of them look tall. There's a short runty one. God, what if that is him? I did not ask anyone how tall he is. Does it matter? Height in a man is nice. But kindness is nicer. A good smile. Gentle hands.

What if he has none of these? What if he is like my brother Godred? We can always spot the latest girl he has taken a fancy to by the bruises. Fingerprints on her neck sometimes, and always something in the eyes like a trapped doe.

I am beautiful. I am beautiful. I lift my chin to elongate my neck. My mother taught me that. Perhaps he has eyes like an eagle and can already see me. I must be like a queen now, just in case. Christ love me, I could throw myself to the deck and weep, I am so scared. No, I am not scared. I am of the line of Ivar. I am beautiful.

Everyone tells me so. It must be true. My father tells me, when he needs something from me. Like a song for a visiting dignitary who needs soaping. Or, say, a marriage to a strange and awkward warrior across the sea.

My mother tells me so, again and again. Straighten your back, slither your hips, bite your lips, pinch your cheeks. Cast your eyes down, flick them up. Smile, don't smile. Be beautiful. It is all you have. It is your currency, your hack silver.

Your father's bastards litter the island. You must stand out.

She is the most beautiful of his cast-off women and I must be the most beautiful of his daughters. Will yourself beautiful, she says. Make it so. Believe it, and it is true. Hold in your stomach. Laugh at their jokes. Not that loud, like a blasted herring-wife. Soft laughs, tinkling ones. Lean over when pouring; too far, you look whorish. Lick your lips. Delicately, child.

She slapped me for slouching, slapped me for giggling, slapped me for lounging. Afterwards she would cry and I would cry and we would talk again about how my face and my body are my power. Without power, I am nothing. A chattel. I must enthral this stranger. It is not enough to make him my husband. Husbands stray; husbands ignore their wives. I must make him need me. Want me. That is the only way to become powerful – through his weakness for me. That's what my mother said.

I can see the sense in it. My father is the most powerful man in these seas. His wife is a nothing. She did not make the most of the early days of his pleasure in her to build her own kingdom within a kingdom. She let it slide, until one day he took his first mistress, and all the flattery and the bribes and the elaborate homages went sideways while the wife looked on. She was humiliated.

I have one lever already, beyond and above my face. My father.

'Come here, my beautiful one,' he said when I went to bid him farewell. He did not come to the jetty to see me off, but at least he granted me an audience.

I walked towards him. Stomach in, lips bitten, chin high.

'Was I wrong,' he said, 'to give you to this upstart?'

I inclined my head with grace, or so I hoped. He does not always expect an answer to his questions.

'But he is becoming awkward, and you, my child, can settle that.'

I was proud of his trust in me.

He had been talking to his champion, and a few of his other leading men. They were drawn against the wall, respectfully waiting for the farewells to be done and their business resumed. I tried not to look at them. At one of them in particular. I felt his eyes on me, though. I knew he was watching. What use is crying for the impossible? At least so my mother said when she found me weeping over him. Baldur the Bold, they call him. Baldur the Beautiful, I whispered to him once, when we were kissing in the forest.

Oh Jesus, watch over me.

My father pulled me to him. He hugged me. That frightened me more than anything, for when did he last do that? When I was seven, perhaps, and forward with my affection. I would run at him and throw my arms around his neck. Do not be opportune, said my mother. Do not hug the king like some common fisherman's daughter. So I did not run to him any more, and he seemed not to notice. At least, he never pulled me into an embrace. He ruffled my hair sometimes. Chucked my cheek.

So on this last day, he pulled me tight against his bristling beard and I felt uncomfortable. Baldur's eyes at my back, my father's unfamiliar smell surrounding me. He let me go, and looked me up and down. 'He will be pleased, unless he is made of stone. Hear this, Ragnhild.' He raised his voice so that his warriors could hear; a promise given to a woman is no promise unless other men hear it.

His kingly voice, then, with the warriors listening in to witness it. 'I have told him, and I am telling you, that you are the favourite of my daughters. He is honoured to get you. If he breaks that trust, if he dishonours you in any way, I will crush him as a dog crushes a rat's skull. Do you understand? You are to be his wife, and he will treat you with honour. As Christ is my witness, your honour will be dear to me.'

There was some shuffling in the corner at this, but of course no one spoke. My father thinks himself a Christian man, a moral man. He thinks himself a dutiful husband and expects his men to treat their wives with respect. He is utterly blind to his own hypocrisy. He can kiss his latest whore with one face, and lecture the islanders on marital morality with another. My mother says that this is one reason why he is a great ruler: he is bullishly convinced of his own purity and clarity of thought, in spite of all evidence to the contrary.

Will my new husband be the same? They need careful managing, men like that. They must believe all ideas are their own; that all dissent is agreement. Lord, what will he be like, the stranger I am to marry? Thorfinn Ottarson has met him, and says he is all that a woman could want in a husband. But Thorfinn would say that. This marriage was his idea; if it goes awry, it will be he who earns my father's displeasure. But how could it go wrong? That implies that there is a choice for me. That I could step down on to that beach and say: 'No. I do not like the look of him. Take me home, Thorfinn. Take me home, and I will marry Baldur the Beautiful and we will have ten children as beautiful as he. I will not marry this strange barbarian.'

I look aside to Thorfinn Ottarson, and try to imagine saying the words aloud. No. No. No. The word is like rising bile in my throat. No. No.

Thorfinn catches my eye and smiles at me, in a manner I assume is meant to be encouraging. Beyond him, standing gripping the prow, is a boy of about seven or eight perhaps. I do not know.

I can't see his face. He is looking towards the beach, all rigid like a hunting dog. I do not know who he is.

I look over his head to the shore. My mother came down to see me go. When I began to cry, she slapped my arm. It is not far enough a journey to cure red eyes and a snotty nose. First impressions are everything. *Everything*. She was stopping herself from crying, and I owed her that much, although I thought I would burst from the keeping it all in.

The wind is fierce on my skin. I think of the popping of tiny red thread veins on my cheek. But now is not the time to shelter. Now is the time to stand tall and proud. I will the boat forward. I plead for it to stop. I cannot decide if I want this meeting to come quicker or to be put off indefinitely. Put off, I think. So that this moment spins out for an eternity, and I never have to step ashore and meet my fate.

1138

somerled

Here he is, then, on the same beach, waiting for a girl. And here she is, walking towards him, all the eyes on them both. He is glad to see that she walks straight and with decided steps, despite the watchers pressing on her with their expectations, their hopes and their malice.

Ragnhild is fair, with blue eyes and an eyebrow arched at him as if to say, here I am. Do you like me? And, God help him, he does like the look of her. He feels a sudden keen pleasure at the thought of sleeping with her, this poppet of a princess with her big eyes, slim body and serious face. The churning in his loins feels like a betrayal, a bricking-up of his beloved in her island cell.

But what can he do?

As he says the necessary words, a boy darts from the boat behind her. Gillecolm. He looks around the beach with quick, smiling eyes. Something dawns on him, Somerled can see it: an awakening. The boy looks from Somerled to Ragnhild and back again.

'Where is my mother?' he says, in a voice too high and too cracked. 'Where is she?'

Ragnhild

I am beautiful. He tells me so. He whispers it in the darkness. 'You are beautiful,' he says. It must be true. His voice is full of sadness. It is the aftermath of love. For he loves me. How can he not?

What we do in the night; what more proof of it do I need? It floods my body. I am there and not there. I am Ragnhild, and I am Freya. It only hurt the first time, and he was gentle. My husband.

There are so many reasons to be proud of this man, this husband. He is a great thinker. A great warrior. His men follow him without question. They are not scared of him, exactly. Not like men are scared of my father. They do what he says because they trust him.

Trust. I trust him. He is kind, and gentle. He is all that I could have hoped for. The relief. Oh Christ, the relief. He is not a man who beats women. He is not a man quick to use his fists. He is not a man to fear. Neither, I think, is he malleable. I have not worked out yet how best to be Ragnhild in his presence. Until I have judged it right, I am careful to hold myself near him as my mother has taught me. I am grace and lightness.

His hall is built on a wild, rocky outcrop. Near us is a long sea loch, at the head of which is a sheltered area by a river. I suggested, with all proper diffidence, that we build a hall there, hidden from the wind and the waves. He laughed.

'And how, my princess, would I see the sea roads, hidden away there like a turnip farmer? My eyes are my strength.'

So we are buffeted out here. I do not leave the hall over-much. The wild wind shivers my hair into knots, and one look at Sigrdrifa's mottled face is enough to know what it can do to a woman's skin. So I stay inside and I spin and I weave and I sing and I forbid myself all thoughts of home. It is gone to me now. I may visit it, perhaps, in a year or two. For now, I must pretend that it does not exist. It is the only way.

Father Padeen was here earlier, leading the prayers for all those not off hunting or fishing or fighting. The boy was there, Gillecolm, the one who made the fuss on the beach at the moment that should have been my triumph. He was praying earnestly, and missed my look of contempt. He has kept out of my way since I have been here, which is to the good. He is my husband's bastard son, I am told. But Somerled does not pay him much heed, and so neither shall I.

I do not think I like Father Padeen. There seems something sly and over-clever about him. He told me that he knows of women who can write; not Ogham, which is carved only by masters on stone. But in old tongues, like Latin, scratched on to parchment with sharpened quills. Absurd, I told him. But I thought how lovely it would be to write a letter to my mother, one that only she can read. I sent Thorfinn Ottarson with a message:

Your daughter is well and happy in her new home. She is treated with all the honour that is her due. She sends her love and her greetings across the sea and hopes this message finds her esteemed mother in good spirits.

He had a similar message for my father. He looks at me with an annoying smugness, this Ottarson. It is known in this place that Somerled enjoys me. I hold my head high for the women, sway my hips for the men, and let them read in it my husband's lavish attention. Feast on this, Oona, I think, as the dwarfish old witch looks on. I do not like her. She treats me like a pet, like a spoiled child.

If I could write a letter to my mother that only she could see, what would it say?

Oh my mother. I miss you. I love you. I miss you.

My husband is a good man. He is gentle, and kind. And oh, my mother, it is such a relief to find him so. He is nice-looking. Medium height, good eyes, a broad smile. He is not short. He could have been anything. Sometimes I lie awake at night, while he breathes near me in the darkness, and I pray so hard in thanks that my brain rings with it. Thank you, Lord, thank you. To have a youngish, gentle husband who is kind to me. What a boon. He could have been like the giant Aed. Grizzled and frightening, with missing teeth and a too violent laugh. He could have been like my brother Godred. You never did like his mother, but even she is frightened by him, they say.

He could have been Baldur, but that was not my fate. You have taught me often enough to be disciplined with my mind. No use lamenting what cannot be.

So I give thanks for what I have, and for what I may have. For all this coupling must produce a child. And love. Surely that will come. How can it not? I think I might love him already. You said it would grow, and I think it is. How do you know, though? What should it feel like?

Oh my mother. I would not write this, as I do not want you to be sad for me. But I am a little lonely. The women disregard me. Life goes on in well-worn patterns, which were woven before I arrived. My attempts to change things are met with bland smiles, and no action. There is no one for me to talk to. And I am alone here.

Better perhaps that I cannot write. Better not to send such a letter, I think. Safer to stick to platitudes.

I look behind me and find that Somerled is standing near, looking at me.

I rise, pulling in my stomach, straightening my hair. I hold up my cheek, and he comes to me and kisses it swiftly with cool, dry lips.

'The rain has gone off,' he says. 'I'm heading out into the hills for the night, hunting. You could come with me.'

I consider this. 'Where would we sleep?'

He smiles as if my question is amusing. Will there come a time, here, when people do not treat me like a child? 'In a shieling, up in the hills. We may get a deer, perhaps two. Or there's salmon in the loch.'

I picture a cold, wet dawn. I think of how my hair will straggle down my face, and the mud smears, and the pinched red nose from sleeping outside. I imagine how his face will sour at the sight of me bedraggled like a fisherwoman.

'I will stay, I think, husband,' I say.

He looks at me for a heartbeat. I cannot read his face. I struggle to know what he is thinking, which makes it hard to please him. The only sure way I have found so far is in silent night-time tumbling.

'Whatever pleases you, my dear,' he says. He leaves me, and the walls close in a little. I pull my shawl closer, and forbid myself from thinking about home.

somerled

S omerled is, to his slight regret, relieved to sail away. He looks behind him once, to the small figure standing on the edge of the shore, watching the reduced fleet depart. The oars are out, pulling them into the Sound of Mull before pointing north. North, to meet Olaf and his fleet. He is sailing as an ally, to take on the rebellious men of the northern isles.

He looks out over his crew, creaking into their familiar rhythm. He will take his turn at the blade on the way north, he thinks. He is getting flabby. He looks down at his body, this traitorous thing that tups the silent princess with such abandoned joy. He finds a release in sex without love that he was not expecting. He does not care over-much if she is enjoying it; and that, he finds to his shame, is liberating. He thinks of their last frenzied coupling, and he leans into the wind.

In the darkness, they have found an illusion of closeness that suits them both. He kisses her young lips in the shadows. He watches the play of light and dark dapple her skin. He took the first time slowly and gently, listening for the quickening of her breath. Trying not to think of another woman alone on an island full of women.

She smiles at him at the right times, casts her eyes downwards in the light and grapples with fervour, pretend or real, in the darkness.

And yet.

'It is not her fault,' Sigrdrifa told him last night, finding him alone on the shore watching the Sound.

'Whose fault is it?'

'And that is a child's question from a big man.'

She sat next to him, grunting on to the rock.

'Is she not a pretty enough girl?'

'Yes. But.'

'But, but. Loki has tricked you and toyed with you and is laughing now. All you can do is live with it. Does she know how she is here?'

He shook his head. 'No. She thinks that it is the usual run of things. A political marriage.'

'And you will not tell her?'

'How can I? She is so young, Mother. I just want to be kind to her.'

His mother sighed. 'She has that quality, poor thing. She invites make-believe. We circle round her on tiptoes. Fill her with half-truths to keep that pretty face smiling. Not like . . .'

She paused, and the missing name filled the night around him, choking him.

Into the darkness she said: 'In the middle time, there is someone you are forgetting.'

'Gillecolm.' He said the name with an unfamiliar heaviness.

'Gillecolm,' she nodded. 'Poor boy is eating his own heart. He misses his mother. And you are telling him nothing. Nothing.'

'I promised her.' He found it difficult to say her name, afraid that if he tried, it would come in a howl. 'How can we tell him that he was the reason for it all? What kind of a burden would that be?'

'So instead you say nothing, hey? Avoid him. Let him be fatherless and motherless and sisterless, poor dear pup.'

'I will try,' he promised.

'Too many secrets,' she said. 'Too many.' They settled into a comfortable quietness.

Now, as he unthinkingly matches the flex of his knees to the rise and fall of the galley, Somerled thinks of the silence that spins itself around him and Ragnhild. Does she find it oppressive too? He finds her pliability depressing and unconvincing. Whatever pleases you, husband. Whatever makes you happy, husband. Whatever you like.

He imagines her mother standing behind her, whispering in her ear. Please him. Bend yourself to his wishes. He knows he should shake her out of it. Ask her, what pleases you? What do you like? But he fears the answers.

And what of Gillecolm? He shakes his head, irritated suddenly. How is it that home has become a knot of problems? What can a man do who has lost his sanctuary?

He thinks of turning the galley around. Screaming his defiance towards Man and sailing to Iona, casting himself at her feet. Throwing his aching head into her lap.

Why doesn't he? He wrestles himself.

'Somerled?' says Aed, nearby. He must have spoken. He looks at Aed as if through a fog. If he follows his heart, all the forces of Man will fall on him. Not just on him – he could bear that. On Oona, and the rest of the women and children. He has no choice. Choices are, by and large, an illusion. Without power. Power must come first; his heart's desires second. He will kiss Olaf's hairy arse. He will build his strength. He will grow in power. And then, then he will put his upside-down world the right way up.

He thinks of his mother's words about Gillecolm. He should have spoken to the boy before he left. He has lied to himself, through the unmooring. Told himself that he tried to find the words to talk to his son.

But, he thinks now, watching the galley rise and fall, pushing its way into northern seas, I did not try very hard. There was too much to do, before the leaving. Too many men to brief, galleys to inspect, stores to account for, prayers to offer. Until all there was time for was a snatched goodbye, under the questioning eye of Ragnhild. He kissed them both and ran for the sea, for the cleansing rush of wind and spray.

~ ~ ~

Olaf the Morsel, King of the Isles by the grace of God, is a giant of a man. He stands almost shoulder to shoulder with Aed, and Somerled resents immediately the crick of his neck to look up at the man. Olaf uses his bulk with great skill. He dominates any space he is in, planting wide feet and lengthening broad shoulders. He does not smile until he has weighed the effect of it. He has never, to anyone's knowledge, laughed.

Somerled watches him. This man defeated his elder brothers by cunning and force, and took the power of all the isles. He has held on to that power for years that stretch into decades. He is a good man to watch, to study.

There is no hatred. Olaf was playing the game, the great tafl play of power and influence. Somerled thinks of Eimhear and little Sigrdrifa in their island tomb. Anger and violence will not get them back, only cunning. He must be as mighty as Olaf; he must number as many ships, as many men. Then let the Morsel tell him who he may or may not love.

Somerled sits with Aed and Sigurd on a small shingle beach, which hangs awkwardly from the edge of rebellious North Uist.

Ruaridh's absence is still alive to them, but none of them talk of it. His men are exaggeratedly gentle with him, like children told to tiptoe round a deathbed. It is infuriating, but he finds the distance between them useful. He thinks that a kind word or a misplaced reminiscence might send him spiralling into public grief; a wailing, stone-throwing, God-cursing storm from which he will never have the strength to emerge.

'Strange land, this,' says Sigurd.

'It is,' Aed nods, picking up stones and running them through his big hands. 'More water than solid earth. Do the men here have webbed feet, do you think?'

'It's good for us,' says Somerled. 'If they stay inland, we should be able to find them. Where is there to hide? No hills. Just water.'

'Imagine living here—' Sigurd begins.

'We do not have time,' says Somerled sharply, 'to play childish games.'

He notes the quick look that passes between his old friends.

Somerled kicks at the fire, sending sparks skywards. His breath catches as he notes the beauty of the flying embers. How odd that the commonplace can sometimes arrest you with its extraordinariness. God's work. Why did he make fire beautiful, when it only needs to be useful? Or do we find it beautiful precisely because it is so essential? It is the type of question Eimhear would love to worry at. Is she watching a fire now? Is she reconciled? Raging? He does not know. Here is another question she would like. Is physical proximity necessary for two souls to remain each other's twin? Will his soul still speak to hers, across all the rage of wind and sea?

He becomes aware that Aed is talking to him. 'Small fights, Somerled. They are when a man becomes careless. When he drops his guard. Especially when he is . . .' Aed searches for the word, and Somerled almost smiles at the man's embarrassment.

Sigurd is nodding with vigour. 'Aye. A man needs something to fight for.'

'Is that true?' Somerled unbends a little. 'Is it not enough to want to stay alive?'

'It is not,' says Aed. 'Life must be more enticing than death, and sometimes that is not always true.'

Somerled has a sudden image of the three of them when they were younger; full of banter and bravado. Everything weighs heavier now.

He pushes himself to his feet and mutters something about lookouts, walking away from the fire and into the black night.

~ ~ ~

The next day, Somerled remembers Aed's words as they finally find the slippery bastards on dry land, caught in that silvery space between the sky and the water's sheen. They are being tested, he knows. Sent in by Olaf alone against the men of North Uist, to prove their friendship.

They rush at the Uist men, with their usual ululating roar of fury. Somerled throws his misery into the cry and it tears his throat. The enemy give before the swords even clash, so great is their terror. But there is something not quite right, some tug at the edge of Somerled's battle cry. They are ceding ground too easily, as if in a pattern.

Before he can work it out properly, he gives the order to stop, regroup. Even as he shouts it, he knows it is going to be difficult to check their battle rush. He shouts it again, and again. Aed hears him – the words penetrate and he comes to an uneasy stop, his axe quivering with the effort. Between them they slow the others and step back. A strange, uneasy silence falls, broken only by the heavy breathing of the confused warriors. The Uist men are not running, as they should be. They too have checked their flight.

'A trap?' says Aed, from the corner of his mouth.

Somerled nods, offering a silent prayer of thanks that he spotted it. His duty to his men outweighs his misery when the swords are drawn. The knowledge comes as a relief and a rush of something he could call love for the big hairy warrior at his side.

'Swine array, at a walk,' he shouts, and they cluster in behind him. 'I lead, Aed,' he says, and the big man concedes with a nod. He probes his way forward, pushing the point of his spear into the ground. His shield is up, and he feels the jar of the spears hitting. They move forward with agonizing slowness. Behind him he hears a cry as a high-flighted spear finds its mark. He walks on. And there it is. He pushes his spear into something that seems like scrubby land, and it gives way. He can't find the bottom with his spear shaft, and it pulls out with a rotten suck.

'Watch out on the right,' he cries. 'Bog to the right, to the right.' The cry carries back down the line, and the wedge flattens behind him into a column. Good men, he thinks. Good men.

He continues slowly, probing ahead and to the side. Ahead of him, some twenty feet away, the Uist men watch him, growling at him in their strange dialect. There, on the left, a similar falling-away of his spear, a similarly odd mash of land and water, each pretending to be the other. They are on a sort of natural bridge or ford, then, across this hidden bog. Jesus, imagine if they had carried on their headlong charge, each abreast of the other, all roaring with battle madness.

He feels a flood of nausea suddenly. A rush of horrifying might-have-beens which threatens to paralyse him. In his head, his men flounder and are picked off, one by one. The grinning Uist men spit their contempt as they skewer them. They are sucked under, bog water bubbling in their lungs.

234

Jesus, Somerled, hold it together. He has lost his song, he realizes. Once he would have sung himself brave. He tries. *I am Somerled. I am Somerled. I am . . . I am . . .*

He has stopped. Aed bumps into him, swearing softly. The Uist men are nervous. They bounce from foot to foot, shake their weapons, roar themselves brawny. The biggest steps forward. From the narrow bog-bridge, this will be like a prow-to-prow galley fight. Somerled bunches himself tight. What use the Loki trick of guessing their plan, if he cannot be Thor as well, barrelling forward to take out his man?

He roars forward, Aed at his shoulder. The big Uist man blinks, and Somerled knows he has him. The man's axe comes forward, too slowly. Somerled glances it away with his shield, and takes out the man's legs with a spray of blood that sends him crashing to the floor like a felled and stupid tree.

They meet the rest of the Uist men head on, sending them scattering backward. The pockets of water splayed across the land turn red, and quickly it is done.

~ ~ ~

'This is the price of betraying your lord,' he says to the old man kneeling at his feet. Outside the pathetic hut they can hear the sound of women screaming.

'But the Orkney lord threatened us with this if we did not swear loyalty to him.' The old man's voice cracks into a boyish wail. A higher scream breaks through the wall. In the corner, the youngest girls huddle. Somerled has ordered them here and they watch him with the wide eyes of cornered hares. He realizes that he has forgotten to tell them that his order was to keep them safe; they must think that his taste runs to undeveloped flesh. He feels an immense, overwhelming disgust. With himself, with his men, with the girls crying in the corner, with this old man who lost the battle and must pay the price.

'What choice did we have?' The old man screams it.

'This is the price of betraying your lord,' says Somerled again, woodenly. Obstinately. He knows that a world of easily broken oaths is an impossible world in which no one can be safe. He knows this as a principle that cannot be violated. It is a theoretical truth that all right-thinking men must understand. And yet here in this smoky hut, confronted by the rawness of the old man's misery and the girls' fear, all seems utterly hopeless.

eimbeaq

We watch the sea, little Sigrdrifa and I. I find the horizon calming, when life here threatens to drown me. I hate the land for its constancy. It never changes. Rocks sit there, stupid and immovable. Even the heather comes and goes with maddening slowness. It changes colour slowly, too, when you are not looking, as if to emphasize time's numbing advance.

But the sea changes its mood in front of your eyes. Waves curl and retreat, each one just different enough from the one before to mesmerize. There is a high spot, on this pathetically small island. Just high enough to kill a leaper. We sit there sometimes, Sigrdrifa and I, watching the light playing on the water. We drink in its endless cycling though blues and greys and greens.

She has stopped asking about home. She has stopped asking about Somerled. I fight to keep my face smooth and cheerful.

If I float on the surface of my life, it is almost bearable.

Our days have a numbing sameness. We rise at dawn, and take our turn with the milking. There are more cows than women on the Island of Women, crowded as it is. Colm Cille banished us both, cows and women, to this overgrown rock. As the saying goes, *Where there is a cow, there will be a woman; and where there is a woman, there will be mischief.* This from the mouth of a saint, so it must be true.

If the day is fair, we can hear the monks' low chanting drifting across the short crossing between Iona and the Island of Women. The sun, if it rises, catches the stone of their church before it draws out the sparkling turquoise of the sea. More often, the morning flops through shades of dark and rain, until we lie suspended in the half-light between a grey sea and a black sky.

As the hymns fade, the first boats begin to ply. The children take the urns of milk, the bowls of curd, the fresh-churned butter down to the water, where the novices will load the boats and banter shyly with the older girls. The novices bring with them loaves of still-warm bread and the dear love of the baker to his wife, who sets her butter-smeared hands on her hips and thanks the Lord it is a Monday and there are five full days before she has to see his miserable face again.

The master stonemason kisses his wife and three girls goodbye, boarding the returning boat with his eldest son. He has stayed an extra night on the women's side, but the man is an artist so he sets his own terms. They say that the cross he is carving is like a living thing under his hands. They say it is so beautiful and so complicated that he is terrified of not being able to finish it, of bringing all the loops and whorls back to where they started.

There is real affection between the man and his family. I turn away, and look towards the sea.

When the boats are gone, we eat a little and pray a lot. I managed early on to escape the worst jobs, proving my utter incompetence in sewing the simplest of cowls. I tend the vegetables. I concentrate with all my might on whatever job is at hand. Pricking out the seedlings. Spreading the manure. Weeding and deadheading and rootling about in the earth. The harder the labour, the less space for thought.

Darkness brings the relief of a warm fire, and some food. We all eat together; simple stuff invariably. Prayers. Bed. I struggle to sleep. Instead I construct elaborate plans of escape, which the morning always reveals to be unworkable. Two perpetual stumbling blocks – my refusal to place myself under the protection of any man who is not Somerled; and the safety that this place provides for little Sigrdrifa. It it were me alone, well, that would be different.

But here I am, and I must try to make the best of it. Oh, how I try.

There is a strange hierarchy here, based on skills I do not possess. The preening head of the pack is the woman who embroiders the abbot's robes. I admit her right to eminence; the neat and intricate stitching is a wonder. I do not admit her right to send me half mad with boredom as she talks of thread width and dye efficacy and needle style to her gaggle of ninny-headed acolytes.

Sigrdrifa has more of a skill for it than I. She is popular here; cosseted for her cheerfulness, praised for her needlework. I have struck a deal with one of the older monks, who works as a scribe in the monastery's library. I smuggle him wine, and he teaches Sigrdrifa her letters and the Latin. I watch her scratching out the *hic haec hoc*s with something approaching envy and a vast pride. She could be a boy, he said once, meaning to please. She takes to it so quickly.

What good it will do her, I do not know. Stuck out here, no good at all. But life has a habit of changing quickly, and it cannot hurt. She is Somerled's daughter, after all.

We hear of him, sometimes. When travellers and pilgrims arrive too late for the crossing, they hop across to us and we feed them. His is a name that crops up, as he grows in power and influence. His success is built on my banishment. Even though I agreed the terms, sometimes I swell with a bitterness I did not expect. I fight it. It will drown the good in me, if I let it.

When his name is spoken, there is always a whispering, a naming of me. Pride makes me silent, when I want to fall at the travellers' feet and cry, yes, I was his woman. How is he? How does he look? What of his wife? What of my son?

But I hold myself in, tight like a closed cockle. They call me proud and prickly here. They think me humourless.

Perhaps they are right. I am losing myself. I drift on the surface, and underneath is a void, a blankness. Even thinking about it makes me dizzy with pain and grief. So I rise at dawn and I milk the cows and I wait for dusk.

Ragnhild

I hate becoming fat. This stomach feels like it belongs to someone else. My face is puffy. My ankles are swollen. Even my fingers are rounded and fat.

I am a stranger to myself. At night, my chest burns. As I roll over, the massive weight of my body wakes me up and I spend the nights sleepless and tearful. I attempt, sometimes, to pull the younger warriors' eyes to me. But they slide past and fix on younger, slimmer girls, and I am enraged and pitiful all at the same time.

Who am I? Who is this fat and slothful stranger living in my body? Who is this girl who can make a room full of women fall silent when she enters? Who is this tearful person, with red eyes in a puffy face?

When the baby comes out, I hope then to snap back to being me. I pray for a boy. A boy will bring me power; consolidate my position. Somerled is still together with my father. When he comes back, I will present him with a boy, and he will bow to me. And if he bows, so will they.

Sigrdrifa is fading. She gabbles in Norse, and talks as if her husband is still alive. Perhaps when she dies the women will treat me more seriously.

In the meantime, I grow and grow. I am breathless. I am heavy, when once I was light.

There is something else. Something troubling.

When Sigrdrifa is in her madness, she names a woman. 'Eimhear,' she says. 'Who are you, moppet? I want Eimhear. I want Sigrdrifa.'

I am impatient. 'You are Sigrdrifa, you old fool.'

'And look who is calling me a fool.'

She laughs, and the drool leaks from her mouth, running down the lines in her chin. She is horrible. I cannot look at her. There are long grey hairs straggling along her jaw, and pink scalp showing underneath her thinning locks. Her hands are claws. She has three teeth.

She garbles of otters.

'Stop talking nonsense, old woman.'

Her chattering is a constant buzzing in the background. I will her to be quiet. I ask her politely. She laughs at me, edging closer to the fire, taking all the heat I need for my baby. I ask Oona to take her in. She stares at me. 'This is her home.' In my head, I scream: it is supposed to be my home! But I say nothing and stare at the wall. Sometimes I want my own mother here so much I have to fight back the tears. I do not want the mad old witch to see me crying.

We had word from Somerled. He will be on his way home soon. I will greet him with a son, and it will be the moment of triumph. I imagine it again and again, holding his son to him and meeting his eyes, and knowing that I am his queen in soul as well as form.

1140

SOMERLED

'God's blood, boy, it's not that difficult.'

He stands over Gillecolm, who sprawls on the floor. The boy's knuckles are bleeding. There is a bruise flowering around his eye. Fingal, Aed's younger boy, stands aside. His breath still comes in ragged gasps. He's exaggerating, no question of it. For it was pitifully easy for him to send Gillecolm sprawling backwards, his wooden sword skittering across the stones.

Gillecolm puts his fist to his mouth and sucks at the blood. A smear of it sits on his cheek, and Somerled fights the urge to raise the boy up and push it away with a tender thumb. It will do him no good. The eyes of the men are on them already, and Gillecolm's ineptitude is bad enough without coddling him.

Is this where I went wrong? wonders Somerled. Loving him too much? Is it this tenderness that has made him soft?

The boy unnerves him. He is a quiet, still child with a broad grin and a happy soul. He is provoking to Ragnhild; she cannot understand him, and the joy that flutters about him like a cloud of butterflies, despite all the reasons in the world for bitterness. He can sit for hours on the rocks with the seals. He knows where the eagles' eggs are. He knows the name of each wild flower of spring.

He can read the sea as well as Sigurd, sense the changing moods of the sky before they rush over the horizon. But he cannot hold a sword like a Christian.

It is no help to be the lord's son; Somerled's band does not work that way. The boy finishes the practice sessions bruised and bleeding from the flat and sharp of the wooden swords. All the patient coaxing, all the irritated barking, all the private lessons cannot make him faster or more instinctive.

Gillecolm pulls himself to his feet, not catching his father's eye. He breathes deeply, clearly willing himself to hold the sword upright to stare along its blunt point at Fingal.

Behind them, there is a shuffling and deliberate quietness. The embarrassment of it all hangs heavy over the sparring boys. Somerled can feel the eyes on his neck, the contained nervous laughter. The pity for him and his boy, barbed with disdain. He longs to spin round and tell them all to go to hell, but he fears that will ratchet up this dripping atmosphere to something unbearable.

Fingal spars with Gillecolm, restraining himself. The champion's boy is light on his feet. The wooden sword is part of his arm, part of the dance. Gillecolm, God keep him, shows all the joins.

Everyone watching knows that Fingal can step up a level. He clearly has his father's surprising softness for his friends. Fine, thinks Somerled, as long as he has his father's ferocity with his enemies.

Will it be like this with his new son? He thinks of the boy. He has his mother's colouring, fair and bright-eyed. He is hungry, strong, packing on weight with each passing month. He is, in the eyes of the world, the legitimate one. When Somerled returned, Ragnhild held the child up to his father like an offering. She crowed of his maleness. He was ready to greet her, to say the necessary words, when he noticed something else. He saw Oona's red eyes and the misery of the women, and the absence of his mother. He looked around, a child's panic lurching in his stomach. Oona shook her head, her tears falling freely.

He pushed past Ragnhild and the baby, desperate to be away from the eyes. He ignored her stricken face. The need for solitude was greater than his grief, fiercer than any lust he had ever known. He pushed through the silence. It was only when he was halfway up the hill, alone and accepting the crushing grief, that he realized he had not even asked the boy's name.

eimhear

He is coming. He is coming.

I roll the words around in my head, but still they make no sense. It is two years since I saw him. Two years. Each minute a cut, each day a scar.

And now he is nearly here. Aed told me, bless him and keep him. The big man jumped down from the galley and waded ashore to shave seconds from the meeting. He is in that galley there, he said, pointing, and I looked along the line of his finger to the most beautiful boat the world has ever seen. In her bow, clutching the beast, a small figure with wind-whipped hair, waving and shouting across the sea.

I wrap my arms around Aed, and he kisses the top of my head and whispers the laments we did not have time for when I left. It feels odd to hold a man, even one so very much like a brother. I can smell blood and sweat on him; and the kiss of the sea. He is hard and unfamiliar, but he reminds me of home, and so I twine my fingers behind his broad back and I hold on and on.

Later we will talk of Oona, my sharp-eyed friend. We will talk of his children, and his pride in them. We will, perhaps, talk of Somerled. But first there is *my* boy, scudding towards me across the sea. My shining boy. My face pressed into Aed's chest, I swallow down the torrent.

Little Sigrdrifa must be here. Aed says he will find her, and I whisper garbled directions to the bay on the other side, where she is hunting for mussels clinging to the low-tide rocks. He moves off, unpeeling himself from me. Our words are an irrelevant babble of joy and friendship and promises. His big gap-toothed grin, and his shaggy beard are like sunshine ripping through cloud in this Island of Women.

He walks away, and here I am.

And here, suddenly, is my boy. My son.

He runs forward and pushes into me, burying his head in my neck. He is nearly as tall as me, all elbows and limbs. He is unmistakably, unbearably mine. I push myself into him, reaching for the soft skin at the nape of his neck where the hair grows in chestnut down. I pull back to search his face, but cannot bear the air between us. I pull him close again, inhaling him. I adjust to the new size of him, the new shape of him, and I whisper his name again and again until the words run into each other like tears.

When you are in a boat in rough seas, the first thing they teach you is to keep one hand for the ship and one for yourself. The hand for the ship anchors you; keeps you safe from the capricious bucking of the seas.

That is how it is in this week with my son. I must keep one hand on his skin to feel safe. I can sense, after a while, that it annoys him a little – this constant amazed touching. But I cannot help it, and he knows this. His kindness outweighs his irritation. He lets me run his fine chestnut hair through my fingers. He lets me kiss his neck as I pass him on the way to fetch things to feed him. He is so thin, my boy. I press food on him. Curds and cured things. Red meat still rich with blood. All manner of things from the sea and the soil. Anything I can find, I offer up to him.

Little Sigrdrifa sits near him. I see their two heads bent together over a book, their hair different shades of the same brown. The two of them together in one place, under one roof, by one fire. Safe.

They catch me watching them and look at each other, amused by me.

There is no point trying to explain to them. No use in articulating this desperate joy. I don't need them to understand, or to love me back. I just need them to be unblemished and fire-flushed, sitting together reading a book.

'Mother,' he says, in the see-saw voice of a boy trying to seem old.

'Hmm?' I watch his lips as they move; try to imprint each plane of his maturing face on my mind.

'You know I must leave tomorrow. The winds being fair, Aed will come for me.'

'I know.'

'I wish I could stay here with you.'

'And I too. But it's no use to wish it. How could you become a man in this place? Who will teach you to fight and boast and be a boor?'

He smiles, but I don't quite trust in it.

'What is it, Gillecolm?'

'Nothing.'

'Is it her?'

He laughs. 'No. It's not her.'

'Is she kind to you?'

He looks straight at me. 'No. But she is not happy, so it is hard to hate her.'

'Does happiness matter so much in this life?'

'It's easy to say that, Mother, when you have a gift for happiness. She does not.'

I catch my breath. When did he become old enough to say things like this, to have compassion for his tormentor?

'But I wish I could stay here.'

He is childish suddenly. I want to gather him up, but I take his hand.

'I wish you could stay too,' says Sigrdrifa. She burrows into him, like a puppy.

I look at him and see something elusive about him, something sad.

'Is there something else bothering you, my darling boy?'

No, he says. No, again, with greater emphasis. But I don't trust him. He wants to please me. My child wants to protect me; and that is the saddest thing I have ever known.

He sails on a clear, fine day. The sea takes the smell of him first. Then his voice. He becomes a blur. A speck. Then the horizon settles to a clear unbroken line, and he is gone.

1148

SOMERLED

The years become fluid, interchangeable, as you grow older. So Aed and Somerled tell each other as they creak to standing, trotting out the old man's platitudes they never thought would be theirs to own.

The seasons come with new births. A daughter to follow Dugald, then three more boys. They snap at each other's heels from the instant they can crawl. Each child adds a physical layer to Ragnhild, like an onion putting its skin back on.

The distance between them grows.

She tried, he thinks. Poor Ragnhild. Oh God, how she tried. At first.

He tried.

Did he?

He doesn't know.

How men can filter their memories. How men can slant their actions, re-imagine their intent. The extraordinary myopia of being human.

He can tell when other men con themselves. He can tell when other men soothe themselves with lies, dulling the pain of their shortcomings with whispered, twisting salves.

He can recognize it in others. He knows that Gillecolm tells himself that he does not mind being a hapless warrior. He knows that Brian tells himself he is waiting for the right girl. He knows that Ragnhild believes that their snarling sons will look after each other, that their love for her will conquer their pride, their ambition.

He watches the weave of other people's lies and yet cannot untangle his own. He looks for them, his hidden lies. He turns on his memory suddenly, trying to surprise it, to catch it unawares, so that it will yield its secrets without flattering its only audience.

Here, then, is what he thinks is true: he did try, but not hard enough. He had other concerns; she is the wrong woman in the wrong skin.

She has never had any sense of what he did, no notion of his machinations, political or military. And he has never tried hard enough to teach her, even as he grew frustrated by her lack of foresight. Slowly, sentence by sentence, word by word, they have stopped talking of anything much. She saves her words for God, with a growing and desperate fervour. A zeal fed by loneliness, perhaps, the poor soul.

He saves his words for his men. Mostly, he is silent.

He has found space enough, on occasion, to lust after her. They have met, sometimes, in frenzied couplings; usually prompted by another man's appraisal of her. She was good-looking, after all. Blonde and pink and curving in all the right places. They have been quite remarkably fecund together. He barely had to touch her for her belly to swell.

He can pity her, too. Pity her the absence of that flooding love that he has known elsewhere. But most of all, when he notices her at all, it is with a consuming irritation. He flinches when she talks, feels the prickles of rage crawling about his skin like spiders. It is not her fault that the way she speaks, with its high-pitched rounded-out vowels, clenches his stomach. Not her fault that her laugh, which cascades with a self-conscious prettiness, makes his hands ball into tight fists. It is not her fault that she is an essentially humourless creature who laughs at wit only when she sees others laughing. It is not her fault that she bears children so easily, with a wide-hipped, slick rushing that leaves Somerled feeling irrationally anticlimactic. It is not her fault that when he meets her tired eyes over the squirming lightness of each new baby, he feels . . . nothing.

It is not her fault that she is not Eimhear.

~ ~ ~

Eimhear. Each year, Gillecolm goes to spend a few weeks with her and little Sigrdrifa on the Island of Women. Let the boy be cosseted by women sometimes, thinks Somerled. He gets little enough of it from his stepmother. She wears her resentment of him openly. He gets the place farthest from the fire. He gets the milk that is on the turn, meat that is more gristle than flesh.

Somerled has tried to counter her little barbs, but there is a silence, too, between him and his son. Gillecolm's utter haplessness with a sword or axe is the problem. His failure in this one great and necessary skill has put up a barrier between Somerled and his son. When not with the other boys his age, Gillecolm spends his time with Padeen, with Aed. When Somerled comes near, the boy flinches, as if expecting another homily on the use of weapons, or the duties of a warrior. Somerled has stopped trying to tackle the boy over it. He stopped, in fact, as soon as Gillecolm grew to eye level with him; but the distance and the flinching linger.

Each year, as he sets off for his mother's place with the bard at his side, he springs aboard with a lightness, an infectious happiness, that has jaded oarsmen grinning in their seats. Each year, Somerled watches him go, torn and made harsh in his goodbyes by something he refuses to name as envy.

Each year, the bard returns with the boy and a message from Eimhear. Just one line. Each one a marking of time, like the first call of the cuckoo. Each one a sear on Somerled's scalded heart.

My knees are like an oarsman's hands from all the praying.

Do you think God is as bored of hearing all these fucking hymns as I am of singing them?

Can you drown in boredom?

1153

SOMERLED

S omerled watches the man crumple into an ornate chair. He is
too small for it; his fingers flutter nervously on the gilt-edged
rests. The man does not know where to look, and fixes his horrified
gaze at some mid-point on the ceiling. It is doubtless higher, more
ornate than any he has seen. Who knew that stone could arch
and bend like this? Who knew that men could walk inside without
crouching, with eyes unclogged by peat smoke? Who knew that a
man could be so wretched with embarrassment that his old body
twists and coils of its own volition?

The white-haired man kneeling clicks his tongue, irritated.
'Hold still,' he whispers sharply. As an afterthought: 'My child.'
The hall is hot; the great fire stoked continually by a boy so that
even the corners are warm. The smell of pigs and crusted dirt rolls
off the seated man in the heat. Sweat betrays him; shameful beads
on his forehead.

Somerled feels light-headed. He and his small band have just
walked into the castle, out of an unyielding drizzle. The dry and the
fire set their wet wool cloaks to steam, and they stand, a little foolishly,
amidst the white puffs. Water pools in the hollows of the rushes
between their feet; it drips off the straggling ends of their beards.

The room is full of crisp, dry men. Some thirty hangers-on, standing in a respectful semicircle around the tableau at the front, where the grimy, rag-clad beggar offers his feet to a king. A low chatter in French behind them; a slow intonation in Latin from a priest beside them. The priest bends his tonsured head, and Somerled can see the dried scab of a shaving cut. A hole in his hair like a reverse halo. Not like the old way of the high shaven forehead. And what was wrong with the old ways?

He wriggles his damp feet in his boots, impatient to peel them off and set his pulpy skin to dry. But first, this absurdity.

'The water, your majesty.' A page, kneeling by the white-haired King David, pours the water into a bowl.

'Your feet,' says the king to the twisting man in the chair.

'My feet?' he says stupidly.

The king snaps a glance across the page's head to one of his retainers, who shifts his weight and slides his eyes to the side, fixing, by chance or design, on the mumbling priest.

'How,' hisses the king, in a voice rich with unuttered expletives, 'am I supposed to wash your feet if you don't put them in the water?'

The man nods. The misery rolls off him. Somerled feels an answering sympathy for the beggar as he dips his feet gingerly into the bowl. He gasps, and pulls them back. The king looks up, and the man's feet fall quickly back into the water with a violence that splashes the liquid over the sides of the bowl and on to the king's fur-lined cloak.

Somerled looks across to the retainer, clearly the man who fished this particular beggar from the town's sewers. He sees the man's eyes close, and his lips whisper a silent appeal.

The beggar's feet are not as foul as you would expect. Either the king's men wash them first, or they line them up, the poor bastards, and choose the least revolting. Still, perhaps he will get a meal from it.

Slowly, the feet are washed. The beggar, at a sign from the king, pulls them out of the bowl and places them on a cloth resting on the king's bended knees. Slowly, and with studied care, the toes are dried. Still the look of acute misery sits on the man's face. Sigrdrifa, his mother, would have laughed herself to tears at this tableau, thinks Somerled.

The beggar wriggles, earning a tut from the kneeling king.

'Poor bastard's ticklish,' Somerled hears Aed whisper to Gillecolm. The boy has the good sense at least to stifle his laugh. Somerled checks himself. Not a boy any longer; a man in his prime.

At last the ordeal is over. A priest comes forward to bless the man and the king. The room claps. It is pie-stuffed with retainers, oozing sycophancy. Somerled and his band join with them politely. The beggar smiles nervously into the crowd, as if the applause is for him.

David stands without a sound, but he pushes himself upright, hands on knees. Sixty-four, thinks Somerled. Twenty years on me. Will I make it to such an age? he asks himself. Christ, I hope not.

David turns and sees Somerled. He pauses for a heartbeat, and Somerled finds that he is holding his breath. He breathes out, irritated with himself. Around them, eyes watch, waiting for the moment of judgement, the exact calibration of greeting that will show them how much respect is due to this big, shaggy barbarian from the west.

'Lord Somerled,' says King David, and walks forward, pulling him out of a bow and clasping arms, wrist upon wrist. Somerled feels the tension in his band slacken, feels the mental rubbing of hands as they calculate the better rooms, better drink and better women that will likely come their way now.

'Your majesty,' he says, looking straight back into the appraising brown eyes. Could he hazard a joke about his feet needing a bit of a scrub? No, perhaps not. Behind the king he sees the beggar being ushered out of a side door, his clean feet sinking into the rushes and grime of the castle floor.

The king looks old, and he looks tired. He seems to have shrunk since Somerled last saw him, his neck sinking into his body and his shoulders rounding. The eyes are sharp in the furrowed face. A face carved by irritation into granite lines. He wears his grief like a breastplate, visibly weighing on him.

It is more than a year now since the death of Henry, the old man's only son and his heir. Somerled feels the bounce in his toes as he thinks of his own sons. Dugald, the eldest by Ragnhild, is fourteen now, and eager to row with the warriors. A good boy. Taciturn, strong. Ranald, the twelve-year-old, will be blooded on his father's return. Angus is just eleven, but tries to seem older. A puzzle, that fierce, competitive child. Olaf, the youngest, is still happy jumping waves. Bethoc is too pious, like her mother. At her age she should be sighing after the warriors, not whipping herself into divine frenzies. None of them smile much, Ragnhild's children, now he thinks of it. The boys can handle a sword, though, not like Gillecolm.

Gillecolm. The blasted boy never *stops* smiling. A smile like his mother. Did she smile so often, so provokingly? At sea, with his legs spread in the easy, rolling way he has and the wind catching his hair and the spray shining his face, Gillecolm wears a smile so wide it will pull the gods' wrath on them all. A smile so fierce it will tear through the clouds and fall upon heaven as a challenge: do your worst, do what you will; this soul is beyond your malice.

Yet he is twenty-three now, not a boy. He should put away his smiles and learn how to hold a sword like a Christian. God's blood, but he is hopeless in a fight. He's only alive because Aed, the ageing champion, sticks to him limpet-tight, cutting down his opponents and dodging the boy's own clumsy, ineffectual hacks.

All Somerled's glee at beating David in the matter of sons leaks away, and a familiar irritation settles on him. What kind of lord's son holds his sword like a virgin on her wedding night?

David, meanwhile, has ushered forward a pale, slight boy. Not yet shaving. Eleven, perhaps?

'This, Lord Somerled, is my heir, Malcolm. My grandson. Returned from a tour of the kingdom.'

The boy's eyes widen. He looks as if it is the first time he has heard himself spoken of as David's heir. It is the first time Somerled has heard it from the old man's lips. The maiden, they call the boy. And is there not a womanish cast to his handsome face? No surprise that he will be king. The old bastard has introduced every English notion going, stuffing his court with French knights and English monks and lawyers. Why would he not now insist on their way of doing this: the throne passing down through the eldest in the male line, no matter if the male line is worthy. Or even bearded.

Malcolm is thin and pale and terrified. The hand gripping his shoulder is white at the knuckles, and the boy looks as if he would shy away if he could. Lord, thinks Somerled. The old man had better last a few years yet – this boy needs time.

Somerled sits at the feast and imagines himself young. It becomes more of an effort with each passing year. He watches the shadows dance on the wall of the king's hall, and wills them to shape themselves into a boy-shaped wraith. Are you pleased? he asks the shadow. Do you know me? Do you know who I am?

The sound of a harp breaks his spell. The shadow melts into a mocking twist of shapes. The king's bard is standing to sing. A song from the Gaelic lands, in honour of the guests. With the first chords Somerled feels his stomach tighten, feels the churning helplessness of being trapped. It is the Lay of Deirdre. He sees Aed register it, and look anxiously towards him. The song has been banned in Somerled's presence, in his own halls. Visiting bards are taken to one side, whispered into submission.

Why? they ask.

Because he doesn't like it.

Why?

What's it to you? It's enough to know that he won't have it. Try crossing Somerled, stranger. See where it gets you.

So they sing him different songs, and thank the bardic gods for the warning, as they watch his grim face and imagine that cold eye turning on them in anger.

Somerled knows that he terrifies men. It is useful. He catches sight of himself, sometimes, in mirrors, in rare calm waters. A stranger looks back. A glowering man. A man held taut between contempt and rage. A man who has never turned handstands in a cold sea to make a girl laugh, who could never even conceive that such an act was possible.

He is like a mussel in a tapped shell. Unreachable.

And now here, in this court, where he cannot dictate the bard's choices, he will have to listen to it. Jesus, Lord. Let me be no man's vassal. I cannot bear this.

Worse, the bard knows his trade. He is clear and beautiful of tone. The French knights, even though his words are a jumble, are as rapt as the rest as he sings of all the beauty of the world and how it came to rest in one woman, Deirdre.

The bard sings as if it were true. As if all the beauty of the world was not Somerled's own, once; held in his hands as he cupped his lover's face with oar-calloused palms.

Somerled has the twofold agony of remembering how she loved this song, and how they were both wrong about its moral. How they failed to understand its portents. What use a seeing eye? Men choose blindness. It is easier that way.

Even the music failed to irritate her, tone deaf as she was. The dear one. She followed the poetry of the words. He remembers her eyes glinting in the firelight, and how she would turn to him, unfailingly, as the bard sang of Deirdre's enchanted season with Naoise, her beloved, on the shores of Loch Etive. She would throw him a secret smile as the bard built Deirdre a bower above a waterfall. There on a flat rock big enough for two, she could sit with her beloved and listen to the water's ripple, watching the moon shine in silver promises on the loch.

Jesus, it is hot in this hall. He sweats, shifts his slick arse on the bench, trying to get comfortable. Aed is trying not to look at him. The big man's fingers tap out the beat on his thigh.

They thought, Somerled and his lover, that the song foreshadowed them. That it spoke across the centuries to their bower on the hillside, to the nights they spent, the two of them, entwined in each other while the business of life continued far below them in the bustling hall.

They thought it was their song, and so it turned out to be.

The bard is ratcheting it up now, introducing the serpent into paradise. Deirdre's dream foretells the doom: how Naoise and his two loyal brothers will end their tale. Small portents of impending grief sidle into their loving hearts.

At last, the spurned King Conor, who loves Deirdre, comes for the brothers. A druid calls a flood, and the three brothers are caught, neck deep in the waters. They beg that their heads should be cleft from their necks in one stroke.

Around Somerled, the warriors are moved. Gillecolm has never heard the tale sung, banned as it is from his father's hall. No. That's not right. He heard it there when it was her hall too. Probably sat on her lap, curling her long hair around his fingers, skin against skin. Pushed his face into her neck to breathe her in, as children do to their mothers. And their mothers let themselves be breathed in

The boy is openly crying, and Somerled wants to wipe the tears. He wants to slap the boy for crying. But his own miserable soul needs some attention. For this is the bit he hates most. The bit where Deirdre has the courage to seek her lover's head, to clean it and to kiss the staring eyes. The strength to leap down into his grave and die with him, clutching his lifeless body to her.

Jesus, why am I so base? Somerled cries the question silently into the bottom of his cup. Why so cowardly? Why so alive?

The music falls to its end. Silence in its wake like an offering. Somerled is caught in this flood of wretchedness, of a self-loathing so profound it makes him clasp the knife in his palm tight enough to cut. He sees Gillecolm turn to him, a smile beginning to form on his tear-tracked face.

'Why must you insist on shaming me?' hisses Somerled. The words cling to the boy like leeches. Somerled watches the colour bleed from his son's face and closes his fist tighter around the blade. The blood drips, shocking and red, on to the king's white tablecloth.

He tries to remember. Her skinny legs waving above the water. Her serious face watching him, ethereal somehow, like a selkie. No. That's not right. He shakes his head, trying to get it straight.

Around him, the business of making camp. The galley beached, the early summer sun dwindling to a polished gold.

Out in the Sound, a fin breaks above the calm waters. A small fin in a great grey back that catches the late sun on its shining surface and throws its sheen back to the watching men on the shore. Late May. Minke whales, perhaps. He turns away, back to his thoughts, noting Gillecolm's cry and his scamper down to the rocky edge of the sea. Somerled sees the delight on his son's face. Like his mother. She loved a whale. Why does that thought not spark a rush of love? Why only this cold irritation?

He drinks, absently. Imagining her pressed against the heather, watching the clouds. She would have run down to the sea to watch the whale. Would she not?

Has he remembered her right? He knows that some of it must be true. He has told himself the stories of her again and again, and they are fixed in his head. Like the North Star.

But the words are brittle things. He can't smell her, or taste her. He can't hear the exact quality of her laugh. He tells himself it was beautiful. He tells himself *she* was beautiful. But her image is constructed of words, not flesh. She is pieced together by his cold memory.

And here is the question. Was he really happy then, or is he dreaming it? Is he using her memory, as a proxy for a joyous soul? Can he blame his questing, unsettled nature on her? Can he shift the burden of his sour life on to her lost shoulders? Perhaps he is just made this way. Perhaps his misery is of his own making. Not hers.

Or perhaps she really was a shining joy. Perhaps it is true that when she was lost, he was lost. There was a boy who dangled his feet in rivers, and lay still to watch the otters play. There was a boy who turned handstands in freezing seas. He existed once. Didn't he?

She wasn't mystical, nor mythical. She bled monthly, and each time railed against it with absurd pointlessness. She was irritable sometimes. She crumbled a little more each year he knew her with the drudgery of eking a life under that wide, forbidding sky. She snapped and raged at small irritations. Sometimes they grew so taut with each other that breaking seemed the only fate. But other times, other times . . . Oh my Lord. Oh Lord, you were witness to that joy. You saw. He does not dream it. He does not pull phantoms from his hopeful youth, and call them her name. Does he?

They bustle around him. He is all stillness, and he knows that it unsettles them. Let them be unsettled, the bastards. He is the lord here.

Fires are made and tended. Food is shared. The low hum of chatter. Around him, a high wall of silence. Respect and deference. He could have it no other way. And yet. Yet. He thinks about calling Aed over, but he sees the big man talking to Gillecolm. He leaves them.

But now, something new. Round the headland comes a galley, fighting hard against the winds. It pulls in, close to shore. Somerled recognizes the big man standing in the stern – one of the king's men. Left behind in the court only days before. The galley skims as close as it dares, and the big man mounts the galley's side, one arm holding the backstay, leaning out over the oars' surging.

'The king is dead,' he shouts. 'The king is dead.'

Somerled ignores the buzzing behind him. Like bees in a poked hive.

'When?'

'Two days after you left him, Lord Somerled. Malcolm is to be crowned. I am sent to spread the word. Spread it, Somerled. Malcolm is our king.'

Somerled waved the galley off, his face impassive.

'Malcolm the Maiden?' says Aed, coming up behind him. He moves quietly, for a big man. It never fails to surprise Somerled, after all these years.

'We shall see,' said Somerled. Beside him, the big man grins.

1153

SOMERLED

A curragh pulls alongside as they sweep towards home with stretched oars and aching backs. Somerled leans over to see his sons looking up at him from the boat. The sun is behind him, and they have to squint. The four of them are crammed in. Olaf, the littlest, grabs a rope thrown by Somerled's pilot, and fastens it to the curragh. Dugald, the eldest, snaps an order from the tiller, and Ranald pulls down the heavy sail.

Angus leaps aboard, leaving the curragh rocking violently behind him.

'Did you hear, Father? About King David.'

'We did.'

Angus deflates a little at this. His brothers clamber up the side to stand with him. Olaf runs to Gillecolm, jumping up at him, wrapping his skinny legs around the young man's waist. The older boys ignore their brother, looking at their father intently.

'Well?' says Dugald, at last.

'Well what, boys? We are hungry and tired, and want to get home.'

Somerled thinks of teasing them, but looks at their shining fierce faces and decides against it.

'Lord help us,' he says, tetchy. 'Would I tell you my plans before they are made? We have your cousins to think of. Mael Coluim and Domhnall.'

'They have the same right as the Maiden,' says Angus.

'King David believes in primogeniture,' says Dugald.

'And are we Normans?' Ranald turns, facing his older brother, bristling. 'Why should it be the elder? It should be the best.'

'What if the elder is the best?' says Dugald.

Their squabbling is grating on him. He wants to savour this moment, the first sight of home. His first pulse-quickening view of the black rocks falling away into the sea, of the hall behind that he helped to build, of the hills where he has roamed and hunted. Where he loved.

Wordlessly, he picks Dugald up. The boy is nearly as big as him now; he couldn't manage it without the aid of surprise. He tips him backwards over the side of the boat. Ranald next, who flails a little. They float, spluttering and shocked, in the long, slow swell. It must be cold, thinks Somerled. It will force them awake.

'Let's see, then,' he says. 'Swim home. The first to touch the door shall be the first among you.'

'Lord Somerled,' says Aed behind him, his voice oddly formal.

He almost regrets it then. But the boys are off, swimming with wild, violent strokes towards the hall. Something rushes by him, a small body. Angus jumps on to the low side of the galley and flings himself at the water in a graceful arc, hovering above the water like a gull spying a herring. In he glides, with barely a ripple.

The band rest on their oars. They can't row forward anyway, churning the water with those slight bodies there. The drama grips them. A gasp as an arm grabs a handful of hair and pushes it down, under the spumy waves. He hears the whispers of bets being placed, wagers laid.

'Let me go after them in the curragh,' Aed whispers behind him. 'Stop this.'

'Too late,' says Somerled. His heart is pumping. 'Would you baby them, Aed? They have a kingdom to carry between them.'

'What if they kill each other?'

It looks violent out there in the water. They twist into each other, the rippling bodies. They pull each other back, and drag each other under. They could be playful dolphins. They are not playing.

'They won't.' But suddenly he is not sure. He grips the forestay fiercely, watching this thing that he has created. Admiring their ambition. Regretting it.

'Father,' says Gillecolm. Somerled can't bear his anguish. Olaf's face is buried in his brother's neck.

'Stop your whining. All right, then.' He nods at the pilot. 'Bring her in. Slow. Half-strokes. Back up on my call.'

They creep behind the boys, gliding slowly across the water.

The women and the warriors left behind have come outside, watching the galley come in. He sees a woman run to the water's edge. Ragnhild, his wife. He can tell her by her bulk, the awkward judder of her body as it wobbles in the unexpected motion. He will pay for this later in cold silences and muttered complaints. No matter; he has learned to think round her chatter and her silence alike.

The boys in the water have separated now. Dugald is the fastest. He's making for the jetty. Angus trails behind him. Ranald is taking the shorter route, towards the black rocks at the base of the hall. It will be fiercely hard to climb out there, with this swell rushing and sucking the jagged, sharp stone. He reaches the rocks at the same time as Dugald grabs hold of the smooth wall of the jetty.

Dugald pulls himself out with ease, Angus coming in behind him. Ranald has more difficulty, but he's nearer the hall. On land, they race, and it seems to the men on the boat that the older two reach the door at the same time, pounding its wood before sinking into the grass. Even from here, they can see that Ranald is in a bad way. His torso streams with salt water and blood. He has cut himself ragged on the sharp edges of the rock, the swell crushing him, dragging him along the barnacles and the sharp limpet shells.

Angus sits on the end of the jetty, trying not to cry. 'It's not fair,' he shouts, as the galley comes alongside. 'Their arms are longer.'

Somerled runs towards the boys, and stops short, shy suddenly, as they turn and look at him with fierce eyes. Behind him, he can hear Angus's plaintive cry. 'It's not fair.'

Over their heads their mother looks at him blankly. A fat, grey-haired stranger. Ranald's blood, diluted with seawater and her own tears, smears her white cheek.

He is furious at their collective silent reproach. It was the boys' choice to rise to his challenge. Their choice. He pushes past them, raging now, into the darkness of his hall.

Ragnhild

I wipe the blood from my son's skin. The bowl is red with it. He tries not to cry as the cloth presses against the scratches. I want to cry for him, but I bite my lip to hold it in.

They sit close to the fire, warming themselves, blankets thrown over bare skin. I want to move among them, my sons, and press my nose into their salty skin. To smell them, and weep over them, and hold them until their bones crack.

I do not. Boys do not need their mother's love. They need her ferocity. Boys need to be told to get up when they fall; to stop weeping when they cry; to hold their chin high and their shoulders square. What use is such tearful tenderness to them? So I fold it inside this stranger's fleshy body.

Bethoc brings more blankets. She stops first at Ranald, the one she likes best, though no one else can get close to him.

'Stop slouching, girl.' I snap at her and watch her flinch. She pulls herself up, however. She is awkward with her changing shape, and hunches over her shoulders to disguise her new breasts. I remember my mother's voice. Straighten your back, slither your hips, bite your lips, pinch your cheeks. Cast your eyes down, flick them up. Smile, don't smile. Be beautiful. It is all you have. It is your currency, your hack silver.

I never saw her again before she died. They are lucky to have me, these children. I will prepare them.

A small voice in my head mutinies. It did not work for you.

I round on it fiercely, pushing myself upright from the stool and pacing the room. What dent could I make on a heart that was already promised? Did my father know, when he sent me here? Did he care?

Gillecolm enters, carrying little Olaf on his shoulders.

'Mother,' shouts Olaf happily. 'There was a race, did you see it?'

'Shh, little man,' says Gillecolm. I wind my fingers into my skirt, to keep from striking him. God curse his tact, his rueful smile, his easy ruffling of Dugald's wet hair.

'I tried to stop it,' he said.

'Not hard enough.'

'Do you think he meant it?' asks Angus, his face tear-streaked.

'Meant what?' I ask Gillecolm the question and his face darkens.

'No matter.'

'Tell me. Dugald?'

Dugald's newly broken voice cuts past Gillecolm. 'He said that the first to the castle would be his heir.'

'I was first,' says Ranald.

'Liar. I was first.'

They bristle at each other. Gillecolm moves between them. 'Easy. I don't think he meant it. He is in a strange mood. The death of David . . .'

He trails off, looking at me apologetically. I turn away.

The boys are still fighting over who was first, and Gillecolm tries again to calm them.

Dugald spits at him. 'You were not even in the race. And you a bastard.'

Gillecolm meets the barb with that easy smile, and I hate him anew. I like to see my sons' spears find their targets.

'Aye,' says Gillecolm. 'You boys are welcome to fight over it. Just let me have a ship, whichever of you wins, and I'll be happy.' In another man it would be a lie, I think, as he wanders off whistling. To find Sigurd's daughter, I expect, who gazes after him like a seal puppy at a culling club.

The boys simmer down after he leaves. I feed them and clothe them. Bethoc bustles between them with pitchers and platters.

We sit by the fire for a while, at peace. Somerled is out there somewhere, seeing to the docking and to his men. I relish the last of the time without him.

'Tell us a story, Mother,' says little Olaf.

'Which one, my princeling?'

'The one where you and Father met.'

I tell them. I tell them how he saw me at a feast and fell madly in love. I tell them how my father would not let me go. I tell them how Somerled took my father and his warriors out on his galley and deliberately scuttled it in mid-channel, drawing out a great iron pin from its hull. My father could not swim. Let me marry your daughter, said Somerled, or I will let you drown. So my father was tricked and defeated, and I married the prince.

Olaf sighs happily at the end of the story, as he always does. I see Dugald watching me over his cup, with eyes so adult, so scathing, that my stomach lurches. I look away and into the fire, watching the leaping flames in silence.

SOMERLED

I t comes the next day, the news. Driving all other thoughts before it like a winter storm. King Olaf of Man is dead. His father-in-law. The man who held the power in the Irish Sea. The man who sat in his stronghold like a wizened sea-spider, his commands strung across the sea, passed from headland to bay, across the waves and through the wind. The man at the centre of it all, his body bent and crouching, his mind thrumming, seething with strategies and plans.

Gone. It is the type of news to suck the air from their discourse. A pause, where speculation and boasting should be.

Olaf's nephews, exiled, came home and struck the old man down. They came under a promise of repentance and peace, and splattered his brains across his own table.

'Death is stalking lords this season,' says Somerled to Aed, later that night. They listen to Ragnhild's quiet sobbing creeping through the hall.

'David, then Olaf.'

Somerled nods. 'East and west of us. Hard bastards, but stable. Now what? Stormy times, Aed.'

'They say that King Stephen's son and heir is ill down south. Like to die,' says Aed. 'Then it will be coming at us from three sides.'

The hall is quiet; huddles of men drink softly. Eyes turn to Somerled, as if he will wear his thoughts on his brow. They sit, the lord and his champion, nearest the fire, their heads inclined to each other. Easy with one another.

'Ragnhild thinks I should avenge him,' says Somerled.

'His son is in Norway?'

'Godred, yes. A snake of a man. Perhaps I should. Olaf was my father-in-law.'

'But not a friend, Somerled.'

'Pah. Friends are for boys. Children.'

Aed grins at him through his great shaggy beard. Somerled feels awash with affection for him.

'Fool,' he says. 'You know my meaning.'

Aed smiles, looking into the fire's sparkling heart.

'Last night, Somerled, I had a dream. I was a fisherman. Do you think of the other lives we might have led? Do you think of all those moments that spin on a sword's arc, or a woman's smile, or a vicious sea?'

'You sound old.'

'I am old. I creak when I fart.'

'You never stop creaking, man.'

'The Manxmen, then. What will you do?'

'I think I will wait. When I was young, I thought waiting was cowardice. Yet sometimes . . .'

Aed nods. 'The nephews have no chance. No support, no backing. Godred will return.'

'Aye, with a Norwegian army at his back. No. Let this play out, I think, like a bard's lay. There can only be a tragic end.'

Aed turns towards him, with that familiar sharpness strangers do not suspect him of. 'A tragic end for whom, Lord Somerled?

~ ~ ~

He talks to Ragnhild of her brother Godred. The news has come that he is sailing back to reclaim his father's land from the murderous nephews. She straightens from her work, putting down the skeins of wool with careful hands.

'He is my brother. I should not talk ill of him.'

'And I am your husband. You should talk the truth to me.'

'Really?' She looks at him, and he feels a familiar unease. Sometimes, when she arches her brows at him, he feels as if he is standing, disorientated, on a foggy clifftop. The disquiet is hard to pin down. He thinks, in the pause, that it springs from his underestimation of her. He is so accustomed to seeing only the surface. The wrinkled and crêped skin of her face. The fat that clings to the lithe body of his memory. Sometimes he watches her lumber from sitting with an air of puzzlement that she is not springing. She looks down with astonishment at her own thick thighs, her stranger's stomach.

Sometimes, as now, she regards him with a face that could be amused, or could be contemptuous; he doesn't know. It is sad that he cannot read her, he thinks. Sadder still how little he really cares.

'Godred,' she says slowly, as if to a foreigner, 'is devil-spawned. Godred is cruel. Godred is hard and vicious, like a blade turned for evil. Is that what you want to hear?'

He sends letters to his friends in Man. Thorfinn Ottarson and others. Not pointed letters. Just to remind them he is there. He mentions Dugald, Olaf's grandson, oh so casually. How strong he is, for a boy. How accomplished. He does what he can imagine Olaf doing – he nudges, hints, prepares.

But first, the Maiden.

~ ~ ~

The rebellion is fierce, pulsing. They push the Normans and the men of Alba back, fighting the way they do best. Small wars on the fringes. Lightning raids. Vicious, bloody little affrays.

They choose ground that wrong-foots the Norman horses. Boggy, heathery ground. Vertiginous slopes that leave them skittery and vulnerable. They aim for the beasts, for their bellies and their legs. On foot, the Normans are more easily taken; great lumbering metal men who stand, feet planted wide in the heather, as Somerled's men dance round them like nimble wolves, sharp-toothed spears seeking out the holes, the weak links in the chain. Once the skin is nicked, they sink slowly, these metal men, bleeding to death in their own metal coffins.

Sometimes, when they do not have time to strip the bodies, they leave them there on the hillside. Somerled imagines them slowly rusting from the outside in, confusing the scavengers, who love a battlefield. The smell of blood and ruptured skin and emptied, shit-scared bowels. Yet the wolves' teeth will scrape on the metal; the birds' talons screech across the links.

~ ~ ~

His nephews are tall, violent boys. They believe they have as good a right to Alba as the Maiden. They are older than their cousins, war-tested. In the evenings, they talk long and hard about their birthright until it is a thing unquestioned – a shiny, bright truth that must be fought and died for.

Gillecolm hates this war. Hates being inland. He was born with salt in his veins, that boy. There is something else troubling him.

He has lost his sparkle. Somerled takes time to notice. He is so used to the boy's laugh grating at him when he is trying to think that its absence is a single discordant note at first. It sets him on edge and he doesn't know why. It sends him snapping for extra scouts, more lookouts.

There it is at last, made obvious. The boy sits at a fire, surrounded by his shield brothers, their boasts and banter a constant thrum, and his face alone still and quiet, lost in staring at the flames.

Somerled wants to ask him what is wrong. He wants to put an arm across the boy's shoulders, whisper in his freckled ear, 'What ails you, my son, my boy?'

He rises from the fireside, the bones in his legs crackling with effort, the muscles tight. His face is warm and red from the fire, but standing it catches a breeze, which cools him down and makes him pause.

He looks across again, his face cast in the shadow of distance from the flames. He watches his boy's misery and hugs it to himself. Silent.

~ ~ ~

There is a pause between battles. A breathing time. They make camp by a loch. They comb out their long, matted hair and see to their kit.

He finds Gillecolm lying on the grass at the edge of the water. The boy is holding a flower, studying it. Somerled stands, for a space, watching him. The boy looks like him, everyone says it. But Somerled can only see Gillecolm's mother. He feels a great rush of tenderness.

Gillecolm turns, a smile on his face. When he sees Somerled, the smile fixes, and he jumps to his feet, the flower hanging limply at his side.

'Sit down, boy,' says Somerled, and although he means it to

be an invitation, it spins on his tongue to become a command. Gillecolm sits, squinting up at him, the sun in his eyes.

'They were your grandmother's favourites,' he says, easing himself down next to the boy. He should not call him a boy, he supposes. How old is he now? In his twenties anyway.

'Really? I was looking closely. Do you ever think, Father, that we don't look hard enough at the small things?'

'I have big enough things to look at,' says Somerled, leaning back on his elbows. It's the first warm day of the year. The first day you can feel the sun etching itself on to your skin. He raises his head to it, sighing a little.

They are quiet for a while. Gillecolm stares into the depths of the pink flower, past the soft petals and into its heart. Somerled thinks of the campaign to come. He thinks of the orders he must give. He remembers, suddenly, that he has forgotten to check that the salted meat supplies are holding up.

'Look, Father.' Gillecolm grips his arm. Overhead, an eagle hangs in the still air. Impossibly large, its feathers are muddied and bedraggled, but it soars above them with a careless grace. Beside him Gillecolm is holding his breath, the bird's beauty reflected in his rapturous face.

Somerled smiles, feeling his son's hand gripping his arm, watching the eagle's imperious flight. Gillecolm drops his hand, the eagle moves on and there is a distance between them again.

'It's about Deirdre,' says Somerled.

The boy turns to look at him.

'Sigurd's daughter,' says Somerled.

'I know who she is.'

'Be civil, boy. Of course you know who she is. You're barely able to go five minutes without a hand on her arse. Is she why you are moping about the place like a calf who's lost the teat?'

Gillecolm's face sets rigid. He looks away, towards the sea. 'We love each other,' he says.

'Well. And that is fine. I will talk to Sigurd. Smooth it all out. A handfasting, and if there are children, we will make sure they are cared for.'

'I want to marry her.'

'Marry her? Be serious. She is the daughter of a thrall.'

'I love her.'

Somerled snorts. 'Did I say you couldn't? But you are not to marry her. I have other plans.'

'But what of *my* plans?'

'What of them? You are my son, and you will marry for the family.'

'I am a bastard.'

'You are my bastard.'

Gillecolm stands, brushing the grass and mud from him.

'And if I will not?' he says, looking down on Somerled.

'Everything you have comes from me.'

'And yet everything I am disappoints you.'

Somerled begins to deny it, but he looks into his son's face and falters. 'Not everything,' he says.

Gillecolm smiles, suddenly absolving him. 'So who is it you want me to marry?'

'The chief of the Russ of Mull. One of his girls.'

'Does she have the family nose?'

Somerled laughs. 'And if she does?'

Gillecolm crouches on his heels beside his father. He looks earnestly at him. 'It is a question of heart,' he says.

'Don't be a child. It is a question of policy. Dugald will put his heart where I tell him.'

'He has a heart, does he? I didn't know.'

Somerled finds himself laughing again, but the boy's next question chokes it off, slides the smile into a frown. 'Father? Was it policy that made you put my mother aside? For Ragnhild?'

Somerled pauses.

'Did you ever ask your mother?'

'No. She was so unhappy, so lost. I just wanted to make her smile. I am asking you. Policy or something else?'

He looks to the heavens as if for guidance. Tell the boy the truth? Let him, now that he is a man, carry some of the guilt? Or lie, and accept his hatred?

He looks at his son, at the tilt of his head that conjures his mother, at the hair that could be cut from her own. 'Policy? Yes,' he says, and watches the boy's face twist with anger. 'I loved her . . .' he begins to say, but Gillecolm is standing and walking away, the flower crumpling in his folded fist.

Gillecolm stops and turns back, the low sun behind him. 'Were you always like this?' he says, his voice cracking. 'Were you ever young?'

eimhear

News reaches us even here, on this little crumb, this boil on the arse of Mull. We are the afterthought to Iona, the pause at the end of the song.

Olaf of Man is dead. The man who sat on his island throne, lifted a finger in command and ruined my life. What should I feel? The laments drift over the water from Iona. Those who understand the music sigh and wilt with the song. I just shrug and spread manure.

Sigrdrifa skips to me across the heather. She is too old for skipping. We left home when she was five, and she is twenty now. The chattering, adventurous child is a young woman. She is self-contained now, quiet. There is some essential relationship with the hollering ball of mischief she once was, but it is hard to discern.

'Olaf dead, Mother,' she says, flopping next to me on the heather. 'Lord, think of it.'

She hands me an oatcake, and we munch companionably for a while, looking across to the strand of pure white sand on Iona's shore.

'Father Padeen sent me a book. All of my own. He was writing to his friend in Canterbury, who sent it to him. He has read it and sent it on to me. Gil told him I was desperate for new things to read.'

She shows it to me, and we marvel at it.

'Read it to me,' I say.

'Lord, I will try. But it must be translated from the Latin, you know, and I am not as fluent as I should be. It is a tract by a fellow called Seneca.'

'I know the name, child. Father Padeen talked of him. He told me that translations of the man were setting Chartres and Canterbury by the ears.'

'He was exiled to an island too. Did you know that?'

'I did not!'

She smiles at me, and we bend our heads again to look at the book. We are transfixed by the marvel of it. The words of a man, a thousand years ago, held in our hands like a jewel.

She hacks at it slowly, piecing out the Latin like a puzzle. It is about the briefness of life. Even the short time we have rushes by, says this philosopher, from the mouth of my daughter, whose grown-upness is a constant, breathtaking source of surprise. All but the very few, he says, find out how to live at the end, just when they are ready to die.

You squander time, he says, as if there is a full and abundant supply. You have all the fears of mortals and the desires of immortals.

Sigrdrifa stops translating. She looks at me to find that I am crying. I never cry.

'Mother, what is it?'

'I am sorry, child. It is a miracle, that is all. The miracle that this man sat in Rome a thousand years ago and wrote these words, and I sit on this rock and listen to them, and we are all connected and unconnected, and the thing is a puzzle and a glory.'

She nods, and takes hold of my hand to kiss it.

It is truth, or a version of truth, that I have told her.

I am thinking too of the time we are squandering, here on this island. The wasteful, wanton slide of minutes, hours. The slow attrition of body and spirit in this waste, waste of a life.

1155

SOMERLED

It started with so much promise. But three years in, the rebellion grinds to a halt. They have won some land, sacked some halls, made themselves a little older, a little richer. But the Maiden clings on. They have galvanized what little support he has, failed to gather sufficient momentum, win new men.

His nephews are like dogs throwing themselves on a locked door, until even they seem more bruised than angry. At last, in a small, half-arsed raid near England, Domhnall, the younger, is captured.

Somerled is, he finds, a little relieved. It gives him an excuse to break it off. He can see that they will not win the great prize. Alba will not fall. He needs more men, more support. A host.

Sanguine, he sends men to treat with the Maiden. Padeen and Brian lead the party. The boy agrees to spare Domhnall's life, to leave him locked away with his father, who has been imprisoned for twenty years now. Twenty years. Somerled shudders to think of it. His sister has been allowed to move to share his captivity. Is she allowed to leave the castle walls? He hopes so.

The terms are reasonable. The borders are the same; the same stretches of hill and water mark the limit of his lordship and the

Maiden's. But he will not be paying tribute, paltry and face-granting though it was.

Men have died, but boys are older and new men have joined him. Broadly, he is content. There is no point throwing over the tafl board in a fury if luck runs against you. Beside, he has other plots to ferment.

An emissary comes from Man. Thorfinn Ottarson, one of the great Manx earls. Somerled tries not to remember the first time Thorfinn came here. He forces himself not to see the man's presence as an omen.

Thorfinn slips around the subject, snakelike. Twists through the pleasantries. He eyes Dugald. Ragnhild's eldest son is sixteen years old. He takes after his mother, with that fair northern colouring. The girls think him handsome; they drip after him, sighing and primping.

Somerled doesn't ask about the boy's love life. He suspects Dugald's heart is safe enough. The boy thinks mainly of swords. He practises long into the night, knitting the muscle on to his shoulders. His brothers join him, their fraternal competition so bone-deep it is like a living thing. A fifth brother to stalk them.

He approves their swordplay. Best to make the attacks and parries as deep as their rivalry. The sense of the sword needs to become a memory in the muscle, so that the blade's edge moves before your mind can catch up. Slice first, think second. Block first, pray after.

He has let Gillecolm marry Sigurd's daughter; better that than another awkward conversation. The boy's happiness shines so fiercely, he walks through the band like an omen. Somerled watches it sometimes, the way Gillecolm and his Deirdre's bliss splits the onlookers. Some answer it with a smile, nostalgic or fond. Some grimace at it, tipped over into bitterness by their conspicuous joy.

And Somerled? He is irritated by the joy and the unthinking responses to it. Sometimes he feels as if he is the only one who thinks. The only one who rises above prick and stomach.

He watches them now. She is pregnant, provokingly rounded, ostentatiously happy. Gillecolm leans in to whisper in her ear, lips scratching the lobe. She laughs, half turned to him. Brian, now one of Somerled's most feared warriors, is watching them too, something wistful on his face.

They are feasting Thorfinn Ottarson. The table is groaning. At the end of the hall, Maud, Somerled's latest woman, is watching him, he knows, waiting to throw him a sultry toss of her head. While Ragnhild is looking away, he points her out to Thorfinn, and watches the man's eyes bulge.

'You're a lucky man, Somerled,' he says.

'Am I? Do you remember when we first met?'

'Yes.' Thorfinn watches her. She knows they are looking, and leans forward into the gaze. Flicks her eyes up at them. Jesus, does she have to be so unsubtle?

'You can have her,' he says, suddenly.

'Seriously?'

'Aye. If you'll stop beating up to windward and tell me why you're here.'

Thorfinn pulls his eyes from Maud's cleavage to look at him.

'Godred. He is a bastard. We're all bastards, but he is something fucking special, Somerled. He had a boy beaten to death last week, for no reason.'

'And? Boys must be beaten.'

'It sounds small, does it not? And yet if you saw it . . . how he is. We all have power, men like us. Like you. What stops you killing a man whose face you do not like? Tupping the wives of your warriors? Taking their land? Beating boys to death for the pleasure of their screams?'

'I wouldn't.'

285

'Yes, but why? You could.'

Somerled is silent for a heartbeat. He points upwards. 'I'm being watched.'

'Jesus, aye.' Thorfinn nods.

Somerled doesn't correct him. He thinks of his mother laughing on her cloud, and hides his smile.

'Imagine you don't give a fuck who is watching. What's to stop you then?'

Somerled says nothing. He swirls his wine in his cup, takes a sip and wishes it were beer.

'The worst of it is how we all behave in the face of it. We cringe before power wielded badly. Stupidly. Cruelly. We become craven. Corrupted. We tell tales on our blood brothers, part our wives' legs for him.'

Somerled tries to keep his face unreadable.

'So, Somerled,' says Thorfinn. 'This is why we have come. Dugald is Olaf's grandson. He has a claim. You are Somerled. We need your help.'

~ ~ ~

He walks up to the crag above Ardtornish Bay, his breath labouring. A grey, blustery day. The cold wind along the Sound reaching up on to this exposed cliff. The waterfalls running down the face of the crag blow back up the rock. Down at the bottom, looking up, the columns of water seem alive. The grey ladies, she called them, and the name has stuck. Here, close up, the illusion is shattered into showering droplets of water.

It's good to get away on his own. No one warned him, when he was young and burning up with ambition. No one warned him that he would never be on his own yet he would feel entirely alone, always. He has been alone since he lost her.

A voice behind him calls his name. Jesus. Christ in heaven. Will they not leave him be?

He turns, and there, striding up the hill behind him, is Aed. Lord, but when did the big man get so bald? Looking down on him, Somerled can see his great burned head. He almost smiles.

'Lord Somerled,' says Aed. 'I am sorry to follow you. But I wanted to talk to you. It's difficult, below.'

Somerled relents. He clasps Aed's arm, wrist on wrist. Pulls him wordlessly to the landward lookout rock. The boy stationed there turns and sees them. He jumps upright with a clatter, his spear falling to the ground and rolling away towards the cliff edge.

Somerled feels the big man beside him tense, but he shakes his head.

'We will relieve you, boy,' he says.

The boy clambers down to retrieve his spear, his face crimson with the shame of dropping it. Jesus, but can he be Sigurd's son? The same colouring. The same wiry frame. A salt spray of memories threatens to flood him: of Sigurd this boy's age, conning the galley, looking back across the bank of oars with a damp grin.

'No matter, no matter,' he says gruffly, and the boy glances up at him with a grateful, nervous nod, before running down the hill towards safety and his mates.

They sit down on the rock, looking out across the Sound. The hills of Mull are wreathed in a grey cloud that hovers just above their heads. They can feel its damp shadow pressing down upon them. The Sound is rough, ridged with white-flecked waves. Down in Loch Aline, the fleet lies at rest in the storm anchorage. They can see the small boats plying a threading between the galleys, and the tiny men swarming across the planking. Making fast, checking rivets and stays, tying everything down.

Order. Preparation. He feels a surge of satisfaction. It's good to have his fleet safe in the loch, under the lee of the crag. A massive bulwark of rock and scree and tree roots between his ships and the coming tempest. Assuming it comes. He looks over towards the blackest clouds, clinging to the mainland hills.

'Lord Somerled,' says Aed at last, breaking the heavy silence. 'I am sorry to ask. But I would stay behind. I do not have another season in me. This is not my war.'

Astonished, Somerled turns to face him.

'You are my champion.'

'By courtesy. Come, lord. You know as well as I that a score of the younger ones could take me. Indeed, are bristling to take me. I can barely sit in a chair without groaning.'

'But . . .'

But I need you. I can't be without you. You are my only friend. You remember.

'I could take care of things here,' says Aed, after a pause.

'I always thought you would die with a sword in your hand.'

'So did I, lord. Yet here I am. And I am old.'

Somerled looks down at his own lined, ridged hands. Tries to imagine them smooth.

'If we followed my mother's gods, Aed, I could refuse you, for your own good. Give you a sword and whip you towards Valhalla.'

'Aye, but we do not. And there is no shame for a Christian in dying old and warm in his bed. Oona has begged me, Somerled.'

They are to leave after the storm has blown itself out. Leave the Maiden, for a while. Turn their eyes to the islands, where they belong.

Aed takes his silence for agreement. So be it. Somerled nods, and Aed smiles. A little rueful, perhaps.

'You are the only man here,' says Somerled, 'more afraid of your wife than of me.'

'True,' says Aed, grinning.

A pause, as they watch the bunching black clouds.

'Should you not wait for the spring, Somerled?'

A spit of anger. 'If you are not coming, Aed, don't tell me how to fight.'

Aed shrugs, waiting.

'Sorry,' says Somerled at last. 'You are right, it is a risk. But Godred has annoyed the Man lords now. He is isolated. If we wait, he may win them back.'

Aed nods. 'Why do it, Somerled?'

'Why do what?'

'Why this war? How big will your fleet need to be before you are happy? How large your territories?'

'Bigger. Larger.' Somerled waves his arm in a great arcing gesture that takes in half the sky.

'Why?'

'Jesus, Aed. What a question.'

'Well?'

A boy comes over the ridge. The new lookout. He walks slowly, diffidently towards the two greatest men in his world. The rain starts. No preamble, no light patter – an angry, drenching rain.

Somerled stands, suppressing the grunt that comes with the creaking of his limbs.

'Race you down,' he says. They begin to run, ignoring the boy's astonished staring. They slide on the scree, brush aside the heather, tumbling downwards in a rush of rain and laughter and loose banter. Until they reach the bottom, still laughing, fighting for breath. He leans over, hands on knees, looking up at Aed's lined face and gap-toothed grin. A youngster comes forward, all deference. A problem with one of the galleys dragging her storm anchor. Somerled straightens his back, squares off his shoulders. Loses the unfamiliar smile. Walks away.

~ ~ ~

It is strange to set sail without Aed by his side. More than strange. Aed stands at the end of the jetty, Oona beside him. His feet are spread unnecessarily wide, as if he thinks himself aboard a pitching deck. How does it feel, Somerled wonders, to watch this fleet catch the tide and the wind?

What a sight it is. What a day. The roaring of an adventure started. The clanking and creaking of eighty rigged sails drawing in to catch the wind. The ridged sea cresting up; the thick sky glowering down. They are suspended in a rush of wind, curving into the Sound, hair whipped and blood high.

More than one thousand oars rasp back on board as the wind pools in the sails. Eighty pilots call the words as the strain falls on the masts. Sails billow, loose ends fluttering. Their shouts mingle, hovering above the galleys like a prayer. The gulls call and skirl.

Somerled stands like a boy up by the otter's head, sinking and rising with the waves. His arms curl round the slippery wood of the otter's neck. The spray on his face is salted; the wind in his hair is wild and wet. His is the first galley, pushing into the forbidding sea; the otter seems alone in this sliver of sea road held between the water and the sky. Mull, off to larboard, sits squeezed between the stubborn low cloud and the flecking of the surf. He turns, for a last sight of Aed, who looks small already. A tiny buffeted figure left behind where the land meets the water.

He brings his focus closer, to where Gillecolm, the first pilot of the fleet, stands at the rudder. Knees loose, riding the kicking of the boat. He can feel her swell and shrink, surge and retreat. The boy looks up, to the top of the mast, out beyond the screaming otter, and at last behind to the following galleys. He turns back to the horizon, catches his father's eye and grins, joyous. Somerled hopes the boy is up to it. It's hard, sometimes, to trust your own kin. His mother told him that.

He looks out past Gillecolm to the boats behind, following him on. The shaggy brown sails stretch across the Sound, making the heathered hills beyond seem drab, lifeless. Jesus, but what a fleet. He remembers setting off from Ireland with his father, a handful of warriors in a few beaten-up galleys. If the boy I was then could see me now. If he could see me!

Somerled wants someone to see what he has done. To understand how far he has come. He wants his mother's gruff voice to pour praise upon his head. But she is dead, and he must sing his own song, to his own heart.

O, the wind-taut sails! O, the luscious curve of the hulls! O, the brave shrug of the prow beasts, shaking off the water in a dazzled spray! O, the sharp curl of the bow wave! O, the sucking and the frothing of the sea!

Look at them, O, look at them. He sends a silent paean to the sky. Is it possible that man has made anything more beautiful? These bold, brawny galleys, riding the wave. He wants to howl his pride. Keep your domed palaces. Keep your vaulted churches. Keep your motted castles. Keep your arched cloisters. This is the only thing worth having – a bold fleet screaming its challenge to all before it.

He runs his tongue across his briny lips and it's as good as the best wine. This is beauty. This is power. And this is mine.

1156

SOMERLED

They head first to Coll, that fertile flat pebble in the sea. Their masts are almost taller than Coll's highest hill. No one can miss them. No one can huddle into the side of a hill, eyes shut, pretending he is not there.

We must look like a host, like death, Somerled wants to say to Aed. There is space enough for just five galleys at the sand's edge. The rest bob on the swell, sails furled, oars biting the water to keep them still.

Somerled jumps down into the thigh-deep waves, and the cold shock of it makes him gasp. He wades out on to the beach, slowly, his eyes focusing on the greeting party. A grey-haired man, backed by a dozen warriors. They are dressed as for war, but everyone standing there on that beach under the cold, dark sky knows that it is hopeless. Death or capitulation. The only possibilities.

Somerled strides forward, a smile sitting on his face. I would not trust this smile, he thinks to himself, and the thought spins the smile into a genuine one. The grey-haired man opposite him is confused, frightened by Somerled's freakish good humour.

'Well now,' says Somerled. 'And you are the Lord of Coll?'

'Aye. Cathal,' says grey-hair, shifting his weight from foot to foot.

'I am Somerled.' He watches the old man's eyes widen in recognition. Fear.

'This,' says Somerled, waving to the man walking up the beach behind him, 'is Thorfinn Ottarson. And this,' he points to Dugald, who fixes his eyes on Cathal, 'is your new lord. My son. Dugald. Lord of Man and the Isles.'

'But,' the man stammers. 'But . . . we heard . . . I mean. Godred. Is he dead?'

'Not yet,' grins Thorfinn.

Somerled cuts him off. 'Confusing, ain't it? Here's the easy part. Me and my men have been sailing, and we're hungry. Feel free to feast your new lord.'

Cathal looks behind Somerled to the rows of warriors staring at him from above the planked sides of the galleys.

'How many?'

'Eighty birlinn is all.'

The old man closes his eyes, imagining, no doubt, his winter hoard ravaged, and his people reduced to quarter rations until spring.

'Come, Cathal. At least it's not eighty Norse longships,' says Somerled, and the old man smiles weakly.

~ ~ ~

With not enough room to beach, most of the men spend the night on the galleys. Food and warmed ale is ferried out to them. Somerled wanders down from Cathal's hall at midnight to watch the fleet dancing on the moonlit waves. A half-moon, now bright, now cloud-shrouded. A shining path picked out along the black water. The galleys drift in and out of sight with the meandering of the clouds. It is cold, but dry. They will be fine out there tonight.

Somerled pulls his cloak about his shoulders. Coming into the cold night from a hot fire sends his skin wild with goose bumps and shivers. He thinks of his son, Gillecolm, out there in the boat. Sharing a pot, sharing a cloak. Laughing at someone's vice, someone else's virtue. He thinks about how the laughter of your brothers can keep you warm on the coldest evening, keep you brave against the perils of dawn.

He turns back to Thorfinn Ottarson's shrewd eyes and Cathal's grudging smile. Behind him, songs and laughter drift across the water.

~ ~ ~

The next morning, the previous night's soft regrets seem absurd. An affectation brought on by eating and drinking too much. He splashes cold water on his face, lets it prise open his hooded eyes.

Cathal is trying, failing, to hide his relief at their departure. Somerled studies his face with an internal smile as he says: 'Your son, Cathal. Ragnar, is it? A fine lad. The child of a late love, I think?'

He watched last night as Cathal cradled his son in his gaze. The boy is about fourteen, with all that age's lanky oscillation between arrogance and childishness.

Cathal brightens with Somerled's praise. 'Yes,' he says. 'My first wife, God rest her, could not bear children. It was a great sadness. The boy is my only . . .' He stops speaking, stops walking, turns to Somerled. In the unforgiving dawn light he looks ancient, a grave-hoverer.

'No,' he says, flatly.

'No? Well now, Cathal. The Maiden, in Alba, has just been knighted by the King of England. In France. Did you know that?

The Continental style of things, I'm told, is for a boy to serve as a page to a great knight until he comes of age. The Maiden caught the notion from the English, I think. His head, they tell me, is full of chivalry. He is proud to be King Henry's vassal. How absurd. Don't you think? To pledge yourself to another man's service when there is no need. On the other hand, if there *is* a need . . .'

He flicks his eyes across to Cathal's son, who stands talking with Ranald. The boys are of a similar age. He can't imagine what they find to talk about.

'We have become such friends, Cathal. I would hate for us to fall out.'

'Speak plain, Lord Somerled. Give me that at least. You want my boy as a hostage?'

'Yes.'

'And I have no choice?'

'No.'

'And if Godred comes and demands my allegiance back to him? And I give it?'

'That, my dear friend, would be a very stupid thing to do.'

The man's face falls in on itself. He is trying not to cry. Somerled feels an unexpected shard of pity. He crushes it, cursing himself.

They sail away, with the boy attached to Somerled's own crew. His face is white, determined. As the old man standing alone on the beach cries his farewells, the boy turns away, fixing his eyes on the open sea.

~ ~ ~

So they hop, that winter, from island to island, taking hostages and hospitality. And more. He watches his younger sons strut. He watches them eye the women, flit off into the shadows before the feasting is done. He has his fill of women too. They are offered up to him. He has earned a reputation as a man with many women, which he finds entirely surprising. Yet they are there, the women, and losing himself in their bodies is a kind of forgetting and a kind of remembering.

The islands will be littered with their bastards, come the next autumn.

He enjoys showing Dugald his new sheep, showing the sheep their new shepherd. Until the muttering grows too loud for Somerled to ignore.

'They want a fight,' says Brian, quietly. They are beached on Jura, in the shadow of the Paps. It is bitterly cold, and wet. Dusk settles on them as they sit, morose and still. The water trickles under the stretched hides, vindictive and icy, seeking out any flesh that is still warm, still dry.

Brian is Somerled's champion now. Less by brawn than by cunning. No one fights Brian if they can help it, even the big men who dwarf him. He is impossible to read, slippery. His closed, calm face is disquieting to those who go into battle screaming, signposting their feints and attacks with shifting eyes.

Somerled nods. 'Of course they do. All this winter sailing, and no silver, no women.'

Brian makes an ambiguous noise.

'Well then, few women. Patience, friend. It will come soon enough. He will come.'

'And when he does, lord?'

Somerled looks at him, wishing he would unbend, just a little. Smile sometimes. He turns to Cathal's boy, who sits in his shadow. 'Fetch my sons,' he says.

Soon, Dugald, Ranald and Angus come forward. Olaf was left behind with his mother, poor scamp, furious at his own youth. 'All my sons, you idiot,' he growls to the boy, who runs away and comes scampering back with Gillecolm.

'Well, boys,' says Somerled, looking at them. 'What now?'

They are not used to being asked their opinion. Angus looks at his older brothers, who gaze at their father.

'We are provoking Godred,' says Ranald. 'Waiting for him.'

'Good.' He gestures at them to sit by his fire. 'And what will he expect when he comes?'

'A fight,' says Angus.

'Clearly. Where? How?'

'He will come by sea, and we will fight him at sea, of course,' says Dugald.

Gillecolm says: 'Your fisher spies are out, Father?'

Somerled nods, and explains to the younger ones that he has sent a fleet of curraghs down to Man, to spy on Godred.

'But how will they find us?' asks Angus.

'Good question, boy. They know our intended route. We started north and are heading south; they are going the opposite way. It is entirely possible we will miss each other. But you should always try, when you can, to know more about your enemies' movements than your enemy knows about yours.'

The boys nod, solemn. He notices that Cathal's son has crept closer to listen, trying to shrink himself into a shadow.

'What will happen when we meet?'

'We will smash him.' Ranald snarls it, like a parody of a warrior. His brothers nod.

They are young; he will forgive it. He looks at Gillecolm.

'Well, Father. He has longships, at least the five he brought from Norway. Probably, from what Thorfinn says, around twenty-five.'

Somerled nods his encouragement. 'Go on.'

'Our birlinn are smaller. Rightly smaller,' he says quickly.

'Longships do not suit the jagged coast here. Ours are handier, more navigable. The stern rudder makes for tighter, quicker turns than the longships' steering oar.'

'But,' says Somerled, looking at Dugald.

'Their longships carry more men. Four or five times more,' says Dugald.

'So what is our best tactic, in a sea battle?'

The boys are silent.

'Snapping hounds,' whispers Cathal's son, Ragnar.

'Quiet,' hisses Dugald.

'Shh. The boy is right. If we board them one by one, they will have us. Too many men. We must be as snapping hounds to a stag. Harry them, hassle them. Attack in pairs, in threes. Men pouring in from both sides.'

The boys nod, wide-eyed. Dugald looks towards Ragnar. Something vicious in his expression unsettles Somerled. He will keep Cathal's son close tonight.

'So it would be best to meet them when we have the wind. If they are to leeward, we can play with them,' says Gillecolm.

'And?'

'A narrow space. So our ability to turn and twist counts for more.'

'A place like?'

'Here.' This from Ranald, who is rewarded with a smile. 'The Sound of Islay.'

Somerled nods his agreement. 'If they have the wind, we will run before it, weather Jura and think again. If we have it, we will bleed them. Let them think they are hunting us. Let them think they have the longer sword.'

They settle in on the beaches, ready to wait. But just the next day a fishing curragh comes spinning into sight. Its sail is stretched taut, its heel pronounced. Over the waves comes the sound of calling. 'Godred is coming. Godred is coming.'

1156

somerled

Fear is a dry mouth. Fear is a tight-clenched fist. A rising of hackles to remind a man how like an animal he is, no matter how precious he values his soul.

Fear is a bittersweet freezing of time, a maw stuffed with exquisite detail: the exact shrillness of the gull's cry, the sheen on the water that sends the grey sea into a sparkle of silver.

Ahead, Godred. His oars spread in banks that dip and catch, pull and rise in perfect harmony. Regular as a song-beat. Dip, catch, pull, rise. Dip, catch, pull, rise. The dragons' eyes snap red, their jaws stretching in a roar of challenge, of fury. They plunge towards the sea, rise again screaming. How long their necks! How high the tumblehome of the longboats' ribs! How large of mast, how bulging of beam are his enemy's galleys!

They pull towards him, against the tide, against the wind. They swoop across the water, tossing the sea aside.

Around him, his men are busy. They are still under sail, the wind with them, pushing them on to those giant beasts ahead. He envies them their tasks. Small but necessary distractions. They ready the spears, checking they will not catch as they pull them from their homes along the thwarts. Near him, the slingshotters gather, picking over the stones that lie in the galley's belly.

Gillecolm, at the rudder, frowns his concentration. He looks up at the fat curve of the sail, across to where the nearest neighbour draws wind, a little too close for comfort. He sees his father's gaze, and throws it back with a smile.

All is in hand. His armour is on; the light-worked mail from Denmark, set with gems that catch and keep the sunlight. He sparkles when he walks, and he thinks himself ridiculous. But it is expected. He reaches down to the sword at his side, feeling, as always, for the imperfect catch in the metalwork. Will he ever learn that this is a new sword, precious beyond measure but somehow depressing in its perfection?

All that is left is for him to stand here at the prow, looking confident, trying to stop the rumbling of his bowels by effort of will alone. He fancies himself propelling the galley forward by the power of fart, and imagines telling Eimhear the joke. He turns his face to the front as he laughs, so the men will not see it.

The boy is there, tucked into his shadow as usual. Somerled keeps him close. He cannot quite tell why. The boy sees him smile.

'Ragnar. Frightened, boy?'

The boy pauses, looking into his face.

'Yes.'

Somerled grins. He likes the boy's honesty. He likes his serious freckled face. He lifts him up, shows him how to wrap his arms and legs around the otter's neck, holding him there just in case. He used to do this with Gillecolm. Before the premature death of the boy's childhood.

Ragnar laughs as he rises and plunges, part of the breathing of the boat up here, the glorious inhale and exhale that sends her onwards. Somerled brings him down at last, worried that it is too cold. What a thing to worry about, when there are Man spears with

301

the boy's runes carved on the shaft. Still, the January air is vicious. The boy wraps wet red hands inside his cloak.

'They have stopped rowing, Lord Somerled.'

Somerled looks past the otter to Godred's crew, oars pressed down in the water to keep them still.

'So they have. Do you know what they're about, boy? Have you fought a battle at sea before now?'

The boy shakes his head. Looks up at him with innocent eyes. Jesus, thinks Somerled. Those eyes will lose their innocence before today is done. Lord keep him safe, though.

'Well. They are grappling together, do you see?' The boy looks out across the water to where, one by one, Godred's boats are lashing themselves together. Two, then three, then four. Five. Like a floating raft.

'Think of the tafl board, Ragnar. The point is to take out the king. So they put the king in the middle of the raft to keep him safe.'

'Will we do the same, lord?'

'No. Their advantage is in size. Ours is in numbers. See how not all of them are joining the raft? The smaller ones will take us on, while we make for the raft and try to take it boat by boat. Like peeling an onion. The *Otter* will hover about the back, however. If they take me, we are done.'

It sounds so simple, like that. So cold-blooded. As if tactics and the directing of galleys were a matter of fireside humming and hawing. As if every decision were not washed in blood.

The priest comes forward now. He is ugly, this fellow, the broad plane of his forehead emphasized by the shaved tonsure. Somerled can't remember his name, but moves aside for him. The smell of incense mixes with the salt air and spills upwards in grey smoke.

He has a low, rich voice, this priest. The warriors stop their work and listen, standing still and quiet. Behind him, beyond the otter's head, the screaming dragons are drawing near.

Christ with me,
Christ before me,
Christ behind me,
Christ in me,
Christ beneath me,
Christ above me,
Christ on my right,
Christ on my left,
Christ when I lie down,
Christ when I sit down,
Christ when I arise,
Christ in the heart of every man who thinks of me,
Christ in the mouth of everyone who speaks of me,
Christ in every eye that sees me,
Christ in every ear that hears me.

Somerled whispers the words. He thinks of St Patrick, who faced down a king with this prayer as his only breastplate. He thinks of the boy he once was, who sang his own poem in his head as the dragons closed in.

~ ~ ~

It begins with a shower of stones and arrows. From where the *Otter* bobs, behind the thicket of galleys, they can watch death raining on the lead ships. It is like sitting dry on a sunny bank, watching a summer squall across the sea. Somewhere in that dark, sharp squall is his son Ranald. Rocks and arrows are raining down on his dear head, seeking to crush that skull Somerled once cradled in the palm of his hand.

Dugald stands next to him, chafing at their safety.

'Easy,' says Somerled. 'We will be in it soon enough. No reason to let the bastards catch or kill either of us. The whole enterprise would be lost before it started.'

'Easy for you, Father. You have proved yourself five hundred times over. I have not. This is my birthright we are fighting for. And Ranald is . . .'

He stops, the sentence trailing off.

They watch in silence as the ships begin to meet. Godred's free longships are surging forward, clustering defensively around the rafted ships at the centre. Somerled's birlinn stick in their pairs. He watches the first attack. One birlinn to the bow of the longship, one to the stern. The biggest, the strongest board first. One at each side, simultaneously, to split the longship's defence. The longships want to close beam on, so their bigger oars can destroy the little birlinn and their men can jump in numbers from the high gunwale on to a deck still reeling from the blow.

Their numbers, their size will not count if Somerled's men can come in from bow and stern in unison.

He's too far to hear it, to smell it. But he has boarded himself often enough. Aed in front, Somerled at his shoulder. He knows this moment so well, he recalls it not as a memory, but as a living thing, so sharp that he stands alongside each of his lead men as they face down the dragons.

Their big man standing alongside the dragon, your big man facing him. Screaming an inarticulate scream of rage and prayer and lust. A demanding roar, an insistent roar that says: 'I will be the one to live. I cannot die. All that I am, all that I will be, all these bones, these hates and loves, these heavy muscles, these eyes.

Impossible! Impossible that they should die.' Such a deal to say, such words of life and love and fear, it comes easier as a scream of rage, of entitlement.

They face each other, the first men. Screaming. Hefting their great double axes, tossing them from hand to hand like toys: look at my strength, look at my skill. Blue veins pop in white skin, running along the oar-built muscles. Their eyes mad with it.

The crash and judder of the boats running on to each other, which fells the unwary before the fighting even begins. Some leap before the crash, some wait. Some, clear-headed even when they are maddened with anger and desire, let the other man come, knowing that he will be off balance, knowing that he will need a dancer's grace to leap from one wave-tossed deck to another, jagged and buckled from the impact, while he keeps his hands free to hack.

Seconds, it takes. That first strike. Rarely do both men hold their ground. One steps back, the other forward. The step forward creates movement, lets in the two men behind, and the two men behind that. The step back means two back, four, ten. Then suddenly the galley is thick with men, grunting and thrusting in a closed space, falling back over the rowing benches, the blood pooling with the salt water in the scuppers.

Somerled knows this. Knows the smell of blood and salt. Knows the raging pleasure of that moment when you are on the front foot pushing forward, and they are dying, the bastards.

Back here, he comes to himself, pulls himself away from the battle. He tries to clear his head. He smells only salt, hears only the rush of the waves and the crying of the gulls. He can see that the first longship has fallen, quickly. He watches men dive off its side and swim towards Jura. Over there, it looks as if the two birlinn have failed to coordinate their attack – the first has been overrun from the longship's bow. They will scupper it, most likely. There are men left over to deal with the stern threat. Two birlinn down. Fools.

There, a longship has run alongside a birlinn, its great bank of oars crushing the smaller boat, which has failed to arc around her. Fools. Three down.

Jesus, but he forgets how hard it is to watch your men fuck up. Did he not give the orders, clear and simple? Did he not spell it out? Now he must float here at the back like some sort of fat, incapable old man, and watch them panic themselves to a defeat, the idiots.

He realizes he has been striking the otter's neck with an open palm, the sound of his fury ringing around the quiet galley. He clenches his fist and pulls it behind his back. He sets his face to be implacable and watches the great battle unfold.

Time passes in unpredictable waves, speeding and slowing with triumph and disaster. One longship is driven on to the shore, where it breaks open and spews out its men to scuttle on the rocks like crabs. One birlinn sunk, another taken, another floating ambiguous and empty, its empty oar holes a mystery. One longship taken and turned on another, using the tide to bring her in beam on beam, the oars on both splintering and snapping like toothpicks.

Honours are even. An eye for an eye. A tooth for a tooth.

Dusk comes early. Somerled feels it coming on, feels the breath of darkness and with it the loom of defeat. Or at least, not victory. And there in the half-light, he sees his chance. A gap, as Godred's free longships are taken or beached or engaged elsewhere. A gap through to the raft of five bound ships, where Godred squats, idle as himself. A gap like the parting of the Red fucking Sea, God-given for the *Otter* and her consorts to charge through.

Somerled shouts for Gillecolm and points to it. Bless the boy, he seizes the situation at once. Somerled lets Dugald sound the battle horn, telling his reserve birlinn to engage, to follow him. The oars rasp out into the water, dark and foamy in the gathering dusk. The horn sounds and sounds. The oars bite and the dragons call them on.

~ ~ ~

Brian does not scream. Brian stands. All the flyting, all the screaming is in his eyes. Somerled has seen how the man's unhappiness concentrates in his cold, malevolent stare. The scream of the longship's bow man falters, and that is when Somerled knows that they will take this ship. Before the otter meets the dragon, before the tearing of wood and leather.

Brian hops across, like a boy playing at rock-jumping. He takes out the bow man almost casually, and before the man has crumpled to the deck, his head flapping absurdly on an unsevered sliver of gristle, Somerled and Dugald are across. Dugald is young to be second, but Somerled wants to give him face.

Somerled pulls his axe down, and though the man dodges, it catches his shoulder. He spins, the great gash in his mail, in his skin, opening ever deeper. Shoulder down, Somerled pushes past the limp sword and barrels him out of the way. Parries a stroke from larboard with the wood of his axe, and brings his helmet to meet the man's nose, which shatters and splays across his face.

He's level with Brian now, more men coming in beside and behind them. His axe needs too much room for this close work, and he pulls his stabbing sword. Sharp, deadly. There's no place for fancy stuff. Feet slip and slide on the blood-wet floor. Quick, low strokes. Unflashy. A man's just as fucked if you take his legs out.

Dugald is still with them. He hears the boy's roar. They are

307

pedalling backwards; jumping sideways into the water. Somewhere behind him he hears the thud of the axe cutting the grappling ropes, and suddenly the longship is swinging free. They've not taken out the stern ropes, so she moves outward, still tied two thwarts up from the stern. A gap too far for reinforcements, although one tries the leap, and lands with a thud and a cry with his belly across the gunwale. He falls heavily back into the sea.

It is perceptibly darker when the last of the defenders jump overboard. The deck is loud with the sobbing breath of exhausted men, and the whimpering of the wounded.

'The next, the next,' screams Somerled, and he shouts an order at the nearest loose birlinn to come up on the bow of the longship next along. Brian leaps to the place at the stern where the two longships are still attached. Its men should be pouring through, the fools, but they are sticking with their own ship.

On then they rush. His feet find purchase on the longship's sloping clinker-built sides. He jumps then, axe first, landing in a tangle of limbs and blade in the next ship. He is disorientated, so he jerks and stabs and thrashes until he can stand upright. Men come in behind him, pushing him forward so they're on the enemy like a pack. He feels something that might be pain in his arm, but he's too raging, too caught in it all to understand.

Looking down, he sees a boy with his teeth sunk in his arm. Blood froths up around the boy's mouth. Dugald grabs the boy's hair and yanks his head back. His lips are a mess of blood and skin, and there is a chunk missing from Somerled's arm. Enraged, he stabs the boy's exposed throat, and kicks him as Dugald throws him to the ground.

They have been overtaken by his men as this little oddity plays out. Somerled is at the back, and realizes with a sudden shock that something is not quite right. It is dark now. The men and boats alike are ill-defined shapes in the cold air.

The next boat along, the middle of the raft and the one on which his enemy cowers, has cast off. He hears the familiar scrape of oars, hears the catch of blade on water and the timekeeper's low call. The bastard is running. Godred is running.

~ ~ ~

Somerled wakes quickly. Dawn is a glimmer; Jura and Islay, hemming them there on the Sound, are grey, indistinct. The sea is calm and strangely lit with a silverish tint. Its gentle, whispering waves rock the boat.

The bench is hard, unyielding. Somerled looks at the sky, where a crescent moon hangs on. He can feel the tightness of the muscles in his shoulders and his back. The weight and heft of his axe boring into his body. He will ache today. His mouth is painfully dry, scraping on itself as he tries to swallow.

He pulls himself upright with an effort. Around him, men are sprawled in their armour. Lying on thwarts, on the deck. Ragnar is curled in the loop of a rope. The oars are lashed to keep them upright in the water, so the longship bobs quietly on the calm sea. Christ, it is cold, though. He shivers, pulls his cloak closer.

By the rudder, there is a figure standing upright. Gillecolm. Somerled walks across to him, stepping over the sleeping bodies, his foot squelching in something that must be blood.

'Why did you let me sleep?' he asks, the words thick on his parched tongue.

Gillecolm hands him a flask of fresh water. He drinks long and deep, ignoring the protest from his shoulder as he lifts his arm. The water is cold, delicious.

'Because you were tired. Besides, there was no need for you to

309

be awake. We can't follow Godred in the dark, not in these waters.'

Somerled thinks of the black rocks in the darkness, waiting to rip the belly out of a boat. Godred will be lucky to make it.

He grunts, not quite wanting to tell the boy he is right. They fought themselves to a standstill, fought until the darkness settled like a blindfold. Dropped where they stood with screaming muscles and longing for sleep.

'I ditched the bodies,' says Gillecolm. 'More theirs than ours.'

Brian looms up beside them quietly. Gillecolm passes him the flask, and breaks some bread. It is hard, long past its best.

'Well,' says Somerled, into the heavy chewing. 'We didn't lose.'

'We didn't win.' Brian's voice is neutral, soft.

The light is spreading now. They can see the boats sitting quietly on the water. They are lucky with this calm, at least. There are boats split open on the rocks; more beached on the shore. There will be a counting later, but it's plain to see that there's no one winner. It's hard to tell who has the upper hand. On the other ships he can see figures moving: mailed, bearded men, stretching and yawning. They all look the same in the half-light.

A small boat, the type of curragh that can be trailed behind a longship, is rowing slowly through the shattered fleets. They follow its jerky progress as they eat, watching it resolve itself into a more defined shape now that the dawn is brighter.

'Lord Somerled? Lord Somerled?' A voice calls low from the drifting boat.

Somerled looks at Brian, and stands, leaning out over the water to shout: 'Here. Who wants me?'

The boat draws under them. Somerled can't get used to the size of the longship. He's dizzy all the way up here, gazing down on the figures in the boat. A man looks up at him, a grimy, blood-spattered man about his own age. He appears exhausted, beaten.

His armour is rich, well worked. The men at the oars rest them in the water, drooping.

Brian and Gillecolm are either side of Somerled, eyeing the man down the shafts of spears. He holds up his hands. 'I want to talk to you, Lord Somerled. I am Conn of Islay.'

They help him up the side of the boat, and he scrambles awkwardly in.

'He ran away. Ran away!' Conn says the words with a childlike wonder on his grizzled face. 'How could he, Lord Somerled? How?'

Somerled shakes his head.

'We knew he was a vicious bastard,' Conn says. 'Vicious is tolerable. Cowardly? No.'

Gillecolm breaks more bread and holds it out to the man, who looks at it shrewdly. He knows what is being offered. Slowly, stretching out a hand, he takes it and eats. Somerled feels himself relax, warm to the conversation.

'Well, Conn, my friend. What can we do?'

Conn looks at him, chewing valiantly on the bread. 'I am a little lord. I can muster a ship. That one there is mine, and she's still mine.'

He points across the water at a longship, one of the smaller ones. The morning is taking shape now, and it is fair. Bright and frosty, and crisp. She's a pretty enough boat – thick-ribbed but dolphin-sleek. Gorgeously, painstakingly painted.

'She is the beauty of the seas,' says Gillecolm.

'Isn't she, though,' and Conn grins so wide that they find themselves grinning back.

'I would like, Lord Somerled, to be my own man entirely. As you are. But I know where I stand. Little lords must bow to big lords, and there's an end to it.'

Somerled nods.

'But I can choose where I bow, can I not? Not being a vassal, like those slaves in the south.'

Somerled meets him halfway. 'My son Dugald, whose claim to Man and the isles comes through his mother's line, would be honoured to take the bow from a lord such as yourself.' He reaches out his hand, and they clasp, hand on wrist.

Afterwards, they sketch out the detail. Conn thinks he can bring most of the other island lords with him; the southern isles, anyway. It is settled that he will take Brian with him to treat with Godred on Man. To make it formal.

'Godred will have to agree,' says Conn. 'He has lost such honour by fleeing. It will be all he can do to keep a hold of Man. You'll be my guest, until it is settled? My hall is there.' He points off to Islay, which lies, frost-covered and iced, beyond their stern.

'And then, Lord Somerled, you will be King of Argyll and Lord of the Isles,' he says, the smile reaching his red-rimmed eyes.

'Dugald will be,' says Somerled quietly. Conn shrugs.

How well it sounds. How lovely the words. Lord of the Isles.

1157

SOMERLED

G odred Crovan crouches in Man like a crab in its hole, peering
out. The seas around him are Somerled's seas; the galleys he
commands pay Somerled homage as they pass. The southern isles
are his. Man is crumbling.

In Dublin, Muirchertach Mac Lochlainn catches the way the
wind is blowing and sends men across the sea to kiss Somerled's
mighty arse. Aed watches them with laughing eyes as they pledge
their enduring friendship.

They shower Somerled with praise, heaping the glories of the
world upon his head. He is the warrior of the age, this Lord of
the Isles. He is the carrion-giver, the son-maker, the silver-ringed,
God-kissed king of the seas. And would he, by the by, care to help
their master in his quest to be king of kings, the son of Tara, the
Lord's chosen one in His rolling land of peat and bog and rocky
shore?

Somerled sees Aed's laughter and yet lets the praise seep in,
toes up. What is the point of risking all, of stretching his boots to
stamp hard in the peat of Argyll and harder in the heather of Mull?
What is the point, if not to tip your chin to a shower of glory, to let
it drench you?

It wears off, he finds. He shrugs himself out of the shower, impatient. He can't bring himself to laugh, as Aed can. He finds instead that he withdraws even more. He worries about the undone ends. He worries about the new threats and lets the recent triumphs fade to a background hum.

Malcolm the Maiden has granted vast strips of land south of the Firth of Clyde to Walter FitzAlan, his grandfather's steward and now his. Added to the grants by David, the land between Somerled and Galloway is now held by this adventurer, this lisping third son of a Breton who rode with Norman spurs to land and glory. FitzAlan holds the land in the new fashion: the king owns the land, the knight holds it in trust for him and the peasants are accounted slaves on their own patch of grass.

Down in Galloway, Fergus's son Uchtred has risen against him. Both have appealed to Somerled for help, and the decision is troubling him more than it deserves. He has never liked Fergus, but that does not matter. He has never met Uchtred, at least not since the boy was a small snot of an infant. But that does not matter either. It should be a simple decision – which winner would most suit him? Yet it is not simple.

He watches his boys closely, he finds. He watches Dugald simmer; Lord of the Isles yet not lord. Man yet not man. Dugald is seventeen and dangerous. Somerled finds the pity of it almost unbearable. He held the boy once, rocked him at night. He wiped away tears when he fell. He pulled him to standing when he learned to walk.

He watches Dugald striding past, his youth blinding, with a painful fizz of pride and envy.

'Let him have his head,' says Aed. A husk of Aed, thin and permanently pained. No one knows what ails him. They watch him shrink and sour. They only know of the pain because he groans

314

sometimes, when it is too great to hide, great keening groans that flush Oona's cheeks.

'Let him have his head?' They sit in Aed's hall, the fire shadowing the floor and the wind swirling beyond the thick walls like something demented. The long winter afternoon stretches. They are too old now to bother joining the young men outside in the wet and wild to chase game. They have proved themselves too many times over.

'Remember your father?'

Somerled nods. Who else here would? No one. His father is a name. An ancestor. Men die and they are forgotten, no matter what they tell themselves when the darkness approaches.

'I think that for some fathers, and some sons, distance can be a saviour. Dugald is called Lord of the Isles, and yet you are lord and he knows it. How would you have taken that?'

Somerled plays idly with his beads, clinking them along the strand that holds them together.

Aed stiffens suddenly, as if a tremor has taken his body by surprise. He holds the table with an old man's hands, gripping at it with white knuckles. He breathes out, slowly, carefully, as if too great an effort might bring on another wave. Somerled watches his hand clutching the table and imagines taking it between his own palms, holding on to it tightly. As you would a beloved one in childbirth. Instead he sits silently while his old friend fights the pain and finds his face again.

'Take Man,' says Aed, with a carefully even tone.

Take Man and give it to Dugald. With Man will come Skye, the small isles north of Ardnamurchan and that tumble of land and loch they call the Outer Hebrides. Lord of all the isles, to be sure. Why not? Muirchertach Mac Lochlainn in Dublin loathes Godred – it would cement their alliance.

It would be like putting an injured dog out of its misery, to take Godred out. If Somerled is engaged in Man, neither side in Galloway can blame him for failing to help – he will not be forced to gamble on a winning side. And if Malcolm's puppyish yapping at him across the Clyde continues, if he is forced to fight to the east, well all of Man's resources and wealth will not go awry. To Man, then. To become lord of all the isles. And then perhaps . . . Perhaps.

He looks across at Ragnhild, who sits straight-backed by the fire, a bundle of wool in her hands. Perhaps it is her turn on an island of women. Who is to tell him no, once Man is his? Power first, Eimhear second. Is that not what he always told himself? Why has he delayed? He could have sailed straight to Iona from the great sea battle. The Battle of Epiphany, they are calling it. Aye, but it would have angered the Manx earls, just when he needed them.

And does Ragnhild deserve to be cast aside, like so much broken crockery? She has done her best, poor soul. He imagines his sons' faces if he turns round and tells them he is swapping their mother for Gillecolm's.

And what of her? Did he not promise he would come back when he had the power to return? Has she not lived there, drowning in boredom and virtue, all these years, waiting for him to dock? What does she even look like? Has she run to fat, like Ragnhild?

Somerled turns back to the fire, his hand cradling his wine like a communion cup. He looks into the flames and tries to pick the colour of her hair from the riot of oranges and reds. He lets himself think of her – a rare indulgence. How can memories alone swirl with so much pain and pleasure? He thinks of her pale back, and the freckles like a star map that traced their way down to her bottom. He thinks of her laugh, and the shake of her breasts as he tupped her.

The worst thing about his memory is the way it has splintered. He has to fight to find a picture of the whole of her in his mind. He

316

holds only parts, fragments. Traces of skin, nuggets of conversations. He wants to replay whole scenes of their life together, in full detail. Instead his mind skips, dissatisfied. Her skinny little-girl legs poke up from the waves as she walks handstands through the shallows. But the face that comes back up through the water is the new mother, clammy and triumphant, and softened permanently by this frog-like baby pushing its way into her breast.

What should I do? he thinks, bewildered by this unfamiliar lack of clarity. He is not used to being indecisive. There is no one to open his mind to. He has sent Padeen to Rome, on the pilgrimage he has always longed for. Aed, he thinks, would call for the galley to sail for Iona and damn the eyes of any who stood in his way. But Aed only has responsibility for himself. Somerled must bear the weight of all of them. He sighs. It was my choice, was it not?

He is lying to himself. He knows it. Fear is holding him back. The indecisiveness is a symptom, not a cause. He is frightened of seeming weak, frightened of arriving at her door and feeling nothing. Frightened of discovering that it is all an illusion, this great love that has sustained him all these years.

Here he is, the most powerful man in this world, and his fear dictates his actions. Even power is trumped by fear. Perhaps, he thinks, that is why the God of my father won out against the gods of my mother. Her gods knew only power; his God knew only fear.

He deals first with the easy part. He sends Brian to Thorfinn, to take the soundings of the Man chieftains. The word comes back that Man is ripe for the taking. He sends a messenger to Dublin, out of courtesy to Muirchertach, and receives back his blessing. The price is Somerled's help in the Irish mainland, once Man and the outer isles are secure. He will pay the price willingly.

~ ~ ~

Fire. Great hanging sheets of fire, reaching up to the stars in a fury of sparks and flame. The smack of heat stuns them into silence. He wrenches off his helmet, which is warm to the touch already. Godred's hall has taken the flames and thrown them skywards, proclaiming to all of Man that a new power is here. A baptism, an inferno for the new Lord of the Isles.

The old one has scuttled off again. To Norway perhaps, or Orkney. It would have been better to take him. But he can be no threat to them now.

Beside him, Dugald's face is more open than he has ever seen it. Transfixed, awed by the simple majesty of a wall of fire and a crumbling dynasty. The orange light cast by the fire warms the boy's skin, makes him ethereal in the darkness.

Somerled watches his son watch the blaze. He watches his men's faces as the roof catches and fires, the crash and burn of the timbers echoing across the bay. How men love destruction. How little they care, when their blood is reddened by victory, that there are treasures melting in that hall. They do not care that it was a wonder of its age, that hall, proclaiming its master's domination of the Western Seas with its vast timbers, its forbidding angles. When he saw it close to, as his fifty-eight galleys sailed brazenly into Man's great bay, spitting spears and arrows, he gawped like a child.

Yet now, with Godred in flight and his men turned or cowed, now it burns and he feels his soul leap and crackle with the flames. Why? he asks himself. Why are we compelled to destroy what is beautiful?

eímbeaR

I know immediately that something does not make sense. These men are too sullen, too shifty to be simple pilgrims as they claim. They arrived at dusk, in a big, sleek galley. They are richly dressed. Their leader, the one who calls himself Olaf, made some strange excuse to Eua for not crossing to Iona, despite the last light sheening on the still water of the Sound.

They claim hospitality and we give it, moving among them with soup and bread. Olaf is restless. He twitches; drums his fingers on the table. He scarcely eats. There is something sinister in his contained energy. He boils like a warrior before a fight; but here we are on the Island of Women, with no one to fight but the cows.

Sigrdrifa is sitting with Padraig, the stonemason's eldest boy. He is a good boy; tall and broad-shouldered like his father. He brought her a bunch of flowers picked from the machair in Iona, and carried across the Sound amid the mocking of his peers. He laughed with them and clasped the flowers tighter, offering them up to her with a diffidence that made me like him all the more. He will be a stonemason like his father. Once I thought she would marry a prince. Now I wish for her the gift of relishing a quiet life. A small, happy life led to the sound of axe chipping at stone.

A life in which there is joy in the two ends of a stone-carved circle meeting.

Somerled once said he loved me for my questing soul. God grant her a restful soul. God grant her . . .

I hear his name. The man Olaf is asking about my daughter. Is she Somerled's daughter? he wants to know. He gets the reply, and his dark face gleams. Across the room, my daughter laughs. She is young and she is pretty, and her innocence cuts through the heavy air of the room like clear water tumbling on granite.

Oh Lord. Oh my Saviour.

I watch him, this Olaf, watching her. He follows her, his gaze intent under hooded lids. His eyes flick up, they flick down. My hand wraps itself around the handle of a knife. I imagine using it, and the rush of his men to avenge him.

I will her to look at me, but she has eyes only for Padraig. The boy shifts in his seat, as if made nervous by the strength of my stare. He looks up to find me watching them, and he blushes red. Oh bless him, and make him strong. I stand, still staring at him, and jerk my head to beckon him to the shadows beyond the fires. He whispers something to Sigrdrifa, and I see her turn and search for my gaze, all imploring hope.

In the corner, I wait for Padraig, and watch Olaf's eyes eat my child.

'Lady,' begins Padraig, his voice a little too loud.

'Shh,' I hiss. One of Olaf's men is watching us. I keep my face smooth, pushing away the deep-frowning fear. In a light whisper I say:

'Look playful, boy, we are watched. She is in danger, I feel it. No. Do not move, I beg you. They must not smoke us. Listen. I will draw this Olaf into talk. You get her away. A boat if you can. Smuggle her to Mull. You have somewhere to go there?'

He nods, and bless him, he keeps calm and pulls on a mask of lightness and banter.

'When shall I bring her back?'

'When they are gone. And if she comes back whole and safe, you shall have her as a bride, if she wishes it. No, boy, stay calm. Only if she wishes it, mind.'

He nods and walks back over to her. She looks up at him, and across at me. She knows something important has passed, but she can't work it out. I watch Olaf watching her frown and I walk forward.

Loudly I say: 'Who are you, to ask for Somerled's daughter?'

'A humble pilgrim.'

There are smirks from his men.

'Are you friend or foe to the Lord Somerled?'

He looks at me properly then, for the first time. He has been more busy eyeing the youngest of the girls, though he is my age or older.

'Who are you to ask the question?'

'I was Somerled's woman. He spat me out on to this island when he married that bitch from Man.'

A few of his men flinch forward at this; but he raises a hand to hold them.

'You are Eimhear? Yet I heard you were a great beauty.'

His cronies laugh.

'Time ravages women, my lord.'

'Why do you call me that?'

'It is clear that you are a man of consequence. Of great worth.'

Beyond his head, I see my daughter slowly rising, holding Padraig's hand. I see her moving back towards the shadows. But still, they need to skirt the back and leave by the door near Olaf.

321

'I can tell you things of Somerled, my lord. For whisky. For what else is there to comfort an old woman in her dotage? I can draw you a map of his lands, and where to land unseen, to creep up behind.'

He leans forward, interested now.

'Do it,' he commands.

I drop to my knees at his feet. With my knife, I scratch on the floor. His men move in to watch, crowding in on me.

'Here is the castle, my lord. Here the entrance to the loch. And here, there is a blind spot for the lookout – who is here.'

'It is a long time since you were there, woman.'

'Aye, but he is a man of habit, who thinks himself safe in his own nest.'

I point again at the place, where a hidden jag of rocks will drown their black souls if they ever think to try it.

They ask me questions. I try to be convincing. Behind their bent heads, Sigrdrifa escapes into the darkness.

~ ~ ~

Later, I hear his drunken shouting. 'Where is she? Where is Somerled's daughter? Where is the bitch?'

The door flies open.

'You know. Where is she?'

'I do not—'

The blow sends me reeling across the room. Pain thunders in my head.

'Where is she?'

A full punch, which cracks my head backwards against the wall. Oh Lord. Oh my Christ. Where are you?

A blow to the stomach. I crouch over, beast-like, spitting blood on to the floor. I hear the sound of his excitement; his sharp-drawn breath, his panting.

He pushes me down, tearing at my dress. I try to scream, and his hand comes over my mouth, over my nose, so that I cannot breathe. This is drowning. This is the water coming over my head. This is not knowing which way is down, which is up. Bubbles flying both ways; panic insisting on an impossible breath.

This is his fist pushing inside me, his quick breath loud in my ear.

This is a pain that swells like a rip tide.

This is him pushing himself inside me, as someone, somewhere, laughs.

He judders and moans. Pulls himself upright. Takes his hand from my mouth. I try to bite it, but he is too quick. I can't even do that much. He laughs. Then he spits in my face, and as his gob slides down my cheek he says: 'Tell Somerled that Godred, son of Olaf, King of Man, fucked his woman.'

1157

Somerled

H e knows something is not right as soon as his feet touch the ground. Gillecolm, who was left in charge with Aed, stands alone to greet him. Was Gillecolm's face always lined, always so sad? No.

'Father,' says the boy without preamble. 'Father, it is Aed.'

'Dead?'

Aed's son Fingal, a brawny man with the look of his father, pushes his way to the front of the boat. His older brother is with Dugald in Man. He did well this season, Fingal, thinks Somerled. I must tell Aed. Aed.

Fingal jumps down next to Somerled. He is Gillecolm's age; they are boyhood friends. Gillecolm looks at his friend as he shakes his head.

'Not dead. A sickness.'

They walk quickly towards Aed's house. One week ago now, Oona found Aed lying still, eyes open. He cannot move, cannot speak. Gillecolm has sent messengers to the wise men in Ireland, to Alba, to Norway, even to London to try to find a cure.

The hall is dark, stuffy from a stoked fire. Aed is propped on furs. His eyes flicker to Somerled when he enters. His mouth is a

324

strange twist, with pap running down the side of it where Oona's spoon has missed. His body is a mockery of itself, an unlikely assembly of skin and bone and wasting muscle.

Somerled pauses in the doorway. It smells of sickness and old age and death. He forces himself to walk in. He kneels heavily by the old man's bed.

'Aed,' he says. 'Aed.'

Oh Jesus.

Fingal stands in the doorway. He pulls off his cloak, and his muscles swell across great broad shoulders. The pulsing health of his young body draws all eyes. Oona, Aed and Somerled watch him as he comes forward. His youth is a reproach and an offering to his father.

He is carrying his axe, his weapon of choice.

He sets the axe next to the bed, and draws his mother's shrunken body into an embrace. Aed's eyes flicker to the axe, and back again to Somerled. He grunts, spittle falling out of his mouth. He grunts again. His eyes flick urgently back to the axe.

'No, Aed. No.'

Then, for the first time in the great span of years they have known and loved each other, Somerled watches Aed cry. The tears run down his twisted, frozen face, and the snot gathers in shameful bubbles at the bottom of his nose.

Somerled, who has not cried since that day long ago when his life ended, feels the answering prickle in his eyes, and to save them both, he leans forward and whispers into his friend's ear, his eyes fixed unblinking on the yellowing wool of the rug Aed rests on.

'I will do it, then, my friend. You have been waiting for me, old man. I will do it.'

~ ~ ~

Afterwards, a kind of madness takes him.

Somerled hides himself in a shieling up in the mountains, cold though it is. He hunkers down, beastlike. He thinks if he has to see a face, he will stab it bloody. If he hears a human voice, he will rip out the throat that made it. Tries not to think beyond the act of being alive. Wake up. Fish. Eat. Sleep. Hunt. Eat. Sleep.

Sometimes he does not bother. He lies under furs and listens to the rain. He listens to the rumble of his belly; feels his bladder rise. He wishes he could find a silence in his own mind. He has outward silence up here. Only the rushing of water and the calling birds break it. Sometimes it makes it worse, amplifying the voices in his head to a terrible shout. Sometimes it soothes.

They leave food for him at the foot of the mountain, like offerings to an ancient god. He will not see them. He especially will not see the-priest-who-is-not-Padeen, who bothered him as he sharpened the axe. Who told him that it would be a sin. Who told him that God would prefer Aed to linger on in his travesty of a body. The priest who scampered alongside him as he walked up the hill from the smithy with the sharpened axe, arguing with him and shouting at him when he would have been alone with his thoughts, alone with his prayers.

It took Fingal and Gillecolm to hold the priest back. Oona was elsewhere. With her daughters and the other women. He could not hear their keening. It was a windy day, made to snatch away the sounds of their grief and scatter them to the horizon.

He wanted to close his eyes. He did not want his last memory of Aed to be this one. He knows the power of memory, Somerled. Knows how one brutal image can chase away the rest, leaving a man to fight to find the happy faces in his mind's eye while the pained, hurt, lost ones crowd in unasked.

But he could not close his eyes and risk missing Aed's proffered neck. He could not let his cowardice make Aed's passing more difficult. There was no great declaration at the end. No outpouring of thanks and love. 'Goodbye, old friend,' said Somerled, and Aed looked up at him with unreadable eyes. When they closed, those dear eyes, Somerled raised Fingal's axe to the sky and let it fall.

~ ~ ~

He comes down the hill at last. He sets his face into a fury that forbids questions. They all scuttle round him, afraid. He is a magician, he finds, a wizard. He can conjure silence from rooms full of chatter. He can send children running with the flick of an eyebrow. He can make servants invisible. He can make women pretend to swoon for him, as he beds them mechanically and to mutual dissatisfaction.

There is one thing this sorcerer cannot do. He cannot conjure love. He cannot spin its invisible threads, pick his boys up and ravel them in twine. He would bind them tighter. But here they are in front of him. Angus with a purple eye and a bloody nose. Ranald all bleeding fists and defiance. They are grown men, near enough. Old enough now to come raiding with him. He should not need to separate them, brawling like drunkards at a feast. Olaf stands behind them, awkward on tall limbs he has not yet learned to use.

He can see Gillecolm in the distance down by the shore. Staying out of it. The boys are talking over one another, words tumbling in a stream of justification, accusation and plaintiveness. He watches Gillecolm as he deftly skins a seal, holding its head with a tenderness at odds with his task. His two small sons, Sigurd and Fergus, watch as he slowly slices the skin away from the flesh, careful not to break it. He works quickly with the point of his knife, easing the skin from the bloodied carcass.

'He took my sword.'

'He said I could.'

'I did not.'

'You're a liar.'

On it rolls. He feels a great weariness settle on him. He wants to topple over into the furs spread behind him, let his head sink into them. He would stretch his limbs out, arching his back. He wants to give himself up to thoughts of Eimhear as he first knew her, spread below him and laughing up at him. He would open his eyes to watch her son carry out a small task competently. He looks over to Gillecolm. The skin is peeling off the seal in one piece, leaving the strange, sad flesh behind. Blood pools in the indents of the rock, and the boys stick their fingers in it, to draw patterns on the white stone surface.

He watches the whorls of the younger boy, Fergus. Sigurd draws fighting stick men, their axes raised and blobby faces drawn of blood screaming defiance at one another.

'Father, you must punish him.'

'Me? You're the liar and the thief.'

'You are.'

He looks up, to where a skua fights the air currents. It battles elegantly, wings spread. It hovers, then concedes, letting itself slip sideways. Or is it pushed?

As he stands, the cup he holds falls to the ground and the last of the wine dribbles out.

The boys stop talking and watch it fall. He pushes past them. Ranald opens his mouth to say something, but stops himself. Somerled looks at them, confused. Is it pity he feels for them? Is it contempt? Perhaps it is guilt. Perhaps their scratching and snarling is his fault. Is it possible to be a king and have sons who love each other as Aed's boys do? Is it possible to have power and bequeath it seamlessly? Can power pass joyously through generations, or will it always corrupt and embitter on its way?

He shakes his head to clear it. Angus and Ranald fall back, looking at each other and back at him.

Silent, he walks away from them, down to the shore. He feels the turf give to rock under his feet. The low clouds threaten rain, but it holds off for now, brooding over a sullen sea.

'Can I help?' he says. Gillecolm looks up. He grins.

'Please.' He gestures at the pile of seals to be skinned. Some ten of them, lying tumbled on top of one another.

Somerled squats beside him. He pulls his knife and reaches for the nearest body. Still warm, the creature. Only a great dent in its head to explain its passivity. Carefully Somerled makes the first cuts.

'I haven't done this for years,' he says.

'It's not my favourite job.'

'Aye, you always loved a seal.' Like your mother.

'Still. I'd not have the boys shiver through a winter because I'm too squeamish to skin one.'

'Jesus, boy. Can you imagine if you refused? You'd never live it down.'

'Lord. I can see the faces on my crew.' They both laugh, and it feels good.

They work quietly, deftly. The pile of skins grows higher.

'They say,' says Gillecolm, 'that the Maiden is earning his name. He does not lie with women.'

'No? Men? Beasts?'

'Nothing.'

Somerled whistles. His blade slips a little, nicking the skin. He curses.

'I should shout at you for that ruined skin, Father.'

'Just try.'

Gillecolm smiles and throws his last skin on the heap. He stands, stretching out of the crouch. 'Father, will you come with the boys and me for some food?'

The boy has his own longhouse, as befits his status. Somerled ducks inside. Deirdre, coming forward from the fire, sees it is him and freezes. It takes Gillecolm and the boys coming in to unroot her. She finds her voice and welcomes him. They warm themselves by the fire, while she rushes about to rustle up an unexpected banquet. She ignores Somerled's pleas for simplicity, pushing them off with trailing sentences.

'No trouble. It's a . . . an honour. Boys,' she hisses. 'Here.'

The meal passes quietly, pleasantly. Somerled is calm and easy in their company. He works hard with Deirdre, who he has largely ignored until now, and makes her smile.

Afterwards, he goes outside and stands still to breathe the sea. On the rocks where the seals were skinned, he sees the water come high, washing away Fergus and Sigurd's seal-blood paintings. The water falls back, leaving no sign that the crimson army has ever been there at all.

I will go, he decides then, in that instant. I will go and find her.

Ragnhild

I know where he is going. He thinks I do not. He is like a boy, bounding about. Excited. The old fool. He whispers in corners with Gillecolm. They go quiet when they see me. As if I am stupid. As if I do not know.

What will he do with her? With me? Will he bring her back here, set her over my head? Will he turn me out? Should I take my boys and flee? But I have nowhere to go. Man is his. The islands are his. I could not get to Alba without him tracking me down first. He could not take the direct affront of his wife sheltering with his greatest enemy. Galloway is no use; it has its own problems fighting the king in Alba.

There is nowhere for me to go. I have lived on this spit of land my entire adult life. I have birthed and raised my children here. I have cried here. It is home, but it has never been home.

I sit entombed in flesh that does not belong to me. Wearing clothes that are too tight. Wearing the heavy gold and silver pieces he fits around my neck and arms because it is expected of him.

Sometimes I dream of another girl, who married Baldur the Beautiful and raised children who had no great birthright to hate each other over. She is slender still. She wears flowers in her hair,

331

not precious stones. Her necklace is a cheap trinket, worn and given in love. She smiles often and does not understand loneliness.

Then I round on myself. Baldur the Beautiful is probably Baldur the Bald and Grumpy now. He probably beats his wife. Her hands are chapped and sore from chores; her back is crooked and her eyes weak. Her children are contemptuous, as the young always are in their secret hearts. Ragnhild the Fair has become Ragnhild the Fat and Sad in every possible life.

So what can I do but stay here? I will stay while he goes off chasing fairies and phantoms. I will weave and work. I will pray and fast. I will see to his household. I will keep his bed warm. I will settle his fractious children. And I will wait for him to decide my fate, like some divine potentate pulling on a string.

Patience.

This is what I teach my daughter. Raging does not help – I learned that a long while since. Embrace your passivity, my daughter, it is the only way. Learn to let the minutes, the hours, slip by. Thank the Lord for uneventful days. Learn to bear, as bear you must, your inability to alter your fate. Men have blunt tools in the face of God's wrath, to be sure. But they have something. We stand defenceless and wait. Wait.

1157

SOMERLED

His kingdom stretches from Ardnamurchan Point down to the Mull of Kintyre. He sets sail to tour his realm; an itinerary designed to end in Iona. A roundabout way to the Island of Women, but one he can justify without reference to his great fear. How can he be fearful of one woman? Even the sea is his. No ship can pass through the sea roads without his knowing, without his approval.

He is the sea god, Aegir. He is older than giants. He is father of the nine wave maidens. His storm-happy daughters carry him to his land-based dominions. The clear wave. The blooded wave. The pitching wave. The frothing wave. The rising wave. The billowing wave. The welling wave. The foam-flecked wave. The cool wave.

Lord, how rich he is now. Silver seems to cream from the surface of the sea, filling his hall, clinking on his men's arms, hanging in drops from his latest girl's ears; weighing tighter, harder, in ever greater chains around his neck.

Padeen has told him of the great king in Byzantium whose crown was so heavy it could not rest unaided on his skull without crushing it. The towering weight of the gold and jewels was suspended on silken ropes hung from the ceiling above the throne. At some point, thinks Somerled, a bare-headed little man must crawl beneath that

333

crown, bring his head up to meet its golden rim and then, only then, call himself a king.

Somerled misses Padeen. He is still in Rome, the creature. The longed-for pilgrimage granted by Somerled after the rebellion against the Maiden. He will think of that war again now that he is Lord of the Isles. The hasty peace he agreed with the Maiden, as his nephew Mael Coluim wailed and vowed to fight on alone, will he keep it? Perhaps.

They start at the far south of his lands, down on Kintyre. They pass the place where his father's hall stood, its charred black skeleton covered now by a fine skin of sand. He stamps down the memories, tramples them viciously. He allows himself, only once, a moment to think about his mother. He waits until no one is watching, just in case he cries. He does not cry; instead he rages, grimly silent. When he tries to find her face, her dear, red-cheeked, flour-smeared face, it is not there. It eludes him, his mind a blur of other things, other features.

Up into Islay, then, where he raises a finger, like a god, and orders a castle built on a nub of rock by a lovely bay. A second Ardtornish, to rule the southern seas. One sentence is all it takes these days.

Build me a castle, he says, and there is nodding, and bowing. Orders ripple down a line, whose end he cannot even see. Once, he stood, pick in hand, and ripped up the peat to set the foundations of his own hall. He remembers the joy of watching it rise from the heather, and how Eimhear and his mother whirled around the finished vaulted room. Arms clasped, they spun in tight circles, like a child's hoop spiralling down a hill.

On Islay, exploring hall by hall, they gather in the tributes. No longer for Godred of Man, but for Dugald, grandson of the dead king. Somerled watches his son accepting the bowing and scraping as if he were born to it. But he only holds it in trust. No one doubts who is really their lord, as their eyes slide past the smooth-faced boy to the glowering man behind him.

They come, on Islay, to an inland loch. Surrounded by low hills, it is, to Somerled's mind, an eerie place. Reeds whisper in the corners; the wind ruffles the fresh water. There are two or three small islands at one end; at the other, the hills taper off to close in the valley.

Ranald turns to him with a shining, raptured face.

'This,' he says. 'This is where we should build.'

'Here?' The borrowed horses rake at the grass, snorting and juddering. Dugald reaches down and pats his mare's neck.

'On those islands,' says Ranald, pointing down.

'But we are *inland*,' says Somerled slowly, as if talking to a child, not a boy of sixteen.

'But think, Father,' says Ranald. 'Think how easy it would be to protect those islands on the loch. No sea attack. No one could get close without you seeing them. And even if they did, they couldn't get at the islands. Nor keep you from fresh water.'

Somerled can see the sense in that. But what a place it is. Overlooked. Imagine setting up your home somewhere without a salt breeze. Imagine the eyes in the darkness, watching.

'What about the waste, the sewage?' he asks, thinking of the low-tide rocks at Ardtornish that serve as a latrine, washed clean twice a day.

Ranald waves an impatient hand, as if such a concern is beneath the notice of a king. Somerled opens his mouth to rebuke the boy, but pauses. He will learn soon enough that concern for his men's bowels is as much a part of kingship as ring-giving. To a king, shit matters like silver.

'If you like it, it is yours,' he says mildly, ignoring the silent start of Conn beside him. 'What is this place anyway?' he asks.

'Finlaggan, Lord Somerled,' Conn says.

Somerled nods, and turns back towards the sea.

~ ~ ~

The next day they move on to Jura, with its men as ferocious as its midges. Perhaps, he thinks, their ferocity comes from the constant jibing at their island's geography: the two great hills rising like breasts above the sea. The men who live in the shadow of the Paps of Jura have heard all the jokes before, and they are dour, touchy with strangers.

~ ~ ~

In Mull, they climb the big hill there for the sport of it. Its strange conical summit is visible from Ardtornish. She always said they would climb it together one day, but he does it, at last, without her. It is cold at the top, clammy with low clouds. Just below the cloud line, on the ridge before the summit, he sits with aching legs and looks out across the Sound to his home. Will it do, now? Now that he is lord of all of it. Lord of the Isles.

He can't see it from here. Iona. The holy isle of Iona that sits, a precious pearl, in the turquoise sea off the tip of Mull. Can he bear it? He has not been there since he lost her.

When he has time, he will breathe life into Iona again. He will reinvigorate its fading abbey. Set a good man at its head. David may be dead, but his legacy is persistent. The tonsured monks of the Roman church are spreading. Monasteries are pushing their roots into the alien heather. It is said that in Alba, the Culdees are in retreat, forced out by the Continental orders. Prayers are barked in Latin. The God of these seas should hear them in Gaelic.

336

Iona. The pulsing heart of the church he knows and loves. The cadences of its prayers in God's own language. The play of sea and sky, cycling through blues and greens and greys. The golden sand on its beaches. The scudding low clouds and the piercing shafts of light that tear a rent in the grey to glint upon the sea. The smallness of the island against the raging of a winter gale. Men clinging on to its heathery safety.

A place to hear God. To see his creation in every changing colour of the place.

But before God, the island like a teardrop in the bay. The Island of Women.

eimheaR

I am with child. I thought I was too old. I am past forty-five, I
think. But I am with child. I know it, and the knowledge is a
kind of madness. I am sick all day. My breasts are tender. I feel a
great and furious lethargy that pulls me down towards the heather
as to a bed.

His child. Godred's child. A thing spawned of violence and fear.
How can I love it? How can I bear the shame?

I pray and I pray. But perhaps God does not hear me. Or he
laughs. Peers over the edge of his cloud and says: what now, my
tiny plaything? What will you do with your free will now, my child?
Will you stay to bear the shame? The abbot's fury, the women's
whispering?

Will you throw yourself from the cliff, my child? Hah! You could
land on your belly and rip Godred's child out, to bob on the tide
like a tadpole. Will you tell your daughter, who does not know
that you parted your legs to keep hers closed? Oh, but I will enjoy
watching that conversation. He laughs, sending waves of thunder
barrelling across the seawater.

I sit, watching the water. I will the waves to numb my mind,
which returns, traitorous thing, to Godred. To the stink of his

breath. To his spit sliding down my cheek. To the blood on my thighs. To my shaking hands and violent sobs. To my passive, still body, which let him do that to me.

The waves are high today. White-flecked. The sea is that strange steel-grey that promises blue but does not quite get there. The light on Iona is golden; a gap in the clouds has opened up like a flower. Perhaps so He can watch my tortured flapping. My struggle for breath. You can't even see the horizon from here. I have been hemmed in by Mull and Iona for nearly twenty years. How have I borne it?

A ship rounds the headland. With a lurch, I recognize the emblem it carries. The sign of the otter. Perhaps it is Gillecolm. It is not his time. Lord, how I would love to see him. It would be such a blessed relief to tell someone what has happened. I will not tell him, though, I know it. I will pull on a mask and hope he can't see through it.

I watch her glide into the cleft in the rock that passes for a bay. She backs her oars and drops anchor, and a man jumps into the shallows. Not a tall man, but broad. He raises his head to look about him, and I recognize him with a shock. Somerled.

I am running down the hill. My foot catches on heather and I nearly fall. I am close to him now. I can see the lines at the corners of his eyes. The grey in his hair. I see the gold and silver clanking on his arms and neck. I see his air of prosperity, the smug bounce in him as he clears the last of the shallows.

I fly at him.

He sees me and begins to smile. It seems to me the final insult, and I slam into him. I scratch him and bite him. My arms flail at him again and again. I spit at him and scream a gibbering nonsense. You are too late, too late. The scream is a thing apart from my body; loud and wild and alarming. The thing inside me that calls itself a baby seems to rise like bile in me, and I am fury.

He staggers backwards. He looks sideways to his ship full of men, and I realize he is embarrassed, and that drives me wilder. Embarrassed. I am a wailing, screeching embarrassment to this great lord, this great fucking potentate who has deigned to drop from the sky.

I hit him again and again, until he falls backwards into the surf. I stand over him, panting and sobbing.

He sits on his arse in the surf and grins. Grins, the bastard.

'Are you happy to see me, then, my Otter?' he says.

I look up at the grey sky, trying to find my breath. I am laughing, I find, not sobbing. Laughing, for all love. He laughs too, until I splash his face with icy water. His ship is heeling over at its anchor, as all the oarsmen stand starboard-side to gawp at this spectacle we make. Two old fools fighting in the cold shallows.

He puts up his hand and I pull him upright.

'Is there a fire? Jesus, but it's cold,' he says, for all the world as if it is twenty days not twenty years.

~ ~ ~

I tell him straight away, with no preamble. I tell him what Godred did.

He looks thunderous. He moves as if to hold me, but I put up a hand. I cannot, I will not be touched by anyone. I try to explain it to him. How my skin is not my own. I pull the blanket around my shoulders, hating even its rough scratch against my skin.

'I can wait,' he says. 'I have had enough practice at not touching you, Eimhear.'

He pauses, and rakes the fire. 'I will kill him,' he says, raising his eyes to meet mine.

I nod.

'The baby. There is a clear solution. Tell everyone it is mine. We are handfasted still – there would be no shame in it for you.'

'They are not stupid – the timing is wrong.'

'People believe what they want to believe. They tend to find it convenient to believe me.'

I look at him as if at a stranger. There is something contained and ferocious about him. It is unnerving. He has to smile before I am easy again; that singular sweet smile I have known and loved a lifetime.

How strange it is, how sharply odd. To be sitting here with him. Morose and lined shadows of the children who played at being a family. But there is something of the essence. I can feel it, spinning between us in the half-light. And what is more, so can he.

I am still peculiar. I can still feel that man's hate on my skin, his spit on my cheek. I am still furious with Somerled. This soft talking is dreamlike – a quietness in the storm. Yet there are flutters of joy to come. It is like that moment in carrying a child when you first feel a movement; it catches you and you stop in wonderment and confusion. Is that flicker in your belly a miracle pulse of growing life, or is it wind?

I smile at the thought and he moves his hand to my face to catch it. I flinch. He pulls back his hand and sits on it, as if to control his impulse.

'Sorry,' I say.

'It is not your fault,' he says. 'It was a message for me, was it not?'

It is always about you, I think, but the thought is not worthy. Neither is it his fault that the world revolves around men and their stupidity.

'What hope have we, if we talk about fault and blame? In any of it,' I say.

'You are a seer. I have always known it.'

'Pshaw. I am a woman who wants to go home and will say any crap that will get me there.'

'You want to come home, truly?'

'No, I would rather stay here. I have a very important cabbage plot to tend. Don't laugh. It is true. But if you insist, I suppose someone else can pull them up. And eat the bastards.'

'What of Sigrdrifa?'

'I think she will stay here with Padraig. The boy's head is full of stone crosses, and he is better served here.'

'I will go and find her soon.'

'She is leaving us together. All tact and embarrassment. Bless her.'

'Does she know? About that man?'

I shake my head. His shadow is long, and I shiver.

'Oh, my Otter. I am sorry.'

I pull my blanket even tighter, like a swaddle. 'If I come with you, what of your wife?'

'I thought of sending her to Man. To run Dugald's household there. I will give her face, load her with riches. She will be happy.'

'She will be humiliated, unless she is very stupid.'

He pauses, and looks unhappy. Here are seas to chart another day, I think.

'Still. I will stay here to have the baby,' I say. 'Let us not heap on the scorn by turning up with a big belly. I will have the baby, and suckle it, and then I will come.'

'But that will be a year, at least.'

'Have we not waited long enough? I will not come home with another man's child in my belly. I will not.'

He looks fierce, and I remember that he is a great lord now, with a passive wife. He is not given to being contradicted. But he

342

nods at last, and smiles, and I am relieved. I suddenly realize that, for all the terrifying boredom, I have been my own chief for nearly twenty years, as much as he has. I will not go home to be his vassal, no matter how much the thought of being there with him is turning me soft and simpering.

'Well,' he says. 'You will have an easy birth, I know it. If you hate the child for being his, we will find it a home. If you love it for being yours, you will bring it with you. God between us and evil, but we will be together, my Otter. First, we must make it clear to listening ears that this baby is mine.'

I cannot be touched. I cannot. He smiles and shakes his head.

'We will go to bed and be chaste as nuns, my darling. Perhaps a little play-acting.'

So in my corner of the hall we lie under blankets and make the noises of love, giggling silently like children. I reach for his hand in the darkness. I turn it over and kiss the oar-calloused skin. He turns my hand and kisses the hoe-calloused skin. I feel the madness in me, the strangeness, ebb from a shriek to a murmur. I am going home.

eimhear

He is not done with me yet, this vengeful deity. I close my eyes and imagine his laughter churning the waves.

I feel the high kick of the baby against my ribs; the great swell of my belly pulling me earthwards. And I watch the woman being handed down on to the jetty. She is larger than I expected; fatter. Her hair is a greying blonde, curled and plaited as if she were ten years younger.

She looks awkward as she climbs from the galley, as if her body does not belong to her.

Gillecolm, at my side, holds my hand tight. He sailed like a fury to get here first, to warn me of her coming. She is on her way to Man, to join her eldest son's household. But why has she come here first? What use is it? What does she want with me?

She stops and looks around, pulling herself upright. Catching her breath, perhaps. Her eyes move past me at first, and swivel back. We stare at each other.

The heavy, violent atmosphere – the watching eyes. It summons up a memory, of the day I jumped down into the shallows at Ardtornish and walked up the beach towards Somerled.

The scene is sharp and clear in my head, and I relish it. I remember his face, that comical fear of the blooded warrior caught in mysteries of the heart he does not quite understand. The panic at the soft edges of love and life creeping up on him, when he's used to the simple clang of metal.

I remember how he took a step forward, and one back, haplessly. I remember how old Sigrdrifa stood behind him, laughing at his obvious discomfort. I remember the eyes of the warriors on me, flicking up and down, assessing me like meat. As if my body mattered. As if he could not have had any choice morsels he fancied – as if what we were to each other was only the promise of entangled limbs.

Here I am again, meeting someone at the edge of the sea and the land. Someone whose life is threaded with mine.

The absurdity of it all hits me, and I feel the griping of laughter at my stomach, fighting for room with this mountainous baby I carry. I start to smile, and then to laugh.

Her face changes. I can't read it, I don't know her. But something in Gillecolm's stance beside me tells me I have made a terrible mistake. This is a woman who does not understand the role of laughter in defeating Him and His plans. My rage would have been kinder than laughter. I have cut her legs from under her before she has even walked two steps on my island. What have I done?

Ragnhild

S he is laughing. Laughing at me. Of all the things I expected, of all the scenes that played out in my imagination, this was not one of them.

My mother's voice echoes in my head. Straighten your back, slither your hips, bite your lips, pinch your cheeks. Cast your eyes down, flick them up. Smile, don't smile. Be beautiful. It is all you have. It is your currency, your hack silver.

But I am not beautiful any more, I scream back. I have nothing. I am left with nothing. And she is laughing at me.

Neither is she beautiful, this witch. She is older, and her face is lined and sunburned. Her hair is faded, washed out of colour. Is that worse? That he is putting me out for this old, worn woman?

She walks towards me, swallowing her smile, made cumbersome by the weight of her belly. Her belly that carries my husband's child. The laughter is lingering in her eyes. What is she laughing at? Why am I so pathetic, so hilarious to her that she must laugh at me?

'Welcome, Lady Ragnhild,' she says. 'I am Eimhear.'

I nod. I know who you are, you witch. Close to, the likeness between her and Gillecolm is uncanny. It is clearer now why I always disliked him, and his sly face.

'Come,' she says. 'We have food prepared. Simple enough, but good.'

I shake my head. I am cold and tired and starving, but I will not eat with this woman. I am conscious that I have not yet spoken. My mouth seems unable to work. She takes the lead, and I hate her for it.

'A walk, then?'

I nod. She motions with her head to her people, her son, and they slip away, until it's just the two of us here on this vile shore. We are beyond earshot of the galley, where my escort watch us with narrowed, prurient eyes. I glare at their captain and he blushes and turns away.

'So,' she says. 'Why are you here?'

'To understand.'

'And do you, now that you are here?'

I shake my head. I cannot quite look at her full in the face. My eyes slide to the side. I feel her gaze upon me.

'No,' I say, with heaviness.

We pause, and the silence between us is filled with the screech and clamour of seabirds. When I get home to Man, I will order heavy shutters, and heavier curtains, and line the walls with tapestries. I will block out the sound. I will have silence.

'You should know,' I say, 'that he is incapable of sticking with one woman. He has paraded them in front of me. Trotted them up and down. Fondled them with my back barely turned. Young ones. Old ones. He is a goat. He is vile.'

'I'm sorry,' she says.

I want to swear at her, like a fishwife. I want to fly at her, scratch her eyes, make her take back her pity. I look away, blinking hard to stop the tears.

'I had no chance,' I say. 'Somerled loved your shadow, all the time. It would have been different. You stole my life, when it had barely begun.'

She laughs at this. Laughs. 'Jesus wept,' she says. 'Some old bastard is laughing at us now. You stole *my* life, Ragnhild. You stole mine. You and your father.'

I turn around and face her then. Her laughter is too much, and I feel something snap. Something deep. I feel a swell of rage so sharp it's almost an ecstasy. Before I recognize what is happening, I spit at her. I spit at that laughing, mocking face. She steps back with an expression of horror. I think she will hit me, assume she will hit me. But she just stares and stares and stares. Until at last I turn and hurry back to the jetty, and the safety of the galley.

eimhear

Her spit slides down my cheek. It sears my skin. It burns. There is hatred in her face, in her eyes. Her brother's eyes.

Deep inside, I feel something give, something go. A click in my pelvis. I feel a trickle of moisture between my legs. A sudden sharp tightening on my great belly. The baby kicks, and it feels vicious. It feels like a warning.

I touch the place where her spit scalds me, and watch her go. My legs begin to shake and I sink down to sit on the rocks. I am frightened, God help me. For the first time in an age, I am terrified.

1157

SOMERLED

He hurries down to the shore, from up near the crags where he has been hunting with Brian. A messenger has brought him news that his daughter is here. Sigrdrifa! She has not been here since they left some twenty years ago. She was a tiny, voluble scrap then, his littlest otter.

It is a glorious, glorious day. Sharp but clear. The sky is blue and the sea sighs. Overhead, the skuas wheel and call. He will take his daughter roaming. Show her all her old favourite spots. She loved the river's tumble into Loch Aline. They will go there, and talk of days gone and the ones they love. They will hunt, perhaps. She seems stronger than Bethoc, more like to draw an arrow than whine to Jesus.

He will throw a feast for her. He shouts at the messenger to find his steward. The hall will ring with the sound of cooking and cleaning and scraping. The smell of meat will send the dogs into a frenzy, and the children will gather at the back to beg for scraps. Lord, what a night they will have to welcome his daughter home.

She is married now, he knows that. To the boy he met, the stonemason. He would not have allowed it, had he known in advance. She should have had a champion; a prince. Still, it is done. He will order up crosses, set him to work, keep them here. Grandchildren, perhaps. Little girls that look like their grandmother turning somersaults in the cold sea and rising up, laughing, from the waves. Little boys to fight with wooden swords, and God love their hypothetical brows, if they are as useless as their uncle, he will laugh it off and gather them up and claim a grandfather's right to be tender.

He tries to move faster down the hill. His old man's knees protest the pace. He tries for the loose-limbed lollop of his youth, which carried him fast down a mountainside but it will not answer.

Perhaps she is here to broker the homecoming for her mother. Perhaps this means that both his otters will be coming home, where they belong. He lets the hope froth up, and he laughs aloud – a great booming laugh that frightens a bird from its perch in the heather. As it flutters away, he sees Sigrdrifa.

There she is. Being handed down by a broad-shouldered fellow; her husband. She is holding a bundle – a baby. He feels his heart leap, and prays it is a girl. A daughter for his daughter. A freckled sprite who will chatter up at her grandfather and take him swimming and laugh as he is upended by a wave.

He finds himself running forward, careless of his dignity. Men stare.

He calls her name, joy in his voice. She looks up at him, and her face checks him. He comes to a halt. She moves forward, crying, the grief ageing her by a hundred years.

'Child. Daughter. What is it?'

She cannot speak. He moves towards her. The baby shrieks, suddenly and loudly.

'Your mother?'

'It was the baby. This baby. She wouldn't come. There was blood. So much blood. My mother,' she says, in a broken voice,

351

'she seemed defeated. Without fight.' She gives up trying to speak, and looks at him with mute despair. He understands, and he is lost.

1160
SOMERLED

He is a stranger. He is a single, quivering point of rage. People are frightened of him. Servers' hands shake as they pour the wine, knowing that a spilled drop will pull his great fury down on their heads. Young warriors grip swords with white clenched fists as he passes. He has donned armour and a helm impenetrable to the human eye. Once, he believed that this encasing was a temporary thing. Eimhear, when she came home, would peel off the necessary layers. Unbuckle the plate, lift the helm. Kiss the bare skin beneath. Perhaps that was only ever an illusion; it is welded on too tight to shift.

He beds women indiscriminately and widely. They are brought to him as offerings from all over his lands, white-faced and nervous, snapping-eyed and keen, young and old, thin and plump. He loses himself in white flesh, cream, bronzed. He needs only a decent pretence at willingness; when you are king, the line between enthusiasm and duty is irrelevant anyway. He knows this as well as they, and why bother pretending otherwise?

He showers them with gold, silver, jewels. Doubling up for those with child. He loses count of the bastards. He has trouble enough with the ones he owns to.

He is a goat, a satyr. Sometimes a flicker of something like shame catches him by the throat, and he forces it away. There is no one left to fan the ember. Padeen died on the road from Rome, disillusioned and bitter, so his companions say. Disgusted by the corruption in Rome. He sent a letter before he died, full of ramblings about his shaken faith. *At home, I thought I could hear Him. Here, He is present in the sea and the sky and the rock. But can my God really be their God? Can my God hear prayers in Gaelic as well as Latin? Can His voice be true in the dust and the stink of the Tiber, and also at home, where the water runs clear as the day He made it? Is my faith a truth spoken in a true language or a lie? If our God is not their God, then who is He? I do not know. You sought to give me knowledge, Somerled. All I have gained is doubt. And that is a terrible, terrible thing.*

Doubt is a terrible thing. Somerled will allow for no doubt now. He let doubt and weakness rule him once and he will not do it again. He will allow for no mistakes in those who follow him. There is only the hard drive forward, the clash of steel on steel, the screaming of the prow beasts.

There is Gillecolm. This son, who once he berated and ignored, has become his crutch. The only one, now, who ever sees him smile. He is the one they send when there is bad news; the only one who will not be spitted on Somerled's fury.

He stands now in front of his father. The hangers-on and the servants are sent away, and Somerled gestures for Gillecolm to sit. The boy smiles, and it lights the room. Does everyone see the glory in that smile, thinks Somerled, or is it the blood between them that makes it so?

'Father,' says Gillecolm. 'We have had some news from the south. The Maiden has granted more lands to Walter FitzAlan. Down Paisley way. Set up on terms as a vassal again, the way they're doing it now. They've moved the monks in, too. Cluniacs, they call themselves.'

Somerled nods. The Maiden is pushing his vision of Alba steadily westward. He has been fighting Fergus in Galloway, demanding his vassalage to the Scottish crown. He's planting his knights along the Clyde, slowly, castle by castle, to where the river meets the sea. Somerled's sea.

'Giving land to this steward, FitzAlan. A deliberate provocation?' says Gillecolm.

'Partly. If I was my neighbour, I would put some muscle at the borders.'

'We never settled terms with the Maiden, did we?'

'No. Just let things slide while we took Man and the isles.'

'Well?'

Somerled thinks, trying to push aside the great weariness that still tugs at him. It is less urgent now, that desire to close his eyes.

He needs air to think, salted air. 'Come with me,' he says, and they duck outside, walking down to the sea. He likes having Gillecolm with him. The boy cannot fight, but his judgement is sound.

'Go to Roxborough,' he says. 'Make terms for me to visit the king. Peace, friendship, all that. We need to buy some time. We are only just back from fighting the Irish wars. The isles are still restless. Godred's in Norway, trying to persuade King Inge the Hunchback to send a fleet against us. We need to watch that.'

Gillecolm nods, accepting the commission. Pray God he is up to it.

~ ~ ~

At first, sitting in Roxborough at the great Christmas feast, he does not notice her. She is the king's mother. She speaks a language he

355

does not understand. The skin around her face is slack, her eyes wrinkled. She is Eimhear's age, perhaps.

He is polite to this queen, this not-Eimhear. His eyes slide past her, to the great long run of Scottish nobles talking, laughing, spitting, chewing, roaring their way through this meal. They fix on a girl talking to Gillecolm. Young, blushing. Her skin is white as sun-bleached rock. Her hair is black, with a sheen on it from the candlelight.

To his right, the boy king is quiet. Somerled feels awkward with him. There is something awry about his frame; his head is too big, his body too thin. His face is set in a pinched frown, as if his crown is too tight for comfort. They say that he is in permanent pain. All his effort is focused on holding in a scream, leaving no air for the usual pleasantries.

Somerled, wrong-footed by the boy's silence, can't decide how to pitch his conversation. Avuncular? Servile? Bluff? He cannot work it out. He feels heavy and stupid from the food and the heat.

Everything is not what it seems here. A boy king who moves like an old man. A world of intrigue and symbols, peopled by Scots nobility who speak only French. Everywhere a stupid, tricksy language that sounds to the Gaelic ear like the rasping of insubstantial birds. Food piled high in glistening piles that will never be eaten. The giants themselves, readying their huge frames for the battle of Ragnarok, could not finish all the birds, beasts and fish that have been slaughtered in their thousands to lie on this table as a symbol of the king's munificence, his wealth.

Malcolm picks at a single thigh bone, cutting the meat from the gristle with delicate strokes. He sips at his wine, wipes his fingers carefully between each course.

Down the table, as the feast winds on, they make some headway. Ribs and bones replace flesh. Half-picked, most of them. Somerled imagines his mother's fury at the waste, pictures her grabbing a carcass and waving it reproachfully at the assembled nobility, jellied skin and small bones flying.

'My lady asks why you are smiling, Lord Somerled.'

He slides back to the present. The boy stands behind him, Ada de Warenne's translator. Somerled turns to look at her, and notices how her green eyes crinkle with amusement. She appraises him, a frank, open look.

'I was thinking of my mother, my lady.'

She slurs French at the boy.

'My lady says, your mother makes you smile?'

He nods. 'My mother made everybody smile. I was thinking that she would be furious, appalled, at the wasted food. She would be gathering it all up, putting it to use.'

The boy relates this to Ada. Her eyebrows rise. He remembers, too late, that her mother was daughter to King Henry II of France. A cosseted princess. He looks down at her hands, which rest lightly on the table. They are milk-white, and soft. Hands used to fur-lined gloves and idleness.

'And would your mother do this herself?'

'My lady, I once saw my mother kill a beached whale with a kitchen knife, and butcher the carcass herself. She was head to toe in blood when she was done.'

She says something to the boy. He twists nervously behind them. She snaps at him in French. Not one to be crossed, this great lady, he thinks.

'My lady says I must translate everything she says. She says – and I am sorry, Lord Somerled – that you are proving to her that you are a barbarian.'

Somerled looks at her. Her eyebrows arch, waiting, and he realizes suddenly that she is bored. She is provoking him, in the hope that he might amuse her. Turn fierce.

'Tell your lady that I *am* a barbarian. I bite.'

As the boy translates, Somerled gnashes his teeth. She laughs, and he joins her. It feels good, to laugh with a clever woman. He notices her long, elegant neck. Sees her properly for the first time. She must have had Malcolm young. She has five children. Hard to tell how it has affected her body, but he tries to look without her noticing.

'I am sorry I have never learned French, your majesty.'

'And I Gaelic. It is a difficult tongue to master. I have tried.'

'It is the language of love and truth and beauty.'

'Yet that is what we claim for our tongue.'

'Can we both be right?'

The boy's whisper in his ear tickles.

'Tell me, Lord Somerled, why are you friends with Henry in England, and not so with my son?'

He reels from her frankness. How much do they know about his dealings with Henry? The supposedly secret talks Somerled has been holding with Henry's emissaries, to sound out the wily English King. To find out how he would react to a strike against Malcolm the Maiden. Her son.

He blusters.

'My loyalty is to my people first.'

She clicks her tongue impatiently.

'Those nephews of yours. Like thorns in my son's side. So irritating.'

'You have one in a dungeon, your majesty. If he is so unimportant, let him go.'

She smiles at him, pityingly, as if he has just let his queen be taken by a pawn.

'Why can we not be allies, Lord Somerled?'

'Why is your son granting land on my borders to his knights? Letting them build castles, take tributes?'

'It is his land. Is he not free to reward his followers?'

'But where will it stop? From where I sit, your majesty, it looks like provocation.'

'Squint, Lord Somerled, and it may look different. Like fear of your growing might, perhaps?'

A servant comes up, curtseying, seeking her attention. She smiles at him before turning to speak to the girl. Somerled looks down the table to where his men sit, checking they are behaving themselves. His eye catches on Brian. The man looks peculiar. He is talking with animation to the Norman knight next to him. A slight, blonde man in a gold-edged cloak. There is a flush in Brian's cheek, a brightness to him that Somerled cannot immediately fathom.

He throws his napkin to the floor and reaches down for it, beating the translator boy to it. Down there, he looks across, under the table. Sure enough, there is a fumbling of hands on Brian's large thighs.

Somerled rises, glad of the king's silence and the queen's inattention. Lord. Can it be right, what he has seen? He looks across to Brian and understands the brightness. It is happiness – Somerled has not seen it on him before. A sin. An abomination; belied by Brian's glow. He hopes no one else has seen it. He feels a rush of irritation at his champion. What a problem to lay at your lord's door. He will forget he has ever seen it. He hopes that it will not take the edge off Brian's skill. Each famous warrior has something that drives his sword, some source of power. With Brian it has always been his misery, guiding his arm, making it stronger, more fearsome to his enemies. Sadness is to Brian as hair is to Samson.

'My lady apologizes, Lord Somerled. She asks you to take some wine with her.'

He watches her eyes over the rim of the cup. Knowing, amused eyes. He begins to think about unpinning her hair, letting it tumble down her back.

They talk, Somerled and Ada, through the boy. They talk of the limitless ambition of Henry down in England. He has subdued Gwynedd, quelled the ferocious Marcher lords in Wales. Somerled does not lay bare his recent dealings with the man. His tentative steps towards an alliance. Henry cannot be ignored. He must be befriended or counted an enemy. A firebrand, like his mother, Matilda. The great-grandson of the Conqueror himself, he is greedy for land, like a beggar for sausages. He wants the borders, the seas, the very rocks.

'I have met his wife, of course,' she says. 'Eleanor of Aquitaine. I knew her as a girl.'

'What is she like?'

'And why does anyone care, Lord Somerled? She could not bear her first husband a son, and he put her aside. Now she has given a boy to Henry. Richard is his name, is it not? Is that not all there is to know about her? Look at me, Lord Somerled. What do you see?'

He is conscious of the translator, squatting behind his ear like a tick. Strange to watch her mouth move, and hear the gravelled, just-broken voice of the boy.

'The mother of a great king, your majesty.'

'You seek to flatter.'

She pauses, and Somerled senses a *but* hanging in the air between them, untranslated.

'A womb. This, Lord Somerled, is the point of women like me. Like Eleanor of Aquitaine. I have five children. This is all there is to me. This mouth? An irrelevance. This face? An irrelevance. This neck? An irrelevance. This body?' She arches her back, just a little.

Somerled swallows, eyes flicking to the boy behind.

'It is not so, my lady.'

'What do you see?'

'I wish I could speak your tongue, to tell you.'

She smiles, amused, and turns away to talk to the lord on the other side. Somerled is prickling with the heat, stifled. He turns to the king.

'A glass with you, your majesty,' he says. The boy king's pale eyes turn on him, and look through him. They raise their glasses. Malcolm drinks deep. Somerled wonders if it is true that Ada has been frantic in her efforts to persuade him to marry. That she sent a naked girl of good family to lie on his bed. The story goes that she lay cold and goose-bumped waiting for him. When he saw her, he was polite, mindful of the eyes beyond the door. He slept on the floor.

Which girl was it? Somerled wonders. He sweeps his eyes across the room, picking out the pretty girls and imagining each of them in turn. Jesus. He should think of something else.

'My lady says,' the boy interrupts his priapic thoughts as if the conversation had never been broken, 'that it is understandable, this obsession with royal wombs. Much as it is irritating for the owner of the womb. She says, is that not the preoccupation of power? How to pass itself on without ruptures?'

'You are wise.'

'They have different customs among your people, I think? Not the firstborn, but the best. Be he a cousin or a younger son.'

'That is the way it has been. Sometimes the firstborn is a weakling.' He winces, trying hard to stop his eyes turning to the boy beside him. She offers him a half-smile.

'It is a stupid custom. Have you not come from fighting in Ireland? Are the wars there not cousin against cousin in an endless battle to be high king? And once crowned, like your friend

Muirchertach Mac Lochlainn, are they not just waiting for the next pretender? A miserable miser waiting to be robbed.'

He nods, thinking through what she has said. 'But without wars, how would the young men prove themselves?'

His answer has disappointed her, he can tell. She looks down at her glass, twists the stem with elegant fingers.

'My lady, there was a Roman emperor, Diocletian. He was a great and wise ruler. But after twenty years of ruling the Empire, he retired. To grow cabbages.'

He has caught her back.

'And what happened to the Empire?'

'Civil war.'

'Of course. And Diocletian?' She struggles with the name.

'He grew lots of cabbages.'

'And how,' comes the boy's voice, dripping into his ear as he watches her lips move, 'do you think he felt, this Diocletian? How would you feel, Lord Somerled?'

'At first, an enormous relief. I would take to my bed. Stay there for a month. See no one. Well, almost no one.'

She smiles.

'I would watch the rain. Fish. Hunt. Read.'

'At first?'

'Yes. And it would not take long,' he says, 'before I was restless, bored.'

'Yes?'

'And very sick of bloody cabbages.'

~ ~ ~

He leaves the next morning, guessing that the shadow in the upper window is Ada watching him leave. He waves, just in case, ignoring the questioning stares of his men. They are not used to this mood, this jauntiness.

As he walks across the damp heather, he whispers a prayer to keep her safe. He is grateful to her. She has given him back something; a tie with another human soul. The knot may be loose, like a slipping bowline, but it is there. He feels it, and the spring in his step that tells him that he is not finished yet. That he is not committed for the rest of his dwindling days to this sad and furious loneliness.

Ada. He thanks her again in his prayer for her cleverness. She knows that he is not done with the Maiden, cannot be done with him while his little lords build castles with arrow slits pointing to Somerled's seas. She knows that they will play out this game until it is over. He is the child of the north and the west, with his tumbling, violent heritage of Norse and Gael. She is the child of the east and the south, with her Norse forefathers swallowed whole by Frankish things, like Fenrir's son Skoll swallowing the sun and allowing the burning inside to erase his own tale.

They will wrestle for this place, for its tongue and its God and its soul. But she is clever, this French queen, and charming, and she has given him a gift of something intangible and precious.

He searches for the word, which shivers beyond his horizon like a sail sighted at dusk. He raises his face to the rain, and finds it there. Joy. For did he not have a clever, spirited queen by his side when he needed her most? He has been so angry, so furious at her leaving him that he forgot to thank her for being there at all. She was a blessing. Her children are a blessing. Gillecolm, the best sailor in the fleet and a diplomat of uncommon skill. Sigrdrifa, all grown-up and quieter than any who knew her tiny self could have expected. But in both of them that gift for happiness their mother had. A happy sigh at the end of a meal, delight in a dolphin dancing in the bow wave, the inhaling of a loved one's skin.

He borrowed her joy, and now he will borrow theirs.

They march on towards the dusk, he and Brian both smiling and whistling, until the rest of the crew are hushed and uneasy, which only makes them laugh all the more.

ragnhilo

I have always hated it here. But I had nowhere else to go. I am not
wanted in Man. It is not the place I left; I recognized none of
it. Baldur is long dead. My mother is long dead. The girls I giggled
with are matrons. Strangers. The place I grew up in is gone; burned
down by Somerled.

My son did not want me there. I was a great and fat
embarrassment to him.

So I came back here. What else was there to do?

The wind is relentless. Grinding. It pounds the rocks, flattens
the grass. It finds holes in the walls. Seeks me out. It whips up the
waves, which crash on the rocks and spray me malevolently. It tugs
at my clothes. Wraps my hair into tight knots.

It keeps me inside these walls. I have paced each inch of this
place. I have sat by the fire, eating, eating. What else is there to
do? I am revolting. A great pig of a woman, with slitty eyes and
puffed-up cheeks and a belly that ripples and judders and sinks to
the floor. My breasts, once stared at, are pendulous things. I do not
look down when I wash. I close my eyes.

My children are all grown up. They laugh at me. I have seen
them. I saw Olaf do an impression of me to Bethoc. He blew up

his cheeks and pushed his flat belly forward and waddled from side to side.

We were at odds from the day I came here, Somerled and I. I did not see it. I was filled with hope, stupid girl that I was, filled with relief that he was youngish and slim and did not seem violent. But we were opposites, right from the start. Was it my fault? Probably. He loves it here. He loves the lash of the wind and salt in his face, and that great long view both ways down the Sound. My trap is his freedom. My end is his beginning.

Perhaps I was always doomed to fail. Perhaps his success demanded my failure. My great fat irrelevance. That was always what I was most frightened of: being irrelevant. And that is what has happened. I am the shrug at the end of the sentence, the pause in the ballad. Even I don't listen to myself any more. I just sit. And I eat.

1164

somerled

I t happens fast, one summer's evening. Two days before he is
due to sail. The final reckoning with Malcolm. His bound men
summoned, his allies called. They have come from Kintyre, from
Man, from Dublin and the western isles. The chief of them are
here, in this great hall, drinking and boasting and summoning
their battle selves.

Ragnhild is sitting next to him, eating a haunch of venison.
They talk, of what? The inconsequential things that long-married
people talk of. Of leaking roofs, reluctant milkers. Of storms to come
and gales they have seen. Of food stores, and silver, and the fishermen's
haul. Of their children, of other people's small lives, small loves.

They do not talk of their sons' violent envy of each other. They
do not talk of Bethoc, their daughter, who refuses every potential
suitor except Jesus, to whom she is passionately, morbidly attached.

They talk instead of a weaving she has done, of Olaf's sword arm
and Angus's skill at the tiller.

And then, suddenly, she stops talking. A glassy look in her eye,
a tremor that runs through her body. Slowly, definitely, she topples
sideways, her grey-blonde hair catching in the blueberry sauce,
trailing a smear of purple juice across the table.

She is on the floor. Entirely still and silent, her blubbery body not moving. The hall is strangely quiet. A hubbub looms on the horizon, like a squall. In the silence before it arrives, Somerled knows that she is gone, knows that he has failed her. He thinks, too, in that silent heartbeat that stretches onwards, of his own great age and the grim gods waiting for him. Oh, my sad, my piteous wife, he thinks as his sons rush forward to throw themselves on their mother's still-warm skin. I am sorry.

~ ~ ~

How is it, he wonders, that they are all so young? They should be playing with wooden swords, these youths who cluster round him, seeking his orders. They should be playing tag across the rock pools, not commanding galleys. He looks out over them. Each the jarl of his own boat. Each an emperor in his own empire of planks and rigging.

They stand in loose confederations. The Dubliners and the Manxmen apart, the men from different isles grouped clannishly. He spots Ragnar, the chief's son from Coll. He is grown now, a warrior flushed with youth and immortality. He sees Somerled's eyes on him, and he grins, taking Somerled back to the small boy who set sail with a stranger and called him lord.

Somerled nods to him. Nine years ago. Lord, how fast a man races to his grave at the end. Nearby is his nephew, Malcolm. Absurdly old, with grizzled grey hair that astonishes Somerled each time he sees the man. His face is grave, watchful. A misting of rain coats them all. Out in Loch Aline, more than a hundred ships ride on their anchors. You could walk from one shore to another across their tight-packed decks. Dance on the heads of the prow beasts. His steward has aged a decade since the host arrived, with the settling, feeding, loading, seething of one hundred and twenty-four galleys, each full to bursting with fractious, belligerent men scraping on each other's honour like flesh on barnacles.

Still, thinks Somerled. What point is there in being the lord if I cannot make the headache and minutiae of supplies someone else's problem? Poor sod. He almost smiles, but catches himself in time. He looks out again at the awesome jumble of galleys. He thinks of Padeen's quiet voice telling him the tales of Troy. The Greek host, sailing the wine-dark sea. He shivers at the thought. Ten years to win the bloody battle, and ten years to get home. What a waste.

He wrenches himself back to the present, where he is standing on a rock, facing them all, feeling old and tired and faintly ridiculous. An echo tugs at him, of the boy he once was. The boy who felt like a fraud but swaggered like a jarl and convinced them all, the fools.

He reaches for his armlet, a thick-worked gold piece of a snake eating its own tail. He is aware that he has been silent too long, and the restless scratching of the heather beneath hundreds of feet signals their impatience.

He holds up his hand for silence. In Gaelic and Norse and the jumbled sailor's chat that straddles both, he lays out the plan. Sail south with the tide. Keep close. If they are separated by the weather, meet here. If not here, there. Camp at the mouth of the Clyde. Before dawn, oars out and a dash upriver. Burn anything made by man. Kill anything that squeals. Make the bastards frightened of us. At Renfrew, we will destroy this castle Walter FitzAlan is building, a provocation to all men of the west. Plunder. Women. All yours.

Then?

He leaves the great question hanging, knowing that only a few – Gillecolm, Ragnar, Brian – will have moved past the thought of the plunder and the women to consider it.

It is a bald speech, a bad speech. No matter. He climbs heavily down from the rock, trying not to wince as his crumbling knee jars. Pain shoots through his body, sending sparks into his head.

'My lord?' says his steward.

Somerled grunts and pushes past him. Time to sleep a little before the tide. To be warm. He thinks, briefly, of sending for a girl. He finds to his astonishment that he misses Ragnhild. He would have liked to go inside now, talk idly with her. Let her fuss him and irritate him and cloy him. He still feels the coils of their long, binding twist of a life together. Who is left from his youth now? Why is he the only one?

~ ~ ~

As soon as it begins, all feels wrong. He has his host, he has his plans. He has three of his sons by him: Gillecolm, Angus, Olaf. He has his champion. He has more than a hundred galleys pulling up the Clyde, stuffed with men. But something is awry. A net cast in the wrong waters; a broken arrow in a still-running deer.

He can't fathom it, but it is making him cross-grained and irritable. They are scared to approach him. Even warier than usual. He has one man whipped for smirking, not recognizing his own voice as he raps the order. He has another demoted, another beached. He doesn't know why, even as he orders it. He is becoming irrational, but the rational part of him watches on and flounders.

They reach Glasgow before dawn. Christ, but what must it seem like to the people who live there? The unimaginable host of longships clamouring out of the dusk. The warriors jumping down into the soft mud of the riverbank, surging up towards your miserable hovel. The glittering screech of two thousand swords pulled, the screaming of your parents, your children, your cousins.

Your pigs. The host outnumbering the people, and every single warrior wanting his sword blooded, so that each God-forgotten peasant is punctured and pricked with a multitude of wounds like a stuck pig. The long lines of warriors queuing for the odds and sods of womanhood they have found hiding, their fingernails black from scrabbling at the dirt, trying to escape, their throats raw and red from the screaming.

The children spitted to stop their crying. The priest calling for his God as they laugh and taunt him. The smell, everywhere, of split stomachs and steaming blood. The emptiness that comes afterwards, as some men nurse their shame, and others count their pathetic gleanings from the hovels; the small lifetime hoards prised from their hiding places.

Somerled, pleading his knee, sits it out. They don't need him. There is no army here, just a confusion of peasants offering themselves to the slaughter. His galley sits beached on the riverbank, and he watches, morose, as the blood trickles in rivulets down the low-tide foreshore to curdle in the shallows. Gillecolm is with him.

Somerled does not say: 'I talked of this to Padeen once. I told him that this was the price a lord must pay to be followed. Besides, we will win if they fear us.'

Somerled does not say: 'I would stop it if I could.'

Gillecolm watches on, his body rigid with pity and contempt. He tries to busy himself with the work of the boat: recoiling untidy ropes, splicing a frayed end here, planing away the splinters there. Each task is unfinished, trailing, and he sits still at last, next to his father. Silent, they watch the day fade and the first crackles of fire breaking out across the rooftops of Glasgow. Sparks reach for the sky.

~ ~ ~

The next morning, the smoke still hangs over the land like a shroud, catching in throats raw from last night's drinking. Men stumble, bleary-eyed, when the alarm sounds. There is panic and puke spreading among Somerled's men, caught by the sudden appearance of Walter FitzAlan at the head of a host. How could he have assembled such a force so fast?

Treachery. He knew of their coming.

Somerled looks through the smoke to the blue sky beyond. He has been praying for rain. They are on flat ground here, and the soil is dry, hard-baked by the sun. Perfect for hooves. Perfect for the metalled horses gathered over there.

He stands with his sons, watching the enemy preparing to break upon them.

Suddenly he is laughing. Laughing so hard, he bends over and grasps his knees, the tears falling from him on to the dry ground. They crowd round him, worried. The thought that they imagine he is cracking up makes him laugh all the harder, so he can't breathe. At last he manages to spit it out, watching Gillecolm's face split with the joke while the others remain bemused.

'Rain,' he splutters. 'Rain. It never stops raining in this fucking country. And now, *now* the sun shines.'

~ ~ ~

They come together in a screech of fury and fear. Walter sends in his foot soldiers first, leaving his horses to pick at the stragglers. From the off, Somerled knows that he has miscalculated. He has eschewed his usual trickery, trusting in the power of his numbers. Yet they have no advantage of surprise and they are fighting on ground so favourable to FitzAlan that he must believe God is kissing his brow.

Perhaps he is, thinks Somerled, as his men begin to fall. Perhaps God is a Norman. Or perhaps he does not care whom slaughters who. He just sits drinking mead from a golden goblet, attended by angels, watching; just as we watch dogs fight for sport.

He is slow. Too old for this. He lets others push on past him, screaming defiance, spitting at the odds.

~ ~ ~

A sudden memory catches him off guard, reels him backwards. So sharp, so clear that he is there, not here on this doomed and bloody battlefield.

They are lying side by side on a flat rock, leaning over. They are at the head of Loch Aline, near where the big river tumbles and splays into the water. The ripples of it do not reach this far. The surface of the loch is flat, so smooth it is as if the dwarves themselves have polished up silver.

They watch their faces. Four of them. Reflected back up. Somerled. Eimhear. Gillecolm. Little Sigrdrifa.

They are quiet, even Sigrdrifa, whose chatter is usually a constant amused and bemused commentary on the world. It is a deep marvel, to see their own faces looking back up at them.

'Hello,' says Sigrdrifa, quietly.

'They're us, stupid,' says Gillecolm, his reflected face smiling wide.

'I look old,' says Eimhear.

'You are as fair as the day I met you.'

'You're not. You are older and uglier.' She laughs so deeply, it catches all four of them.

373

He tickles her, and Gillecolm joins in. She falls on to her back, laughing and protesting. Sigrdrifa snakes her arms around his neck, pulling with all her might, like a mouse restraining a bear. 'No, Daddy. My Daddy.'

Her voice floats like a wraith across the battlefield. He reaches for it, tries to catch it with his sword.

He feels the pity of his younger children's solemnity. Their great and vicious hatred of each other. He imagines the contained delight that the boys will feel at his death.

Lord Jesus. Sometimes life seems like one long fucking funeral.

The dead parade like ghosts on inspection before him. Gillebrigte, Sigrdrifa. His first and best band, with Aed leading, Sigurd and Ruaridh behind, making obscene gestures about the angels to make him laugh. Ragnhild; poor, miserable, unloved Ragnhild. And Eimhear. Oh my love.

The dead. Where are they? Where am I going? Jesus, who knows.

He sees it then. He sees Gillecolm's beloved body lying on a pyre of mud and blood. He is crooked; all his angles off slightly, as if he is a boy playing a trick, bending his limbs to see how far they can move. Beneath his helmet, his brown beard is blood-crusted.

He was so proud of that beard, of its slow and determined advance. He watched for it years before it could hope to appear, stroking his face compulsively as if to hurry its growth. Anointed it with oils, and combed it, amid the mockery of the other boys.

The lance has pierced his neck. Somerled struggles to look at it. For all the corpses he has seen, for all the blood, for all the eviscerating, shattering ways a man can die, this is the worst. The horror. The bright spill of his son's life leaking out on to a shit-strewn floor.

He remembers Gillecolm's mother holding the baby up to him; the fierce joy and pride on her face that blazed through that storm-racked night like a beacon. And he remembers her half-forgotten voice. 'In essence, my summer heart, it is all meaningless. This life, this death.'

Standing lost on the battlefield, his son's body at his side, he still does not know. Was she right all along? Was the question even worth asking? 'Why? Because we are here, because we are here,' she said.

His head is a fog. He can't think; can't breathe. Gillecolm dead, and the others snarling like wolf cubs, waiting for him to die so they can fall on each other, teeth bared and searching for the nearest brother's throat.

He kneels by Gillecolm and lifts his son's head from the mud. His blood is too precious to fall on this cursed flat plain. It should be in the sea, his poor boy's blood, floating on the tide. Somerled puts his mouth to the wound, and drinks. He swallows Gillecolm's blood, tasting the warmth of it, feeling it sink through his throat, down into his stomach. They shall not have my son's blood. They shall not have it.

He can hear the thrumming of the horses' hooves now. They are coming in again, the bastards. And he looks around at his men, the few that are left, with the fear rolling off them in sour waves of shit and muttering. We will lose this, he thinks. Those bastards on their great horses, with their French lisps and perfume, they will beat us. We are done.

He thinks then of the other men who have thrown and lost. Donald Bane, the land-stealing bastard, blinded and mocked by his nephew. Fergus of Galloway, humiliated and being slowly bored to death in some grim English monastery.

Jesus wept.

That's not for me, you bastards. Not for me. He lies Gillecolm back down. He is slow, deliberately tender.

He pulls off his helmet, and the cold wind sweeping in from the sea meets his clammy forehead, filling him with a delicious, sensual pleasure. His mouth is sticky with blood.

He stands, turning to his men, the best of them right there with him. Olaf, God be praised, is at the back somewhere. Angus looks at him with wide eyes. He reaches out a hand to touch the boy's cheek. No time for this, no time.

'Run,' he shouts. 'We are done here.'

'Lord!' screams Brian from a bloody beard. 'Fuck. What? Fuck.'

You inarticulate fucker, thinks Somerled, smiling. I hope you make it.

'Run!' he shouts again. Angus looks at him. A face flushed with fear. 'Go, my boy,' says Somerled. He wishes he has time; wishes for a space to sit and tell the boy to be good to his brothers. Don't fight. Don't tear it all apart. But the end is coming fast, too fast, so he screams at them once more. And so ingrained is his command that they begin to move, avoiding each other's eyes, giving in to the fear that calls them to run, run fast and far. He turns away from them, from his living son, towards the pounding beat of the hooves that shake the ground beneath his feet and roar inside his head.

He has time to think one last thing before the horses are upon him. He thinks, yes, there was death. But there was joy. He screams it at the horses coming for him, his legs planted wide in the heather.

'There was joy!'

The lead knight, implacable behind his black helm, holds up his sword, and Somerled raises his bare head, watching its point glinting in the sun.

He screams his defiance and begins to run forward. In his head, for the first time in too many years, he hears his song. *I am Somerled. Death-bringer. Life-giver. Norman-killer. Otter-lover. I am Somerled. I am joy.* When the scream finishes and the Norman sword begins its arching downward slice, he hears an echo, a vibration.

He hears her laughter, drifting towards him on the salt-wet wind.

historical note

This afternoon, I went walking.

Up past the ruins of Armadale Castle, the base of Somerled's descendants, Clan Donald. Up through woodland and then grazing land. Past the sheep and on to open moorland. Along a muddy track, and up a heathered slope to the top of Armadale Hill.

The sun shone, the clouds lifted. Across the Sound of Sleat, the summits of Knoydart shrugged off their usual fog shroud. The browns and greens twisted and tumbled down the ancient rock towards a cold blue sea. At that heart-stopping moment, a problem resolved itself.

From the very beginning of this project I have been dogged by a sense of hubris. I should not write about this place; this wild tip of our islands. I do not belong. My heritage is Ireland and Yorkshire, mangled through a London childhood. There is an absurdity in floating in to the Highlands, wafting about the hills and scuttling south when the nights grow long and dark.

But today, on Armadale Hill, the final draft of *The Winter Isles* buzzing on my laptop in the Clan Donald library far below, I realized that none of my concerns really matter. Hubris be damned. What counts, as Father Padeen once said to Sigrdrifa, is love.

I have been visiting the Highlands and Islands of Scotland since I was fifteen, when I first fell in love with all the intensity of a teenager. My passion was sparked by the remote, boggy hills near Cape Wrath. I have since explored much of the Western seaboard where this story is set. From the Summer Isles to Lewis, Iona to beautiful Barra and beyond. It was on Islay with my husband – obviously a Scot – that I first began to read about the tangled mesh of Viking and Gael cultures which produced the early Lords of the Isles.

Not much is known about the real Somerled. He is, like all the best heroes, a conflation of myth, conjecture and a few facts. MacDonald legend has him as a Gaelic warrior fighting to expel the heathen Norse. But this is not a straightforward tale of colonization and revolt; it is a tangled to-and-fro of violence, absorption and assimilation. Somerled himself seems to typify this. His name was Norse but his father and grandfather had Gaelic names. Recent DNA studies on Somerled's army of descendants suggest that he had a Norse patrilineal heritage.

In these waters, power counted for its own sake; not as an expression of an anachronistic nationalism. The best works I have read on the era include: *Domination and Lordship (Scotland 1070–1230)*, Richard Oram; *From Pictland to Alba (789–1070)*, Alex Woolf; *Irish Sea Studies 900–1200*, Benjamin Hudson; *The Kingdom of the Isles*, R. Andrew MacDonald; *The Sea Kingdoms*, Alistair Moffat; *Early Medieval Ireland*, Dáibhí Ó Cróinín; *Viking Pirates and Christian Princes*, Benjamin Hudson; and *Somerled, Hammer of the Norse*, Kathleen MacPhee. I am particularly indebted to *Somerled: And the Emergence of Gaelic Scotland*, John Marsden.

If this book inspires you to buy another, please make it *The Triumph Tree*, edited by Thomas Owen Clancy. A collection of early Scottish poetry from 550AD to 1350AD, in Gaelic, Norse, Latin,

Welsh and Old English, it contains some extraordinary, evocative lines.

The legend of Somerled was forged in the world of *The Triumph Tree*. The legendary Somerled lived in a cave with his dispossessed father. He was fishing for salmon when he was asked to fight the Vikings. He invented the stern rudder which characterized the birlinn – a craft which came to dominate the Irish Sea. He tricked the Vikings with the old trick of swapping the cow hides to make his men appear more numerous.

Somerled only appears in records towards the end of his life. He seems to have participated in various rebellions against the Anglo-Norman influenced Canmore Kings. By 1160 he is referred to in Scottish records as Somerled sit-by-the-King at a Christmas feast. His death in 1164 at a battle in Renfrew appears in a number of places. Two Clan Donald traditions suggest that he was betrayed, or even assassinated on the eve of battle. '*Carmen de Morte Sumerledi*', a near contemporary Latin poem by a cleric hostile to Somerled, claims that he died in battle early on. I have chosen this latter fate; clan historians dislike their heroes falling in battle – far better to have them betrayed or tricked.

Somerled's marriage to Ragnhild appears in the *Chronicle of Man*, as well as the *Orkneyinga Saga*. Legend tells the story that he was madly in love with the young princess and tricked her father into allowing the marriage. I am deeply suspicious of dynastic marriages that are later overlaid with romance. Besides, Somerled's oldest son, named as Gillecolm, is recorded in some traditions as dying next to him at Renfrew – pointing to an earlier significant relationship. Eimhear, and her story, are my invention.

The Island of Women does lie next to Iona, and is believed by some to have fulfilled the function I ascribe to it.

The Battle of Epiphany is in the records, as is Somerled's further excursion into Man in 1158. I am indebted to Wallace Clark for his book about recreating a voyage in a Highland galley, *Aileach: The Lord of the Isles Voyage.* I have accepted Mr Clark's hypothesis for the siting of the Battle of Epiphany, as well as drawing inspiration from his vivid recreation of galley sailing.

Somerled's descendants include, among others, the MacDonald clan, as well as the MacDougalls and MacAllisters. The Donald in question is his grandson, Ranald's son. On Somerled's death, his sons by Ragnhild fought bitterly amongst themselves over the Lordship of the Isles. Legend foretells this fraternal warfare with the story of the swimming race; although in the legendary version one of the brothers hacks off his own hand and chucks it at the shore in order to win.

Somerled ultimately failed in pushing back the Anglo-Norman influenced Canmore Kings, with their push towards feudalism, monasticism and urbanization. History is full of fascinating counter-factuals, but the what ifs here are fascinating. How different would Scotland have been, had Somerled and his horde of Gaels and Manx and Dublin Norse won at Renfrew, pushing the Anglo-Normans back to the Borders?

A question to mull over a whisky. Those to whom I owe many drams include my agent Andrew Gordon who believed in this book, and gave utterly invaluable advice. Thank you. Sara O'Keeffe and Louise Cullen at Corvus have been fabulous and supportive. My copy-editor Jane Selley was meticulous and put-upon. Thanks too to Maddie West, who among many other moments of greatness, came up with the title.

Thanks to my wonderful girls who have tramped much heather without too much whining and bribery. Lara, Romilly and Claudia – I love you beyond measure. Much love, too, to Dad, Glencora,

Elishna and Hector. The Skippers, the Roes, the Moores and the Talyarkhans – you can all be in my clan, any time. Thanks to my Mother, whose wisdom and determination to laugh at fate provided my template for Gaelic womanhood. Thanks and love to my Scottish clan-in-law, particularly Bill and Sarah West.

This book is for Colin, with whom I hope to stand on many a wild shore, with a fog rising and a dram waiting.